BUILDING 41

Andy Mellett Brown

Copyright © 2016 Andy Mellett Brown

All rights reserved.

ISBN:1523949325
ISBN-13:978-1523949328

In memory of the late David Hodges, G6IXH, without whose friendship I might never have discovered Bletchley Park or come to know Harry Stammers.

Acknowledgements

Thanks must firstly go, once again, to my wonderful wife Patricia, for putting up with me constantly wittering on about Harry, Ellen, Elsie and Co, for making countless cups of tea and for encouraging me to write in the first place (yes, it was her fault). Thanks also to my test readers for Building 41, Pat Housego and Joanne Hunter and to my proofreaders across the series, including Doris Brown and Sue Packer, without whom there would be even more mistekes than there are. Also to Janice Issitt for her wonderful photographs. To my many and varied Facebook friends for clicking "Like" and sharing my posts about the books. To the twits for tweeting. To everyone who has bought my books, and especially to those of you who have said nice things about them at amazon.co.uk. Oh and to my dog, Yaesu, for keeping my feet warm over many nights, when we sat up writing instead of heading up the wooden hills to Bedfordshire. Thank you.

CHAPTER ONE

Friday, May 9, 1941

The U-boat slipped through the icy waters of the North Atlantic, the low hum of her Siemens-Schuckert electric motors inaudible to the arctic terns wheeling in the cloud-laden skies above her.

'Level at thirty metres,' reported the helmsman.

The control room crew, to a man, turned and stared at their captain in silence. Lettmann drew a long breath, his bearded face impassive. These men, many no older than boys, were depending on him. Pale and sweating, their eyes staring at him expectantly from stubbly chinned faces. And not only these men and the other ratings and officers who together formed the U-boat's crew but also their families. Their mothers and brothers. Sons and daughters. Lovers. Friends. All of them.

While he would never have admitted it to his crew, the burden weighed heavily on **Kapitänleutnant Fritz-Julius** Lettmann. It had been his choice to join the U-bootwaffe and his great honour to take a command. His first two crews had been elite volunteers, carefully selected from among the Kriegsmarine's finest, but mounting losses had led to the selection of ever younger men. Men who, though trained at the Unterseebootsabwehrschule in Kiel or more likely at Pillau on the Baltic, or at Gotenhafen, had been given little more than two or three months training before being selected for active service.

Lettmann peered toward the wireless room. 'Well?' he called out.

A face, framed by a set of headphones, appeared in the passageway. The wireless operator raised his hand and for several moments the two men locked eyes. Then the wireless operator slowly shook his head.

Two or three months of training was not enough to prepare a man for a month or more at sea, confined for the duration to living in such cramped conditions with fifty other crewmen and the stench that they and the diesel engines generated.

'Up periscope,' Lettmann said, breaking eye contact with the wireless man.

'Up periscope,' a voice echoed the command.

It was barely enough to prepare a man for the monotony of life aboard a U-boat, let alone for the terrors of undersea warfare. When, with fifty metres or more of seawater above their heads, all that even the most experienced submariner could do was to wait for the boom of a depth charge, praying that the U-boat's hull would not be torn open like a sardine can on the supper table.

Lettmann turned and flipped the handles of the periscope into the horizontal as the scope came up. He raised his goggles and peered into the view finder. 'Bow up three,' he said, quietly.

The control room crew waited in silence.

He turned the periscope slowly. 'Stern down five. Come up.'

A restrained voice echoed the command.

'Stern up. Three, zero.' Lettmann glanced over his shoulder at the man he had heard approaching. His forehead was covered in sweat and his hands in a thick layer of black grease.

'Surface,' said Lettmann.

'Bow set to blow.'

BUILDING 41

Above them, the surface of the Atlantic began to boil and slowly, out of the depths, U-110's bow and then her conning tower rose up out of the water, like a great, steel-grey sea dragon.
'We must press on with repairs,' said the bearded engineer.
Lettmann faced him. 'Is it the gasket then?'
The engineer nodded. 'Number two.'
'That is all?'
The engineer shrugged. 'I am a mechanic not a fortune teller. We will know that when the head is off.'
'How long?'
'Three hours. *If* it is only the gasket.'
Lettmann glanced down at his watch. 'You have two, Schröder.'
'Two hours?' the engineer scoffed and turned away.
Lettmann placed a hand on the man's shoulder.
Schröder turned again to face him.
'You heard me. Two and no more,' Lettmann said, his eyes steady.
The engineer shook his head. He was still shaking it as he walked away.
Lettmann reached for his tin cup, took a mouthful of coffee and closed his eyes. What weighed most heavily on him was the thought that if these young men died in the effort, neither they nor their families would ever know the reason for their sacrifice. Of all the men on board, only Lettmann knew. And perhaps one other.
'Sir? Are we going up?'
Lettmann sighed, put down his cup and stared at the watch officer. 'You go on ahead, Heinz. I'll be up shortly.'
'Very good, Sir.'

First Watch Officer Heinz Federick pulled on a rain coat and hauled himself up the ladder toward the bridge deck. After almost four weeks at sea he was a little lighter than he had been when they'd left port at Lorient but still it was an effort. Reaching up, he braced himself then released the clip, sprung the lid and ducked the curtain of sea water that crashed in through the open hatch. When the water had subsided, he heaved himself up, stepped out onto the deck and took a deep lungful of clean air.

It was raining. Hard. He pulled the Zeiss binoculars from beneath his coat and dragged the coat's hood over his head. The wind was gusting from the north-west, sending the waves up and back on themselves, in plumes of white spray that burst onto the submarine's deck as the bow rose and fell in the swell. At least the night's storm had abated. He observed the bank of still angry, steel grey clouds to the south-east. He spat a mouthful of salty water at them in disgust.

'Permission to come up,' called a voice from below.

'Come up, then,' Federick yelled, lifting the binoculars and turning in a wide arc, scanning the horizon.

'Anything?'

Federick completed the turn. 'Not yet,' he said, removing the binoculars from around his neck and handing them to the second watch officer.

'I don't like it. We're too close to shore to be sitting here like ducks in a pond.'

'You worry too much, Günter.'

'Do you think so?'

'Orders are orders,' said Federick, without emotion.

Vogel snorted. 'Ours is not to reason why…' He raised the binoculars and peered westwards. 'But whose orders, Oberleutnant,' he said, under his breath. 'Whose orders?'

Lettmann stood in the doorway to the wireless room. The operator glanced up at him. 'Nothing, yet.'

Lettmann looked down at his watch. 'Keep listening.'

'Was it altogether wise to surface?'

Lettmann eased himself into the only available seat. 'It is a gamble, Matthäus. But I want both those engines. Shroeder asked for three hours. I gave him two. We make the schedule. And then

BUILDING 41

we run. I'd rather not be limping all the way to Kiel, with half the Royal Navy on our tail.'

Matthäus Krause leant back in his seat, linked his hands behind his head and stretched his shoulders. 'Ah, Kiel,' he said, closing his eyes. 'Beer, a comfortable bed and the best damned whore houses in Germany.' He opened his eyes and stared at his captain. 'Three good reasons to return with our tails intact.'

Lettmann's face showed no emotion. 'You have a one track mind.'

'A little harsh, perhaps but not entirely inaccurate,' the other man replied.

They both fell silent.

In normal circumstances, Lettmann reflected, Krause would have been right to question his decision to surface so close to the coast. And to stay surfaced while repairs were carried out. It was more than a gamble. In any other circumstance it would have been sheer recklessness. But these were anything but normal circumstances. Lettmann's determination to make it back to Kiel was driven, not by the port's whore houses, but by the necessity of their mission and the reputation of those who had ordered it.

'Let us hope,' said Krause, 'that this particular gamble pays off.'

'Do you have the signal ready?'

Krause slid open a drawer to his left and removed a folder. He handed it to his captain. 'Do you know what it says?'

Lettmann stared at him. 'No more than do you,' he said, leafing though the contents of the folder. In truth, while they had both been briefed, neither man knew the meaning of the signal, nor the extent of the other's knowledge or wholly trusted his true purpose. Lettmann knew that this had been the intention behind their separate briefing. It was standard Abwehr practice. 'Just be ready. As soon as we have contact, transmit the message and record the reply.'

Krause tilted his head in acknowledgement of the order.

'And then I want this destroyed,' he said, returning the papers to the file and handing it back to the wireless man. 'No mistakes Matthäus.' Lettmann got to his feet. 'You know what the consequences will be if we fail. For us both.'

Lettmann left the radio man contemplating his words. Krause would be in no doubt about the consequences for them both if they failed, whatever his purpose. Their mission had been authorised at the highest level. Perhaps, by the Führer himself. Failure would be as good as a signature on both their death warrants.

'Sir, a message from the bridge,' said Ledersteger, one of the crew's younger ratings, as Lettmann stepped back into the control room. 'They have contact.'

Lettmann cursed under his breath and checked his watch. 'Danke, Ledersteger.' He strode toward the ladder to the bridge and slid on a coat. 'Coming up,' he called into the voice tube. He climbed the ladder and stepped out onto the bridge. 'What is it, Vogel,' he shouted, against the sound of the crashing sea.

'A convoy, Sir. To the starboard. Bearing, forty degrees.'

'Where are they heading?'

'South-west. Straight across our path.' Vogel handed him the binoculars.

Lettmann peered toward the horizon. 'Estimated number?'

'Twenty plus.'

'Escort?'

'Uncertain.'

'Damn it,' Lettmann muttered. He turned and shouted into the voice tube. 'How long before we have engines?' He waited.

'The Chief says an hour at least, Sir,' came the reply.

'Not soon enough. They'll spot us,' yelled Federick, the anxiety in his voice self-evident.

A plume of water crashed over the three men.

'I know that, Federick,' Lettmann shouted. 'Clear the bridge.'

'But, Sir...' Federick spluttered, his mouth full of spray.

'If we can't run, we will have to hide. Until we can wait no longer. I said, clear the bridge.'

Vogel and Federick headed for the hatch.

Lettmann lifted the binoculars and stared at the approaching convoy. So it was a gamble that was not going to go in their favour. 'God damn them to Hell,' he said between clenched teeth. He turned, stepped onto the ladder, pulled and locked down the hatch and slid down the tube.

'Take us down,' said Lettmann, as soon as he had removed his coat.

'Diving stations.'

Lettmann waited while the boat submerged. 'Come to periscope depth.'

'Periscope depth.'

'Up periscope.' Lettmann gazed through the scope.

'Contact, Sir.'

'Bearing?' Lettmann said, without taking his eyes from the scope.

'Forty-two degrees.'

Lettmann turned the periscope. 'Right full rudder. Both motors, ahead full.'

'Right full rudder, Sir'

'Take us down.' Lettmann kept his voice flat. Calm. So as not to alarm the men.

'Aye, Sir.'

Lettmann scratched his chin.

'Contact closing. Range, two thousand metres. Speed twenty-five knots. It looks like a destroyer, Sir.'

'Faster then.' Lettmann swallowed a curse. The schedule meant that this was no time to play cat and mouse. They would have to surface again. Soon.

'Depth, fifty metres.'

'All right, let's see whether they have spotted us. Kill unnecessary lights. Silent speed,' Lettmann ordered.

'Silent speed, Sir.'

'Keep taking us down.'

'Sixty metres.'

'They're closing fast, Sir.' The stress in the young seaman's voice was plain.

'Steady. Hold your nerve,' Lettmann hissed, his words as sharp as steel.

'Seventy.'

Not yet.

'Destroyer almost above us, Sir.'

'Quiet now. They're fishing.'

From above, they could hear the low throb of the destroyer's engines.

'Eighty,' came a voice. This time subdued.

The boat creaked. Fear buzzed about the crew like a swarm of angry bees.

'Relax. It's just the pressure on the hull,' Lettmann said, willing his voice to remain emotionless. If the destroyer had located them they would know it in the next few minutes. They would know it from the boom of a depth charge. Lettmann tried to breathe easily. Fear was like a virus that would pass from one man to another until they were all infected, slowing their reaction times and causing disorder. But it was a virus that he could counter. He reached for his coffee cup and emptied it, casually. He caught Ledersteger's eye as he moved to return the cup to its resting place. None of the men would have dared such a thing. Lettmann watched the young rating's eyes widen and then relax as he silently replaced the cup.

Ledersteger smiled, almost imperceptibly.

'Well?' Lettmann said, breaking the silence at last.

'She's turning, Sir,' came the restrained reply.

Lettmann's eyes flicked to the depth gauge. 'Level out at ninety metres,' he said, glancing at his watch. *Come on. Come on.*

'Contact has turned back. She's moving away to starboard, Sir.'

'Like I said, just fishing.'

'Contact fading.'

Lettmann felt the release of tension as each of the crewmen began to breathe again. 'Hold.' They were not out of the woods yet.

'Contact receding, Sir'

'Patience, gentlemen.'

They waited in silence.

'I can hardly hear her.'

Lettmann allowed himself a smile. 'Take us in towards the coast. Motors ahead full.'

'Motors ahead full,' came the reply.

Lettmann glanced towards the wireless room. 'How long have we got Matthäus?' he called out.

The radio man's head appeared in the passage way. 'Forty minutes. No more.'

Damn it. They needed to be on the surface.

'Sir, the convoy is too close,' Federick whispered, as though reading Lettmann's thoughts. 'The escort will spot us the moment we surface.'

'That's a chance we'll have to take. You've got twenty minutes helmsman. Get us in as close as you can. They won't be expecting that.'

'Aye, Sir.'

'Lights.'

The submarine's lights flickered from red to orange.

CHAPTER TWO

Lettmann made his way through the submarine, nodding to his crewmen and barking orders as he passed. 'Clear that away König. Quickly,' he said as he approached two ratings, one of them watching the other hauling a sack across the gangway. 'Assist him Schuster, you lazy bastard.'

'Yes, Sir. Sorry, Sir,' Schuster said, aware suddenly of his captain's presence.

'And Schuster?' Lettmann barked again, as he passed them.

'Sir?'

'You stink as bad as those rotting bloody cabbages,' he said, nodding toward the sack. 'Do something about it. Or the next time we're on the surface, God help me, I'll throw you overboard myself.'

'Yes, Sir,' Schuster replied, grinning broadly.

As he stepped through the watertight hatch, into the engine room, Lettmann was hit by a wall of oil and diesel fumes. Shroeder had spotted him almost immediately. 'Well?' Lettmann said, when he was within earshot.

'We've patched her up but she won't take full RPM,' the chief engineer replied, wiping his black hands on an oily rag.

'Damn it, you know the score. I'm depending on those engines to get us back to Kiel in one piece.'

BUILDING 41

Shroeder shrugged. 'I told you that we needed three hours. We've patched her up in half that.'

Lettmann locked eyes with his chief engineer. Shroeder could be a surly bastard, but he was also one of the Kriegsmarine's finest engineers. If patching her up was the best that he could do in the time that they had, then it was the best that could be done by any man. Lettmann sighed. 'Very well. But be ready. Once this business is done, we're going to have to run and the faster we do it, the safer we will all be.'

'Yes, Sir. We'll give it our best shot.'

'Of that, Chief, I have not the slightest doubt,' Lettmann said, clasping his chief engineer's muscled arm.

Lettmann stared through the periscope but visibility was poor in the swell. He looked at his watch. They were all but out of time. 'Anything exciting out there?'

'Position reports only Sir. Faint.'

'Surface, then.'

'All set to blow.'

It was now or never. As U-110's conning tower broke through the waves, Lettmann was already in the wireless room. His eyes were on Krause, who was listening to the hiss in his headphones. Lettmann waited. After several minutes, Krause looked up and shook his head.

'Damn it. Where are they? If this has been for nothing…' muttered Lettmann.

Krause's eyes returned to the radio. Lettmann watched him making tiny adjustments to the dial. He knew that the longer they remained on the surface, the more likely it was that they would be spotted. If they were spotted again, they might have only minutes to complete the schedule. Miss the schedule and they were dead men. Stay up too long and they were dead men. With the coast off to their port side, even the options for escape were limited. Lettmann looked at the clock on the wall and then down at Krause.

The wireless operator glanced up and shook his head again, his forehead covered in sweat. The odds were narrowing with every passing second. They both knew it.

Without warning there was a low, distant boom that reverberated around the submarine's interior. And then another.

Federick's face appeared in the doorway. 'It's one of ours, Sir. Distant. Firing on the escort.'

One of ours... 'Do we know which boat?'

Federick shook his head. 'They must have been tracking the convoy, Sir.'

'Good of them to keep us informed,' Lettmann replied caustically, turning to Krause. 'Put out a call.'

The radio man stared at him. 'If we do that, every ship in that convoy will hear us.'

Krause was right. But waiting for a non-existent signal, when the unexpected intervention of another U-boat had already put the convoy on high alert, was not only pointless, it was also wasteful. The U-boat's attack, if it was sustained, might keep the escort tied up just long enough for them to make contact and slip away. But they needed to act quickly. 'I said, put out a call.'

Krause stared at him.

'That's an order, Funkmaat.'

Krause reached for the morse key.

'Contact, Sir,' yelled a voice from the control room.

Lettmann cursed, silently. 'Make the call. Now. Or I will relieve you of your station and do it myself.'

The radio man began to tap out the coded call.

'Repeat it,' Lettmann ordered, when the radio man had paused.

Krause signalled the message again.

They both waited in silence.

'Well?' said Lettmann, when he could wait no longer.

A rating appeared in the door way. 'Sir?'

'Silence,' Lettmann barked.

'But, Sir...'

BUILDING 41

Lettmann turned. The rating was red in the face and sweating. 'Did you not understand the order, Ledersteger? I said, silence.' He turned back to the wireless operator.

Krause shook his head.

There was another low boom. Closer this time.

'Again,' said Lettmann.

Krause nodded and keyed the message for a third time. Lettmann translated the first few code blocks in his mind: - "*WJXD BQOY HDIU...*"

Then he turned. 'What is it Ledersteger?'

'Contact, Sir. Two. Heading straight for us. Could be freighters.'

'Freighters, my arse.' As he said it, Lettmann felt a hand on his arm. His eyes flicked from the rating to the radio man.

Krause nodded.

Lettmann turned. 'Battle stations,' he shouted, as he ran along the gangway toward the control room. 'Linder?' he barked.

Linder appeared in front of him.

'With Krause. I want a report as soon as he has completed the exchange. Do you understand?'

'Yes, Sir,' Linder replied, turning away.

Lettmann grabbed his arm. 'The *moment* it is completed,' he said with emphasis.

'Yes, Sir.'

'Federick, Vogel, Dietmar' Lettmann yelled, searching out each man's face in the chaos. 'With me to the bridge. Now.'

Lettmann peered through the binoculars towards the rapidly approaching vessels. 'Destroyers,' he shouted over the roar of the wind and the crashing of the waves against the U-boat's hull.

'How long before we can dive?' Federick shouted in response.

'Longer than those two are going to give us.'

Behind his back, Federick and Vogel exchanged glances.

'We must dive, Sir,' Vogel yelled.

'No. Not until we have completed the exchange,' Lettmann returned.

'But, Sir...'

'I said, not until Krause has the response.'

Federick approached him and spoke into his ear, as quietly as the waves would allow. 'Think of the crew, Fritz. We're sitting ducks. If we're sent to the bottom, whatever Krause does manage to receive will go with us.'

'And if we leave without completing the exchange, it may as well be to the bottom, Heinz, believe me.'

Federick did not reply.

'All ahead, full. Left rudder,' Lettmann said, staring at his watch officer.

Federick hesitated. Then turned and relayed the message.

'Anything from Linder?' Lettmann shouted.

Federick shook his head. 'Nothing.'

'Prepare tubes one to four for surface firing.'

Federick stared at his captain.

Lettmann shoved him aside. 'Prepare tubes one to four for surface firing,' he shouted into the voice tube.

It was a few seconds before the reply came. 'Tubes one to four flooded.'

He turned and met Federick's eyes again. 'Stand by to attack.'

'Bearing three hundred and forty degrees,' shouted Vogel.

Lettmann waited. 'The larger vessel. We'll take her first.'

Vogel was watching the approaching enemy through his binoculars. 'Range one thousand metres.'

There was a flash from the nearest destroyer. Lettmann heard the whistle of the shell above the sound of the waves. The sea exploded just metres from them, swamping the bridge in a plume of white spray. The U-boat rose up, the men on the bridge grappling to stay on their feet.

'Target identified,' came a voice from below.

BUILDING 41

'Open the caps. Lock on tubes one and two. Follow for bearing.' Lettmann peered at the approaching destroyer. Another muzzle flash.

'Fire when matched!' Lettmann yelled.

'Fire one.'

There was an immense explosion. All of them were thrown to the deck. The U-boat listed heavily to port.

'Fire two.'

Lettmann clambered to his feet. 'Clear the bridge,' he yelled. As soon as the other men were clear, Lettmann followed. He slammed the hatch behind him and slid down the ladder.

Inside, the U-boat was in chaos. Water was pouring in through several breaches.

'Out of my way. Quickly.' He yelled. 'Federick, take the scope. Prepare to dive,' he shouted over his shoulder. 'On my word. Not a moment sooner.'

There was a distant boom and the U-boat shuddered.

Lettmann clambered over the debris that had fallen to the control room floor and halted at the wireless room door. Krause was bent over his log book, recording the incoming message in four letter groups. Lettmann watched him anxiously. *Hurry, man. Hurry.*

There was another explosion, the U-boat convulsing violently. Smoke began to fill the passageway. Lettmann could hear men shouting from the direction of the engine room.

Too late. Too damned late.

'We've lost power, Sir. The batteries must be flooded,' yelled a voice from the control room. It was Federick's. He came staggering towards Lettmann, his uniform sodden, his face ashen and streaked with blood from a deep gash on his forehead.

Without the electric motors they would be unable to move submerged. Lettmann hesitated.

'What's your order, Sir?'

Lettmann thought of the many young men on board.

'Shall we dive, Sir?' Federick shouted.

'Dive? Are you mad? The hull is breached and we've no power, man.'

Lettmann watched Federick's face go slack. He had the experience, at least, to know that they were beaten. He pushed Federick aside. 'Last stop. Everybody out,' he shouted.

'Abandon ship?' Federick's expression portrayed his disbelief at the order.

Lettmann grasped his arm and stared into his face. 'Get everyone out onto the deck, Heinz. Keep them away from the gun. Hands in the air. They will not fire. They're British.'

'Yes, Sir.'

Lettmann was coughing now, the smoke and fumes filling his nostrils and lungs. He turned back toward the radio man. 'Give it up Krause. Bring the codebooks and the machine.'

There was panic aboard U-110 as the crew fought their way along the gangway, up through the conning tower and out onto the deck. Lettmann stood at the bottom of the ladder, helping those who had been injured and yelling orders, until he was hoarse.

A grim faced Karl Shroeder followed the last of his men.

'Where the hell is Matthäus?' Lettmann yelled.

'I don't know. The wireless room was empty,' Shroeder answered. 'Shall I go back?'

'No, I'll do it. You get out. You've done enough.'

The two men stared at each other. 'I'm sorry, Sir,' said Shroeder.

'Sorry? What the hell for? This is my responsibility,' Lettmann replied.

'It has been an honour to serve with you, Kapitänleutnant.'

The two men embraced.

'I hear that the British have some very comfortable prisoner of war camps.' He held the chief engineer at arms length. 'Now get the hell out and that is an order.'

Shroeder's expression was grim. He nodded, turned and disappeared up the ladder.

BUILDING 41

Lettmann began to make his way toward the radio room when there was the unmistakeable sound of automatic gunfire from above. 'Schweine!' he yelled, running back to the ladder. 'I said hands in the air, no firing,' he yelled.

But it was not the crew of U-110 who had opened fire. As Lettmann stared upwards, a body fell across the open hatch, blood running from a gaping wound in the man's chest. Lettmann climbed the ladder, reached up and pushed the body aside. It was Karl Shroeder's, though he was barely recognisable. His face had been all but obliterated.

Lettmann peered out onto the deck. The destroyer was no more than one hundred metres off the U-boat's port bow. It was firing at them, seemingly indiscriminately and with every available gun. Lettman's crew were either dead or were throwing themselves into the sea.

For a moment Lettmann stood at the top of the ladder, unable to speak. He had failed. Utterly. Failed the mission. Failed his men. All of them. What in God's name were the British doing? 'We've surrendered you bastards,' he yelled.

But his plea was answered by another volley of machine gun fire and the sound of screaming from the remaining crew. Lettmann hauled the hatch shut and locked it, then he let himself slide down the ladder. No more than a few feet from the bottom, the submarine suddenly lurched violently and he lost his footing. As he slipped, Kriegsmarine Kapitänleutnant Fritz-Julius Lettmann struck his head a vicious blow against the submarine's hull and lost consciousness.

CHAPTER THREE

The noise was deafening. Everyone who could find a gun was firing it at the U-boat, as the crew spewed forth from the conning tower and ran toward the deck gun. The first of our shells, which had struck the submarine's bow, had caused several of the Germans to throw themselves into the water. But it was the hail of machine gun fire that had caused panic. Men were tumbling over each other in their haste to abandon the stricken vessel. I saw several of them thrown up by the swell and dashed against the side of the submarine, their lifeless bodies slipping slowly back into the sea and disappearing beneath the waves.

'Petty Officer Warren?'

I barely heard the gunner's mate above all the noise. 'Yes, what is it?' I shouted.

'You're wanted for the boarding party, Sir. I am to issue you with this.'

He handed me a standard service revolver. I looked at the gun and wondered what the devil use it would be, clambering up the side of the U-boat, or down the conning tower, feet first, if anyone was still aboard.

'Lieutenant Harding wants you down below, Sir.'

I followed him across the deck to the stairs, revolver in hand.

BUILDING 41

I was to be one of eight men, led by Harding, to take Bulldog's twenty foot whaler across to the stricken and listing U-boat. The whaler was of the traditional type, pointed at both ends, with five rowing positions. Two on one side and three on the other. I was to take one of the oars.

We clambered into the boat and waited for the order: - "Away armed boarding party."

I was completely terrified and, by the look of the others, I was not the only one. Baker was shaking so violently that he barely seemed able to hold an oar, let alone to use it. Powell was as white as a sheet and quite unable to speak.

'Why the rush, Sir?' I said to Harding, as he made his way past us, revolver in hand.

'Because if they have any sense at all, Warren, they will have made efforts to scuttle her and send her to the bottom.'

'A bloody good job too, if you ask me,' I said, offering no apology when Harding looked at me as though he thought me an imbecile.

'Which is why I am not asking you, Warren.'

That was all the explanation I was given or was going to be given, by the sound of it.

The whaler was lowered from Bulldog until we were about six feet from the waves. We all held our breath until the order was given to "out pins" at which point the pins holding the weight of the whaler were knocked out. It was then up to Harding to watch the waves and, at the opportune moment, to give the command "slip", at which point ropes would be pulled and the boat lowered onto the crest of a wave. It was a difficult enough manoeuvre at the best of times, but in heavy seas it was particularly perilous. None of us were keen to end up in the cold Atlantic, especially a few feet from Bulldog's hull and in seas that were as likely to dash us against the ship's side, as they were to wash over our heads and send us to the bottom.

When the command finally came, it was a struggle to hold onto my breakfast but in the end the boat flopped down onto the sea without incident and we were away, rowing as though our lives depended on it, which I suppose they did. With the sea so angry, it would have been a simple thing for the whaler to be thrown back against Bulldog's hull, breaking up the little boat and drowning us all.

We approached U-110 on the side facing Bulldog, which was windward with waves breaking over the side of the submarine's hull. It is not an easy thing to board an abandoned submarine, if indeed she was abandoned, even in calmer seas. In rough seas, it was dangerous in the extreme and it took us several attempts to get close enough to secure a rope. But eventually, we did secure one and all eight of us clambered aboard U-110, service revolvers at the ready.

The submarine gave every impression of having been abandoned. I had witnessed, from the whaler, several bodies being tossed about in the waves. I had seen dead bodies before, but I couldn't help but regret that we had fired, so indiscriminately, on the U-boat's crew. While some of them had appeared to be running for the deck gun, they had not fired a single round at us and most of them had thrust their hands into the air following the initial volley of machine gun fire from Bulldog. I suppose that war is war. These men had, after all, been firing torpedoes at us only minutes before.

There was nobody on the deck of U-110 and only dead bodies in the conning tower. All with dreadful machine gun wounds. But what was odd was that the watertight hatch had been closed. Had they been intending to scuttle her, they would certainly have left the hatch open. It made no sense and we were all sure that we were going to be fired on the moment the hatch was released. But Harding was determined not to use a hand grenade. If there were secrets on board, he wanted them intact.

BUILDING 41

It was Harding, to his credit, who opened the hatch and went, feet first, down the ladder. He must have felt terribly vulnerable as he lowered himself down. He had no choice but to holster his revolver, as he needed both hands to hold on, so he could not have attempted to return fire had he been fired upon from below.

In the event, Harding encountered no resistance at all and, when he was down, called up for the rest of us to follow, which we did. I was the second man down.

The U-boat captain was lying at the bottom of the ladder with the most dreadful gash across the side of his right temple. His right leg was bent awkwardly beneath him. I knew, instantly, that he was the captain because of the insignia on the shoulder of his seaman's sweater. It was evident that Harding had already examined him because he was stood, pointing his revolver directly at the man, which I took to mean that he was still alive. When Baker was down, Harding attempted to rouse him with some success. Baker and I hauled the German to his feet and Harding, revolver in hand, pushed him forward into the control room to act as a shield in the event that any further U-boat crew were present and inclined to resistance. The man could hardly walk at all for the injury to his leg but somehow managed to stay upright.

What struck me immediately was how eerie an empty submarine feels after the heat of battle. The control room was a dreadful mess but completely silent, save for a worrying hissing sound that was probably coming from the batteries or a leak in the hull, and a faint, rapid tapping sound. The air in the control room stank. A mixture of sweat, smoke, human waste from the toilet and rotten eggs, probably from the hissing batteries. The submarine was also listing by fifteen degrees or so, making staying upright particularly difficult. Especially for the U-boat captain, who was staggering around to such an extent that I was sure he was going to collapse. Harding was ruthless in his insistence that the captain should lead the way which was fortuitous because, as we approached the wireless room, the source of the tapping sound was revealed. I heard the U-boat captain shout something in German and saw, briefly, the terrified look in the wireless operator's eyes as he reached for his weapon. Then Harding shot him in the face, sending blood and pieces of brain and bone spewing across the room.

The wireless operator had evidently been tapping characters into a black cipher machine, which, we later discovered, was screwed down to the wireless room desk. It looked somewhat like a typewriter, with three rows of keys, three further rows of characters that lit in a strange order when a key was pressed, and a set of silver rotors above them. It was still switched on, as were the U-boat's wireless receiver and transmitter.

The wireless room was in some disarray, with papers and books strewn around the floor. Harding gave orders to Powell, who had by now joined us with the others, to guard the captain, and to me to gather all of the papers together, while he led the search of the remainder of the submarine. Some of the papers were spattered with the wireless operator's blood. I had to shake off some of the bits which was a gruesome task that I will never forget. When I had completed the job, I looked up and noticed the captain watching me. The look he gave me was one of pure hatred. I was briefly taken aback by it. I suppose, on reflection, that it was understandable that he should have hated us at that moment. We had, after all, dispensed with his entire crew and seen the rest of them jump to their deaths, into the sea. But, at the time, his hatred had seemed both unwarranted and unfair. I was simply following orders, doing my job as he and his men had been doing theirs when they encountered us.

I don't know if that is what made me take the small, red codebook that I found beneath the wireless operator's table, and walk across to the captain, leafing through its pages of hand written ciphered text, grinning at him nonchalantly and watching his obvious fury with a certain amount of pleasure. Nor am I certain whether it was why, having so enjoyed his discomfort, I chose to tuck the little codebook, secretly, into the inside pocket of my tunic, rather than to gather it together with all of the other papers, the cipher machine and the other equipment that we passed back through the submarine, up the conning tower and out into the waiting motor boat. But that is what I did.

We were on U-110 for almost six hours, gathering equipment and trying to make the boat watertight, before a tow was safely attached and we were able to evacuate and return to Bulldog. As I climbed back onto Bulldog's deck, I felt my inside pocket secretly and with some trepidation, as I had never before, nor did I ever subsequently, take any kind of trophy from the operations with which I was involved while on active service. On this occasion I consoled myself with the thought that, years later, I might at least be able, not just to tell my children and grand children about what I had done during the war, but to show them. That is what I told myself but unfortunately, due to yet more foolishness on my part, it was not to be so.

CHAPTER FOUR

Thursday, November 9, 1944

The bus from Bletchley clattered into the village, splashing water onto the grass verge as it pulled up to disgorge the little group of Park girls who were billeted in the rooms above the shops lining the main street. It was stationary for a few minutes only, before the driver sounded the horn and pulled back out into the road, the bus' engine labouring to gather momentum before he changed gear with a lingering clunk, sending a puff of filthy grey smoke billowing out into the night.

At the back of the bus, a young woman waved as the girls' outlines faded slowly into the darkness. When they were no longer visible, she settled back into her seat, stifled a yawn and closed her eyes. Even in sleep there was no escape from the countless log sheets. She'd been staring at them for so long, that it was though they had burned an imprint in her mind. Like looking into the sun.

It wouldn't have been so maddening had they been able to read the damned logs, but the messages they contained were always ciphered.

She opened her eyes and stared out into the darkness, her view blurred by the tiny droplets of rainwater, running in horizontal rivulets across the windows of the bus, as it made its way out of the village.

BUILDING 41

Checking the logs of German Kriegsmarine and Luftwaffe traffic might be dull, but at least it was more stimulating than the work of the intercept operators who had created them. Sat at their stations for hours on end, translating Morse code into cipher text, with no idea at all of the meaning of their intercepts. It would have driven her crazy. Beyond crazy.

Thank goodness that Mr Welchman had revealed, to the log readers at least, that their work had contributed to the breaking of the German machine ciphers. It had given them all a renewed sense of purpose and, for a while at least, some enthusiasm for the work but it was relentless nonetheless.

Welchman had seen fit to break their work into cycles, at the end of which a report was produced and then, blessedly, they were allowed a day off and, once in a while, a weekend. *A whole weekend.* She sighed at the thought. With the report due in tomorrow, she should at least have been looking forward to a day off in Cambridge or Oxford. Or to an evening at the Au petit coin de France in Carnaby Street with Roddy, the young man from Hut Four who she'd met in Soho, quite by chance, late one Saturday afternoon. They had spent the whole evening together, both reciting their cover stories before he had announced that he needed to catch a train back to Bletchley and they had discovered that they were, in fact, colleagues.

'Next stop, The Galleon,' shouted the driver, rousing her from her despondency with a jolt.

She should have been looking forward to a day off, but on this occasion, even that had been denied her. She fastened the buttons on her coat, retrieved the little mirror from her handbag, checked her hair and, dropping the mirror back into her bag, got to her feet and made her way along the aisle. 'Be a darling and drop me as close to the door as you can, would you?' she said to the driver. 'It is positively ghastly out there and my hair took an absolute age.'

'Righto,' the driver replied cheerily. 'Meeting a young man, are we, Miss?'

'A young man?' she said, as he pulled the bus over and got to his feet. 'Who needs a young man,' she added airily, 'when I have you, Tommy Higgins?' She leant across and kissed him on the cheek. It made him blush. She knew that it would.

'Good night, Miss,' he said, red faced and flustered.

'We live in hope,' she called out over her shoulder, as she headed off in the direction of the pub. 'We live in hope.'

The saloon bar at The Galleon was already busy. She brushed the rain from her coat and glanced about the bar through the haze of tobacco smoke. It had filled the space below the ceiling and was sinking slowly towards the floor, like a bank of fog descending on the wheat fields. She caught the landlord's eye.

'Well, blow me, if it ain't Elsie Sidthorpe,' he called out.

She removed her coat, shook it and, throwing it over her arm, made her way toward the bar.

'They've 'ardly been and given you a day off, 'ave they,' he added, grinning.

'Chance would be a very fine thing,' she replied, shaking her head. 'Pour me a drink do, Sidney. Before I expire.'

'Busy day?'

She stared at him.

He flashed her another grin. 'What'll it be?'

'I suppose that a Pimm's is out of the question?' she said, hopefully.

'Pimm's? Lawd, listen to her,' he said, turning to the row of old men who were lined up along the bar like a row of crows on a telegraph cable. 'Thinks she's in one of those fancy London drinking 'oles.'

'Aye,' observed one of the old men, between puffs on his pipe. 'In my day, women knew their place.'

'In your day, Arthur,' she replied, giving the old man a withering look, 'I dare say that Mrs Creslaw spent her days washing out your smalls and was grateful for it.' She paused while the old man

BUILDING 41

choked on his tobacco smoke. 'It may surprise you to know that modern women aim a little higher.'

The landlord folded his arms across his chest. 'And she don't mean the rest of your laundry, Arthur.'

The old man snorted, knocked out his pipe in the ashtray on the bar and shuffled off towards the door.

'Silly 'ole bugger,' whispered the landlord. 'Now what'll it be?'

'I take it from the question that for once there is actually a choice?' she said, mocking him.

'For you, Elsie, I'd have driven to the brewery and back myself but as luck would have it, they saved me the trouble and delivered four barrels this morning. Two of mild and two of stout.'

'In that case, Landlord, I will have one half of your finest mild. No,' she added, looking over her shoulder. 'Make that two. And we will have them in the snug, if you will,' she said, exaggerating her accent.

'Very good, m'am,' he replied, mimicking her. 'That'll be a shilling, then,' he said with a straight face.

'Do stop fluttering your eye lashes at him, Elsie. You will give the poor man entirely the wrong idea.'

Elsie dismissed her friend with the wave of a hand. 'Oh, don't be such a spoilsport,' she said, reaching for her glass and draining it. 'Shall we have another?'

'Don't you think you've had enough?'

'Darling, one can never have too much of a good thing. Didn't you know?'

Her companion glared at her.

It had always seemed to Elsie to be such an unlikely friendship. Their backgrounds were, after all, entirely different and, on the face of it, they'd had little in common, save that they had both chosen to join the ATS and found themselves posted, within a few months of each other, to Beaumanor.

Meeting her for the first time at the Leicestershire listening station had been unsettling. She had seemed to see past the pretence almost immediately. How could she know that her outwardly ebullient personality masked a woman who had, since her school days, been unable to maintain all but the most perfunctory of relationships? Even with the many male admirers that her good looks had attracted and with whom she'd appeared so enduringly popular.

It had been her parents doing. They had deposited her at the boarding school for girls with great enthusiasm but, in truth, it had been more for the freedom that the school offered them than for what it was likely to offer Elsie. She had positively despised it, of course. But secretly. She had learned quickly that it didn't do at all to isolate oneself from the other girls, or indeed, from the school's teaching staff who were vindictive, almost without exception, and not at all averse to making an example of a child who was foolish enough to stand out. Elsie had surmised as much within her first term at the school. And so, blessed as she was with a lively, intelligent mind, she had set about masking her true feelings behind a facade of confidence and perpetual cheeriness that, she soon found, became a good deal easier with practice. In the doing of it, she had discovered an ability not so much to *play* the part, as to *become* it. To adopt an altogether different personality and to think and to feel as somebody else might think and feel.

There had been benefits that came from perfecting the technique as a young woman, as well as draw backs. Perhaps her new friend had sensed her inner loneliness. The extent to which she longed for the intimacy that her mask had denied her. The trouble was that she had become so versed at wearing it, that she was no longer sure whether she was capable of playing the part of the person behind the facade. Not that she would ever have admitted it.

Elsie stared at the woman seated opposite her. Having seen, seemingly effortlessly, through the pretence, what had surprised Elsie most of all was that she had appeared to accept both its

BUILDING 41

continued presence and the existence of the woman behind the veil. It was the first time that Elsie had experienced the like of it and, though the mask had not yet allowed her to acknowledge it, the first time that she had experienced something approaching true friendship.

When their transfer from Beaumanor to Bletchley had been announced, Elsie had worried, secretly, that they would be assigned to different sections and would drift apart. Thankfully, on their arrival at Bletchley, they'd been assigned to the same hut and, most happily of all, to adjoining desks.

'In any case, I am not fluttering my eyes at him. I simply feel sorry for the poor man, that is all. Sitting there, on his own like that, when I dare say he has been away at sea for months.'

Her friend wasn't a prude. Elsie had established as much from their many whispered conversations about their male colleagues. When Elsie had suggested that they set about scoring them for eligibility, on a scale of one to ten, she had been reluctant at first but with a little persuasion, had soon entered into the spirit of the thing.

Roddy had, of course, come out on top, although it had surprised Elsie that they had agreed about him. Their taste in men was normally something else that they didn't share. As was Elsie's willingness to engage in a little direct investigation, especially when it came to Roddy. For her friend, however, the exercise had thus far proven purely theoretical.

Elsie leant across the table. 'I'd say that he's at least an eight, wouldn't you? On first impression.' she whispered. 'Not quite in Roddy's league, of course, but a definite also ran.'

Her friend glanced at the sailor. 'Tell me, Elsie, what *do* you find so attractive about a brute in uniform?'

'Oh, darling, do you have to be such a snob?'

'I am not a snob,' replied her friend petulantly. 'You will take that back.'

Elsie ignored her demand. 'He would be a near perfect match,' she said, glancing past her friend at the sailor and noting, with satisfaction, that he was watching them.

'What do you mean by that? A match? For whom?'

'For you, darling. Now that I have Roddy, we need to make up a foursome. It would be a perfect scream.'

Her friend's eyes were smouldering to such an extent that they looked like they might spout fire at any moment. Elsie sighed. 'Well, if you're going to insist on passing, I might very well have to hold him in reserve, myself.'

'You will do no such thing,' exclaimed her friend. 'Do you know, if I didn't keep you in check, Elsie Sidthorpe, I dare say that you'd be smuggling every sorry looking tommy back to your hut and getting yourself into the most frightful trouble.'

'Tommy? He is a chief petty officer at the very least.'

They both turned as the sailor, having downed the rest of his pint, pulled back his chair and stood up.

'Good school, I'd say,' said Elsie. 'Look at the way he holds himself. From a long standing naval family. Father was a captain. Now retired, of course. To the family pile somewhere in the home counties,' she enthused. 'A little land. A boat on the Thames, perhaps.'

The sailor looked towards them and smiled.

'Oxfordshire, I'd say,' Elsie continued, with certainty. 'Henley-on-Thames.'

Her friend turned towards her. 'Oh, honestly Elsie, how can you possibly tell that he comes from Henley-on-Thames, for heaven's sake?'

'Years of practice, darling.'

'Years of drinking, more like,' her friend scoffed.

The sailor had picked up his kit bag and was walking toward them.

'Now look what you have done,' her friend whispered, her face flushing madly.

BUILDING 41

'Excuse me ladies,' he said when he had reached them. 'I see that your glasses are empty. Could I, perhaps, offer you both a drink?' The accent was unmistakably Cockney although he was making an effort to mask it.

'Thank you. That would be perfectly splendid...' Elsie hesitated, glancing at the insignia on his jacket.

His eyes followed hers. 'Petty Officer,' he said looking up and holding out his hand. 'Ronald Warren. But you can call me Ronnie. Everybody does.'

Her friend glanced at her.

Elsie ignored her triumphalism. 'Elsie Sidthorpe,' she said, holding out her hand. 'And this is...'

'Martha,' her friend interrupted.

He took her hand.

'Martha Watts.'

'Delighted, I'm sure,' he said, still doing his best to match their accents.

The two women stared at each other for a moment and then burst into peels of laughter.

'Isn't he an absolute hoot?' Elsie said, as the sailor made his way, unsteadily, toward the bar.

'He's a bit full of himself, if you ask me. To hear him talk, you'd think that he'd single-handedly sunk half the German fleet. I bet he's never even seen a U-boat, let alone boarded one.'

Elsie giggled. 'You cannot blame a man for trying. He wants to impress you, darling.'

Martha pulled a face.

Elsie leant forward. 'You know what they say about sailors don't you?'

Martha's face was a mixture of disapproval and despair. 'No, I most certainly do not.'

'They say,' Elsie whispered, holding her hand to her mouth, 'that they have a girl in every port.'

'It would not surprise me.'

Elsie considered another retort.

'And, before you say another word,' Martha said, interrupting the reply that had been forming on Elsie's lips. 'Bletchley is most definitely not a port and I have, in any case, absolutely no intention of becoming one of his conquests.'

Elsie blinked. Whatever it was that she was going to say was now lost in the comfortable haze that had settled around her.

'As for you, Elsie Sidthorpe,' Martha added, lowering her voice, 'might I remind you that you are already attached to a certain young man from Hut Four?'

'Attached, darling. Not… shackled,' Elsie hiccuped. She glanced towards the bar. By the look of it, she was not the only one to have had one drink too many. The sailor was not so much weaving his way back towards them, as listing from side to side like a rudderless schooner. Quite how he was managing to hold onto the tray, on which he had balanced three glasses, was a mystery to her.

'I said, quite clearly, that I didn't want another one,' Martha complained when she spotted the glasses.

'Oh, do go and help him, darling. The poor man is going to end up in a heap on the floor.'

Martha gave her a look like daggers.

'Very well, then I will,' Elsie said, clambering to her feet. At which point the room began to spin. She grinned foolishly and sat back down.

'Oh, honestly Elsie, you're a perfect state,' Martha said, getting to her feet. She marched the short distance to the sailor, who was listing slightly to port and held out her hand.

Elsie couldn't hear the exchange between them but she noted with satisfaction that Martha had held out her arm. Ronnie Warren took it and allowed himself to be piloted back to their table.

'Petty Officer Warren, might I say how much we have enjoyed your splendid company, this evening,' Elsie said as he flopped down into his seat.

BUILDING 41

'The pleasure's been all mine,' Warren said, grinning.
'However, there is one matter which I feel we must clear up.'
Martha's expression betrayed her mistrust.
'The very beautiful, and might I say very *single*, Miss Watts, has,' she said, warming to the task, 'though she is, of course, far too well mannered to raise the matter with you directly, expressed a certain level of scepticism as to the accuracy of your earlier claims regarding submarines.'
Martha's face had flushed crimson.
The sailor looked at her blankly.
'In short, Ronnie, if I can call you that?'
He tipped his head in assent.
'Miss Watts thinks it entirely unlikely that, in reality, you have indeed been aboard one of Herr Dönitz's infamous U-boats.'
'Oh, does she now?' he said, folding his arms across his chest.
'She does,' Elsie said, hiccuping again.
'Well, let me tell you,' he said turning toward Martha who was looking like she'd swallowed a toad. 'That not only have I been aboard one, I have the evidence with me to prove it.'
Martha had opened her mouth to speak but had evidently thought better of it.
He reached for his bag and started to untie the drawstring.
'Elsie, really' Martha said, flashing her eyes at her friend. 'There is no need,' she said, turning back to the sailor. 'She is just teasing.'
'Not at all,' he said, evidently finding what he was looking for and pulling it from the bag.
The book had a soft red cover with a white paper label. On it, stamped in bold red letters, were two words in German.
Martha's expression told Elsie that she was not alone in recognising them.
'I liberated this myself,' Warren said, waving the book about in the air, like the trophy that it evidently was, 'from the wireless room on U-110. After we'd put a bullet in the wireless operator's head.'

She caught Martha's eye.

'The Kapitänleutnant was none too pleased, I can tell you,' he said at the top of his voice.

Martha turned towards him. 'Show me,' she said, urgently.

He handed her the book.

Elsie watched her leaf through its pages. 'Well?'

'Where on Earth did you get it?' Martha said in a tight whisper.

'I told you. From a German U-boat,' Warren replied, sounding for all the world like a small boy caught with his hands in the biscuit tin.

'Who else knows that you have it?'

'Well, nobody does. I mean, I thought I'd…'

Martha interrupted him. 'You shouldn't have it, Ronnie. Really you shouldn't.'

'It's just a little keepsake…' Warren looked like it was beginning to dawn on him that revealing the book might not have been his finest moment.

'Is one of you going to tell me what it is?' Elsie said, now thoroughly intrigued.

Martha gave her a piercing stare and vehemently shook her head.

'There's no harm in it, is there?' Warren said, looking crestfallen.

'Put it back in your bag and not another word about it,' Martha said, handing the book back to him and looking around the pub nervously. 'If I were you, I'd hand the thing in, at your earliest opportunity.'

'Well I can hardly do that now can I?'

'Why not?' Martha snapped.

'Well, I've had the blessed thing for three years.'

'*Three years*?' Martha said, her eyes bulging ever so slightly, Elsie noted.

'Yes. May 1941 it was.'

'You have been walking around with that in your kit bag for three years?'

Warren nodded.

BUILDING 41

Martha reached for her glass and emptied it. Then she put the glass on the table, sat back in her seat and closed her eyes.

'Mr Warren, might I congratulate you?' Elsie announced, hiccupping yet again. 'I have been trying, all evening, to persuade my friend to unwind with a drink. Your little surprise seems to have succeeded where my very best efforts had altogether failed.'

Martha opened her eyes and, for a moment, the two women held each other's gaze.

'I don't suppose that you have any other little wonders in that bag?' Elsie said, turning to the sailor. 'American cigarettes would be wonderful. I am positively gasping.'

Warren shook his head.

'Oh come now, you must have obtained all sorts of treasures on your travels,' she teased him.

'Well, there's half a dozen yards of American knicker elastic I got from a merchant seaman at Portsmouth docks, if that is any good?'

Elsie opened her mouth to speak but thought better of it.

Warren reached for his glass and drained it. 'I tell you what,' he said. 'I'll go and see if the landlord has any cigarettes. You're not the only one who fancies a smoke.' He hauled himself to his feet and lurched off towards the bar.

'Well?' Elsie said, as soon as he was out of earshot. 'What was in the book that put you in such a terrible spin?'

'Don't give me that. You saw the label as well as I.'

'"Geheim Reichssache",' Elsie said. 'Intriguing.' She reached for the kit bag.

'What are you doing?'

'Oh come on, let me see.'

Martha looked panic stricken, grabbed the kit bag and pulled it from her grasp. 'Are you mad? Warren is going to get himself into the most dreadful trouble for taking it.'

'So we will take the book and save him the trouble.'

'You will do no such thing.'

'Now look here. Either you tell me or I am going to have to insist on examining the book for myself,' she said, trying to look serious but failing utterly.

'Elsie, this is no laughing matter.'

Elsie said nothing but hiccuped again.

Martha sighed. 'Oh, very well.' She leant across the table and whispered in her ear.

'Really?'

Martha nodded.

'How absolutely splendid that it should have fallen into our hands.'

'It has not fallen into our hands.'

Elsie nodded sagely. 'We can hand it into the Naval Section in the morning. Mr Birch will know what to do with it.'

'And how, precisely, are you going to explain how it came to be in your possession?'

She looked at Martha blankly.

'Elsie, I absolutely forbid it.'

'Oh, very well,' Elsie said, her voice sulky, like a child's.

At that moment, there was a commotion at the bar.

'For the love of God, what now?' Martha said, turning.

'It seems that our wayward Petty Officer requires your assistance.'

He was standing with his back to the bar, another tray of drinks in one hand, beckoning towards them with the other. A little group of men at the bar were also waving at her, in between bouts of bawdy laughter.

'This is positively the last time I ever go drinking with you, Elsie Sidthorpe, I swear it,' Martha said, getting to her feet.

'Tush, tush,' replied Elsie, waving her away. 'Do not forget the cigarettes.'

Martha turned and stomped off toward the bar.

BUILDING 41

Elsie hesitated and then, watching the bar carefully for any sign that she was being observed, slid across into the seat beside the kit bag, pulled the drawstring and pushed her hand inside.

CHAPTER FIVE

Martha Watts opened her eyes. She had been vaguely aware of a noise from the lane outside her bedroom window. Muffled voices. Doors banging in the distance. That she had managed to hear anything above the sound of her friend's incessant snoring was a minor miracle. She had tried nudging her. She had even managed to turn Elsie onto her side but to absolutely no avail.

Martha turned on to her back and stared towards the ceiling, her thoughts drifting randomly. *Cold.* The thought had registered itself in her mind quite without warning. *Dear Lord but I am freezing!* She pulled her hand from beneath the sheet that, thankfully, still covered her and felt about in the darkness for the rough woollen blanket. She'd found it in a trunk at the foot of the bed on the day she'd moved into the little cottage. It had kept her warm every night she'd spent in the billet since.

After a short search her hand found the blanket's edge. *Oh, for heaven's sake.* Elsie had wrapped it around herself greedily.

Martha yawned, noting in the light from the lamp in the lane outside her window, the vapour trail that floated up from her mouth towards the ceiling, as though her soul was departing her. She reached for the clock on the table beside her bed, held it up to the light and groaned. Untangling herself from the single sheet, she slid out of bed, padded across to the window and peered out into the darkness. A light shone dully from an upstairs window in the pub at the top of the lane but there was no sign at all of the source of the voices that had disturbed her. She turned, reached for her dressing gown and made her way out of the room, closing the door softly behind her.

Martha Watts knelt in front of the flickering fire, her thoughts wandering among the flames. Why did Elsie insist on taking such risks? When the landlord had finally called last orders, she had been quite incapable of making her way back to the Park. Ronnie Warren, who had fared little better, had offered to escort her and, had it not been for Martha's insistence that she spend the night at her billet, Elsie would have gone, too.

It was not the first time. Elsie had the advantage both of beauty and of intelligence and, with a background like hers and with a fair wind, she might want for nothing in life. Yet she seemed so entirely immune to caution. So keen to flirt with disaster. Did she really wish to bring it about? At times it had seemed so. But even at their first meeting, Martha had sensed in her friend, that beneath the facade, lurked a lonely, rootless soul who, whether through choice or circumstance, seemed to be adrift in the world.

Martha sighed and poked the fire. It was a good thing for Elsie that Martha had made her see sense. Warren had appeared a decent enough sort of chap, but really. It had been perfectly obvious that he'd drunk as much as the two of them combined. Imagine them both. Arriving back at the Park's gates, in such a perfect state. Assuming, of course, that they'd been capable of finding their way back in the darkness, which Martha very much doubted.

She clambered to her feet, her thoughts turning to the weekend ahead. Elsie would have to fend for herself for a few days. She had been granted two days of leave and she'd absolutely no intention of spending them in Bletchley. It had been more than a month since she'd last seen her mother or spent a night in her own bed. Tonight, come hell or high water, she was going home.

She turned and began to tidy away the clutter of the evening before. They had arrived back at the little cottage shortly after eleven and had both gone straight to bed. Elsie had been so drunk that she had needed Martha's help to get undressed, but not before she had deposited her bag, her coat and her shoes in three different corners of the living room.

As Martha retrieved the now crumpled coat, something slid from its inside pocket and flopped onto the floor at her feet. It took her a moment to register what it was. She stared at it in open mouthed disbelief. Transfixed. How on Earth had Elsie managed it? Warren had put it back in the bag and... The answer came to her in a flash. She had left Elsie to rescue Warren from the bar. For two minutes. *Just two.*

Elsie had gone too far. If she handed it in, there would be questions and either she'd be forced to reveal how she had come by it - in which case, Ronnie Warren's career in the Navy could very well be over - or Elsie could find herself suspected of... Martha's hands were trembling as she reached down and snatched up the book. What was Elsie thinking?

She hadn't been thinking. That was just it. She'd been drunk and, once again, had taken the most dreadful risk. Warren had been surprised - perhaps even shocked - by Martha's reaction. She had put that down to his limited intellect. Elsie had no such excuse. To have involved herself in this was an act of sheer recklessness.

She turned and thundered up the stairs, with every intention of dragging her friend from the bed. But as she flung the door open and peered into the room, her resolve had wavered and then slowly evaporated. Elsie had wrapped herself around her pillow and was snoring quietly. Her skin reflected the half-light from the window, like pale porcelain. So perfect and fragile that had she broken the silence with the harsh words she had been framing in her mind only moments before, her friend might have shattered into a myriad of tiny pieces. As Martha gazed at her, it was as though, in sleep, Elsie's mask had faded, exposing the vulnerability of the

BUILDING 41

young woman beneath. For all her bravado, Elsie looked, at that moment, like a small child, asleep and at peace with the world and Martha knew that it was a peace that she could not shatter. She turned and quietly closed the door, a plan already forming in her mind.

She descended the stairs, a good deal more quietly than she had ascended them, found her shoes and coat, slipped the book into her pocket, and left quietly by the cottage's front door.

Outside, the lane was silent, save for the sound of the dawn's chorus. It was bitterly cold and her breath left a trail of vapour as she laboured up the lane toward the pub, still muttering to herself. The light that she had observed from her bedroom was still glowing from an upstairs window. She made her way around to the back of the building and, locating the landlord's door, took a breath before hammering on the door with her clenched fist.

The sudden sound sent a pair of blackbirds screeching their alarm calls up into the trees. She glanced over her shoulder nervously. Then she hammered again. Shortly, there were footsteps from inside and the sound of bolts being drawn back. The door swung open.

'What the bloody 'ell do you want now…' The landlord stopped when he saw her. 'Martha?'

She stared at him. 'I'm sorry. I…'

'What in God's name's the matter, woman?'

'Mr Warren. The sailor, who was drinking with us last night,' she said, her speech hurried. 'Well with Elsie mostly. I mean, I hardly…'

'Petty Officer Warren? What about him?' the landlord interrupted.

'He is staying here, isn't he?'

'He was…'

'I need to see him…' Martha hesitated, as the landlord's words registered. 'What do you mean he *was*?'

The landlord stared at her.

'Sidney? Hurry up and close that ruddy door,' said a voice from inside. A face appeared in the hallway behind him. 'Lord, love us, but you'll catch your death. Sidney, for heaven's sake bring the poor girl inside. Before she freezes solid.'

Martha smiled weakly. 'Come in, lovey,' the woman said, ushering her inside. 'Sidney, you clot. What were you thinking?'

'I'm terribly sorry to disturb you,' Martha apologised. 'But I really must see Mr Warren. It is a most important matter.'

'Well isn't Mr Warren the popular one?' the landlord's wife said, her hands on her hips.

The landlord stared at her. 'It wouldn't have something to do with that book would it?'

'What book?' She hadn't wanted to sound evasive but she knew that she had.

'I thought so,' said the landlord. 'You'd better sit down.'

'You said that Warren *was* staying here,' Martha said, once the landlords's wife had given them their tea and retreated from the little parlour, into the kitchen.

'That's right. He was. Until about an hour ago. Odd fellas. Didn't like the look of them at all.'

'Fellows?'

The landlord nodded. 'Two of them, there were. Damn near bashed my door in.'

The accusation was plain. 'I'm sorry. I thought that you might still be asleep.'

'And I might have been, too,' the landlord continued. 'Just before five, it was. Woke me and Marie up, the noise they were making.'

'What did they want?'

'Warren. Insisted on it in fact.' He hesitated. 'Said they had orders to search him and his room.'

'Really? Whatever for?' Martha said, trying to sound like she didn't know.

'Said that they had received anonymous information. Well, what did he expect? The damn fool. Shouting his mouth off about German submarines. Asking for trouble, he was. And trouble is exactly what he got.'

'Somebody must have overheard him,' Martha said, as if to herself.

'Well it wasn't me, if that is what you're thinking. Though he would have deserved it.'

'No. No, of course not. I wonder who it was?'

'Buggered if I know. Could have been anyone.'

Her mind was racing. 'You mentioned something about a book,' she said, trying to sound only vaguely interested. 'Were they asking about it?'

The landlord took a mouthful of tea. 'That's right.'

'What did you tell them?'

'I told them that I had no idea what they were talking about. That Warren had got himself plastered and had made a damn fool of himself. Which is the truth, right enough.'

Martha said nothing.

'I told them that I didn't see no book. I said that he'd been bragging altogether too loudly about boarding some submarine or other, but that was all.'

Martha looked down into her lap.

'They wanted to know who he'd been talking to.'

Martha's head came up.

'I told them that he'd spent most of the evening propping up the bar, talking to whoever was daft enough to listen to him... Well, I didn't want to drop you and Elsie in it, now did I?'

Martha smiled, weakly. 'I rather think that Elsie is going to drop herself in it one day, despite both our best efforts.'

'Sounds about right to me. I don't know what she'd do without us,' he said grinning.

Martha returned the smile. 'The book, I...'

'I don't know about any book and I don't want to know about it,' the landlord interrupted.

Martha could feel the shape of the book beneath her coat. 'Do you think he will tell them?'

The landlord appeared to consider the question. 'Warren's in enough trouble as it is. I doubt that he's going to want to get himself, or two nice young ladies from Bletchley, into any more.'

Martha looked down at her hands again. She hoped fervently that he was right.

CHAPTER SIX

Sunday, April 17, 2005

I pushed the key into the lock and opened the door with a twist of my wrist. There it was again. Even more noticeable in the darkness somehow, than in daylight. An underlying odour of mustiness. I was sure that it was coming from beneath the floorboards. Damp, seeping in from outside. Maybe a leaking drain pipe. That's the trouble with old houses. Always another job to do. You start one and it leads to another. We'd taken up the carpet and now I was going to have to lift the floor boards, damn it. I stepped over the threshold and eased the door closed behind me, trying to avoid the already familiar clack of the lock as it engaged the door frame.

The dining room was an obstacle course of packing cases. A little clearer than it had been on the day we moved in but not much. Neither of us had found the time to unpack. Not properly, anyway.

Thankfully, enough orange light from the sodium street lamp outside was filtering in through the temporary curtains that we'd put up, to enable me to pick my way cautiously toward the kitchen at the rear of the house. With a little luck I might make it, without ending up on my arse.

The kitchen was in near total darkness. I groped for the light switch and stepped onto something hard, sending it skittering across the floor. Even with my ears still buzzing, the sound it made was like a klaxon. 'For fuck's sake,' I muttered to myself in irritation.

We hadn't argued about the cat. Which was something, at least. Because we'd argued about pretty much everything else. Twice now, it had ended in tears. I'd done my best to explain away the tension. After all, along with divorce and bereavement, wasn't moving house supposed to be one of life's great stresses? But if I had thought that she'd swallowed it, half an hour in the back of a taxi with Mike, on the way to the station from the gig we'd attended in London, had destroyed that particular illusion.

I'd known Mikkel Eglund since our days together at university and Jane Mears, his new partner, since I'd started at Bletchley Park. They had become our two closest friends. On reflection, it was hardly surprising that she had chosen to confide in them. The previous year's events had brought us all closer together. Still, I had not reacted well when, sitting in the back of the taxi, Mike had told me how upset she'd been and how worried they both were. Giving him a hard time had been unfair and I was already regretting it.

Ignoring the mess, I walked across to the stove and touched the kettle with the tip of my finger. It was still warm. I lifted it to check whether there were was enough water. There wasn't. So I filled it from the tap, re-fitted the lid, replaced the kettle on the stove and lit the gas.

Mike had been right. I'd been on a short fuse ever since the piece in The Sun. Not just at home but at work. With everyone.

We'd all had to learn to live with the media interest and it did have an upside. I'd been flavour of the moment until The Sun had run that bloody story. Then it had all gone to hell on a handcart. One minute I'd been a national hero. The little guy, who had taken on and exposed Max Banks MP who, at the time, had been hotly tipped to become the country's next Prime Minister. The next, I

BUILDING 41

was a man with a secret past. Then worse, a man with something to hide.

And then there had been the Radio 4 interview. What a total disaster that had been. I'd just lost it. The following morning there'd been paparazzi camped outside my Golders Green flat. When, a couple of weeks later, we'd finally moved to Leighton Buzzard, the Bedfordshire town made famous by sand, Gossard's bra factory and Kaja-bloody-googoo, the paparazzi had arrived along with the removal lorries.

In truth, though, while the press intrusion certainly hadn't helped, it wasn't the cause of the tension between us. I just wanted to tell her in my own good time. Why was that such a problem? The trouble was that Mike now knew the real cause. He knew it because, like an idiot, I'd told him. Which meant that in no time at all Jane would know too. Hell, he'd probably already told her. I should have kept my mouth shut.

While I waited for the kettle to boil, I found a dustpan and brush and started to sweep up the little circles of dried cat food that I'd inadvertently distributed around the kitchen floor. It had been Mike's revelation that she had spoken to them, that had got to me. Had I really been such a shit to live with? So unapproachable that she could not have come to me?

I knew that I had. It was having it pointed out that had been so hard to swallow. Partly, I suppose, because it had forced me to acknowledge the gulf that had opened up between us, where none had existed before. I emptied the dustpan and stood, staring at the kettle as it began to boil. I just needed time. Why couldn't she see it?

The kettle began to shrill. As I reached out to kill the whistle, I thought I heard a voice. I opened the kitchen door and tiptoed across to the foot of the stairs. 'Are you awake?' I said quietly, half-hoping that she wasn't.

'I am now. Thanks to the racket you're making,' replied Ellen Carmichael. She sounded wide awake. Like she hadn't been asleep at all.

'Sorry. I stepped on Jade's food bowl. Do you want tea? I've just boiled the kettle.'

'Yes, all right and will you please put the chain on the door before you come up?'

Just for the record, I always put the chain on the door before going to bed. But she still had to remind me. Why do women do that? We'd already argued about it.

'Of course,' I replied, resigned to another argument.

'Well you didn't last night.'

How is that you can love someone, I mean really love them, like I love Ellen, yet still find yourself harbouring a secret desire to throttle them in their sleep? 'Actually, I did.'

'No. Actually, you didn't and there's no need to be defensive.'

Strike one. Her latest tactic. There was no real way to counter it. I mean, how do you respond to someone who accuses you of being defensive? Say, "No, I'm not"? Damned if you do and damned if you don't. Such a clever ploy.

'I just want to feel safe,' she continued. 'I would have thought that you'd have understood that.'

Strike two. The vulnerability thing. Guaranteed to kill off any possible counter argument. Strategic genius. You have got to hand it to women. When it comes to psychological warfare, men are definitely the inferior sex. It had to stop. We had barely unpacked and we were already at each other's throats.

Maybe it was my inexperience. I'd never lived with anyone before. Apart from family. Until I met Ellen, I'd never even wanted to. Just a day before meeting her I'd been telling Jane, over lunch, that I'd every intention of staying single. Less than a year later and here we were, living together. Bickering about everything. Maybe I just wasn't cut out for it.

'Are you coming up or do you have work to do?' she called out.

BUILDING 41

'No, I'm knackered. I'll just get the tea.'

'Well, don't forget the chain, all right?' she said, her voice a little softer. 'And the back door.'

'I won't.'

'How was the band?' she said, as I pulled my shirt off over my head.

'Pretty good,' I replied, tugging my arms out of the sleeves. 'Sime was on great form too…' I caught her eye. She was pulling a face. 'Sime? You remember, I told you about him? He was DJ'ing?'

'Oh. Right.'

Like she was interested. I waited.

'And Mike?' she tried again.

'What about him?'

She hesitated. 'Did he enjoy it?'

'Seemed to. You know Mike.'

She reached for her tea. 'Did he manage okay?'

She was trying to sound only casually interested but I knew what she was doing. 'Mike was fine.'

It was barely ten months since Mike had been shot and left for dead in the woods, south of Little Wymondley in Hertfordshire by Stephens, the MP's driver. One bullet had passed clean through his shoulder. The other had smashed the bones of his right foot, so that it was a miracle that he was walking at all.

Ellen watched me unbuckle my belt. I slid off my jeans and threw them over the chair at the foot of the bed. It was a cheap, metal framed bed we'd bought from Argos, with the last of the money from the sale of my flat. Ellen had painted it pale green, which sounds pretty grim but I quite like it. In a painted-metal kind of way.

'What did you two talk about?'

It was so obvious. 'Talk? At the 100 Club? You are kidding. My ears are still buzzing.'

'Afterwards, then. You must have gone for a drink?'

I shook my head. 'He wanted to get home.' I was naked now. I usually sleep that way. Unless it is really cold. 'He was worried that Jane would be waiting up for him,' I said, getting in beside her.

'He could have called her.'

I reached for my tea. 'Guess so, but he didn't.'

'Oh.'

It was amazing how much disappointment she could get into one small word. *This has to stop.* I took a breath. 'You put him up to it, didn't you?' It sounded more accusatory than I had intended.

Ellen looked away and for a moment I thought that she was going to deny it. 'I asked him to talk to you, yes.'

'So what, you couldn't speak to me yourself?'

'Harry, I've tried, but…'

'But what? I damn near bite your head off? That's what you told them, isn't it?'

'Well, don't you?' she returned.

'That's not the point.'

She was staring at me. 'So, what is the point? Are you going to tell me?'

It really wasn't her fault. None of it was. I didn't really blame her for talking to them. Even if it had dented my ego. I felt her take hold of my hand.

'Look. Harry. Whatever it is, talk to me.'

I didn't know where to begin.

'Please?'

'I wanted to get it straight. That's all. I'd have spoken to you about it in the end. I just wanted to do it in my own time.'

Ellen hauled herself upright, tucked a pillow behind her back and faced me.

'I needed time but what with the bloody press,' I said, nodding towards the window. 'The house and everything else…' I still didn't know where to begin.

BUILDING 41

Ellen said nothing. She was a good listener. I had to give her that.

'I'm sorry,' I said quietly. It seemed like the right place to start. The only place to start.

'For?'

'For being such a shit. For taking it out on you.'

She leant across and kissed my forehead with such tenderness that the emotion of it caught in my throat. 'You're the best thing that's ever happened to me,' I said. 'You know that, don't you?'

Ellen's face creased into a half smile. 'Er.. Yes. Actually, I do. But you could make it easier, you know.'

I hadn't chosen to make it difficult.

'You've been a bloody nightmare these last few weeks. Like a bear with a sore head.'

She was right. I had. I couldn't deny it.

'The pants on the bathroom floor, I can deal with,' she said with mock sincerity.

I smiled. 'I did warn you about that.' I had. Leaving my pants on the bathroom floor was a habit I took pride in. It was a standing joke between us though, like the pants, it was probably wearing a bit thin.

'It's the silence, Harry,' she added. 'The constant denial that anything is wrong, when I know that there is. You've been pushing me away.'

'I'm sorry. I never meant…'

'I know,' she interrupted. 'I know that dealing with what happened has been hard for you. Especially with the press and all that. It's not been easy for me either you know. When I close my eyes at night, I still get flash backs to the bottom of that lift shaft. The sound of Marcus falling and the state of him when he hit the bottom. I don't think I'll ever forget that.'

Marcus Dawson. He'd joined us at Belsize Park. More than that, he'd led the descent into the shelter in search of some sign of Martha Watts, the Bletchley log reader who had been missing since

1944, a mystery that Ellen's Great Aunt Elsie, herself a Bletchley veteran, had set me the task of unravelling. Marcus, Ellen and I had abseiled down the lift shaft but when we'd swapped places, on the return leg, and Tomasz Dobrowski had severed the rope, it had been Marcus, rather than me, who had fallen best part of eighty feet. He had still not fully recovered from his terrible injuries. Nobody was really sure that he ever would.

I squeezed Ellen's hand. 'You and me, both.'

'The darkness in that hell hole…' she said, shuddering. 'With nothing but a sixty year old corpse to keep me company. Dear God, what she must have gone through…' Ellen said, reflecting on the log reader's fate. A fate which, some sixty years later, Ellen had very nearly shared.

I'd been so wrapped up in myself that somehow I'd stopped thinking about Ellen. I would never be able to imagine what it had been like for her, shut away in the pitch black, one hundred feet below Belsize Park with the remains of Martha Watts.

'It's Ted, isn't it?' Ellen said suddenly.

Was it that obvious? I nodded.

'Well I'm not stupid. I thought that it was the house at first. Maybe even that it was living with me…'

'No. It was never that.'

'But you're worse each time you go to see him. I'm beginning to dread it. Do you know that?'

'It's not you, Ellen. It has nothing to do with us.'

She was waiting for me to say more.

I sighed. 'That time I went to see him. Just before we moved in. Do you remember?'

Ellen nodded. 'Of course.'

'He spoke to me.'

'He what?' Ellen exclaimed.

'Don't get too excited,' I continued. 'When I say "spoke", it wasn't much more than mumbling, to begin with, anyway.'

'Still, that's fantastic,' Ellen said, clasping my hand.

BUILDING 41

My father had suffered a stroke. Shortly before we began the search for Martha Watts. While he had survived it and had eventually regained consciousness, he'd been unable to communicate in any kind of meaningful fashion and certainly hadn't spoken since. I'd feared that he might never speak again and that, with his silence, all hope of discovering the truth about my mother might be lost. I nodded but it was a half-hearted effort.

'Isn't it?' Ellen added, like she suspected what might be coming.

I stared at her. 'He thinks that she may still be alive.'

'He what?' she gasped. 'Your mother? Oh my God. Does he know where she is?'

I shook my head. 'I don't think so.'

'Then how does he know that she is still alive?'

'I don't think he does. Not with any certainty. But he thinks so.'

'He told you that? I mean, directly. He told you that he thinks she is still alive?'

I nodded and then hesitated. 'His speech is very slurred and, to be honest, a lot of what he says doesn't make any sense.' I hesitated again. 'It's hard to listen to.'

'I would imagine so,' she said, missing the point.

'I mean that he hates her, Ellen. A lot of it is pure bile.'

'Oh.' She grimaced.

'It's hard to listen to him bad mouthing her and to hear the hatred.'

Ellen's excitement had already died. 'I'm sorry. That must be awful for you.'

We both sat, staring at the moon through the bedroom window. Ellen had been asking me to put a blind up ever since we moved in. It was another of the jobs I hadn't got around to doing.

'Do you think he might be right?' she said, suddenly. 'That she really might be alive?'

'That's the problem, isn't it? How the hell do I know whether anything he says is right? Half of it makes no bloody sense and the rest certainly doesn't tally with the way I remember it '

'You were only eight when your mum left, Harry. You experienced her leaving from the perspective of an eight year old child. Ted's memories and yours will be entirely different. They're bound to be.'

'You can say that again.'

'What do you mean?'

'Well, for starters he reckons that she disappeared in 1977 rather than '78, which would have made me seven years old at the time, not eight.'

'But you've always said that it happened when you were eight.'

'I always thought that it happened when I was eight.'

Which was the point. It wasn't just the things that Ted had told me that I'd been struggling to come to terms with. It was the thought that my memories might be little more than fantasy. 'I've got a series of events in my head,' I said, by way of explanation. 'Pictures. Voices. Feelings. Snapshots that I have held onto all these years. Because they were all I had to hold onto. Now I don't even know whether they're real. They could be nothing but fantasies. Stories that I made up in order to make sense of it all.'

Ellen said nothing.

'You must have told yourself something from your childhood, that isn't strictly true. Enhanced it a bit. What your dad did in the war. You know, some piece of family folklore. So many times that you began to believe it. So that it became real. A part of you?'

'We all do that. Create a narrative. About the person we are. The person we want to be.'

'Yeah and then someone comes along and exposes it and you feel…' I hesitated.

'What do you feel?' she said, squeezing my hand.

I thought about it. 'Like I don't even know my own past. Like I'm a bloody fraud.'

'Harry, you're hardly a fraud for remembering things from your childhood a little differently to your father. For filling in the gaps.'

BUILDING 41

I smiled. 'You want a bet? If what Ted says is true, then even my name is fake.'

Ellen stared at me, like she knew something big was coming. 'What do you mean? What does he say?'

Ridiculously, I found it hard to meet her eyes.

'Harry?'

'He says that he's not my father, Ellen.'

'He what?' she gaped.

'He says that Mum lied about that. Actually he says that everything about her was a lie. That she used him. Used all of us. That is was all a pack of lies.'

'You are kidding?'

I shook my head. 'I wish I was.'

'God, almighty. You poor thing.'

'Have you told Kate?'

We were in the kitchen, drinking coffee. I'd been dying for a cigarette. Ellen was pretty tolerant of my smoking but I knew she didn't like it in the house, which was fair enough. So I was standing by the back door trying to blow the smoke out into the night. With limited success, it has to be said. I shook my head. 'I don't think I'm ready for the inevitable "told you so" moment.'

'Do you really think she would?'

'I know she would. Kate is a daddy's girl. Always was. She never understood why I blamed him.'

'She was that much younger than you. She probably doesn't even remember your mother. Your dad was the only real parent she ever had. It's only natural that in her eyes he could do no wrong.'

'Maybe she was right,' I said, smiling ruefully. 'Maybe he did do no wrong.'

'Look, perhaps it was not his fault that your mother disappeared. Perhaps,' Ellen said with emphasis. 'But wiping her out of your lives like she had never existed. Refusing to allow you even to talk about her. Whichever way Kate might try to dress that up now, that was just plain wrong. Whatever your mother did, she was… is still your mother,' Ellen corrected herself. 'He had no right to try to take that away from you.'

She was right. I'd spent a long time hating him for it.

'What are you going to do?' Ellen asked, after a pause.

I blew out a long column of smoke. 'I don't know. I guess I'll keep talking to him or trying to. It's not easy. The last time I was over there, he spent most of it glowering at me. Like it's my fault, for God's sake.'

Ellen said nothing.

'I only got it out of him in the first place because I started yelling at him. Telling him what a selfish old bugger he is. That we have a right to know.'

'You do have a right to know.'

'I know that. You know that. But you should have seen his face, Ellen. So much…' I searched for the word. 'Rage,' I said at last. 'If he could have, I'm sure he'd have leapt out of bed and throttled me.'

Ellen reached for the coffee jug. 'You want another one?'

I nodded. 'Please.'

'It'll keep you awake.'

I shrugged. 'When he gets really worked up,' I continued, 'he starts yelling. No words at first. Just grunts and snorts. That's how it was the first time. I was wiping away the saliva from his chin, when he said something. Once he'd said it, it was like he'd rediscovered how. He repeated it. Over and over.'

Ellen's eyes asked the question.

'"Bitch". That's what he said. "Bitch".'

Ellen flinched.

Ted had always been such a stable and resilient man. I suppose he'd needed to be, bringing up two children on his own. While I'd often railed against him, I'd never seen him lose his self control.

Or swear. Or cry, actually. His strength had been a constant in our lives. Until now. 'I went back. The following evening.'

Ellen nodded. 'I wondered why you did.'

'He became agitated as soon as I entered the room. Refusing to look at me. Mumbling, to himself. Mostly incoherent. So I just sat beside him and waited. It was the strangest thing. Suddenly he was talking.'

'And?'

I shrugged. 'He said that she was a liar. That she lied to him. To all of us. That nothing about her was real.'

'Real? Did he actually use the word?' She seemed surprised.

I nodded.

'Odd word to use.'

'Why?'

She pulled a face. 'If someone betrays you. Lies to you. You're going to feel hurt. Angry. Furious, even. You might call them all sorts of angry, hurtful things. But to say that nothing about her was *real* implies that he thought the deception went deeper. You know, like she was living the lie. I mean really living it. Not just lying to the three of you.'

I took a final draw on my cigarette and stubbed out the butt on the outside wall, sending a little shower of sparks cascading to the ground like a tiny firework. 'You know, I've been thinking about that.'

'What?'

'That she might have been leading some sort of double life.'

Ellen stared at me. 'You don't think she had another family or something, do you?' she said, suddenly. 'I mean, people do.'

I ran my hand through my hair. Another of my habits, along with the pants on the floor thing. 'No, I don't think that's what he meant.'

'Then what?'

I shrugged. 'I'm not sure.' Ted's meaning had been far from clear but he'd said something else that had got me thinking. 'He mentioned the people who came to see us. You know, at the house. After she went. Do you remember me telling you about them?'

Ellen nodded.

I was replaying the scene in my head. Again. There'd been a knock at the door. I'd been upstairs, playing on the landing or maybe in my room. I couldn't remember which. When I had come down there had been a man and a woman standing in the hall. I could see their shapes now, in my mind, silhouetted against the sunlight streaming in through the open door. He'd shown them into the front room. It was only used on special occasions and mostly for guests. He'd told us to wait outside. I'd stood facing the closed door, waiting. Holding Kate's hand.

Ellen was watching me.

'Ted said they wanted us to go with them.'

'Go with them?' Ellen asked. 'Go where?'

'I have absolutely no idea, but I think there may have been raised voices. Like they were arguing about it. I remember feeling scared. You know, like you do when you're a kid. Afraid of what was going to happen to us and I remember Kate, crying.'

'God, it sounds awful. Fancy leaving you standing there? You must have been absolutely terrified.'

I shrugged.

'Did Ted say anything about who they were?'

I shook my head. He hadn't. Not a word.

'Police? Like you said?'

That was certainly how I had remembered it. The story I'd told myself a thousand times. 'I don't know. I'm not sure that anybody ever actually told me that they were police. Ted certainly didn't.'

'But no uniforms?'

'I don't think so. I was a little kid. Can you remember anything, I mean in that kind of detail, from when you were seven or eight?'

'Not much, but then nothing that extreme ever happened to me, thank God.'

BUILDING 41

I lit another cigarette. 'Does it really matter whether they were police?'

Ellen shrugged. She was staring into my eyes but her thoughts were elsewhere. 'Could she have been in some kind of trouble, do you think?' she said suddenly. 'Something that threatened your safety. It might explain the raised voices.'

I shrugged. 'How the hell do I know? How will I ever know, unless Ted tells me? And let's face it,' I added, my tone revealing the underlying bitterness I was feeling, 'if he isn't my father, why would he bother?'

'Oh, come on,' Ellen said, sounding irritated for the first time. 'Now you're just playing the victim. Whether he's your biological father or not, Ted Stammers went to a great deal of trouble to bring up you and your sister. You can conclude from that he loves you. He was wrong not to talk about her. To try to banish her from your lives...' She hesitated. 'Do you know what I think?'

I shook my head.

'I think that he did that because she'd hurt him so terribly that it was the only way that he could cope. Not because he didn't love her but because he did. And not because he wasn't your father.'

I blew out a column of smoke. 'I get the feeling that he didn't know about that until after she'd left.'

Ellen looked surprised. 'What makes you say that?'

'I don't know. He kept saying she *admitted it*. Like it was later.'

'God, it must have been a nightmare. Can you imagine what he went through?'

'Maybe, everything came to a head and she told him. Perhaps it was a last ditch attempt to persuade him to forgive her. To go with her.'

Ellen looked doubtful. 'How was telling him that you were not his son ever going to persuade him?'

I shrugged. 'Perhaps honesty was her only chance in the end.'

'Well, it certainly didn't work, did it?' Ellen said, shaking her head.

I said nothing.

'I mean, far from bringing him around, it led him to spend the next twenty-five years denying her very existence. Hardly the most successful strategy in the world, was it?'

I had been thinking about his reaction to discovering that I was not his son. Trying to imagine how he must have felt. To have suddenly lost a child, like that. A humiliation and a bereavement all rolled into one. And yet he had refused to let me go. Kept me there with him. Every day. A reminder of his loss and his humiliation.

Perhaps Ellen was right. That banishing her from our lives had been his coping mechanism. If, as well as betraying him, she'd also exposed us all to some sort of danger, then he would have had more than enough reason to want her gone from our lives. As that idea struck me, another took hold. Something else that Ted had said. It had seemed so implausible that I'd dismissed it, but suddenly the word was reverberating around my head like a bell. Or a bomb. I ran my hand through my hair.

Ellen was staring at me.

'Am I really that transparent?' I said, pulling a face.

'It's that thing you do with your hand,' she said, mimicking the gesture.

'Yeah, well you might want to sit down for this.'

'What?'

'It is probably…' I hesitated. 'I mean, it is so off the wall…'

'What is?'

'Something else that Ted said.'

'What did Ted say?'

'He mentioned a bomb. Several times.'

'A bomb,' she repeated, like she didn't believe it. Like she was doing what I had done. Dismissing it as nonsense. Which it probably was.

'I know. It's nuts, isn't it?'

'Err… yes.'

I shrugged. 'If she was in some kind of trouble…'

BUILDING 41

'Oh come on.'

'Ellen, I'm not saying that it makes any sense.'

She stared at me. 'What exactly did he say. About this bomb?'

I thought about it. 'I think he was describing a conversation they'd had.'

'About a bomb?' she said, like I wasn't making it any more believable.

'Yes.' I hesitated. 'Oh, I don't know. That's what it sounded like but it was garbled. I really don't know.'

She shook her head. 'Jesus.'

It looked like she was beginning to get a sense of where my head had been for the last couple of weeks.

'I take it that's it. That there's nothing else?'

I nodded. 'Oh actually,' I said, remembering. 'There was something else.'

She glared at me.

'He mentioned a name.'

'A name?'

'He said that somebody else knew. About what, I have no idea. Just that she knew. He kept repeating it.'

'She? Who?'

'Somebody called "Rosemary".'

CHAPTER SEVEN

Sunday, July 11, 1976

She sat with her head bowed and her eyes closed, listening to the sounds of shuffling feet and hushed voices, echoing around the vaulted ceiling high above her, like the wings of a thousand tiny birds. She was never wholly at ease in such places and least of all in the presence of the man who had summoned her to meet him here. The nature of their business felt like an affront. Something she had no business bringing into God's house. This morning, however, the almighty would surely not begrudge her this short respite. The heat outside was unbearable. It had been blazing, without respite, every day for the best part of the last month.

She sensed rather than heard his arrival. Something in the air around her had shifted, subtly. She knew, without opening her eyes, that he was there, beside her. 'You wished to see me,' she said, making little effort to mask her antipathy toward him.

He said nothing.

She waited.

'And here you are,' he answered at last.

It was a simple statement. Intended, no doubt, to remind her of their relative status. *Here I am, indeed.* She opened her eyes.

He was staring toward the front of the church, his attention apparently held by an elderly woman arranging flowers in front of

BUILDING 41

a truly vast gothic pulpit, in dark wood. His appearance was the same as it ever was. Nondescript. No distinguishing marks. Nothing out of the ordinary. Bland. Though she had long since concluded that he must be her junior, perhaps by a significant margin, she had no real idea of his age. 'A little off your beaten track, aren't you?' she suggested, her eyes following his.

'I have other business here. I thought I might kill two birds with one stone.'

'Such an unfortunate phrase.' She flashed him a perfunctory smile, which he did not return.

'Shall we?' he said, getting slowly to his feet.

She hesitated and then rose.

He had turned and, without waiting, strode away toward the vestibule at the back the church and to the wide doorway beyond.

'Jimmy Dobson...' Smith said, as they followed the gravel path that wound its way around the side of the Church to the little memorial garden at the rear.

'What of him?'

'We share an interest in him,' he said casually, as though only vaguely interested in her response. When she said nothing, he went on. 'Though I am not entirely certain what yours is.'

She waited.

'Remind me,' he prompted.

'I am surprised that there is any need. F-branch must surely keep you briefed.'

Smith said nothing.

'Very well,' she said after a pause. 'Dobson apparently has no history. He has no nationality, no doctor and he doesn't pay tax.'

'So it would appear.'

'In point of fact, there does not appear to be any record of him at all, prior to his arrival in England.'

'This is of interest to you because?' Smith said, testily.

They had approached a small wooden bench, in the shade of an over-hanging oak tree. 'Shall we?' she suggested.

Smith gestured his assent.

'Dobson is using a false identity,' she said, lowering herself onto the seat.

Smith sat beside her.

'One that has thus far proven entirely impenetrable. Despite our best efforts. Seemingly yours as well as mine. This is not something that is easily achieved. Which means that his presence here must have some significant purpose.'

'That purpose being?'

She tried to keep her face impassive.

'You have a lead,' he said, his eyes staring off, into the distance.

She hesitated. On the face of it, Smith's interest in Jimmy Dobson was straight forward enough. While Dobson's employer - the Nationalist Union of Great Britain - was undoubtedly on the rise, the Service remained divided about the threat that it posed. F-branch had assigned Smith to assess the risk posed by the ultra right wing party. Which meant that he had a legitimate interest in monitoring Jimmy Dobson, the NUGB's new head of security.

There was, though, more to it than that. There always was where Smith was concerned. Another, hidden agenda. Until she discovered it and even if she did, Smith could not be trusted, least of all with the true reason for her interest in Jimmy Dobson.

'You said "thus far". I take it that you meant until now,' Smith said, matter of factly.

She could not afford to directly obstruct him. Smith was a powerful man, with powerful allies. He was also, notionally at least, her superior. She chose her words carefully. 'There is some other purpose to Dobson's presence here in England. His role at the Nationalist Union is merely a cover.'

'Or perhaps he is simply hiding,' Smith said. 'Laying low, while whatever prompted his change of identity blows over.'

She didn't believe that any more than he did. 'Then why, if his intention is to lay low, take such a high profile job at the NUGB? One that was so certain to attract our attention? Mr Dobson has some other purpose. I wish to know what it is.'

'Speculation, nothing more,' Smith said dismissively. He took a handkerchief from his trouser pocket and used it to wipe the sweat from his forehead. It was an unusual admission of weakness.

'Perhaps,' she conceded.

'Unless of course, you have discovered something that reveals this *purpose*.'

Smith was no fool.

'Tell me,' he said, simply.

It was a direct challenge and one which she could not ignore. 'I have been watching Mr Dobson, closely. When he is not acting as the NUGB's enforcer-general, he has been trying to trace someone.'

'Who?' Smith demanded.

'His name is Ronald Warren.'

'Why? What does Dobson want with him?'

She smiled. 'If I knew that, then Dobson's purpose might be a good deal clearer than it is.'

Smith snorted. 'You are, of course, assuming that Dobson's interest in this Warren and his role at the NUGB are not connected in some way.'

'If there is a link then I have not found it. Warren has no particular political affiliation and no criminal record. In fact, Warren has very little record at all. He retired for health reasons, in 1964, from a singularly undistinguished career in the Royal Navy and now lives alone, on his Navy pension.'

Which was true, so far as it went. Warren's career had not, however, been entirely without incident. An apparently minor and unresolved matter, with no obvious link to Jimmy Dobson, but troubling nonetheless. She had managed to expunge it from Warren's record as a precautionary measure.

'Perhaps then, the sooner Dobson traces him, the better,' Smith said, after a moment's further thought.

'A high risk strategy, given Dobson's recent record with a baseball bat.'

'Then suggest to Warren that he takes a course in self defence,' Smith replied.

'Actually, I am considering moving Warren to a safe house, while I attempt to discover the reason for Dobson's interest in him. If it becomes necessary, I'd also like to bring Dobson in for questioning.'

Smith turned and faced her. 'Whatever Dobson's interest in your retired sailor, our imperative is that the NUGB do not become aware of our interest in them. If you move Warren, even with a cover story, Dobson will suspect. Bringing him in is simply out of the question.'

'With respect, that may be your imperative. It is not mine,' she said, cautiously.

'What is your imperative, exactly?' Smith said, facing her. 'You seem disproportionately concerned with the safety of someone who, according to you, is apparently of such low value.'

'Warren is an ex-serviceman,' she shot back. 'I deem him to be at risk. We have a duty to protect him and I intend to do exactly that. In any case, perhaps it is time to let Mr Dobson know that we have noticed him. If he has something to hide, perhaps that knowledge will prompt an error.'

Smith was thoughtful. 'No,' he said shortly. 'What you are suggesting is impossible,' he said, getting to his feet. Evidently her audience with him was over.

Rosemary Sellers closed her eyes and listened to the sound of Smith's receding foot steps on the gravel path.

CHAPTER EIGHT

Monday, November 13, 1944

Elsie Sidthorpe stepped from the train carriage onto the platform at Bletchley Station, pulling her coat tightly about her and wishing for the hundredth time that it was May. Or June, better still. It was bitterly cold on the platform and the carriage had been barely any warmer. Above her, the steel grey clouds looked ominously heavy, as though they might suddenly disgorge a great carpet of snow. She hoped, fervently, that they would not, at least until she'd arrived back at the Park. She glanced at her watch. She was due there, at her desk in a little less than thirty minutes. Her desk. Beside what would now be an empty desk. Martha's desk.

When, on Saturday morning, a weeping Mrs Watts had told her over the telephone, that Martha had not arrived home the previous evening and that there had been no sign of her since, Elsie had not hesitated. She had gone straight to McFarlane, the balding Scot who managed the hut roster and begged him to allow her to go to London. After all, she had been due a Sunday off and would have had it too, had several of the girls not come down with the flu. McFarlane had been surprisingly sympathetic, confirming Elsie's suspicion that he had a soft spot for the now missing log reader. At the end of Saturday's shift, Elsie had rushed to gather together her things and to make it it to the station in time for the eighteen thirty-four to Euston. She had run across the station forecourt, as the train had pulled in and had clambered aboard the London train with only seconds to spare.

'Elsie?'

She hadn't been the only passenger to alight at Bletchley. The platform was a writhing mass of bodies, hats, winter coats and baggage. She scanned the crowd for the source of the familiar voice.

'Elsie?' he said, emerging from the melee.

Framed by a shock of fiery red hair, which he had inherited from his father, Roddy's wide, open face typically shone with an enthusiasm for life. It had been one of the things that had attracted her to him. But the disquiet she noted in his eyes, as he pushed his way toward her, made her heart flutter with anxiety.

'Roddy?'

'Hello, darling,' he said, smiling broadly, but the lie of it was in his eyes.

'What's wrong?' she said in a low voice, as he slid one hand easily around her waist and, with the other, reached for her bag.

'Not here,' he whispered, brushing her cheek with his lips. 'Behave normally. I've got a car outside.'

'A car? Whatever for?' she replied, already alarmed.

He was staring at her. Urging her on with his eyes. 'Come on,' he said, tugging at her arm.

She allowed him to steer her along the platform, her sense of alarm deepening. Then, through the busy ticket office and out onto the station forecourt.

'This way,' he said, directing her toward a familiar little car, parked between a red Post Office van and a black taxi. He opened the boot and they placed the bags inside. 'Quickly,' he said moving to the passenger door.

Elsie didn't think she'd ever seen him looking so anxious. 'What are you doing with Johnny's Flying Ten?' she asked, as soon as they were both seated.

BUILDING 41

He started the engine and eased the car out from its parking space.

'Roddy? What is going on?'

'Johnny thought it might be better to take the Ten, rather than mine.' Little beads of sweat had formed on his forehead, despite the cold.

'Why? Is there something wrong with yours? Where are we going?' He had turned left, away from the Park.

'What in God's name happened at the Galleon on Thursday evening, Elsie?' he said, suddenly.

She stared at him. 'What do you think happened? I had a few drinks with Martha. It was a most enjoyable evening, as a matter of fact. That is Martha, by the way. The same Martha who didn't arrive home on Friday. If you are remotely interested?'

Roddy flushed. 'Yes, of course I'm interested. I'm sorry. Is there any news?'

'None at all. Poor Mrs Watts is in the most dreadful state,' Elsie said, irritably.

'Oh Lord. I am sorry. Really, I am. But I rather think we have other pressing matters to attend to.'

'What other pressing…' she hesitated. 'Now look here, Roddy. Where exactly are we going? I've got to be back at the hut and…'

'Elsie.'

'I cannot possibly be late. It was terribly good of Bob McFarlane to give me the day off. I can't…'

'Elsie,' Roddy said, raising his voice.

Elsie stared at him but said nothing.

'Yesterday afternoon, just as I was finishing up, two men came into Hut Four. Without further ado, I was frog marched up to the mansion. In full view of everyone, I might add. Where I was interrogated in the most unpleasant fashion.'

'Two men?'

'Yes, and before you ask who they were, I have absolutely no idea.'

'What did they want?'

'They wanted to know what you were doing at the Galleon on Thursday evening for one thing and your movements since. They also wanted to know the nature of our relationship,' Roddy said as though it had been an impertinence. 'I mean, honestly…'

'I trust that you were discreet,' she interrupted him.

'And some nonsense about a sailor by the name of…'

'Warren,' she said, finishing his sentence for him. She had already guessed that this was going to be about the petty officer.

He glanced at her. 'Yes, Warren. I said that I'd never heard of the man, which they seemed to find rather difficult to believe. You and he were apparently behaving like lifelong friends.'

'If you are going to rant, would you at least keep your eyes on the road?' she said, glaring at him. Roddy had turned onto the Buckingham Road, away from Bletchley Park.

'Then, this morning, the same two chaps were hanging about at breakfast. Damn it if they didn't follow me back to the camp. Or try to. I managed to…'

'What, exactly, did they want to know about Warren?' Elsie broke in.

Roddy paused. 'They wanted to know how you came to be talking to him. Whether you had arranged to meet him there.'

'What nonsense,' Elsie said, scornfully and with a confidence that belied the nervousness she was feeling.

'They seemed to think that he might have passed something to you.'

Elsie snorted, derisively, 'Whatever were they talking about?' But she had dismissed the suggestion a little too easily.

'Elsie, I think you need to take this seriously. They implied that this might have been some kind of exchange. That you met him there for that purpose.'

'Exchange?' Elsie had paled. 'What did you say to that?'

'I said that if you did, then it was news to me. That I'd never even heard of Warren. Which, by the way I haven't.'

BUILDING 41

She'd caught the inflection in his voice. 'Meaning what exactly?'

'Meaning that you made no mention of this Warren chap when we spoke on Friday.'

'Oh, but I am terribly sorry,' she said with as much sarcasm as she could muster. 'I didn't realise that when you asked whether I'd had a nice time, you were expecting an account of everyone I spoke to. Honestly, Roddy, we might be courting but you are not my keeper.'

There was another awkward pause.

'I'm sorry,' Elsie said at last. 'I did not arrange to meet Warren. Until Thursday evening, I'd never clapped eyes on him. He was just there. He offered us a drink and I agreed. If the truth be told, I was rather hoping that he and Martha might get along, but you know what Martha is like. At the end of the evening, we said goodnight and that was the last I saw of him.' Which was not, of course, the whole story. She had decided not to mention taking the codebook from Warren's bag, or the relief that she had felt when, over breakfast on Friday morning, Martha had told her that she had returned it to him.

Roddy seemed to be processing her words. He had a habit of doing that - of retreating into his head when faced with something difficult or uncomfortable. While she tried not to show it, Elsie was having some uncomfortable thoughts of her own. If the two men who had interrogated Roddy were looking for her, they must surely have already found Warren and searched his room at The Galleon. If they were looking for the codebook, then why had they not found it? Martha had returned it to him early on Friday morning. Had Warren hidden the book and blamed its disappearance on Elsie and Martha? At which point, an even more uncomfortable thought began to take shape in her mind.

'They're going to want to question you, you know,' Roddy said suddenly.

'I would have expected them to be waiting for me at the station.'

'Ah. Yes. Well, that was my doing. I told them that you drove down to London.'

She stared at him.

'Otherwise, they would surely have been waiting for you. I wanted to warn you. To give you a chance to think. In case you've…'

'In case I've what?' she cut him short.

'Done something you shouldn't?' he said, like he knew, full well, that she had.

She said nothing.

'Well, you do seem to make rather a habit of it,' he said, glancing from the road, toward her and back again.

'What do you mean by that?' she said indignantly.

'Oh come on Elsie, you are always getting up to some mischief or other. We all notice the risks you take, you know.'

'Oh, really? And who, exactly, are we talking about here?'

'Well Martha for one. She worries about you incessantly.'

The mention of Martha's name brought a vision of her friend's face into Elsie's mind. She dismissed it. 'Did anyone see you leaving in the car?'

'What?'

'It was a perfectly simple question. Did anyone see you leaving?' she repeated, irritably.

'No. Johnny keeps the Ten at The Belles. I walked over…'

'And you're certain that you were not followed?'

'Reasonably.'

'Take me back to the Park, Roddy,' she said, suddenly resolute.

'Are you sure?'

'Stop off at Church Green and we'll swap places. They're bound to be waiting for me. It will be better for you if we don't arrive together. Find Johnny and tell him that he leant me his car. For the trip to London.'

Roddy hesitated and then nodded.

BUILDING 41

'And thank him for me.'

*****

'I've already told you. Until Thursday I had never met Petty Officer Warren. Martha and I were spending an evening together before her trip to London. Mr Warren joined us and I'm rather afraid that we may have all had rather too much to drink. He said a few things about submarines that, with hindsight, he probably should have kept to himself. I would imagine that he was trying to impress us. Foolish, perhaps, but hardly a crime,' Elsie said, trying to sound confident, though she was feeling anything but.

'As the poster says, Miss Sidthorpe, *careless talk costs lives*,' suggested the man seated across the desk. 'Working here, I would have thought you would have understood that better than most.'

He was a middle-aged man with greying hair and a charcoal grey suit. In fact, pretty much everything about him was grey.

'I do understand it. As a matter of fact, Martha told Mr Warren to keep his voice down. More than once.'

The man stared at her, without expression.

She held his eyes.

'You say that the purpose of your visit to London was to see Mrs Watts,' said the second man. He had taken up a position directly behind her, so that she could not see him. If his strategy was intended to unnerve her then it was working.

'I say it because it is the truth, Mr…' she said, attempting to look at him over her shoulder.

'Our names are not important,' said the man sitting opposite.

'To you, perhaps but I would rather like to know them, nonetheless,' she replied, looking at him like she expected a response. 'If you don't mind?'

He ignored her.

'There is a piece of paper and a pencil on the table in front of you,' said the man behind her. 'You will list the names of everyone you have spoken to since your rendezvous with Warren. And I do mean everyone.'

'It was most certainly not a *rendezvous*,' Elsie corrected him. 'A chance meeting. Nothing more.'

'So you say,' the man in the grey suit replied. 'The list, Miss Sidthorpe,' he said, sliding the paper and pencil toward her in one, smooth movement.

It took her little more than a few minutes to complete it. She slid the list back across the desk.

He examined it, without comment. Then he stood up, passed the paper to the man behind her and, after a few seconds, returned to his seat empty handed. 'Why were you so outspoken with the air raid wardens at Gospel Oak?'

She had been more than outspoken. She had been positively rude. But how in God's name had news of it reached their ears? 'Because,' she replied evenly, 'I found it perplexing that they should be offering Mrs Watts an explanation for Martha's disappearance that was and is so obviously nonsensical.'

The man across the desk snorted. 'What qualifies you to say so? I would imagine that the wardens have a little more experience of missing men and women than do you.'

'A perfectly reasonable assumption and one that, until two days ago, I might have shared. However, informing Mrs Watts that Martha was killed in Friday's air raid, when that is the least likely explanation for her disappearance, suggests otherwise.'

'Unlikely perhaps but by no means impossible.'

'As good as,' Elsie shot back. 'But for the avoidance of doubt, I retraced her steps. The fact is that none of the streets along the route she would have taken suffered any bomb damage during Friday's raid. An observation, incidentally, that the wardens later confirmed. The closest that any bomb fell was at Aldgate. Miles from Martha's route.'

'Then perhaps she was at Aldgate,' said the suited man. 'Or elsewhere,' he added, pointedly.

BUILDING 41

'Nonsense. She had no reason to be there or anywhere else.'

He snorted again. 'You cannot possibly know that.'

He was right, in theory only. 'But I know my friend,' she said, with conviction. 'Martha told her mother that she would be on the eighteen-thirty from Bletchley, so that Mrs Watts would know when to expect her. Going elsewhere would have delayed her and worried her mother terribly. Something that Martha simply would not have done.'

'Unless it was necessary for her to be elsewhere, for some reason,' said the grey suited man.

'A secret errand or, perhaps, a delivery,' added the man behind her.

'What errand? What delivery? What are you talking about?'

Neither man replied.

'We have a witness who saw Petty Officer Warren showing you and Miss Watts a note book, which our witness says Warren produced from his kit bag. A note book which is no longer in his possession.'

It was the first piece of positive information that they had given her and, for the first time, Elsie was uncertain about how to respond. Martha had returned the codebook to Warren. That was what she had said. 'Then, your witness must be mistaken,' she said, daring her interrogator to disbelieve her. If they were relying on a witness and the codebook was missing then Warren had almost certainly denied ever having it. Which meant, either that he had hidden it, destroyed it or... 'I have absolutely no recollection of any notebook,' she said, carefully.

The man in the suit stared at her.

'I do remember him saying that he had half a dozen yards of American knicker elastic in his bag,' Elsie added, trying to buy herself some thinking time. 'It is strange the things that you remember when you've had too much to drink, don't you think?' It was, perhaps, not the most helpful of statements to have made in the circumstances. She replayed her conversation with Martha over the breakfast table. Then she replayed it again.

'You have a habit, do you, of meeting men in public houses and drinking so much that you cannot remember what follows,' said the man behind her.

'Now look here,' she said, getting to her feet and spinning around, in one smooth movement. 'I do not appreciate…'

'Sit down, Miss Sidthorpe,' said the second man.

It was her first real look at him. He'd been lurking at the back of the room when she had entered. What struck her immediately was his age. He had to be seventy if he were a day. Certainly he was a good deal older than his voice had portrayed. He was wearing a white shirt, with the sleeves rolled up.

'I said, *sit down*.'

He said it with such menace in his voice, that she had to sit in order to prevent her knees from buckling beneath her. If Martha had not returned the codebook, then where was it? Had she taken it with her to London? There was no question in Elsie's mind that Martha's one and only motive for doing so would have been to protect her. Their insinuation that she might have done so on some errand for Warren was arrant nonsense. Simply out of the question. Anyone who knew Martha would have said so.

'Might I remind you, Miss Sidthorpe, that you signed the Official Secrets Act when you came here.'

If Martha had taken the codebook to London, could she have been followed? By whoever had overheard their conversation in The Galleon, perhaps? Realising the danger, could she have taken flight and be hiding? Or worse? The realisation that Martha might have compromised her own safety in order to protect Elsie's was beginning to dawn on her. 'Actually, I signed it when I arrived at Beaumanor,' she said, struggling to contain the sudden anxiety that was threatening to envelop her. 'My former posting…'

'And that Bletchley and its staff are under military command?'

Elsie swallowed hard and nodded.

BUILDING 41

'I am going to ask you once more. What became of the note book that Warren showed you?'

'I am sorry,' she said as evenly as she could. It was a gamble, but if Warren had denied ever having had the codebook, then admitting its existence now would mean a court martial. Her testimony against him would send him to prison at the very least. If Martha had taken the book with her to London, then an admission might make them both look like traitors, whether Martha was found or not.

Elsie had been a fool to have taken the codebook from Warren's kit bag. Whatever fate had befallen her friend, it had begun with that single act of foolishness. The very least that she could do now was to protect her reputation. 'There was no note book,' she said with finality.

'Very well, Miss Sidthorpe,' said the suited man. 'That will be all. For now.'

Elsie should have been feeling relieved that the interrogation was over and, so far as it went, she was. But her dominant emotion, as she stood up and walked towards the hut door wasn't relief. It was an overwhelming sense of guilt, that her actions might have led to her friend's disappearance.

'One more thing,' said the suited man. 'You will make no further enquiries concerning the fate of Miss Watts. Like her mother, you will accept the explanation that has been proffered. Miss Watts was killed in an air raid and her body consumed in the resulting fire. You will ask no further questions. In fact, it would be better for you if you forgot about her altogether. Do you understand?'

Elsie hesitated, her eyes filling with tears.

'Miss Sidthorpe, there are matters of national security at stake here. You will do your duty. Do I make myself absolutely clear?'

Elsie nodded. 'Yes, quite' she said, but she knew, in her heart, that if it took her a lifetime, she would never be able to rest until she had discovered the truth about what had happened to her friend.

CHAPTER NINE

Sunday, April 17, 2005

I opened my eyes, reached out with my hand and ran my finger down the contours of Ellen's back. She had been through so much. Laying there beside her, watching her body rise and fall with each breath, the events of the last year seemed almost surreal. Heroes and villains. Gun wielding maniacs and paparazzi. The toppling of Max Banks. The appalling injuries suffered by Mike and Marcus and the gruesome murder of Tomasz Dabrowski. Not exactly what she could have been bargaining for when, less than year ago, she and Elsie had talked me into looking for Martha Watts.

Who would have blamed Ellen, had she decided to call time on our relationship? Not Jane or Mike, who both knew how demanding the last few months had been. Certainly not me, that was for damn sure. But Ellen hadn't called time on it and lying beside her, I felt like a very lucky man indeed.

We'd continued discussing Ted's revelations until Ellen had reminded me that we had to be up early in the morning. By the time we'd climbed the stairs together, much of the tension that had been building between us for weeks seemed to have evaporated and we felt like a couple again. The kind of couple I wanted us to be.

BUILDING 41

I yawned, reached out for my mobile phone and checked the time. I'd only been asleep for a few hours but I felt pretty good, despite Jade's best efforts. For some reason Ellen's large, black cat had taken to climbing onto my shoulder and sleeping there at night, stretched out like a sphinx, paws neatly arranged in front of her. I smiled to myself. Life certainly had a habit of throwing up all sorts of surprises. Had anyone told me, a year ago, that in twelve months time I'd be sharing my bed with a beautiful woman I'd have doubted them. Had they suggested an overweight cat with tuna breath, I'd have said they were completely crazy. Yet here I was. Feeling pretty bloody pleased with myself. I reached out and stroked Ellen's hair. 'Wake up, sleepy head,' I said, quietly.

She stirred. 'Hmm?'

'It's half past seven. You wanted to be out by half eight.'

'No…' she groaned, still half asleep.

'Yes, you did. You told Elsie we'd be there by half eleven,' I persisted.

'It won't take us that long to get to there,' she mumbled.

'Yes, it will. The road through Saxstead, up to Yoxford was a nightmare last time. Remember?'

'All right, but it's your turn to make the tea.'

'No, it isn't. I made it yesterday,' I complained. But it was a half-hearted attempt at resistance. Ellen's turn or not, I was soon up and making us tea and toast and feeling pretty good about it.

We took Ellen's Saab. There was no garage at the new house so my Spitfire was stored, for the time being, at Mike and Jane's place. I didn't want to get rid of her. I'd sweated blood keeping that car roadworthy. But we didn't really need two cars and a scooter. Sooner or later the Spitfire would probably have to go. But not yet. Ellen tended to use the Saab to drive over to the shop that she ran in Barnet with Nicky, her business partner. I was perfectly happy catching the train up to Bletchley. I'd been doing the journey from Golders Green for long enough. The short journey up from

Leighton Buzzard was a breeze in comparison and, with the weather improving, I was planning on using the Lambretta whenever I could. Maybe later in the week if the good weather held.

'You know what Ted told you?' Ellen said suddenly.

She'd been reading, as she often did when I drove. Usually a book. Sometimes, as on this occasion, a newspaper. I could never have done that. Looking down for any length of time in the car always made me feel travel sick. 'Any bit in particular?'

'About not being your father.'

'Uh-huh,' I said, making a hard left in front of the little school at Husborne Crawley. It always struck me as being a funny little place. No houses but a junior school. Where did the kids come from?

'What are you going to do about it? I mean, if you don't get anything more from him.'

'I don't know.'

'Up to now it's all been about discovering what happened to your mother, hasn't it? About finding her. Now you've got two parents to look for,' she hesitated. 'If you want to, of course.'

The thought had crossed my mind.

'Do you?' she said, turning towards me.

'Oh, come on. You know me. Research is what I do. Do you really think that, knowing what I now know,…'

'Which isn't a great deal,' Ellen interjected.

'Granted,' I agreed. 'But do you really think that I could just leave it at that?'

Ellen folded the newspaper, tucked it behind the passenger door handle and turned to face me. 'I know, but Ted is your father, in every way but the biological one. Is it really so important to find the person who did the deed?'

'It's not just that,' I hesitated, thinking about it. 'But, yes, since you ask. I guess it is. I mean, when the time comes to have kids, wouldn't you want to know who their…' I realised what I'd said

BUILDING 41

and stopped myself. We'd been together for less than a year. The subject of children had never come up and I had absolutely no idea why I was raising it now. I glanced across at her. She was smiling. Which I took to be a good sign. I looked back at the road ahead and swallowed.

'Harry Stammers,' she said, the timbre of her voice full of excitement. 'I didn't know you were thinking about children.'

Oh shit. Was I thinking about children? 'No. Well I'm not, I just...'

'You're not?' Now she sounded disappointed.

'No. I mean, well yes, I suppose... But...'

Ellen laughed.

I needed to stop digging.

'I'm pulling your leg,' she giggled.

I said nothing.

'Carry on.'

'You know what I mean,' I said, relieved to be getting the conversation back onto safer ground. 'Anyway, it isn't just about that. Knowing where you come from isn't just about the mechanics of it, is it? There's the story. The reason. The relationship that created you. Otherwise it feels like there is some great yawning gap.' I hesitated. 'I'm talking bollocks, aren't I?'

Ellen was thoughtful. 'No, you're not. That is exactly why he should have told you.'

I said nothing. I was thinking that perhaps this was what I should have explained to Ted instead of yelling at him and calling him a selfish old bugger.

'It makes me so bloody mad and it is not even my business. Keeping it all from you. It was so damaging.'

'It is your business,' I said, reaching for her hand. 'It will always be your business. That's where I went wrong. Thinking that this was just about me.'

I risked another glance in her direction. She was watching me. 'From here on in, we do things together,' I said, perhaps a bit too sentimentally but I was feeling it.

'That's fine by me,' she said happily. 'Although I'd rather not do hospital together,' she said, suddenly breaking eye contact.

I corrected the car's course in time to avoid the grass verge.

*****

Elsie Sidthorpe sat beside the window of her first floor room, looking out across the common with its twin water towers dominating the western skyline. How, whoever had erected the more recent of the two, had gained planning permission was a complete mystery. If, of course, they had planning permission in 1937 when, according to Gavin, the nursing home's gardener, the ghastly thing had been erected. "Art Deco" was apparently how it was described in the town's tourist manual. Elsie sniffed. There was nothing remotely artistic or decorative about it.

The weather had been good all week and this morning the sky was almost completely blue, spoiled only by the occasional puff of wispy white cloud that had been blown in off the North Sea in the light shoreward breeze. Already, cars were lining up along both sides of York Road. It was the same throughout much the year, but especially in the summertime when the town heaved with tourists and day trippers, mostly from Norwich and Ipswich. Thankfully, Elsie reflected, the masses of London's East End preferred the likes of Southend. Even the more adventurous of them rarely ventured beyond Walton-on-the-Naze and certainly not as far north as Southwold. Whoever had decided to close the town's railway line, all those years before, had done the place a very great service indeed, as far as Elsie was concerned. 'Let us be thankful for small mercies,' she muttered to herself. A thought that was interrupted by a gentle tapping on the door.

BUILDING 41

Elsie raised a hand to her throat, her fingers gently caressing the fine gold chain that hung around her neck. 'Yes?' She called out. 'Who is it?' Her voice sounded thin, even to her own ears.

'It is Natalia,' said a voice with an East European accent.

Elsie smiled.

The door opened just wide enough to admit the girl's familiar face. 'May I come in?' she said, peering around the door.

'Yes, of course. I have been waiting for you.'

Natalia stepped into the room. 'I am sorry. I was way... way... how do you say it?'

'Waylaid?'

'Yes, that is it. I was waylaid. It is a funny word. I was waylaid by Mrs White. You know how she speaks very much.'

'It comes from the Middle Dutch word "wegelagen", which means to lay in wait.' Elsie said. She had, for the last six months, been on a mission to improve Natalia's English and under her tutelage, the girl had certainly made progress. 'You could, more accurately, have said "I was delayed by Mrs White" unless, of course, she was truly lying in wait for you?'

Natalia looked confused.

'Never mind, dear. Did you bring the flowers?'

Natalia produced a bouquet of chrysanthemums, with a flourish, from behind her back. 'Yes. I brought them from the florist in the town this morning.'

'Bought, Dear. Brought means to bring. Bought means to buy.'

'I *bought* them from the florist in the town,' Natalia corrected herself, trying to mimic Elsie's Received Pronunciation. She grinned.

'Very good, dear. How much did they cost?' Elsie asked, reaching for her handbag.

'No, you must not pay. They are a gift from me. To you,' Natalia said, walking towards her.

'Oh, but you mustn't. Not on the pittance that they pay you,' Elsie replied, searching for her purse.

'You are teaching me English,' Natalia pleaded. 'You must let me. Please. It would make me very happy.'

Elsie hesitated.

'They will make your room look beautiful,' Natalia added. 'For your visitors.'

Elsie reached for the nurse's hand. 'You are so kind,' she said, squeezing it. 'And so pretty, too,' she added. 'I expect all the men chase you. You must be careful, dear. Men are often not what they seem.'

'Yes, I know,' Natalia replied, awkwardly. She released Elsie's hand and walked across to the little kitchenette at the far end of the room.

'Take, that man on the bench outside,' Elsie continued.

Natalia had found a vase and returned with the flowers. 'Where shall I put them?' she said, doing her best to change the subject.

'Over there,' Elsie replied. 'That would be splendid. Thank you.'

Natalia placed the flowers on the little shelf beside the television.

'He might look like a tourist but he isn't, you know.'

Natalia smiled. 'What time are they arriving?'

'I asked Ellen to be here by eleven-thirty. We have a table booked at…' she hesitated. 'Oh now, there we are. I seem to have forgotten.'

'You have a table booked at The Swan. At twelve fifteen,' Natalia said. 'We put it in your diary together. Do you remember?'

'Yes of course. What would I do without you, Natalia?'

The nurse smiled. 'Do you need anything else?'

Elsie glanced out of the window and down toward the bench at the edge of the common. 'When they arrive, would you mind awfully bringing them in through the back door. I don't want him to know that they are here, you see.'

Natalia walked across to the window and glanced down at the bench. Then she turned and knelt in front of Elsie's chair, taking hold of both the old lady's hands. 'Elsie, the man on the bench. It

BUILDING 41

is Mr Grayson. You know, Eric. From Room Four,' she said quietly. 'Yesterday, you had breakfast with him.'

'Oh, no. I don't think so.'

'Yes. You did. You said that he smelled of fish.'

'Smelt, dear. They say "smelled" in America. Though heaven knows why.'

*****

'Natalia says that you've been worrying again?' Ellen said, spearing a brussels sprout with the end of her fork.

'Such a lovely girl, Natalia,' Elsie replied. 'I don't know what I would do without her. Really, I don't.'

The Swan was as busy as ever and, as ever, the average age of attendees looked to be pushing seventy-five. Southwold's population, or that part of it that ate at The Swan at any rate, was not a youthful one.

We'd eaten at The Swan on a handful of occasions in the nine months or so that Ellen and I had been visiting Elsie together. Elsie preferred it to any of the town's other restaurants. Which was a little unfortunate. Southwold hosted several restaurants that were easily as good, if not better than The Swan. Still, having found a place that she liked and with which she had become familiar, Elsie seemed reluctant to eat anywhere else.

'Stop changing the subject Gran,' Ellen said, between mouthfuls. 'If you're feeling worried, you need to tell us. Otherwise, how can we help you?'

We exchanged glances. Ellen poked out her tongue.

'Help? Why would I need any help, darling? I've told you, they look after me wonderfully well. I couldn't be any happier.'

Ellen looked at her, doubtfully. 'That is not what Natalia tells us. She says that you've been worrying again, about the people you see from your window.'

Elsie's face seemed to darken. 'My window? I see all sorts of people from my window,' she said. 'Doing all sorts of things, I might add. You wouldn't believe me if I told you.'

Ellen shook her head. 'Isn't she infuriating?' she said, turning toward me.

'Ellen's right,' I offered. 'And I should know. The Stammers family are experts at bottling things up.' I reached for my wine glass.

'Ain't that the truth,' said Ellen, holding out hers.

I clanked my glass against it.

'How is your father?' Elsie asked.

I hesitated. Sometimes, like now, Elsie was capable of startling flashes of insight, indicating not just a healthy mind but a razor sharp intellect that meant that she could hold her own in any conversation. At other times, she appeared confused to the point of bewilderment. Had I been unaware that she was suffering from the onset of dementia, I might have thought her capable of switching back and forth from lucidity to confusion at will. Even knowing what I knew about Elsie's condition, I harboured a secret suspicion that she used the technique to avoid answering awkward questions. Though I'd never have had said so, of course.

'Ted's started talking.' Ellen said, casually.

'Talking? Really?' Elsie said, turning toward me. Her piercing blue eyes were watching me intently.

I nodded. 'Yes, he really is.'

'That is wonderful news. I am so pleased for you and your sister…' she hesitated.

'Kate,' I finished the sentence for her.

'Kate. Yes. How wonderful for you and Kate.'

'He's been in a bit of quandary, actually, haven't you Harry?' Ellen interjected. 'About telling Kate.'

'A quandary? But why?'

I wasn't sure I wanted to have this conversation. I picked up my wine glass. 'It's the things that Dad has been saying,' I said, trying

BUILDING 41

to think of a way of avoiding it. 'He's still very confused. I didn't want to trouble her with it. Kate's been through a lot, too.'

'Harry is one of those men who think that we girls,' Ellen said, winking at her great aunt, 'need protecting.'

'Protecting from what?' Elsie asked.

I noticed the edge to her question. As though she was trying to discover what Ted had been saying. 'It's a bit awkward, actually,' I said and left it at that. In part, to see how she would respond.

Elsie had picked up her wine glass. 'Well don't keep us in suspense, darling,' she said, expansively. Like she was playing to an audience. Which, by the looks on the faces of the people at the table next to ours, she was. 'What exactly has he been saying?'

I looked at Ellen. If she had noticed anything odd about the way that Elsie was behaving, she was masking it well.

I turned to Elsie. 'Well,' I said quietly, 'he says that he isn't my father for one thing.' I didn't particularly want the people on the next table to hear it. While they didn't appear to have recognised me, it was possible that they might if I gave them reason to look hard enough. The last thing I needed was another newspaper headline.

Elsie put down her glass, heavily. 'What?' she gasped.

I nodded. 'I know. It was quite a shock.'

'Did he tell you who is?'

Elsie's reaction puzzled me. 'I'm not sure that he knows,' I said, honestly. Perhaps I was reading too much into it. Elsie had always struck me as slightly eccentric and, in the few months since her dementia had been diagnosed, Ellen and I had both noticed a deterioration, albeit slight.

'I'm going to try to talk to him again next week,' I added.

'Are you all right, Gran?' Ellen said, evidently concerned.

Elsie seemed suddenly flustered 'Has he said anything about your mother?' she asked, altogether too loudly.

'Quite a bit, actually,' I said, dropping my voice. 'Most of which is unrepeatable. In particular, he says that he thinks she is still alive. Ellen and I have been talking about how we might go about tracing her, haven't we... '

Elsie's hand, which had flown to her neck, had caught her glass, sending red wine spewing across the table.

'Gran?' Ellen was already on her feet.

'Oh, my goodness, I'm sorry,' Elsie stammered, looking suddenly confused and impossibly frail. 'I seem to have made a terrible mess of things.'

Ellen circled the table and put her arm around her great aunt's shoulders. 'It's all right Gran. Really it is. It's only wine.'

'Such a terrible mess,' Elsie repeated, her eyes brimming with tears.

I had hailed a waitress who had come dashing across to the table with a cloth.

'There's no need to upset yourself,' Ellen said, trying to comfort her.

'No, but Ellen, dear,' Elsie said suddenly reaching for her great niece's hands and clutching them tightly. 'You mustn't go raking up the past. Look at all the trouble it caused us the last time. All my fault. Don't you see? I should have listened to Martha.'

'What do you mean?' Ellen was looking confused. She glanced at me, but I had no idea what Elsie meant. I shrugged.

'Could we have some water, do you think?' Ellen said to the waitress, who disappeared in search of it.

I felt a sudden wave of sympathy for Elsie. At that moment she looked impossibly frail. I tried to think of something reassuring to say. 'If trouble is what you're worrying about, Elsie, then please don't. There's no need. I won't be letting Ellen within a hundred miles of it. Not ever again. I promise.'

But Elsie was no longer listening.

'Gran?'

She was staring toward the window. It overlooked the town's main square. Her face was as white as a sheet. 'We must go. We're not safe here,' she said with sudden lucidity.

BUILDING 41

The elderly women on the next table were staring at us.

Ellen looked across at me, her face full of concern.

'What's wrong, Elsie?' I said, trying to follow her eyes and seeing nothing. I got up and went to the window. Outside, the square looked the same as I would have expected it to look on any Sunday afternoon in April. A row of cars in front of the little car park by the butcher's shop. The same car park where I'd first seen Ellen, getting out of her Saab, less than a year before. A smattering of pedestrians. I scanned their faces, one by one. 'There's nothing there,' I said, turning back towards the table. *Except that...*

Elsie was attempting to get to her feet.

'Harry, go and get the car would you? I think we should take her back. Don't worry about the bill, I'll sort that out. Here,' Ellen said, handing me the keys to the Saab. 'Just pull up outside. I'll bring her out.'

'Are you sure?'

'Yes, yes,' Elsie was muttering. 'Take me home, dear. Natalia will know what to do.'

'Just go and get the car. All right?' Ellen said.

'Sure,' I said, trying to give her a reassuring smile.

When I pulled open the doors and stepped out onto the pavement outside the hotel, I again found himself scanning the faces of the people in the square. It would have been easy to dismiss Elsie's alarm as nothing more than the paranoia that confusion can sometimes bring. But, while I could see nothing to justify it, something was tugging at my subconscious. Making the hairs on my arms stand on end. Whatever Elsie had or had not seen, something was not right. I could sense it.

CHAPTER TEN

Wednesday, July 21, 1976

He climbed the steps awkwardly and stood swaying at the top, fumbling with a set of keys that he could barely see in the darkness and muttering obscenities. Rather more loudly, as it turned out, than he realised. With hindsight, the final pint had probably not been such a good idea. It had been somebody's birthday over at The Mariner. He'd already forgotten whose. A free pint was not to be sniffed at, whether one too many or not.

'Are you all right?'

He couldn't quite place the voice. 'What?'

'I said, are you all right?'

'Of course, I'm all right,' he said to the voice, still unaware of its source.

He tried to focus on the figure who had stepped over the low wall between his property and the next. The man was holding out his hand.

'Give us your keys then. I'm not standing here all bloody night.'

He handed them over without argument.

'Good night was it?' the man said, holding the keys so that he could see them in the light from the lamp opposite the junction.

'Good enough. Nothing to write home about.'

BUILDING 41

'Why do you carry all these bloody keys, man? You've only got one front door. If you just took the one key, you might not end up stood out here every night, cursing live a navvy.'

'It's my eyes. Can't see like I used to.'

'Nothing to do with the five pints of ale you sink every night then?' the man snorted. 'Out of the way,' he added after a short pause. He reached past and pushed the key into the lock. The door opened easily. 'There you go.'

'Brian, you are a gentleman.'

'Are you all right now?' Brian said, guiding him forward with an arm around his shoulders.

'I am.'

'Right. Good night then.'

'Good night.'

'And keep the bloody noise down. The missus is trying to sleep.'

'I will.'

The door slammed behind him. He stood, still swaying, on his hall mat, trying to remember where the light switch was. Failing, he took several steps forward, which was the last thing he remembered before coming-to, tied to a dining room chair with the worst headache he'd ever experienced in his life.

The room came into focus gradually, through a swirling fog of colour and sound. It was the first thing that he noticed. The television. It was on. He didn't remember doing that. The second thing that he noticed was the pain. It was centred in the back of his head but was pulsing, in sharp bursts, down his neck, into his arms and on, into his hands. His awareness of the pain came to him slowly, its severity escalating until he thought he might pass out. But he didn't pass out. Because, as his vision cleared, he became aware of the shape of a man seated opposite him.

The man was wearing sun glasses. Which, even in his confused state, appeared incongruous. He was broad, but not fat, with long, black hair and enormous side burns. Like Mungo Jerry's.

'In a moment,' announced the man with the sideburns, 'I am going to remove the tape from your mouth. When I do, you will answer my questions. Fully and without hesitation.' He paused. 'Otherwise, you will remain silent.'

He nodded.

'You will speak clearly but quietly. If you scream or call out, I will tape your mouth again and then I will hurt you. Do you understand?'

He stared at the man and then nodded again.

'Do not doubt me. If you do, it will be the last mistake you make.'

He watched the man stand and walk the short distance to his side. He braced himself but still it didn't prevent the pain and the dizziness that briefly overcame him when the man tore the tape from his mouth. He closed his eyes and waited for it to subside. When he opened them again, the man had reseated himself. He had produced a gun form his pocket and was screwing what appeared to be a silencer to its barrel. 'It is a German gun. It was my father's.'

He swallowed. As his mind cleared, he examined the man's features as closely as the sun glasses permitted. But he could glean no clue as to the man's identity.

'Do you recognise me?'

He shook his head. 'No,' he said, roughly. It was the truth.

'There is no reason why you should, I suppose. We have never met.'

If they had never met, then what did this man want with him? Why was he here? Had he come to rob him? In which case, he'd come to the wrong house. What other purpose could he have?

'You did, however, meet my father. Once. A long time ago,' the man said and then lapsed into silence.

He tried to think.

'You do not remember, but the manner of your meeting left a lasting impression on my father.'

BUILDING 41

'Who are you?'

'I am Günther Möller. My surname would have been Lettmann had my father not been forced to change it when he returned to Germany after the war.'

Lettmann. Möller. The names still meant nothing.

The man called Möller, who had now attached the silencer to the end of the gun barrel, stood up and walked towards him.

Instinctively, he pulled against the tape that bound his wrists to the chair back. But to no avail.

Möller raised the gun and held it over his head.

He felt the end of the barrel touch the top of his scalp.

'Were I to pull the trigger now, how far do you suppose the bullet would travel down through your body before coming to a stop? My guess would be several inches, at least, into the top section of your spinal chord.'

'What do you want?'

'Good. Let us get to the point,' Möller said, sliding the tip of the gun's barrel across his captive's scalp and slowly down his forehead, so that it came to rest at a point directly between his eyes. 'Let's see whether I can jog your memory a little. I hope so. For your sake. Otherwise, I may have to scramble it entirely.'

He waited.

'It is May 1944 and, having murdered most of the crew, you are standing in the wireless room of U-110.' Möller paused. 'Do you remember now, Mr Warren?'

He did.

'Well do you?' Möller said, pushing the gun barrel hard against his captive's forehead.

'Yes.'

'Do you remember how your Captain… Harding, wasn't it?'

'Yes.'

'How Captain Harding put a bullet into the face of the German wireless operator?'

'Yes. I remember.' He would never forget it.

'Rather like I could put a bullet into your face now.'

He said nothing.

'The wireless operator's name was Krause, by the way. Matthäus Krause. A good man, with a wife and a young child, back in Bremen, where he grew up. Did you know that?'

'No.'

'No, I do not imagine that you would. He was just another Kraut to you, wasn't he?'

He said nothing.

'Wasn't he?' Möller said, raising his voice for the first time.

'It was wartime. We were doing our jobs, just like the crew of the U-boat had been doing theirs.'

'Yes, that's right,' Möller said, smiling. 'But you did something, that day, that your job neither required nor permitted. Didn't you?'

Was Möller talking about the killing of the U-boat crew? He'd always felt ashamed of that. They had been surrendering. Young men. Some, no older than boys. 'It was Harding who gave the order. It was a terrible thing that he did.' He could have spared them. He should have spared them. 'But it was war. Terrible things happen in wartime.'

'You are right, of course. Terrible things. Like the death of your Captain Harding. He was killed, by the way. Three weeks before the war ended. While on shore leave. An incendiary bomb. It hit the house, in Daggenham, where he was lodging with his wife and children. They were all burned to death. Did you know that?'

'No. No, I didn't know that.'

'Justice of sorts, I suppose. But no, I was not talking about Harding's cowardly massacre of a defenceless U-boat crew. I was talking about you. You took something that was not yours, didn't you?'

But how…

Möller laughed. 'You are wondering how, all these years later, I could possibly know about the book?'

He said nothing.

BUILDING 41

Möller's face changed in an instant. 'You would do well to remember my instructions. You will answer my questions fully and without hesitation,' he said, icily.

'Why are you doing this?'

'I am doing this, because I want back that which you took.'

'Your father was Lettmann?' he said, the identity of the man finally dawning on him. 'The commander of U-110?'

'Well done, Mr Warren. My father saw you take it. But then you knew that, didn't you?'

He said nothing.

Möller pointed the gun at his right foot.

The thud of the shot, fired through the silencer, barely registered. The pain, on the other hand, boiled up his right leg, into his chest and came spewing out of his mouth. When the initial shock of it had subsided, he was left sobbing, his head bowed, saliva dribbling from his mouth.

'One warning. You could hardly have expected two.'

A pool of blood had appeared between his feet.

'That you took the book from the wireless room of U-110 is not in dispute. Thankfully for you, I need not ask you to confirm this. What you will tell me, however, is the book's whereabouts now.'

'I don't have it,' he said, looking up and into the face of his assailant. 'I haven't seen it for over thirty years.'

Möller turned the gun around in his hand so that he was holding the barrel. Then he struck him such a vicious blow across the side of his face with the gun's butt that, along with the chair on which he was restrained, he was knocked sideways and would have toppled onto the floor, had Möller not grabbed him and hauled him upright.

Möller waited.

He tried to speak but the pain in his jaw prevented it.

'I would keep trying, if I were you. Your life depends on you telling me exactly where the book is now.'

'It was taken,' he managed with some effort, between broken teeth.

'When?'

He said nothing.

Möller tucked the gun into his inside pocket. Then he punched his captive in the face with his fist.

Blood flowed freely from his nose. 'In 1944,' he spat, after a few moments.

'That's better. Where?'

'A pub called The Galleon, near Bletchley. It was taken from my bag.'

'Taken? Who took it?'

'I don't know. Please,' he begged. 'I don't know who took it.'

Möller punched him again.

He felt his right eye beginning to swell and close.

'Who took it?'

'I'd been drinking with two women,' he sobbed. 'Maybe one of them. I don't know.'

'What were their names?' Möller said, removing the gun from his pocket.

'I don't know. Honestly. I don't know.'

'I will ask you once more. One warning. You will answer me or I will decorate that wall over there with your brains. What were the names of the women with whom you had been drinking when the book was taken?'

He bowed his head. When he looked up, Möller was pointing the gun directly at his face. 'One was called Elsie and the other one was Martha. I don't remember their surnames.'

Möller said nothing.

'It was thirty years ago for Christ's sake,' he cried out. 'I was with them for a couple of hours. I was drunk. They were just two girls. Would you remember their names, thirty years later?'

'Yes,' Möller replied, without emotion. 'As a matter of fact, I would.'

BUILDING 41

They were the last words that former Royal Navy, Petty Officer Ronald Warren heard before he died.

*****

The smell of blood, as she entered Ronnie Warren's corner house in Hove, was unmistakeable but still, it did not prepare Rosemary Sellers for the sight that greeted her as she passed from the hallway into the little living room at the building's rear. She stared at the body, unable to tear her eyes away. Warren was still taped to the dining room chair on which he'd been murdered. While there was blood spattered down the front of his shirt and pooling between his feet, his corpse below the neck appeared, at first sight, to have been unharmed. It was above the neck that most of damage had, more obviously, been inflicted. His face below the eye line looked like he'd been beaten, savagely, with a blunt instrument. Possibly a fist. Above the eye line, in the middle of his forehead, was a neat, burgundy-coloured gunshot wound.

She circled the body, still unable to look away. A section of the rear of his skull was missing altogether having been blown away by the exiting bullet. Blood and gore had been sprayed across the floor and the wall behind.

But it was not the corpse itself that so horrified her. She had seen corpses before and some in a worse state than this. It was the knowledge that it was a death that could have been prevented. That should have been prevented. That *she* should have prevented. And worse, the pit of guilt into which she had felt herself falling, knowing as she did, without so much as a shadow of any doubt, that it had been due to her actions that he had been tortured and then destroyed, as thoroughly as the scene now before her suggested.

'Not a pretty sight, is he?'

She had gasped and begun the defensive turn in the same instant that the thought had registered in her mind that the murderer was long gone.

He had taken a step backwards. 'I'm sorry. I didn't meant to startle you,' he said, looking genuinely apologetic.

'Dear Lord,' she said, her hand involuntarily reaching for her throat. 'I thought that you had finished here.'

'Oh, we have. He'll be off to the morgue shortly. I thought I'd take one last look. With everyone out of the way. It helps sometimes.'

He was a good looking man. Tall, with short blond hair and unusually well spoken, she thought, for a policeman. 'I'm sorry, she stammered. 'I'm disturbing you.'

'DI Windsor,' he said, offering her his hand. 'East Sussex CID,' he added.

She shook it. 'Rosemary Sellers.'

There was an awkward pause, during which they both turned and stared at the body.

'Can I ask you something?' he said, breaking the silence.

'You can always ask, Detective Inspector.'

Windsor circled the body. He stopped when he was facing her. 'The man who did this.'

'Or woman,' she corrected him, playing for time.

The DI smiled. 'If it was woman, she had one hell of a fist.'

She tipped her head in agreement. 'You're the detective here.'

'I take it that you know the name of the perpetrator.'

'And I take it that since that was not a question, you do not require an answer.'

'Would I get one if I did? Strictly off the record, of course.'

She considered the question and then dismissed it. 'Tell me DI Windsor, what makes you think that I know the name of the perpetrator?'

He stared at her, the traces of a smile playing on his lips. 'Just before I left the station I took a call from the Deputy Chief

BUILDING 41

Constable, giving me certain directions as to the extent of my enquiries and their likely outcome.'

'Really?' she replied, feigning surprise. In truth it came as no surprise at all.

But Windsor had evidently been hoping for more. When it was not forthcoming, he continued. 'Which I take to mean that someone somewhere regards these as matters that do not concern us mere mortals.'

'But you are concerned nonetheless?'

He knelt down in front of the body and removed a pen from his top pocket. He used it to lift the sleeve of warren's jacket, sufficient to reveal a tattoo on his wrist. 'Royal Navy. But I expect you knew that already,' he said, glancing up at her.

She inclined her head. 'Petty Officer, retired.'

'Whatever he did,' he said, dropping the shirt sleeve and sliding the pen back into his pocket, 'I doubt very much that he deserved to end his days like this.'

She knew precisely what Warren had done. 'No, DI Windsor,' she said, suddenly struggling to contain the unexpected rawness of her emotions, 'he did not.'

Windsor was watching her reaction. 'You also know why he was killed.'

She turned away, walked toward the window and pulled the curtain aside.

'The mortuary van,' he said. 'They're early. Under orders to clear this little mess away as quickly as possible, no doubt, before the press pack arrives. Or to sweep it under the carpet,' he added.

She watched the black van reverse into the space between two squad cars.

'I must go,' she said, turning towards the door.

'Doesn't it bother you?' he said quickly.

She turned to face him. 'Bother me?' she shot back.

'That a life can be extinguished. Erased. And nobody gives a bloody damn.'

'Oh, it bothers me DI Windsor. It bothers me a very great deal,' she said, trying to hold back the wave of guilt that had formed in her stomach and was threatening to engulf her. She turned hurriedly and headed for the door, but before she had reached it his hand was on her shoulder. He spun her around so that they were facing each other.

'This was your fault?'

She struggled, unable to answer him.

'How?' he said, still gripping her arm.

'I could have prevented it,' she managed. 'I owed him that much.'

'Why?'

She stared into his eyes.

He released her.

'I was a fool,' she said. And with that, she had pulled open the door and was gone.

*****

Smith entered *The Silver Cross* on the corner of Craig's Court and Whitehall. He stood, ostensibly brushing the rain from his coat but in fact scanning the pub's interior, more from force of habit than from any real concern. He had been summoned to the Controller's office many times but was no more able now to fathom its location than he had been on the first occasion. Any watcher was wasting their time.

The security arrangements surrounding access to the tunnels below Whitehall and, via them, to the Controller's office were certainly effective. Reportedly, they had never been breached. Still, they irritated him, being both unnecessary and exaggerated to the point of melodrama. So far as he was concerned, whoever had come up with the idea had been reading too much Fleming.

Smith approached the bar but, rather than ordering a drink, he took the door to the side. It opened into a narrow hallway, about

BUILDING 41

half way along which was a silver-coloured telephone booth mounted on the wall.

In order to gain access to the tunnels, it was firstly necessary to dial the number of the intended tunnel entrance, preceded by the letter "Q", from a specific telephone. They were all sited a matter of yards from their respective tunnel entrances. Most were in regular public call boxes but in some cases they were located elsewhere. One was in the foyer of a well known West End hotel. Two were, like the so-called *Q-phone* beside which he now stood, in public houses. They were known as "Q-phones" because the letter "Q" had been added to their rotary dials, beneath the number "7".

Smith made the call and waited for the acknowledgement. Once given, he would have two minutes to make it to the tunnel entrance in Craig's Court and to buzz the intercom. In the event, he did so with seconds to spare.

Having gained access, it was then a case of riding the lift down to the tunnels. The lift at Craig's Court was not for the faint hearted. The lights in the shaft were triggered, on and off, by the lift car's progress, but occasionally the switch would malfunction and the carriage would be plunged into darkness. It had happened to Smith on the first occasion he'd used the entrance at Craig's Court. The darkness had been like no other he had ever experienced in his life.

At the bottom of the shaft, the car's arrival triggered the tunnel lights. They came on with a series of clicks as fluorescent tubes lit, one after the other, running away into the distance like a fairground attraction.

No matter how often he made the trip, Smith always rehearsed the route, before setting off into the tunnels. It was not a particularly long walk, but there were no signs, and maps of the tunnel system were strictly forbidden. Without extreme caution, it would be easy to become lost, since the tunnels mostly all looked the same.

The main tunnels were served by a particularly effective ventilation system that blew fresh air down from above and then sucked it out again at various disguised points around the West End of London. However, no such ventilation system existed in the side tunnel into which Smith had now turned. He had already begun to sweat.

After walking for five minutes, the side tunnel terminated at what appeared to be a modern lift door. Smith pressed the call button. The door slid open. As he entered the lift carriage, he noted the camera that was tracking his movements. Unusually, there were no floor buttons, nor indeed any controls inside the lift at all. He waited. Shortly the doors slid closed and the lift began to rise.

When the lift doors opened again, Smith stepped out into a windowless corridor with a high, plastered ceiling and oak panelled walls. The corridor gave every impression of belonging to one of London's gentlemen's clubs. Whether it did in fact, or else where it was located, Smith had thus far been unable to establish.

He turned right and passed along the corridor, counting doors to his right as he passed them. At the fifth door, he stopped, knocked, waited for a response and then entered.

Like the corridor, the room into which he had stepped, had no windows. It was otherwise an opulent room, with a plush green carpet and a great Victorian fire place as its centrepiece. It was dominated at one end by a huge mahogany desk, above which was hung a vast portrait, in oil, of the late Edward, Duke of Windsor.

'Smith,' said a small, balding man seated at the desk.

Smith knew the man and his reputation well enough to recognise the raptorial features behind the smile. 'Sir,' replied Smith, approaching him.

The balding man stood up. 'You know Andrews,' he said, indicating a third man, seated in one of three leather armchairs arranged around a low table to Smith's right.

Andrews nodded, but didn't stand.

'A drink perhaps?'

BUILDING 41

'Scotch,' Smith replied, watching him pour the drink from a decanter on his desk.

'Shall we?' He handed Smith his Scotch and gestured toward the vacant arm chairs.

'The loss of Mr Warren,' the balding man said, once they were seated, 'was a disappointment.'

'Yes,' Smith said simply. 'It was.'

'An unpleasant business by all accounts.'

Smith tilted his head in acknowledgement but said nothing.

'Perhaps you would care to explain how it was that the target was able to access Warren unobserved, when we had the house under close surveillance,' the balding man said, smoothly.

'I can't explain it. The only possible access to the property was through the front, which as you say is under close surveillance. The rear had been and still is secured.'

'Nevertheless,' interjected Andrews, 'he did gain access to it, did he not?'

Smith said nothing.

'It would appear that our target is a talented man indeed,' Andrews added. 'Not only was he able to gain access but he was also able to neutralise the listening devices, without arousing suspicion and to interrogate and then murder Warren without detection.'

'I am well aware of that,' Smith replied, unable to hide his irritation.

'Who is our man next door?' Andrews asked.

'Harcourt.'

Andrews scratched his chin. 'Harcourt is experienced enough. How in God's name did he miss the incursion?'

'The target found and then moved our devices into Warren's bedroom. When Harcourt let Warren in through the front door, he quickly and quietly overcame him. Once he had him bound and gagged he put the television on in the room where he had him and the radio on in his bedroom. All that Harcourt heard was a concert.'

'A concert?'

'Status Quo. Apparently.'

Smith had offered it as a statement of fact but for some reason, the reference to the rock band had evidently annoyed Andrews. 'Do you have any idea, Smith,' Andrews asked irritably, 'any idea at all, what was said between the two men before Warren was murdered.'

'No. None.'

Andrews shook his head. 'At very least we will need to redouble our efforts.'

'Indeed.'

There was a pause during which Smith emptied his whisky glass.

'You assured us that you had this under control,' the balding man said, flatly.

Smith turned to face him. 'I did. Until the intervention by Sellers. I have been warning of the risk that she posed for some time.'

'I'm sorry, but I really don't see what Sellers has got to do with this,' interjected Andrews. 'Warren was a long term asset under our protection. His loss, along with any advantage gained by the target is your failure, Smith, not hers.'

'Sellers was and is a liability. I warned you that if the target became aware of her, he might decide to move more quickly. Which is precisely what happened here.'

'We don't know that it had anything to with Sellers, who in any case, might I remind you, is another of our key assets,' added Andrews.

'Did you know,' Smith said, staring at him, 'that she was proposing to move Warren to a safe location? Or that she was planning on bringing the target in for questioning?'

The two men exchanged glances.

Smith saw it. 'You didn't?'

BUILDING 41

'Of course we knew,' snapped Andrews. 'It would not have been permitted.'

Smith doubted that they knew it at all. 'The fact is that until Sellers started sniffing around, there was no indication that the target was about to make a move. It is almost certain that, becoming aware of her interest in him, he decided to act and to do so covertly. Assuming, correctly, that Warren was under surveillance he took steps to identify and to take out the listening devices in the house at Arthur Street.'

The two men said nothing. Smith was certain that they knew that he was right.

'However, all may not be lost. If we move swiftly to remove Sellers, and this fiasco gives us every reason to do so, and we are careful about our remaining surveillance, then he may well conclude that she was working on her own.'

'Rosemary Sellers is not under our direct control, Smith, as you well know,' said the balding man. 'Had she been, we would not have had her assigned to the target in the first place.'

'But her failure,' Smith said with emphasis, 'presents us with an opportunity to lobby for her removal, does it not?'

The balding man stared at him and then turned to Andrews. 'Her interference complicates matters.'

Andrews nodded.

'Perhaps it is time that Rosemary Sellers was retired.'

CHAPTER ELEVEN

Sunday, April 17, 2005

I closed the car door with my elbow and followed Ellen into the house, clutching the takeaway that we'd picked up from the McDonald's on the bypass.

'We should have stayed over,' Ellen said, dumping her bag on the dining room table. 'I feel awful about leaving her.'

After the incident at The Swan, we'd taken Elsie back to the nursing home and waited with her for Natalia to arrive, the three of us talking quietly together, mostly about Ellen's childhood. It had seemed to calm her so that when the Russian nurse appeared she had been able to settle Elsie to bed without further upset.

The cause of Elsie's reaction at the restaurant remained a mystery. I can only describe the expression on her face, as she had stared toward the window, as being one of abject terror but she had offered no subsequent explanation and neither Ellen nor I had been inclined to question her further.

Natalia had done her best to reassure us. 'Try not to worry. Elsie gets things mixed up. Sometimes she thinks she sees things that are not there.'

'Sees things? You mean like hallucinations?' Ellen had asked.

Natalia had been choosing her words carefully. Or trying to. The trouble was that she was clearly selecting them from a limited vocabulary. 'No. I would not call them that. It is like the things that she sees get mixed up with the memories in her head.'

Ellen had glanced at me, perhaps for reassurance but I all I could do was shrug.

'Maybe a shadow or perhaps a car outside in the street. Or a person. Things that make her remember,' Natalia added, walking across to the window.

'Like the people on the bench down there?' Ellen had followed her.

Natalia nodded. 'Yes. She thinks they are people from her past. That they are watching her.'

'Does she say who, precisely, she thinks they are?' Ellen had asked.

Natalia had hesitated. 'No.'

I'd noticed the hesitation and wondered about it. I was still wondering about it.

'This is normal, right? For someone with… her condition?'

Natalia's eyes had flicked from Ellen's to mine and back again. 'It is not for me to say. For this you must ask her doctor.'

'Yes but she talks to you, Natalia. I know she does. She tells you things. Doesn't she?'

'But I am not a doctor…'

'Have you asked her who these people are that she thinks are watching her?' Ellen had persisted.

Natalia had stared at her.

'Please?'

Natalia's expression suggested that she was weighing up how much to tell us. 'She calls them *watchers*,' she said suddenly.

'Watchers?' Ellen and I both echoed.

'This is her word.'

'What does she mean?' Ellen had asked before I could.

'I think she means *spies*.'

I followed Ellen into the kitchen.

'I could have asked Nicky to cover the shop for the next few days,' she said irritably.

I had a pretty good idea what was coming next.

'You don't think I should go back, do you?'

I was right. That she could even be thinking about driving all the way back to Southwold was testament to the extent of her ill ease. 'No, I don't,' I said, trying to sound decisive.

Ellen stared at me. I could sense what was coming.

'Look, I know how worried you are,' I said, trying to head off the argument before it was made. 'I'm worried about her too. But there's nothing more we can do and you heard what Natalia said. She lives less than ten minutes away. If Elsie needs her, she'll be there.'

'I know. It's just... I've never seen Gran like that.'

I thought she was going to burst into tears. I put my arms around her. 'If anything else happens and it won't, they'll call us.'

She nodded.

I held her at arms length. 'Okay?'

She nodded again.

'Come on, let's eat. It's late and I'm bloody starving.'

'What time is it?'

I looked at my watch. 'Five to eleven.'

'Damn. I told Nicky I'd call her when we got back.'

If she did that, then the two women would be on the phone for an age and there was a fair chance that Ellen would talk herself into driving back to Southwold.

'Nicky can wait until the morning Come on. Eat.' I handed Ellen her burger.

'I hate eating junk food. Especially just before bed,' she complained but she took it anyway. 'We should have stopped somewhere. I told you so.'

She had told me so but I'd been worried that, had we stopped, she'd have wanted to turn back. So I'd made excuses and driven

BUILDING 41

on. Thankfully Ellen had seemed too preoccupied by her thoughts to complain. Even now, the complaint was half-hearted.

'Come on,' I said, putting an arm around her shoulder again and steering her into the dining room. 'When we've eaten, I'll make us some tea.'

'Let's have it in bed,' she suggested.

'Fine by me,' I said, grinning.

She flicked my arm with the back of her hand. 'Do you ever think about anything else?'

I considered the question. 'Since meeting you? Rarely.'

'That was one hell of a day,' Ellen said, yawning.

We were in bed, drinking tea, both of us with pillows tucked behind our heads. Jade was sprawled across my legs, purring loudly. 'It was weird all round,' I agreed.

'Weird?'

Perhaps it wasn't the best choice of words.

'What was weird?' Ellen repeated.

'Well, Elsie's reaction, for one,' I said, having thought about it. 'When I told her about Ted not being my father.'

Ellen shifted so that she was facing me. 'What about it?'

I needed to choose my words carefully. The last thing I wanted was to upset her or to prompt an argument. We'd managed to get through twenty-four hours without one, for what seemed like the first time in weeks. 'It just seemed odd. There can't be many things as unsettling as discovering that you're not who you thought you were, right?'

'Sure,' Ellen agreed.

I thought some more. 'I mean, when I told you I think you said something like "Oh God, you poor thing".'

'Something like that,' Ellen nodded.

I paused.

'So what did Gran say? I can't remember.'

I heard the defensiveness in her voice. 'Her actual words were "Did he tell you who is?"'

Ellen said nothing. Instead she sipped her tea and sat staring into space.

I decided not to press the point.

'Everything about today was odd,' Ellen said suddenly. 'What in God's name did she see in that hotel window, Harry? Did you see the look on her face?'

I had seen it, all right.

'It gives me the creeps, just thinking about it,' she added

It hadn't been the look on Elsie's face, or her odd response to my revelations about Ted that had unsettled me most.

'What?' Ellen was staring at me.

'No, nothing,' I said, trying to avoid a further question, but there was no way that she was going to let me leave it at that.

'Harry…' Ellen pressed.

'I had a feeling, that's all.'

Ellen knew exactly what I was talking about. 'When?'

'Standing at the window, looking out into the market square and then again when I went outside to get the car.'

We had discussed these feelings before. Ellen had experienced my reaction to them in the tunnels at Belsize Park when I'd put my hand on the door handle to the room in which, we later discovered, Martha Watts had been knocked unconscious and from which she'd been dragged to her eventual death.

It is difficult to describe them. On that occasion it had been a sudden and almost overwhelming sense of anxiety. On other occasions, it has been a deep sense of foreboding. Once I'd seen the long dead face of Martha Watts staring in at me through a Tube train window. Fortunately Ellen had given these feelings a name because I sure as hell wasn't, even now, willing to see them as any kind of sixth sense. She had called it *intuition*.

'Describe this *feeling*.'

BUILDING 41

Just thinking about it made the hairs on my arms stand on end again. 'You're not going to like it.'

She studied my face. 'Try me.'

'You know that feeling you get?' I continued. 'On the back of your neck. When someone comes up behind you. The feeling that, at any moment, they're going to grasp your shoulders?'

Ellen pulled a face. 'Not really, no, and I'm not sure I want to.'

'Well, it was like that,' I said, ignoring her. 'Only worse. A lot worse. Like I had one of those little red dots from a rifle scope on the back of my head. You know?'

Ellen looked horror struck. 'Oh, thanks a lot,' she exclaimed. 'I feel so much better now.'

'Well, I did warn you.'

Ellen shook her head. 'Most men wish their partners sweet dreams. You send me off to sleep with the thought that there's some crazed gunman out there, with his laser sights trained on Gran's nursing home window.'

For a moment, I thought she was being serious. 'I'm sorry. I didn't mean to freak you out.'

Ellen was shaking her head. 'You and your bloody intuition.' But she was smiling.

I grinned. 'Let's see, I could always give you something else to think about.'

Ellen put her tea cup down on the little cupboard beside her bed and reached out to turn off her lamp. 'OK, Mr Sixth-Sense Stammers,' she said, in the darkness.

I felt her face on my chest and her fingers making circles on my stomach. 'Don't call it that. Sixth sense is mumbo jumbo. Intuition I can cope with.'

'What does that intuition of yours tell you is going to happen next? Like, in the next twenty minutes?'

I closed my eyes. I had a pretty good idea. Ellen was the only woman I'd ever met who was turned on by stress. 'Twenty minutes? I don't reckon you've got the staying power.'

'Oh yeah? We'll see about that.'
And with that, any thought of sleep was quickly vanquished.

I'd been dreaming. Some tangled nonsense. A car chase through winding country lanes. I'm not sure whether I was in pursuit or being pursued. It is strange how quickly the detail of such dreams vanish with consciousness. All I remember now is seeing Ted in the light from the headlights. His face slamming against the windscreen as the car ploughed into him. The music playing on the car stereo. And Ellen screaming two words, while pressing something into my hand.

'Harry?'

The song on the radio was The Jam's "Girl On The Phone".

'It's your mobile.'

'What?'

'Your phone, Harry.'

My ring tone.

'Just answer it, will you?'

I pressed the answer button and held the phone to my ear. 'Who is it?' I said, still half asleep. 'Kate? What's wrong?' I was suddenly wide awake. 'What's wrong with Dad?' I knew what she was going to say. The same two words from my dream. "He's dead."

CHAPTER TWELVE

Tuesday, April 19, 2005

I stood at the archive window, gazing out across the windswept lake toward the mansion, waiting for the percolator to finish. It felt wrong to be angry with him. It was not, after all, Ted's fault that he'd suffered another stroke or that this time it had killed him. Nevertheless and exactly as I'd always feared, Ted had taken the great majority of his secrets with him to the next life. As for this one, his memories were gone. Forever.

What little I had managed to drag from him had been tantalising but how much more did I really know as a result? If anything, it seemed to me that I knew less. Now, as well as having a mother to find, if in fact she was still alive, there was the small matter of my father. In that respect, Ted's revelations had been a complete surprise.

Putting aside his determined refusal, since the day she had disappeared, to so much as mention my mother's name, Ted had been a good father to Kate and me. I'd never really given him credit for it and now it was too late for that too.

I still hadn't spoken to Kate. Now that he was dead, how was I ever going to be able to tell her that we were only half-siblings. If that wasn't bad enough, what if Ted hadn't been her father, either?

He had not mentioned her during his final few weeks but it had to be a possibility.

Ted's death had left more questions unanswered than I'd ever imagined needed to be asked and I was more than angry. I was bloody furious. He'd robbed me. Not just of a name, but of any real hope of ever discovering the truth.

Now, of course, my only hope was to find my mother. Elizabeth Stammers. If she was alive, as Ted had suggested, then she was the one person who could, if she chose to, tell me what I needed to know. But she had stayed away for twenty-eight years. *Twenty-eight years*. That was not a woman who wanted to be found. According to Ted, everything about her had been a lie. Was there any possibility that she would be willing to tell me the truth, even if I could find her? Now that Ted was gone, there was surely little or no hope of discovering the identity of my father, without her.

There was one other possibility, albeit a slim one. Another name. A name that Ted had mentioned and which had triggered a vague memory. *Rosemary.* I had been trying to form a picture of her in my mind. But all I had managed was an image of a sickly, bed-ridden woman with piercing blue eyes. She had been there, I was sure of it, when Kate and I had stayed at Aunty Simone's, shortly before my mother disappeared. *Aunty Simone.* Another shadowy figure from my past. I had no real idea of who she was, where we had stayed and certainly no knowledge of where she lived now. I remembered Simone as a black woman and therefore presumably not my real aunt, but that was about the extent of it. Except for the name *Rosemary* and the fact that the more I had thought about her, the more familiar she had seemed to become. There was something about her. Some wider significance. A link with the present. Maybe.

Which left Ted's surreal but definite use of the word "bomb" during his later mumbled rantings about my mother. There had been a string of IRA bombings in London in the mid seventies. I knew that much. It was entirely possible that Ted had some personal experience of them. But what if anything did this have to do with my mother? Had he used the word just once, I might very well have ignored it, but during one of our later exchanges, when Ted had used a string of garbled expletives to describe her, he'd used the word again. In fact, he'd yelled it as though mimicking her and had become so distressed that one of the nurses had given him a sedative to settle him. What the hell was I supposed to make of it? My mother had a been a school teacher. What could she have possibly had to do with a bombing?

'A penny for them?'

The voice was both unexpected and familiar. 'Jane.'

Jane Mears was the Park's senior administrator. An intensely private woman and direct to the point of rudeness, Jane was less than popular with just about all of her colleagues, bar me. I liked her. I had since the day we'd met. She'd helped me with something. A piece of research. We'd struck up what most of our colleagues would have - and probably did - describe as an unlikely friendship. A friendship that had been cemented, later, by the part she had played in the search for Martha Watts and, most especially, in Ellen's rescue from the tunnels below Belsize Park. On that occasion, Jane had almost certainly managed to put a bullet into our assailant. It was her one big failure, as far as I was concerned, that the bullet hadn't landed between his eyes and finished the bastard off altogether.

'What the bloody hell are you doing here? I thought I told you to take the week off.'

I smiled inwardly. Jane had such a wonderful way with words 'You did and so did Ellen.'

'Then why are you here?'

I shrugged. 'What was I going to do at home? Sit around all day, twiddling my thumbs? The funeral's not for another fortnight.'

'Had I known you were coming in I'd have told you to come and get your own bloody post,' she said, holding out a bundle of envelopes. 'Here.'

I took them.

'No need to thank me,' she said bluntly.

'I wasn't going to.'

It was all part of our well rehearsed banter. She'd turned and had begun to walk away.

'I suppose Mike told you.'

'Told me what?' she asked, swivelling round to face me again.

'About my…' I hesitated. What the bloody hell was I supposed to call him now? 'About Ted reckoning he's not my father.'

'Of course he told me,' she said, matter of factly. 'You look like shit, by the way.'

'Thanks.'

'My pleasure. So what are you going to do?'

'What do you mean, what am I going to do?'

Jane stared at me. 'Don't give me that.'

I returned the stare.

She shook her head. 'So you were looking for one parent. Now you're going to have to find two. When are you planning on getting started?'

I reached for the percolator. 'Coffee?'

'No.'

'No, thank you,' I said emptying some coffee into a chipped cup which I'd rescued from the draining board. 'Did your parents teach you no manners at all?'

'Fuck off.'

'Charming.' I grinned. 'It's a good job that I love you.'

'Eughhh…' she pulled a face and turned away again.

'As soon as possible,' I said, without really thinking about it.

Jane carried on walking. 'Good. It will be therapeutic for you. For both of us. Lunch.' she called out over her shoulder. It was more an appointment than an invitation.

'Oh, hang on,' I thought suddenly. 'I'm supposed to be having lunch with Petra.'

Jane was at the door that led out onto the landing. 'Petra?'

BUILDING 41

She knew perfectly well who Petra was. 'Neufeld. The new research assistant. I said we'd...'

'Cancel it,' Jane interrupted. 'This is more important.'

Neufeld was the new Enigma specialist from Heidelberg and while, nominally at least, she was *my* research assistant, I'd hardly seen her since she'd started. Which was why I'd promised to give her a couple of hours. 'Jane, I can't...'

'Yes, you can.'

I descended the metal archive steps, crossed the roadway that led up from the main gate and followed the footpath around the lake towards the mansion. It was good to be out in the fresh air. I'd been stuck in the archive all morning, sifting through several boxes of photographs and documents that had been donated to the Park by the family of a recently deceased veteran. She had worked in the "Freebornery" - the name given to the team accommodated in C-block during the latter part of the war, punching data onto cards with the team's Hollerith machines and filing them in the card index.

It was the machines and the history of the companies that made them, as much as their operators, that fascinated me most. Designed by Herman Hollerith in the USA during the latter part of the nineteenth century and later produced by Hollerith's company IBM, the Hollerith tabulating machines used at Bletchley had been built, under licence, by the British Tabulating Machine Company Limited, which following merger had become International Computers Limited or 'ICL' . Both, now big names in the IT Industry.

As for the C-block operators, they had consumed around two million Hollerith cards each week. Imagine that. *Two million*. They must have produced a veritable mountain of index cards by the war's end.

I'd almost circumvented the lake, my head still full of Hollerith machines and punch cards, when I heard an unfamiliar voice. My approach appeared to have gone unnoticed by the young woman who was sitting on a wooden bench, set back from the pathway and partly secluded by the surrounding trees. She was speaking in hushed tones into her mobile phone. I found myself straining to hear what she was saying, more from a desire to test my German than to eavesdrop on her actual conversation. While I can read German to a reasonable standard, my understanding of the spoken language is poor, to say the least, and after a few seconds of clandestine listening, I had all but given up. Besides, I guessed from her manner that this was not a conversation that she wished to be overheard. I coughed to announce my presence. It seemed like the decent thing to do. She ended the call abruptly.

'Petra,' I said, trying to look like I had not been listening to the conversation. Which I had, though I'd understood next to nothing. 'I'm sorry. I did't mean to disturb you.'

I knew practically nothing about Neufeld. I'd had minimal involvement with her appointment, which had apparently been the result of an arrangement between the local university and Neufeld's university in Germany. Which I knew to be Heidelberg. Heidelberg is one of Germany's finest educational institutions, more or less on a par with Oxford here. I also knew that she had studied cryptography, and that she had written a very well regarded paper on the development of Enigma, Germany's wartime cipher machine, but that was about the extent of my knowledge of the German researcher.

Lookswise, Neufeld was tall and slim but not skinny, with bottle blonde hair that might have been prettier had it not been cut so short. It had taken me until our second brief meeting, though, to work out what was so striking about her face. And then I'd sussed it. Her eyebrows were impossibly straight. It made her expression difficult to read, which coupled with her accent, had left me ever so slightly unnerved by the encounter, on both occasions.

Neufeld's rock chick image added to the overall effect. It wasn't a look that I'd normally have gone for, but I've got to say that it worked a treat in Neufeld's case. On each occasion I'd seen her, she'd been dressed entirely in black. Plus, I'd worked out that she came to work on two wheels, which gave us something in common. I knew it, because I'd seen her with a black, full-face crash helmet. Mind you, I doubted somehow that her ride was going to be two-stroke and made in Milan.

True to form, this morning she was wearing tight black trousers, a black roll-neck sweater and a short black leather jacket. She looked up and nodded, but said nothing.

'Actually, I'm glad I caught you,' I said, smiling. 'Would you mind if we skipped lunch and met later on this afternoon?'

'No,' she shrugged, like she wasn't really bothered.

'Only...' I hesitated. I guessed she deserved some sort of explanation. 'I... er...'

She was pretending to ignore me, which was surprisingly unsettling.

'I need to catch up with somebody.'

She shrugged again, like she really didn't care.

'Well, anyway,' I added, running a hand through my hair. 'If you don't mind a short postponement, I've cleared my diary this afternoon. I'm sure we'll get a lot more done in my office, than we would have managed in the canteen.'

'You are seeing another woman?' she said suddenly, her expression unreadable.

It was an oddly awkward moment and for a moment I was completely wrong-footed. 'Well, I um...' I said trying to get a grip. It had to be a language thing.

'She is pretty, perhaps?'

Nope. Not a language thing. I stared at her, entirely lost for words.

Then she smiled, almost imperceptibly. She had been joking. Of course she had.

'I'm not sure I'd describe her as that,' I said trying to make light of it. 'Though for Christ's sake don't tell her that I said so.' I was feeling utterly foolish.

'Do, I know her?' Neufeld said, suddenly straight faced once more. 'It is okay,' she added. 'I am not the jealous type.'

If I'm being honest, she was coming across more as the loony tunes type but I was not about to say so. 'Jane. From the main office.'

'Mears,' Neufeld said like the name had left a bad taste in her mouth. 'She does not like me, I think.'

'Really? What makes you say that?' I asked, glad for the shift in focus and intrigued all rolled into one. If she was going to say something critical of Jane then I might at least be able to salvage something useful from the conversation.

'She and I had… how do you say… a run in?'

'An argument? About what?'

'It was nothing,' the German said, evasively.

I wasn't about to let it go. Opportunities like that don't come along very often. 'No, really. If Jane has some problem with you, I should know about it.'

'Very well, but I will tell you when we meet,' she added. 'I do not wish to keep you from your *hot date*.' She pronounced her final two words with the kind of precision that only a foreign language speaker can.

Perhaps it was a cultural thing, I reflected. The mock-serious sense of humour. Mike was a little like that, although he was Norwegian, rather than German. People who didn't know him often mistook his humour for provocation. I shifted my weight from one foot to the other. 'Well anyway. Look, I'd better get going,' I said, glancing over my shoulder toward the mansion.

'I will come to your office,' she said, like it was a done deal. 'At two o'clock.'

I checked my watch and nodded. 'Sure.'

'If you are late, I will wait.'

BUILDING 41

I got the feeling that it was not going to be a good idea to be late.

'You're late,' Jane announced, once I'd spotted her and weaved my way across to her table.

'Sorry,' I replied, pulling out a seat. 'I was talking to Neufeld. I'm meeting her at two.'

I glanced around the mock-forties canteen. It was heaving.

'About what?' Jane replied, sounding only mildly interested.

'I told you. I was supposed to be meeting with her over lunch.' I was still running through the conversation with Neufeld in my head. It didn't seem any less strange on review.

Jane gave me that knowing stare that only Jane can.

I ran my hand through my hair, realised I was doing it and tried to stop myself. 'It was an odd conversation, that's all.'

'Odd? Why?'

Odd as in unnerving but there was no way that I was going to admit it. 'Oh, it was nothing,' I said and then decided to play my trump card. 'She told me that you two had a run in.' Might as well strike while the iron was still hot.

'Did she now?' Jane said, crossing her arms.

'She did. What was that all about?'

Jane's features were more readable than Neufeld's. My guess was that she was trying to decide whether to tell me to "fuck off", which would not have been unusual. Or to "fuck right off", which would have been only slightly more so.

'I caught her going through the veterans' index.'

'So? She's a researcher.'

Jane stared at me. 'It was the subject of her *research,*' she said with emphasis, 'that concerned me.'

'Really? What was the subject?' I persisted. I was annoying her. I could tell.

'She was reading the files on Martha Watts and on Ellen's Great Aunt Elsie.'

The reason for which was not immediately obvious but it was hardly crime of the century.

'She's a cryptology specialist,' Jane said, as if reading my thoughts. 'Why would she want to know about Martha Watts and Elsie Sidthorpe?'

I shrugged. 'The files are hardly confidential.'

'That's not the point. She was looking through them for her own personal interest. In you, I suspect.'

'Oh, come on,' I said, dismissing the suggestion. 'Why would Neufeld be interested in me?'

'When I challenged her about it, she got arsey,' Jane replied, side stepping the question. 'So I reminded her that I am the office manager and that next time she wants to access the index, she comes to me.'

Jane was overstepping the mark. 'Actually, you know, she's a research assistant. Which makes me her line manager. So perhaps next time you have a problem with her, you'd raise it with me and let me deal with it?'

Jane gave me a look like daggers. 'My office. My index. My business.'

God, she could be a stubborn cow. 'Yes but my research assistant. My responsibility. That's all I'm saying. Next time, let me know. Okay?'

Jane stared at me and then shrugged. 'Okay.'

That's the thing about Jane. She is about as direct as they come, but take a similarly direct line with her and she is fine with it. If anything she seems to have more respect for you if you do.

'Are you eating?' I asked her, after a short pause.

'It's lunch time isn't it?'

I ignored the sarcasm, which for Jane was pretty standard stuff. 'It's okay. I'll get it. What do you want?'

'Something with salad. Surprise me.'

'Drink? Coffee maybe?'

'Orange juice. Caffeine is bad for you.'

BUILDING 41

'Which might worry me if the dishwater they serve up in here, masquerading as coffee, had any caffeine in it. Frankly, I'm not convinced that the beans they use in here have ever seen a coffee plantation.'

Jane ignored me.

'Orange juice it is then,' I said, beating a swift retreat.

'How's your sister taken it?' Jane asked, in between mouthfuls.

I'd opted for a pie that purported to be steak and ale but didn't much taste like either. I was already regretting it. 'Kate? Badly,' I replied. 'She's devastated, actually.'

'But you're not?'

I just wasn't. 'I'm trying to be. I know that's the script, but it's hard to be devastated by the loss of a man who has just told you that he's not your father. As well as what a bitch your mother was.'

Jane said nothing.

I took another mouthful. 'I'll miss him,' I said when I'd swallowed, 'eventually. Right now, I'm just so pissed off with him that if he wasn't already dead, I'd probably strangle the old bugger.'

Jane shook her head.

'What? I should show my father a little more respect? He wasn't though, was he?'

'Whatever he was. Whatever he did...' Jane began.

'He was still my...' I interrupted. 'What was he, exactly?' I said, scratching my chin in mock contemplation.

'You can be such a dickhead. Do you know that?'

It was my turn to shrug.

'He was the man who brought you up. Who fed you, watered you, wiped your shitty arse and put you to bed. He cared for you, Harry.'

I felt my face flush. I knew how I must sound.

'Does it really matter so much that he might not have been your biological father?'

'Do you know what?' I said, pausing, but when Jane didn't reply, I continued. 'No. Actually, it doesn't. What matters so much is that he kept the truth from us. From me. It matters to me that all he did in his last few weeks was make matters a whole lot worse.'

Jane put down her fork. 'Worse?' she said, still chewing. 'How's that?'

'I would have thought it was obvious.' I could feel my temper rising and with it, the volume of my voice. People were listening. 'So he thought that she might be alive,' I said, lowering my voice. 'Great. I don't know whether she is or whether she isn't. How has that made it more likely that I will find her? She was a liar and a fraud. Everything about her was false. That's what he said. So where does that get me, exactly?'

Jane said nothing.

I considered another mouthful, thought better of it and pushed away my plate.

'Go on,' said Jane. 'What else did he tell you?'

'Nothing,' I said, dismissively. She was right, I was being a dickhead.

She stared at me.

'All right. He mentioned a name.'

'What name?'

'"Rosemary".'

'Who is?'

'I don't know. I think I remember a woman called Rosemary who was staying at the flat where Mum left us, me and Kate, for a couple of nights shortly before she disappeared.'

'Whose flat?'

'We called her "Aunty Simone". But she wasn't. She was black.'

'Doesn't mean she couldn't have been your aunt.'

I stared at her trying to do the daggers thing. 'You don't say?'

Jane actually laughed.

BUILDING 41

I grinned, in spite of myself. 'Simone was a friend of my mother's. I know that much and bugger all else. I don't even know what her surname was.'

'You are sure that this Rosemary was there?'

I nodded. 'She was ill. I remember her being in bed. Or sitting by the window in her room.'

Jane was thoughtful. 'What did your father say about her, exactly?'

I sighed, wearily. Right then, I was feeling it. 'Not a lot. He mentioned her name. More than once. He said that she "knew".'

'Knew what?'

'Your guess is as good as mine. What a liar my mum was, perhaps?'

We both picked up our drinks and stared into them.

'What about this bomb thing?' Jane said, without warning.

I looked up. How the bloody hell…

'Ellen told me. And before you go off on one,' she added, 'Ellen tells me everything.'

I opened my mouth to speak but she was having none of it.

'And to be perfectly honest, you should be thankful that she does, Harry. Because had she not spoken to Mike and me about all of this, you'd probably be sat in that new house of yours on your own. So grow a pair and get over it.'

The truth. Not always what you want to hear but it seldom does you any lasting harm.

'So, what about it?' Jane pressed.

'He used the word. That's all. At first, I thought that he was just rambling. There were bombs going off all over the place in the seventies. I thought maybe he was remembering one of them. But he repeated the word. In fact he shouted it. Like a warning or something.'

Jane was thoughtful. 'Drink your coffee,' she said after a few moments. 'It's getting cold and you don't want to be late for Mata Hari.'

Bizarrely, I found myself doing as I was told. The lukewarm coffee tasted even worse than it did when it was hot.

'It's not true, though, is it?' Jane said, suddenly. 'All that old guff about your father having told you nothing.'

I put down my now empty coffee cup.

'You've got loads more than you had before. Ted thought she was still alive. So there is a good chance that she is. Those two people who turned up at your house wanted you all to go with them. Which raises the possibility that she had been trying to protect you. So where was she going and why? Because it sounds an awful lot like some kind of witness protection to me. If so, then what had she witnessed that had got her into so much trouble that meant that she could not stay? Something to do with a bombing perhaps?'

That was Ellen's theory too, but it was just too far fetched for me. My face must have shown that I wasn't buying it.

'She'd been leading a double life. That's what your father said, wasn't it?'

'My father,' I echoed, sarcastically. I couldn't help myself.

Jane looked like to she wanted to punch me in the face, which she probably did. 'Oh, for God's sake. Get over yourself.'

If we'd been standing beside each other, I would have ducked. As it was, I was keeping an eye on her knife and fork.

'Look,' she said, her features softening. 'I can see how much that has thrown you. Which is fair enough. It would throw most of us. But get past it and try to think about what he actually said. What he was trying to tell you. When Ellen told me, I couldn't believe how much further forward this takes you. How much he's given you to work with.'

I snorted. I just couldn't get past the anger.

Jane did the daggers thing again. She was good at it. Better than me. 'Think about it. What kind of person leads a double life, so secret that not even her family knows about it?'

I smiled wryly. 'Ted had a word for it.'

'Oh, for God's sake. It is so obvious. Ted was too hurt to see it. Or to deal with it. Forget about Ted and think about what he told you.'

'Meaning what?' I snapped, a little more abruptly than I had intended.

She stared at me. 'Let's try again. Who leads a double life so secret that not even their family knows about it?'

I said nothing, but I was thinking.

'When they're exposed,' Jane continued, 'what kind of person might be offered a new name and a new identity. Given the chance to start over again.'

'Someone working undercover?'

Jane raised an approving eyebrow.

'A copper?' I was thinking out loud. 'You're saying that my mother was a police officer?'

She leant back in her chair and folded her arms. 'Well, why not?'

'Because she was a school teacher.'

'She was a school teacher who, according to Ted, lived a double life, who one day in 1978…'

'Seven,' I interrupted.

'What?'

'It was '77.'

Jane frowned. 'Was it?'

I nodded. I could see the cogs turning behind her eyes.

'Who one day in 1977 vanished,' Jane continued, like she was thinking something but not voicing it. 'Having been offered a new identity and by the sound of it, not just for herself but for all of you.'

We both fell silent.

Was it even plausible? I tried to play the scenario through in my head. It was such a radical departure from the narrative I'd always held onto.

'1977,' Jane said, suddenly. 'Are you absolutely certain that was the year she disappeared?'

'No,' I replied. 'I'm absolutely certain of nothing but that is what Ted told me. What about it?'

Jane glanced at her watch. 'Too late. Time's up. You've got an appointment with your slightly strange German research assistant.'

I glanced down at my own watch.

Jane was already on her feet. 'You'll have to wait. And Harry?'

'What?'

'Be careful with Neufeld, okay?'

'Why?'

'Because I say so. Call it feminine intuition.'

CHAPTER THIRTEEN

I eased on my crash helmet and reached into the pocket of my parka for my wraparound sunglasses. Ellen, and Jane come to think of it, were always nagging me about getting a full face helmet. They are right about them being safer. Hit the ground at speed and you at least stand a reasonable chance of retaining your jaw. Trouble is, they just don't look right. Not on a scooter. I fastened the chin strap and kicked the starter over a couple of times before she spluttered into life, with a reassuring putt-putt-putt. I'd had the Series Three for five years or so now and the restoration was almost complete. Just a few finishing touches and she'd be as good as the day she left the Lambretta factory in Milan. Maybe better. Certainly a finer paint job, that was for sure. I'd paid through the nose for it but it had been worth every penny. She looked dead sharp in red and white. I slid onto the seat, shoved her off the stand and rode her down to the gate.

'Knocking off early, Stammers?' called out Stan, as I pulled up beside the gate house. Stan, the gateman, fancied himself as a bit of a biker.

'Early? It's half past five. Some of us have got homes to go to,' I called back.

'You ought to try a proper bike, mate. What does that thing do? Forty-five with the wind behind you.'

'It's not about the speed, pal, it's about the style. You lot wouldn't recognise style if she crept up on you from behind and kissed your fat, lardy arse. All that grease under your finger nails. It's not normal.'

'Better than riding about on that bloody hair dryer of yours,' the gateman shot back, pressing the button beside the door of the gatehouse to raise the barrier.

I revved the engine, pulled in the clutch lever and dropped her into first gear. 'Yeah, yeah, yeah.'

'See you tomorrow,' Stan called out as I pulled away, sending a cloud of two-stroke smoke billowing back towards the gatehouse. I could see Stan in several mirrors, waving the smoke away with his hands. I grinned, rode down the little slip road and out onto Sherwood Drive. Stan wasn't a bad sort of bloke, really. We engaged in the same old mods and rockers routine whenever I rode the Lambretta into work and he was on the gate. It was all good fun. Stan reckoned he rode a Bonneville but I'd never actually seen him on it. He always came to work in a beaten up old Vauxhall Astra, as far as I could tell.

I opened the throttle and let the scooter stretch her legs. The engine responded eagerly. I found myself thinking about Petra Neufeld. While I'd spent an unexpectedly enjoyable afternoon with the German researcher, there was definitely something odd about her. For one thing, she had almost entirely avoided the subject of her Enigma research, which was, after all, the reason for her secondment to Bletchley. Instead she'd spent most of the afternoon trying to steer our conversation onto the subject of the search for Martha Watts and how we - Ellen and I - had come to the conclusion that the log reader's body was concealed in the cell behind the steel door in the tunnel below Belsize Park Underground station. She'd known about the purse and the train ticket, which was no great surprise. Their discovery had been widely reported. According to Neufeld, there had been as much coverage in the German press as there had been in the British

BUILDING 41

tabloids. Surprisingly though, she'd also known about Elsie, whose story and privacy had been guarded more carefully, mainly at Elsie's behest. Neufeld had been particularly keen to learn of Elsie's wartime role at the Park and had asked about her later life. I'd revealed as little as possible. Although that was, in part, down to how little I actually knew about it, a thought that hadn't really occurred to me before. But my reticence had done little to blunt Neufeld's enthusiasm. Her intensity had been unsettling, but there was also something fascinating about her. Something which, despite Jane's warning, I couldn't help liking. Maybe even because of it.

I buzzed across the junction with Queensway and headed southeast along the Water Eaton Road, narrowly avoiding a white transit van, as it pulled out into the lane in front of me. The driver had evidently decided that a scooter didn't count as oncoming traffic at the first of the road's single lane chicanes. *Wanker.*

I thought about Jane. The revelation that my mother had left in 1977 had triggered something. I knew that look. She'd be on her way home right now, thinking it through, whatever it was. If I was lucky, she'd tell me about it in the morning, but only if she was good and ready. Otherwise she'd leave me in suspense. *Cow.* What the bloody hell happened in 1977? The Silver Jubilee? The Sex Pistols. Man United winning the FA Cup? I decided to google it when I got home.

Jane had been right about Ted's revelations. I had been too caught up in the emotions of it all. Too angry to see anything that Ted had offered me, in any kind of positive light. Perhaps it was time to let it go. Ted had done what he had done. There was no undoing it now. No going back. What was the point of holding on to all that shit? Was it getting me anywhere?

The funeral. I'd been avoiding that too. I was going to have to face it, sooner or later. Thank God that Kate was making all the arrangements.

Kate. She had insisted and, in truth, I'd had been happy to let her get on with it. Still, she'd be struggling with the enormity of it all. She'd adored him. I felt a pang of guilt.

Attending the funeral was going to be difficult enough. Pretending to everyone that I was gutted, when in truth, I was… What was I? How did I really feel about it, when all was said and done? Was I ready to make peace with him? So he'd died with only a fraction of the story told but at least he had tried. Hadn't he?

The trouble was that every time I thought about him, I found myself getting angry. Like I was getting angry now. Grinding my bloody teeth together under the chin strap of my scooter helmet. How could he? I mean, how could he have told me that I was not his son and then died, while the news was still sinking in? It was bloody typical of Ted. He'd screwed with our heads all along.

Which was, of course, completely absurd. I knew it was. Ted had hardly chosen the moment. I'd dragged it out of him. He'd probably never have told me at all had I not goaded him into it. At least he'd tried to do the right thing in the end, even if he had been unable to hide his bitterness. And who could really blame him for that, if even half of what he had said was true? Is that how I wanted to end my days? Still bitter thirty years from now. What was the point of continuing to blame him? It was water under the bridge and Ted was gone. I felt sad. For the first time, really. I swallowed and tried not to think about it.

1977. What the hell happened in '77? I was still thinking about it when I pulled up outside the house, bumped the scooter up the curb and in through the front gate. As I heaved the Lambretta up onto its stand I noticed the neighbour's curtain twitch.

We hadn't met them yet. The neighbours. Not properly, anyway. An older couple. Both retired, I reckoned. I tried to remember their names and couldn't. Ellen had spoken to one of them over the garden fence. She'd seemed friendly enough. Neither of us had met the husband yet. Though I'd seen him peering from behind the curtain. Just as he was doing now.

BUILDING 41

The one-man neighbourhood watch routine might have bothered some people but it didn't bother me. Far from it. If it meant that he kept an eye on the place while we were at work, that was fine by me. The old boy must have had a field day when we first moved in, with the paparazzi camped outside. I caught his eye and nodded in what I hoped was a friendly fashion. He flashed me a grin and disappeared behind the curtain.

Once I'd chained up the scooter, I let myself into the house, draped my parka across the back of a dining room chair, turned on the computer and put the kettle on while I waited for the machine to boot. A few minutes later I was sat at the PC with a coffee in one hand and a mouse in the other, scrolling through a long list of search engine results. I was still there when, an hour later, I heard a key in the front door and remembered that I'd promised to pick up supper from the supermarket on the way home.

*****

Jane Mears leant back in her seat. 'Well, now there's a thing,' she said suddenly.

Mikel Eglund looked up from his book.

Jane glanced over her shoulder. 'Is the printer working?'

'Sure. Why wouldn't it be?'

'The damn thing is always out of ink.'

'I did warn you.'

'About what?' She turned and stared at him.

'I told you we should have bought a laser-jet.'

'No, you bloody didn't.'

'Yes, I bloody did.' He was grinning.

'All right, smart arse. Come and have a look at this.'

'What is it?' Mike said, dragging himself up from the sofa.

'1977. I knew it.'

'Knew what?'

Jane waited until Mike was standing behind her, peering over her shoulder at the monitor screen. '1977. The A1 bombing.'

Mike stared at the screen. 'What about it?'

'I think it might be linked in some way to the disappearance of Harry's mother.'

'Yeah? Cool. Why?'

'I don't know. Yet.'

Mike stepped back, folded his arms and waited.

Jane continued to read. 'You know, the circumstances surrounding the bombing were never fully explained.'

Mike said nothing.

'The papers blamed it on the IRA.'

'No big surprises there then.'

'Oh, shut up.'

'Well, Baader-Meinhof never made it across the Channel and Osama Bin Laden was probably still doing his civil engineering degree in 1977.'

'Osama Bin Laden did a civil engineering degree?' Jane said, staring at him.

'Sure he did. Shame he didn't stick with building things, instead of blowing them up.'

Jane shook her head then turned back to the screen. 'Anyway. The explosive was traced to the IRA, but they always denied having anything to do with it.'

Mike said nothing.

'The only person who was ever charged was Peter Owen, leader of the Nationalist Union of Great Britain.'

'Never heard of him.'

Jane looked over her shoulder again. 'You've never heard of Peter Owen?'

Mike shrugged. 'I was six years old in 1977 and we were still living in Fredrikstad.'

'Owen was done for conspiracy to cause explosions for which he was sentenced to thirty-five years in prison. It was alleged, at the trial, that he'd been conspiring with the IRA. Doesn't that strike you as ever so slightly unlikely?'

'Why?'

'He was the leader of the NUGB. Right wing nationalists, Mike. What the hell would he have been doing working with the Irish Republican Army?'

'I thought you said they denied it.'

'They did, but Owen didn't. In fact he offered no defence at all. Never uttered a word according to reports, although most of the trial was conducted in secret.'

Mike said nothing.

'And another thing. The explosion itself happened in a field in Hertfordshire, off the A1, following a chase through North London. The van containing the bomb crashed and exploded, killing the driver, but there's nothing said in any of the reports about the driver's identity.'

'There probably wasn't much left of him.'

'Oh come on. There must have been a body, even if it was badly burned. But there's nothing in the reports at all.'

'Sounds like a job for Mulder and Scully,' Mike said grinning.

'Be serious, Mike.'

Mike shrugged. 'What's this got to do with Harry's mother, anyway?'

'She went missing in 1977, right?'

'If you say so.'

'According to Harry, after her disappearance, Ted received a visit from persons unknown. Harry remembers it. Ted told Harry that they wanted Ted and the children to go with them.'

'So?'

'It sounds to me like they were being offered new identities. Some form of witness protection? Ted also mentioned the word "bomb". More than once.'

'Yeah, but there were bombs going off in London all the time in the seventies.'

'In the seventies, yes there were. Not in '77 though. With the exception of the bomb we're talking about, there were no bombings on the UK mainland in 1977 or '78 as a matter of fact. So if Ted was describing a specific incident at about the time of his wife's disappearance, this has to have been it. There were no others.'

Mike scratched his chin. 'If he was describing a specific incident. I thought you said that Harry wasn't sure.'

'Harry isn't sure, but the fact is that Ted used the word.'

'So what are you saying?'

'I'm saying that perhaps - and granted, it is a perhaps - Elizabeth Stammers was in some way involved with this bombing. Ted talked about her leading a double life. So maybe she was working undercover. She witnesses something. The plot is foiled. The plotters, apart from Owen, evade detection. So she's at risk and, by association, so are Harry, Kate and Ted. So they are all offered witness protection. Which Ted refuses.'

Mike started to speak.

Jane interrupted him. 'Which Ted refuses, because his wife chooses that moment to tell him that he's not Harry's father.'

Mike closed his mouth again.

'It was not her finest moment, granted, but maybe she didn't have a choice. Maybe she wanted a fresh start. She could hardly have asked Ted to go with her and then a few months say "Oh and by the way..."'

'But if they were at risk, how comes nothing ever happened to Harry and his sister? Or Ted, for that matter?'

Jane sighed. 'Now that, I don't know.'

'And if Ted wasn't his father, who is?'

'Or that. But hey, give me a break, will you? That was one evening's work and I've barely got started.'

'You're a genius,' Mike said sarcastically.

Jane scowled at him. 'There's one thing I'd like to know.'

'Just one?'

'For starters.'

'Which is?'

'The date when she left. My guess is sometime around August 22nd. Perhaps a day or two before. If I'm right then that would just about nail it.'

'Does Harry know the date?'

'No. He doesn't.'

CHAPTER FOURTEEN

Wednesday, April 20, 2005

Smith swung the Mercedes in a wide arc and pulled up in front of a low fence. Beyond it, was the entrance to the harbour and on the far bank, the white sands of Walberswick, dotted with holiday makers out walking in the late afternoon sunshine. The tide had already turned, sending seawater rushing in through the narrow harbour entrance, into the River Blyth which in turn would flood the salt marshes north and east of the little Suffolk village of Blythburgh.

Smith had been coming to the area for many years, and while his visits were infrequent and more so since the recruitment of the girl, he'd made it his business to get to know the place and to establish a small network of contacts. It had been through one such contact - the landlord at The Bell Inn at Walberswick - that he'd been able to recruit her. She had proved surprisingly reliable, sending him periodic reports as agreed and keeping him informed of any developments, of which there had been none for long periods. Until now, in fact.

Smith switched off the engine, removed the key from the ignition and eased himself out of the car. He stood for a few moments, scanning the car park. Four cars. All empty. A little group of people surrounding the blue and white hut, selling refreshments alongside buckets and spades, beside the harbour road. Two women, one very overweight man in shorts and two young children, one in a buggy. Possibly others, out of view. He walked towards them.

As he often did whenever he visited Southwold, he'd dispensed with his usual grey suit and had opted for more casual attire. This time, a pair of chinos, a short sleeved shirt and a pair of brown loafers. It was not a look with which he felt particularly comfortable but at least he blended in. His feet crunched on the gravel as he walked across to the hut.

He waited until the overweight man had departed with one of the women and the two children and then approached the kiosk. The second woman nodded as he met her eyes. 'Two ninety-nines,' she said, addressing the young man who was serving.

'That'll be three pounds ten, love.'

She paid him, took the two ice creams and handed one of them to Smith.

He took the ice cream and turned, gesturing for her to follow which she did without comment. He headed for the harbour. 'Isn't it rather early in the season for ice-cream?' he said when they were out of earshot of the hut.

'It is never too early for your English ice cream,' she said, with a thick Russian accent. 'Sometimes I bring Elsie. She loves ice cream. I would take it back for her but it melts.'

'How is she?'

The young Russian hesitated. 'Not so good. The incident at the hotel upset her. She spends much time, watching from her window.'

'Has she said anything more?'

'Not since I called you.'

'Have you had any further contact from Carmichael and Stammers?'

'Yes. Ellen called this morning to let her know about the funeral, and to find out how she is.'

'Elsie is definitely going to the funeral?'

'Yes.' Natalia glanced at him. 'Why? Should she not go?'

Smith hesitated. 'Elsie may do as she pleases, of course. I am simply interested in her reasons.'

'She wishes to be there to support Ellen. She says that she is worried about Harry and the strain that his father's death might be putting on their relationship.'

'She told you that?'

'Yes.'

While the explanation she had given the nurse might be true in part, what was more interesting, Smith reflected, was what it revealed about her mental state and, in particular, her continuing capacity for deception. Elsie might be fifteen years his senior, but perhaps she was not quite the feeble-minded geriatric she pretended to be. 'What else did you tell Carmichael?'

'I told her what I told you. That the incident has unsettled her. Nothing more.'

They crossed the road opposite the lifeboat station and continued toward the harbour.

'The man who you have observed, describe him to me again.'

The girl smiled. 'I can do better than this.'

Smith glanced at her.

'I took this,' she said, putting her hand into the bag slung across her shoulder. 'From Elsie's bedroom window.' She removed an envelope and handed it to him.

Smith took it from her. 'I did not ask you to take photographs.'

'I know. Don't worry. I was careful. He did not see me.'

'I hope not.' Smith removed the photographs from the envelope. 'For your sake,' he added, looking at each of the pictures in turn. 'Was this the first time you noticed this man?'

'No. I have seen him outside, several times.'

'How many times, exactly?'

She hesitated. 'Three.'

'Always on the bench?'

BUILDING 41

'Yes. Always.'

'When was the last time?'

'On Thursday, last week. It was in the morning. That is when I took the pictures.'

'You have not seen him again? Not since the incident at the hotel?'

'No.'

'I take it that Elsie has also seen him?'

'Yes, but I don't think that she recognised him until the incident on Sunday. Her eyesight is not so good. She thinks that everyone who sits on that bench is watching her.'

He put the pictures back in the envelope. 'Are these the only printed copies?'

She nodded.

'You have the digital images?'

'Yes.'

'Delete them.'

She said nothing.

'Delete them and inform me when you have.'

'Very well.'

'If he turns up again, make no further attempt to photograph him and make absolutely certain that he does not suspect you.'

The Russian nodded.

'He is exceptionally dangerous, Natalia. If he thinks that you are watching him, he will want to know who you are working for and, when he has wrung that out of you, he is quite likely to kill you. Do you understand?'

'Of course.'

She had sounded dismissive. Smith noticed it. 'He has a reputation,' he said, softening his tone. 'For enjoying his female victims before he murders them. I do not wish you to become his latest entertainment.'

'What then, am I to do, if he comes to the home again?'

'Call me. I'm going to be staying here until the funeral at least. Maybe longer.'

'In Southwold?' she asked.

'Nearby,' he replied.

'This man,' the Russian said after a few moments. 'Will he harm Elsie? She is very afraid of him.'

'No, I do not believe so. He wants something that only she can give him. Elsie is an elderly woman. He will have to be careful or he will lose her. I really don't think that he will want to do that.'

'He is trying to frighten her?'

Smith nodded. 'Yes, I believe so. He is trying to unnerve her. To frighten her into some hasty overreaction.'

'He hopes that she will reveal this thing?'

'Yes, I think that is exactly what he hopes.'

They had reached the first of the harbour's landing platforms. A small fishing boat had tied up and men were unloading crates from the boat onto a bright red pick-up truck. When they had passed it, Smith added 'I want you to keep a close eye on her. He may well be right that she will react.'

The Russian nodded. 'I will.'

They had drawn level with a wide wooden bench at the side of the roadway. Smith turned and gestured for them to sit. 'You have done well,' he said, glancing out across the harbour toward a small group of children, playing on the far bank. 'Is there anything else that you need?'

'No. Except,' she added, 'that there is something that I wish to ask.'

Smith waited.

'When I agreed to work for you, you promised me that we would be doing…' She appeared to be struggling to find the words. 'That I would be working on the side of good. That I would be protecting Elsie.'

Smith said nothing.

BUILDING 41

'In my country, there are people such as you, Mr Smith. Many people. They are not on the side of good. If you want a happy life, you do not get mixed up with them.'

'This is not Russia,' Smith said, curtly.

'No, it is not.'

'It was your choice to work for me. Have I not met my side of the bargain?'

'Yes, but I need to know that when this is over, I will be free. To go where I please. To do as I wish.'

Smith was thoughtful. 'I can promise you that this man,' he said, holding up the envelope containing the photographs, 'is most definitely not on the side of good. As to what happens when this is over, that will be up to you. You have my word.'

She nodded.

'Although,' he said, smiling 'if you continue to do as well as you have done, then we may be able to find other uses for your talents.' He held up his hand as she begin to object. 'You will be free to choose. As you were free to choose when you accepted my original offer.'

She nodded again.

'This is Great Britain Natalia and we are not the KGB. You have nothing to fear from us. If you offer us your service, we will not let you down. You can be sure of that. We always look after our own.'

Natalia said nothing.

Smith got back into the Mercedes and pulled the door closed. He sat for several, long moments in silence, watching a small fishing boat navigate the harbour entrance. It was a perilous enterprise in the strong current, but the captain of the craft had undoubtedly managed it many times before and did so on this occasion without mishap. When it was safely in the harbour Smith reached across to the car's glove box and retrieved his mobile phone. He dialled a number and waited.

'Progress?' he asked when the call was answered. He listened to the response. 'Keep working on him and watch for any sign.' He listened again. 'I am relying on your vigilance.' He waited. 'I must know the moment anyone makes a move. Do you understand?' He listened to the response. 'Work on him. Gain his confidence and quickly. We're running out of time.' He ended the call, leant back in his seat and let out a long sigh.

CHAPTER FIFTEEN

I trotted up the stairs to the archive, invigorated by the ride in on the scooter. I'd taken the back roads to avoid the bypass. The Lambretta was capable enough on the dual carriageway but it was so much more fun on country roads, especially early in the morning when the traffic was light. Anyone who tells you that you can't bank a scooter into bends has never ridden one.

I fished about in my parka pocket for my keys, but oddly, when I tried the key in the door, it was already unlocked. I was thinking about how early it was. About how it was way too early for anybody else to have started work. I'd only come in this early myself to get in an hour or two's research before Jane arrived.

Last night had been a wash out. By the time I'd been to the supermarket, returned with the ingredients for the promised curry, prepared, cooked, served, eaten and washed up, most of the evening had been burned. What was left of it, Ellen wanted to spend curled up on the sofa in front of the television. After the rocky few months we'd just survived, I was more than happy to comply. Despite the fact that I was itching to take a closer look at 1977.

I opened the door slowly, stepped inside and stood rock still, listening for any sound of movement, but there was none. Neither had any of the lights been switched on. The first floor archive consisted of a long corridor with a kitchen and toilet at one end and rooms off to the left and right. The corridor had no windows and the rooms that did were mostly filled, from floor to ceiling, with shelving on which was stacked part of the contents of the Bletchley Park archive. Documents, equipment, endless rows of paraphernalia loosely - some very loosely - associated with the Park and the activities of its various inhabitants over the last sixty years. As a consequence, very little if any light made it into the corridor from the outside. Which made it necessary to switch on the lights, even in the summertime. If, that is, you didn't want to trip, arse over tit, over some stray item that had found its way into the corridor without permission.

I hung my helmet on the coat stand by the door. Then, thinking better of it, returned it to my head. If someone was going to try to cave my skull in with a baseball bat before legging it with some item of bounty under their arm, I might as well make it difficult for them. It wasn't as paranoid a thought as it might seem. The Park had been burgled several times and, famously, had even lost an Enigma machine. It had finally been returned by Jeremy Paxman, the BBC Newsnight presenter, after months of protracted ransom negotiations with the thief.

I reached out a hand and switched on the main lights. There was no way I was walking the short distance to my office in the dark. The fluorescent tubes hummed, clicked, flickered and then came on. Still no sign of any movement.

I considered retreating to the gatehouse to summon Stan, but if I did that I'd never hear the end of it. Stan would eat out on the story for months. The great Harry Stammers. The people's champion. The man who had brought down Max Banks. Scared of his own shadow. Death by the hand of an unknown assailant would be moderately preferable.

So I took a walking stick from the coat stand. God knows who it belonged to. It had been there so long, no one could even remember. And made my way along the corridor toward my office. Slowly and with a good deal of caution.

BUILDING 41

About two thirds of the way there, I heard a sound. Somebody moving about perhaps. I called out. 'Hello?'

'Oh. Hi Harry,' said a voice from immediately behind me. The woman to which it belonged had emerged from the doorway of the room I'd just passed.

I turned on my heel, brandishing the walking stick like a sword. 'Sweet Jesus. What the fuck are you doing here?'

Neufeld. Dressed all in black. Grinning. Those ridiculous eyebrows, straight as a die.

'I'm researching. This is the archive. I'm a researcher. Remember?'

'For fuck's sake,' I barked. 'I know you're a fucking researcher. I just wasn't expecting you to be researching this early.'

Neufeld shrugged. 'Here, I am.'

'How the fuck did you get in?'

She stared at me. 'Through the door. Is there some other way? Some secret tunnel perhaps?' she said, like she'd said something prophetic.

I stared back at her. 'I meant how did you get a key?'

'Oh, that was easy. The man, Stan. He sits in that little building beside…'

'Yes, I know who Stan is,' I snapped.

'He told me to listen out for your motorcycle. Well, actually, he called it a… *vacuum cleaner?* Is that how you say it?'

She knew exactly how we say it.

'I was so fascinated by the contents of room…' She turned and looked toward the door. 'Seven,' she continued, 'that I did not hear it.'

She was grinning broadly, now. She looked a bloody site more attractive when she did that. In fact she was looking a bloody site more attractive today, full stop. 'Yes, well I'll be having a word with Stan, the man…'

Now she was laughing.

'He is not supposed…' I hesitated. 'What's so bloody funny?'

'Are you going to take off your helmet and put down that stick? You look like Michael Schumacher on a bad day. A really bad day.'

'All right. All right. It's not that funny.'

'Oh yes. It is,' she said, still laughing. 'I wish, very much, that I had a camera. I could have sold the pictures to your British press. I would have made more Euros from them than you are paying me, that's for bloody sure,' she said, trying to mimic my accent.

I had to laugh. She was odd. She wore black and she was German. But I was liking her a little more today than I had liked her yesterday and I had a feeling that I was going to like her a bit more tomorrow.

'Why don't you go and take your coat off,' she said, when she'd finished laughing. 'You look like you need coffee.'

Coffee was a good idea. I nodded. 'Thanks.' Plus, of course, Jane didn't like her in the slightest. Which was a definite bonus. I watched her walk off towards the kitchen. She had an arse from heaven. Although, it was probably tattooed or something. Which, at that particular moment, was a strangely alluring prospect. Strange because I'm not normally a big fan of tattoos on women, but I reckoned I could have made an exception in Neufeld's case.

I made it to my office, dropped my helmet on a chair by the door and walked across to my desk. I wondered about asking Neufeld whether she wanted to move up to the archive. For some God-alone known reason she had accepted an offer of accommodation in the bungalow, a couple of doors up from the Major, the Park's bombastic but well loved CEO. He must be driving her half crazy and there was plenty of space in the room next door. It might need a bit of reorganisation but she could sort that out easily enough. It would be nice having someone else around the place.

I took off my coat, hung it on the back of the door, sat down at my desk and switched on my PC. Neufeld moving up to the archive would put Jane's nose well and truly out of joint. Technically Jane was my junior, but the way she behaved you'd have thought she was the boss. Mostly I was content to let her. She

BUILDING 41

was a bloody site better at managing me than I am. Occasionally, however, I liked to seize the initiative. Just to remind her that she didn't have exclusive rights. And sometimes, just to wind her up.

'I didn't know whether you wanted sugar,' Neufeld said, reappearing in the doorway. She was holding two cups. 'So I didn't.'

'That's fine.'

She was hovering.

'Come in. Take a seat.'

She smiled.

'What did you find in Room Seven? Anything interesting?' If she hadn't found something interesting in Room Seven than there was something wrong with her.

'Many things. Where did it all come from?'

'Some of it has been here for donkeys' years.'

'Donkeys' years?' She should have been raising an eyebrow, but the damn things didn't budge.

'Oh, sorry. I meant that it's been here for a long time.'

She looked at me blankly.

'Donkeys. They are particularly long lived?' I offered.

'Ah. I see.'

'Anyway,' I continued, 'as word got out about efforts to save Bletchley Park from demolition, people began to donate stuff. Some of it with a Bletchley connection. Equipment that had been ferreted away for years. Some of it was just stuff that people thought might fit somewhere. Sometimes people brought whole collections with them, like the chap who runs the Diplomatic Wireless Service exhibition in Hut One. Have you been in there yet?'

She shook her head.

'Well do. It is an incredible collection. You won't believe some of the stuff he's got in there.'

'Like what?'

I thought about it. 'How about a working Rockex machine?'

The Rockex was a British one-time tape cipher machine. The original model was first produced in 1943, but a few of the later types were still in use into the early eighties.

'Rockex? There is such a machine here?' she asked, her eyes sparkling with interest.

I nodded. 'Brand new. Never been used in anger. Straight out of the stores at Hanslope Park.'

Neufeld was impressed, though don't ask me how I could tell, given those eyebrows.

'Or, if that hasn't sufficiently whetted your appetite, how about a working Piccolo system. Exactly like the set up used in pretty much every British embassy around the world during the cold war.'

'No. That is just too good,' Neufeld said, excitedly.

'He's a great bloke too. You could learn a great deal from him. He'll adore you.'

'Why do you say so?'

'Petra. You're young. You're female and you love cipher machines. He's an old, ex Diplomatic Wireless Service man. He's spent a lifetime travelling the world maintaining radio and cipher installations. A fascinating job but a bit niche, let's face it. Show a bit of interest and you'll be his best friend.'

'You will introduce me to him?'

'Sure. We'll go over there later if you like. He should be in after one o'clock. He usually is.'

I picked up my cup and swallowed some coffee. 'You didn't answer my question.'

She looked lost.

'About what you were looking at in Room Seven.'

'I think it was aeronautical navigation equipment. Not my field. But still very interesting.'

I nodded. 'That's exactly what it is.'

'What has that got to do with Bletchley Park?'

'As a matter of fact, there is a connection, but not all of the stuff here has one. Like I said, as word spread about Bletchley, people

BUILDING 41

began to bring us things. All sorts of things. Perhaps an elderly family member had died and relatives had discovered something in a garage or a loft. Stuff that they couldn't identify but thought might be important. Some of it was and some of it wasn't.'

'But there is such a lot of it.'

'I know and each month there is even more. People still come. Regularly. That navigation equipment you were looking at is a fairly recent donation. Came in a couple of months ago.'

Neufeld was watching me closely.

It never ceased to amaze me what people would turn up with. I'd taken in part of the cockpit instrumentation of an English Electric Lightning once. Painted on the side of each of the instruments were the words "HANDLE LIKE EGGS". It had always amused me. There was no mistaking their meaning.

'What is the connection?'

'Sorry?' I'd been thinking about the instruments from the Lightning.

'You said that there is a connection between aeronautical navigation and Bletchley. What is it?'

'The Civil Aviation Authority was here from just before the end of the war, all the way through to the Park's closure. They had their signals training establishment...' I was interrupted by the telephone on my desk. 'Excuse me a moment,' I said, picking up the receiver. 'Stammers.' I watched Neufeld while I listened to the voice on the other end of the line. She was trying not to look at me but she was definitely listening. 'Hang on a moment.' I covered the mouthpiece with my hand. 'Petra, could you give me a few minutes?'

'Sure,' she said, getting to her feet. 'I must get back, anyway.'

'Actually,' I added as an afterthought, 'I wanted to talk to you about whether you'd like to move down here to the archive.'

Neufeld smiled. 'Maybe.'

'Can we talk about it later?'

'Sure.'

She was already on her way out. I waited until she had left the room. 'Hi Jane, sorry,'
'Who was that?' Jane asked, the suspicion in her voice obvious.
'Neufeld.'
'What's she doing there?'
'I asked her the same thing. She was here when I arrived. Scared the shit out of me. When I found the door open, I thought we'd been burgled. Anyway,' I said changing the subject, 'to what do I owe this small pleasure.'
'I thought you might fancy breakfast.'
'Breakfast? You don't eat breakfast.'
'Yes, I do. Just never here or with you.'
'So why break the habit of a lifetime?'
'I've got something to tell you.'
'You love me. I know that. I've told you before, I'm already taken.'
'Funny man.'
'Don't tell me you're pregnant?'
'Harry?'
I hesitated. 'What?'
'Do yourself a favour and shut your mouth.'
I said nothing, but smiled to myself. Winding her up was easy.
'Canteen. Ten minutes. Orange juice and toast. Brown. No butter.'
'You eat dry toast?'
'I said, shut up.'
'Fine.'
The line went dead. I adored Jane. I always had. There was nobody in the word quite like her. Which was fortunate, really. One was more than enough.

'So let me get this straight,' I was trying to keep the incredulity out of my voice and not making a great job of it. 'You are saying that my mother was involved in some way with the Nationalist Union of Great Britain?'

'I believe so, yes.'

I'd found us a table and was buttering my toast. How Jane was going to eat hers dry I could not imagine. 'So what are you saying? That she was some kind of right wing nutter?'

'I don't know what her motive was, Harry.'

I'd learned always to take Jane seriously. I trusted her. Possibly more than I trusted anyone apart from Ellen. But I was finding this difficult to swallow.

Jane hesitated. 'Do you remember what your mother looked like?'

A picture flashed into my head.

'I remember you telling me that your father destroyed all the photographs you had of her. So do you remember what your mother looked like?'

'Kind of.'

'Meaning?'

'Meaning, I have a picture of her in my head, but when I try to concentrate on her face it's indistinct. Blurry. The harder I try, the more indistinct it becomes. Do you know what I mean?'

'Yes. I know exactly what you mean.'

'All I have is three grainy, black and white pictures of her when she was a teenager.' They'd been taken of her in a park somewhere. My grandmother had given them to me before she died. 'And that's it.'

Jane said nothing.

'Why?'

She hesitated and then reached for her bag. 'Because of this,' she said, removing a plastic sleeve from which she produced a sheet of paper. 'The man in the middle is Peter Owen, the leader of the NUGB. It was taken at an event he attended at the Friday Society in June 1977.'

I was watching her. She looked ever so slightly nervous. She handed me the sheet of paper. It was a printed photograph.

'The Friday Society is a conservative club in London,' she added. 'The fact that Owen was invited to speak there was a big deal at the time. Until then, the NUGB had been dismissed as a bit of a one trick pony. The speech was something of a triumph, apparently.'

There were five figures in all. Three men and two women. I took Jane's word for it that Owen was the tall man in the middle of the picture. I had no idea who the others were.

'Recognise any of them?'

'Nope.' I didn't. None of them.

'Look again at the woman on Owen's right. The one holding his arm.'

I examined the picture again. The woman on Owen's right was pretty and slim with shoulder length dark brown hair. She was wearing an evening dress. The photograph itself was not particularly sharp or close up. But it was clear enough to recognise the woman's discomfort. Like she didn't want to be there, or be photographed, or both. 'Who is she?'

'I think she's your mother, Harry.'

'What?' I gaped at Jane and then back down at the picture.

'What was your mother's maiden name?'

'Muir,' I said, absently. 'Elizabeth Muir.'

'I thought so.'

'Why?' I was still staring at the picture.

'The picture appeared in a Conservative Party pamphlet. Oddly, the woman on Owen's right isn't named. Because all of the others are. She is referred to only as Owen's Communications Officer. But I found another reference to her.' She removed a second sheet from the plastic sleeve and handed it to me. 'It's a piece Owen wrote for the Telegraph. Look at the note at the bottom. It names the person who submitted it to the news desk.'

I read it out loud. 'E.Muir, NUGB Press Office.'

BUILDING 41

Jane said nothing.

Was it her? Muir wasn't a particularly uncommon name. It didn't have to be her. 'I don't know. It could be. I just don't know.'

Jane waited.

But it was. I knew it. I put the picture down on the table in front of me, ran my hand through my hair and looked at Jane. 'It is her,' I said at last. 'Isn't it?'

Jane met my eyes and held them for a moment. Then she nodded. 'Yes. It's too much of a coincidence not to be. I think it is very likely, if not entirely certain, that this,' she said, pointing to the woman in the photograph, 'is your mother. She was already Elizabeth Stammers by then, of course. She was using her maiden name and was definitely working for Peter Owen.'

*****

I was not entirely sure why I was feeling so flat. At least, after years of knowing almost nothing, I'd discovered something about my mother. Of course, the discovery of her association with a convicted right wing terrorist had hardly filled me with joy. But I don't think it was this that had depressed me.

Perhaps it was that the slightly fuzzy picture of my mother standing bedside Owen had served only to emphasise how little I really knew of her. The fragmentary memories I'd held onto since my childhood. Memories that I'd treasured. Guarded jealously against Ted's denial. Perhaps it was the realisation that they were of someone else entirely. A mother who, in reality, did not exist. Who had never existed. I think it was the realisation that I didn't know the woman in the photograph at all. The real Elizabeth Stammers. She might as well have been a complete stranger. Because that is what she was to me…

'Are you going to eat that?' Ellen's voice floated into my consciousness.

'Hmm?'

We were sitting at the dining room table. Ellen had made pasta. I'd hardly touched it. It had been three days since our conversation and Jane and I had not discussed it since. If anything, I'd got the feeling that she'd been avoiding me. Giving me some space, I guessed. Even Jane had her sensitive side.

'You know, this was always going to happen,' Ellen said, gently.

'What?'

'Discovering the truth about your mother. It was never going to be comfortable. Whatever led her to leave you all behind. It was never going to be a happy set of circumstances was it?'

'No, I don't suppose it was.'

'That's the nature of the truth. Unfortunately it's not always the truth that we want to hear,' Ellen reflected.

'I know that Ellen. I always knew that. It's just that I look at that picture and I think "Who the hell are you?"'

Ellen reached across the table and took my hand. 'Do you still want to find out? That's the thing. You've got something to work with now, but do you want to?'

I thought about it. 'Do you know what?' I said, suddenly resolute.

Ellen looked at me searchingly and shook her head.

'I'm going to try to put it out of my mind until after the funeral. I said I'd pop over to see Kate tomorrow evening. She needs me. She's been putting on a brave face but I know her. She'll be all over the place and you know what Jonathan is like. Bloody useless. I'll pick it all up again once the funeral is out of the way.'

'Go easy on Jonathan. It won't help Kate if the two of you are at loggerheads.'

To say that Jonathan Longhurst, Kate's barrister husband, and I don't get along would be an understatement. The trouble is that he just can't lose his courtroom persona. Every conversation with him is an argument to be won or, more likely in my case, lost. Whenever I see him, I inevitably end up wanting to punch the man in the face. 'Don't worry. I'll give him a wide berth.'

BUILDING 41

Ellen smiled. 'It might be for the best.'

CHAPTER SIXTEEN

Friday, April 19, 2005

'It's here,' Kate announced, turning towards us hurriedly. 'Is everyone ready?'

I was as ready as I was ever going to be.

Kate looked tired and drawn, which was surely how she must have been feeling. She was wearing a navy dress, a short black jacket and a hat that, unless it had been hired, which knowing Kate I very much doubted, was probably destined to remain in a cupboard until the next family funeral. I wondered who would be the unlucky beneficiary.

'Now remember,' Kate said, looking at me, 'you and Ellen are with Jonathan and me in the front car. Elsie…' She hesitated. 'You don't mind me calling you Elsie, do you?' Kate asked, awkwardly.

I had almost forgotten that this was the first time that Kate and Elsie had met.

'No of course not, my dear.'

'You're with Aunty Geraldine's party. Is that all right?'

'As long as Geraldine doesn't mind. I wouldn't want to impose.'

Elsie had seemed in great shape. I'd been surprised when she had said that she wanted to attend the funeral. She had never met Ted, but had insisted that she wanted to pay her respects, one family to the other. Ellen was pleased. I think she was hoping that it would give them a proper chance to catch up after the trauma of events at the hotel.

'Don't be silly,' replied Aunty Geraldine. 'We don't mind at all, do we Arthur?' She didn't wait for her husband's reply. 'No, not one bit. You stick with us Elsie and don't you be worrying, Ellen. We'll take good care of her, won't we Arthur.'

I glanced at Uncle Arthur who had opened his mouth to speak but that was about as far as he got.

'We certainly will,' added Geraldine. She was a large, imposing woman in her mid seventies who had always reminded me of Hyacinth Bucket. She was wearing a dark skirt with large grey spots, which flopped, shapelessly from her waist, such as Aunty Geraldine had one. It made her look like a Dalek.

There was a slow, deliberate knock on the door.

'Now, everyone. If we can have family first please. Followed by neighbours and friends. Jonathan, can you make sure you lock up when everyone is out.'

Jonathan Longhurst inclined his head. He was wearing what looked to me like an extremely expensive, but not very well fitting slate grey suit.

Kate had disappeared into the hall to speak to the undertaker. She soon reappeared and ushered us all to follow.

Ellen took my arm and together we walked out of the house, into the sunshine. The hearse had drawn up on the wide gravel drive. There were five black cars behind it. All Jaguar saloons.

'Do you think Elsie will be all right?' Ellen whispered as Elsie came out with Aunty Geraldine. 'I'd hate her to have one of her turns.'

'You can go with her, you know. If you're worried. I'll be fine.'

'Perhaps I will on the way back. I'd rather stay with you until we get there,' she said, squeezing my arm. I knew that she didn't want to leave me. It was reassuring to know that she had my back.

We found our way to the car and, once the procession was ready, the funeral director, who was dressed in a black top hat and tails, led the way along the ample drive. He was on foot, holding out a silver-topped stick in front of him, as though trouping the colour. I was struck by the absurdity of it but I also found it touching in a way that I really hadn't anticipated. Once we reached the top of the drive the cortege turned left onto the road. The street was lined with people. It looked like half the neighbourhood had turned out. They bowed their heads as the hearse passed by. I was quite overcome. It was a mixture of grief and something approaching pride, I think. I did my best to contain my emotions but Ellen certainly noticed. She gripped my arm tightly.

We were passing a little crowd that had gathered toward the end of the street when, out of nowhere, a photographer stepped forward and ran across the road toward our car.

Ellen sighed, 'Oh, for heaven's sake. I thought we were past all this.'

I'm not entirely certain why I did what I did next. Probably a combination of things. Months of putting up with the cameras. Losing my father. In more ways than one. Maybe just the emotion of the day. But to say that the red mist descended wouldn't quite do it justice.

The photographer was now trotting along beside our car, holding the camera almost to the glass, clacking away automatically as it took multiple shots. Before Ellen had realised what I was doing, I had buzzed the window and grabbed the camera.

'Harry, no!' It was Kate.

She'd turned around and was yelling at me but I wasn't taking any notice. I'm not even really sure that I heard her. I had snatched the camera and pulled it with such force that the photographer had been forced to duck to allow the strap to slip over his head. Otherwise I think I would have throttled the bastard. 'Do you want it back,' I was yelling, threatening to hurl it at him.

'Harry!'

'Well, do you?' I bellowed.

BUILDING 41

The driver had evidently noticed the fracas that was developing behind him. He drew the car to a slow stop, flashing the hearse and the funeral director in front of him. The whole procession halted.

I had opened the door and climbed out. 'Bloody parasite. Why don't you just leave us alone?' I yelled, brandishing the camera like a weapon.

Ellen must have clambered out behind me. 'Harry, please,' she said, taking hold of my arm.

'Give it back, you maniac,' the photographer shouted.

Over his shoulder, I caught the fleeting image of a man I thought I recognised. He was dressed in a grey suit. I couldn't quite place him. He was in my field of vision for just a second or two before my attention was drawn back by the driver.

'I'll take that, Sir.' He'd thrusted himself between us.

I stared at him, ready to take him on too if need be.

'Mr Stammers?' the driver said calmly, holding out his hand.

I had become aware of the people in the crowd. They were watching me, I suppose in astonishment. I felt suddenly embarrassed.

'Sir? The camera?'

I held it out in front of me.

He took it, examined it closely and removed something from the camera's body. 'Here,' he said, handing it to me.

'Harry, please,' Ellen said, pulling me by the arm.

It was the camera's memory card. I hesitated.

'Please. Lets just get back into the car,' she pleaded.

'Leave this to me, Mr Stammers,' the driver said. He had now been joined by the funeral director.

I turned and clambered back into the car, enjoying, somehow, the photographer's protestations. I was watching through the open window. The driver had turned and had thrust the camera at the photographer. 'Now. Show some respect, man,' he said bluntly.

'Bloody lunatic,' the photographer returned.

'I said, show - some - respect,' he said, like he'd do something about it if the photographer didn't.

The photographer had snatched back the now empty camera.

The driver said something to him that I didn't quite catch. My attention had been drawn away again. To the guy in the grey suit. I watched him turn away and disappear into the crowd that had gathered around the cars. But still, I couldn't quite place him.

Ellen had, by now, climbed in beside me. Kate was looking ashen. Jonathan was looking ever so slightly amused but had not said a word. Had Kate and Ellen not been there I might very well have smacked him in the face, just for good measure.

The driver had also now got back into the car.

'I'm sorry,' I said, thickly. The anger and grief that had boiled within me, had already subsided. The cortege started to move again. 'I'm sorry,' I said again, running my hand through my hair. 'I shouldn't have reacted like that. I don't know what came over me.'

'It's all right,' Kate said, her voice cracking with emotion. 'You were right to be angry.'

I was surprised.

'The bastard had no right. Dad would have done the same. He'd have been proud of you.'

I thought that she was right about that. Ted Stammers would never have tolerated such a thing.

Ellen Carmichael found her great aunt sitting on a bench in the sunshine at the far end of the garden of remembrance. 'Are you all right?'

Elsie nodded.

'Are you sure?'

'Quite sure. I was watching you and Harry. You both look exhausted.'

BUILDING 41

After the drama of the journey to the crematorium, the funeral had passed without further incident. Harry had personally apologised to those who had been in the cortege. The consensus, so far as Ellen had been able to establish, was that his reaction had been understandable. Still, she had been relieved when the curtains had finally closed on the coffin and they'd all slowly made their way outside to admire the flowers and exchange polite condolences.

'I think Harry will just be glad when it's all over.'

Elsie nodded.

'We should go. Our car is waiting,' Ellen said, holding out her hand.

Elsie took it and stood, awkwardly. 'You're not going back with Harry?'

'No. Harry is going with Kate and Jonathan.'

'Will he be all right without you?'

'It's a forty-five minute journey Gran.' Ellen smiled. 'I think he can manage.'

'What about Geraldine and Arthur?'

'Their daughter is collecting them, apparently. So I thought I'd keep you company.'

Elsie nodded.

'Come on.'

Elsie took her arm and together, they made their way along the gravel path toward the waiting car.

'Is Harry all right, do you think?' Elsie said, once they were both seated and the car had pulled away.

'I think so,' Ellen replied. 'I'm sorry if he seemed a bit...' She hesitated, searching for the right word. 'Absent,' she said, finally. 'It's been a very difficult time for him, Gran.'

'I am sure that it has. The loss of his father must have come as quite a shock.'

Ellen smiled, ruefully. 'That's just it. He'd already lost his father. What is really worrying him is the thought that, with Ted's passing, any hope of discovering the truth about his mother might have passed with him.'

'The truth,' Elsie said, as though thinking out loud, 'is an illusive thing. Even when you discover it, it's rarely what you were expecting.'

It was an insightful comment and Ellen wondered what thought had prompted it. 'He can't even be certain that she's really still alive.'

Elsie stared at her. 'Harry's mother?'

Ellen looked down into her lap.

'Oh dear, did you tell me about it? Have I forgotten already?'

'No,' Ellen replied. 'I didn't want to worry you. Not after…' she hesitated. 'Well, anyway.'

'You must,' Elsie said, taking her hand. 'Ellen, my dear. If there is something that is troubling you both, you must tell me. Perhaps I can help.'

Ellen realised how much she had missed confiding in her great aunt. 'We told you about what Ted had said before he died. Do you remember?'

'About him not being Harry's father, you mean?'

Ellen nodded. 'Yes, but that wasn't all. Some of what Ted said about Harry's mother, well all of it really, was terribly hurtful.'

'Which is why it is sometimes better to leave the past in the past,' Elsie reflected.

Ellen caught the hint of bitterness in her tone. 'Perhaps. And perhaps some men would have left it there but Harry has spent most of his life wondering about her. To a point, you know, finding Martha last year highlighted to him just how absurd it was that he had never looked for her. Not in any kind of concerted way.'

Elsie said nothing but something in her face told Ellen that she was finding the conversation difficult. 'It wasn't your fault, Gran. But it got Harry thinking about looking for her and about how wrong Ted had been to have kept everything from him.'

BUILDING 41

'Perhaps Ted was protecting him. None of us know what was going through the poor man's mind.'

Which was another odd comment. 'That's as maybe, but Harry certainly found out. The things Ted told him really upset him. He barely spoke to me for those few weeks you know. I think he was trying to come to terms with it.'

'I didn't know that,' Elsie whispered.

Ellen hesitated. 'I know you didn't. I didn't want to trouble you with it. Harry can be a bit like that. He's a bit of an introvert, to be honest. Anyway,' she continued, 'he's been talking to Jane. You remember Jane, don't you?'

Elsie nodded.

'Jane did some digging around and it turns out that shortly before she disappeared, Harry's mother was working for the Nationalist Union of Great Britain.'

'Surely not,' Elsie said, after a moment's thought. 'She was a teacher, wasn't she?'

Ellen nodded. 'She was.'

'Well then, Jane must be mistaken.'

Ellen shook her head. 'I don't think so. Jane found an old photograph on the internet. It shows Harry's mother standing next to Peter Owen. He was the leader of the NUGB.'

'If you say so,' Elsie said, dismissively.

Ellen stared at her great aunt. She was definitely trying to avoid eye contact.

'Owen went to prison, you know.' Ellen continued. 'Conspiracy to cause an explosion. Do you remember it?'

Elsie had turned away and was gazing out of the window. 'Explosion?' she said absently, like she hadn't been listening.

'Yes. In 1977.'

Elsie said nothing.

'Jane thinks that she might have been involved in some way.'

'Involved? Harry's mother?' Elsie said, suddenly alert. 'But that's ridiculous.'

'It sounds crazy doesn't it? But if she was working with Owen at around the time of the bombing then maybe it's not as crazy as all that. It might just explain why she left them.'

'What do you mean?'

'Harry remembers two people coming to the house. Shortly after she disappeared.' Ellen waited. When Elsie did not reply, she continued. 'Ted told Harry that they wanted them - Harry, Kate and Ted - to go with them. Harry thinks that they might have been offering the family some kind of protection. He's thinking it over but I know what he's like. He's already got Jane looking further into it.'

'I really don't think that it is a good idea you know,' Elsie said suddenly. 'All this raking up of the past.'

Ellen stared at her.

'The past is better left in the past,' Elsie added.

The irony of the comment was not lost on Ellen. 'You're a fine one to speak,' she said, without thinking.

'That was different,' Elsie snapped. 'Martha would have wanted to be found. Harry's mother obviously doesn't or she would have revealed herself by now. What is the point in trying to find her if she does not want to be found? It will cause nothing but grief for both of them. Has Harry thought about that, I wonder?'

Ellen stared at her in surprise. Elsie had lived for sixty years with a desire to find her missing friend and the guilt of having failed to do so. Surely she knew better than most why it was important to Harry to find his mother. Even if, ultimately, there might be no happy reunion.

'To be perfectly honest,' Elsie added, 'it seems to me that Harry is being rather selfish.'

'Selfish? How on earth is he being selfish?' Ellen said, snatching her hand away.

'Harry's mother clearly does't want to be found, for reasons known only to her. Harry seems hell bent on ignoring what his mother wants. Wouldn't you call that selfish?'

BUILDING 41

The comment was so unlike her that for a moment Ellen was lost for words. 'No, of course I wouldn't,' she said, shocked. 'Doesn't Harry deserve to know the truth? Don't you think that she owes him that much?'

Elsie appeared flustered now. 'We can't know why she did what she did.'

Ellen could feel her temper rising. 'Why are you defending her? Harry's mother walked away from a husband and two young children. She didn't even say goodbye. She may have had good reason. Perhaps she was even trying to protect them, but that doesn't mean that Harry doesn't deserve an explanation.'

'I am not defending her. I am simply saying that Harry should think carefully before he goes raking up a past which he knows nothing about. Perhaps you should think about telling him that. You are his partner, after all. He might listen to you.'

Ellen was appalled. 'I can't believe you just said that.'

'I'm sorry if you think I'm being harsh but you both need to think about this form his mother's perspective. If, as you seem to think, she was in need of protection, then perhaps she still is. Why else would she have stayed away? If Harry goes raking this all up, he might very well put her in danger. Perhaps he should think about that too.'

Ellen could feel her face burning. 'That's enough,' she said, holding up her hand. I don't want to hear any more. I told you because I thought you'd understand.'

'I do understand,' Elise persisted, 'but…'

'I think you've said enough,' Ellen interrupted.

They spent the remaining journey in silence, looking out of different windows and both deep in thought.

CHAPTER SEVENTEEN

It was the day after the funeral and Ellen was pacing. 'I just can't understand it, Harry. Really I can't. She is absolutely adamant that you shouldn't be searching for your mother and she refused point blank to apologise for calling you selfish.'

'I didn't ask her to apologise for calling me selfish.'

'No, I know you didn't but I did. She's no right to say that about you. No right at all.'

We were in the kitchen. Ellen had just got back from taking Elsie home. I'd successfully avoided that particular pleasure by volunteering to run an old acquaintance from Ted's army days, over to Luton for his flight back to Belfast. 'You know, it really doesn't bother me that she thinks I'm being selfish. Perhaps I am.'

'Well it bothers me,' Ellen snapped, 'and you're not. You've every right to know why your mother left. It is outrageous that Ted kept it from you all these years. And whatever her reasons, your mother owes you an explanation.'

'Hey.' I slid an am around her waist and pulled her towards me. 'Forget about it. It's no big deal.'

She allowed me to kiss her but she was obviously still fuming.

'Look, maybe something touched a nerve. How much do you really know about Elsie's past?'

Ellen shrugged.

BUILDING 41

'I mean we've all got skeletons in our cupboards. Perhaps this has reminded her of some skeleton of her own. And don't forget…'

'What?'

I hesitated. 'Don't forget what her doctor said about her condition. She is going to get things muddled and when she does, she could feel afraid, confused, even angry.'

'She didn't sound very confused to me. In fact…' She left the comment hanging in the air.

I stared at her. 'What?'

'Oh, I don't know,' she said, waving me away irritably.

I waited.

'It was just so unlike her, Harry. What's happening to her? Her behaviour has been so erratic lately. I just don't know where I am with her anymore.'

I'd been thinking about Elsie. Maybe it was her illness, but it had sometimes seemed to me as though there was more going on behind that confused persona than she was letting on. 'Come here,' I said, taking Ellen in my arms and hugging her. 'It's hard, but she's an old lady. So she thinks I'm being selfish. Who knows why she feels that way? In the end, you know, it doesn't really matter. Give her some space and then we'll pop over to see her together. She'll probably have forgotten all about it.'

'It's just that we've never fallen out before, Gran and me,' Ellen continued. 'Not once. She has always been on my side. Even when I was a teenager. When I got up to all sorts of mischief and did some really stupid things. She never judged me. Not ever. She was always there for me. Not once did she ever let me down.'

'I don't think she's judging you now, Ellen.'

'No? Well she's sure as hell judging you. *Selfish*. Can you believe that?'

I shrugged. It was no use. 'I tell you what, it's a nice evening. Why don't we take a walk along the canal?'

Ellen pulled a face, sighed and then smiled weakly. 'That would be nice,' she said finally.

'Maybe drop into The Three Locks for a pint?'

Ellen grinned and nodded.

'I could give Jane and Mike a ring, if you like. See if they're free to join us?'

'Yes, all right.'

I kissed her on the cheek.

'I'm not letting it go, you know. I'm going to have it out with her, the next time we speak. Although the way I'm feeling right now, there might not be a next time.'

But she didn't mean it. I knew she didn't.

'So how are you doing, bud?' Mike asked, easing himself into the chair that Jane had pulled out for him.

We had decided to sit inside the canal side pub. There'd been a chilly breeze along the canal and Mike's foot had been playing up. The pub was almost empty, so we'd had our pick of the tables.

'I'm fine. Just glad to get the funeral out of the way,' I answered, honestly.

Jane was unusually quiet. Like her head was elsewhere.

Mike had noticed me watching her. 'She's been beavering away at the bomb plot thing,' he said, reaching for his glass.

'Mike, now is not the time,' Jane admonished him.

We all looked at her.

'Not the time for what?' I said, intrigued.

'It can wait.'

'If you mean it can wait until we've got over the funeral, don't worry about it. I'm fine. If you've discovered something, then I want to hear it.'

'Are you sure?'

I nodded. 'Absolutely.'

She looked at Ellen who followed suit.

BUILDING 41

Jane shrugged. 'Okay. So, Peter Owen,' she began. 'The only man who was ever prosecuted for the A1 bombing. If you believe the newspaper reports, you'd think that he was the only suspect.'

'So?' I said, unable to contain my curiosity.

'Doesn't that strike you as rather strange?'

I looked at Ellen. We both shrugged.

'Owen was the leader of the Nationalist Union of Great Britain. The explanation goes, so far as there is one, that he'd been conspiring with the IRA to cause an explosion in Central London. Something on a grand scale. A high profile target perhaps.'

'Something like the Brighton bombing in... when was it?' I pulled a face.

'Eighty-six. Much later, but yes, something on that scale.'

We were all silent.

'What's strange about that?' Ellen said, eventually.

'To begin with,' Jane replied, 'what was he doing working with the IRA? If he was working with them. They were hardly allies. Owen was a unionist. Why would he have been working with the Irish republicans? Secondly, why did they never claim responsibility or even acknowledge their involvement? Not to this day?'

I was trying to work out where she was going. 'So?'

'One other thing,' she said, ignoring my question. 'If Owen was conspiring, is it feasible that he was the only one? I mean, among the NUGB leadership?'

I shrugged.

'Because none of the other senior figures of the NUGB were ever implicated, let alone prosecuted.'

I thought about it. 'What did happen to them?'

'That's the thing. After Owen's arrest, the NUGB imploded and within a few months it had splintered into several tiny groups, all of them a shadow of the Nationalist Union's former self. The NUGB's big names seem to have just melted away. Disappeared from public view altogether. I've been trying to trace them.'

'And?' I said, intrigued.

'I can't. Take John Taggart, the Deputy Leader. The reports say that he retired. He was a Scot. From the islands. Try googling him. Nothing. I mean not a single word after '77. I've scoured the internet. News archives. The lot. Not a trace.'

'Is that really so strange?' Ellen managed.

'He was the deputy leader of a party with a national profile. At one point they were making serious electoral progress. He was a big figure.'

Ellen looked at her blankly. 'Well, I've never heard of him.'

'It's the same with the entire leadership group. You'd have thought that they were all in that van.'

'Maybe they were,' said Mike. 'Kaboom. Cremated like Hitler in his bunker.'

Jane blanched. 'For God's sake, Mike. I'm sorry Harry.'

I had to smile. Mike's sense of humour was legendary. 'So what's your theory?' I said, waving away the Norwegian's faux pas.

'Cover up,' Jane said confidently. 'It stinks to heaven. All of it.'

'Which is all very well, but where does it get us?' I said, emptying my pint glass and waving it suggestively at Mike, before putting it down on the pub table.

He ignored me.

'Not very far,' Jane conceded. 'Except for one thing.'

We all stared at her.

'One of them didn't disappear,' Jane continued. 'Or rather he did disappear and then re-appeared again. Quite a few years later, as it happens.'

'Who?' I said in perfect time with Ellen. I caught Mike's eye. The Norwegian was clearly aware of the imminent revelation. I could see the mischief in his face.

'Are you sure you want to do this now?' Jane said, staring at me.

'Sure.'

BUILDING 41

Jane reached into her pocket and removed a folded sheet of paper. 'This man,' she said.

I held out my hand.

Jane hesitated.

'You know, in any other circumstances I might think you were trying to milk this,' I said, straight faced.

'Well don't say I didn't warn you,' she said handing me the folded sheet.

I unfolded it and stared. It was a photocopy of a newspaper article.

'It's not easy to find pictures of any of them,' Jane said. 'And it is especially difficult to find pictures of him,' she said, gesturing toward the paper in my hand.

I was still staring.

'It was taken outside Hackney Police Station. According to the caption, he'd been helping police with their enquiries.'

'Who is it?' Ellen said, craning her neck to see.

'It can't be,' I managed.

'It is,' Mike said.

He had better reason than any of us to remember the man in the picture.

'It is,' Mike said again. 'Sure, he looks a bit different. Younger and more hair. Shit loads more hair in fact. But hell, I'd know that face anywhere. It's him.'

'This names him as Jimmy Dobson. The NUGB's Head of Security,' Ellen said.

'Yes, it does,' Jane said, gravely.

Ellen had, by now, taken the picture from my hand and was staring at it. 'Oh my God. This is Stephens. It is, isn't it?' she said, turning to me as if for reassurance that she wasn't seeing things.

I nodded.

'What the hell?' Ellen added.

My mind was reeling. Stephens. The man who had kidnapped Ellen. The man who had tried to prevent us from rescuing her.

With whom we - or rather Jane - had exchanged gun fire in the tunnels below Belsize Park. The man who had tried to kill Mike and who had, almost certainly, murdered Tomasz Dabrowski.

'There's something else.'

We all stared at her again. I was still trying to get my head around the revelation.

'You might want to get in another round. You're going to need it,' Jane said like she meant it.

'What?' Ellen and I both said in unison. Again.

Jane took a breath. 'Like I said, the picture was taken outside Hackney Police Station. On Friday, April 29, 1977. Some months prior to the bombing. Dobson had apparently been helping the police with their enquiries. Which got me thinking about what, exactly, he'd been helping them with.'

'The article says that it was a murder inquiry,' Ellen said, scanning the short piece below the picture.

'I know,' Jane said. 'So I did a bit of digging. There were quite a few murders in London in the few weeks leading up April 29, but if you narrow it down to the week before, there were just five and one stands out.'

I was waiting for the big reveal. Because there was surely going to be one. I could feel it coming.

'His name was Karl Dixon, an eighteen year old black kid from Tottenham. There'd been an anti-racist rally in Wood Green earlier that day to counter a demonstration by guess who?'

'The NUGB?' I suggested.

'Correct,' Jane replied. 'Predictably there'd been trouble. Nothing really major but a few shops got trashed and looted. The local press later called it "The Battle of Wood Green". As far as I can see, it was hardly a battle, but you know the press.'

I knew the press all right.

'Anyhow, later that day, Dixon had been walking back towards the bus station when he was assaulted. Multiple stab wounds to the

BUILDING 41

chest and groin. He was already dead when the ambulance arrived. And guess what?'

Nobody spoke.

'The murderer was never found. Another unsolved crime. There seem to have been quite a few unsolved racially motivated crimes at the time.'

'So sad,' said Ellen, missing the point.

'Here's the really interesting thing,' Jane said, glancing first at Ellen and then at me. 'Karl Dixon had been at the rally with his girlfriend. Her name was Sonia Smithson. He'd walked her home before he was killed. Smithson was younger than him by a year or so. She was still at school. The same school where they had met, actually.'

'So?' I asked.

'So, your mother was a school teacher in North London during the seventies, wasn't she?'

I nodded. I had a feeling I knew what was coming.

'Where was she teaching in 1977? Do you know the name of the school?'

I nodded again. 'Yes. It was St David and St Katharine, in Hornsey. I discovered that, years ago.'

Jane nodded. 'I thought it might have been. The same school where Sonia Smithson met Karl Dixon.' Jane leant back in her seat. 'Your mother probably taught them both, Harry.'

I was struggling to make all the connections. Karl Dixon and his girlfriend had been at the same school where my mother had taught for several years in the 1970's. It was likely, if not certain that she had taught them both. In 1977, Dixon had been murdered. Jimmy Dobson was questioned about the murder. He was photographed leaving Hackney Police Station. Dobson was Head of Security at the NUGB where, evidently, my mother had been working, secretly, with Peter Owen, for reasons that we were yet to fathom. Owen had been conspiring with the IRA but when the resulting bomb plot had been foiled, Owen had gone to prison.

Dobson, the rest of the NUGB leadership and my mother had all disappeared. If I had interpreted Ted's words correctly, she'd been offered a new identity, along with Kate, Ted and I. Ted had refused to cooperate, unable to trust the woman whose double life had just been revealed, along with the fact that Ted was not my biological father. Seventeen years later, Dobson had reappeared as "Stephens" a driver for Max Banks MP. When Ellen and I had accepted the task of finding Martha Watts, it had been Stephens who had attempted to stop us. He had kidnapped Ellen and, directed by Hilary Banks-Wallington, the MP's mother, imprisoned her in the same cell to which we had subsequently discovered that Arthur Wallington, his father, had dragged an unconscious Martha Watts and left her to die in 1944. All of these incidents were connected to the man called Dobson/Stephens.

'But why?' I said out loud.

They all turned and stared at me.

'Why,' I said again. 'It all comes back to Stephens, doesn't it?'

Jane nodded. 'It certainly looks that way.'

'Why? What's his game? Who the fuck is he? Dobson or Stephens?'

'Or neither,' Jane added. 'Stephens is definitely our man, but we have absolutely no idea who he really is. As you say Harry, he seems to be the key to the whole thing. Which is the most significant mystery of all.'

'What do you mean?' Ellen asked.

'I mean, that there is a whole thing. All of this seems to be linked. Martha Watts in 1944. Karl Dixon and your mother, Harry. Peter Owen. The '77 bombing. The Banks-Wallingtons last year. Belsize Park and what we did there. Stephens, Dobson. All of it. Linked.'

'And one other thing,' I said, solemnly. I turned towards Ellen. 'Elsie. She was there with Martha in 1944. She was there with us last year. In fact it was Elsie who set us the task of finding Martha Watts which was what pitted us against Stephens in the first place.'

BUILDING 41

'But she had nothing to do with the events in 1977...' Ellen hesitated. 'Did she?' she said uncertainly. 'Harry?'

I'd paled. I'd remembered something. Or rather I had placed a name and an image together in my head, quite unexpectedly making the final connection.

'Harry, what is it?' Ellen's face was full of concern.

'Fuck.' It was all that I could manage. The image in my mind was of a middle aged woman with piercing blue eyes. Staring at me. Sitting by her window in the flat where we had stayed as children, in the days before my mother had abandoned us. And another image of an older woman with the same blue eyes. Sitting by a window in the room she now occupied in a different place. 'Fuck,' I said again. The name was "Rosemary" but the face belonged to Elsie Sidthorpe.

CHAPTER EIGHTEEN

Sunday, May 1, 2005

Günther Möller checked his watch, turned and sat down heavily on the painted wooden bench. He watched, without really seeing, a small boy tugging at a kite string, while a man, clearly too old to be the boy's father, made repeated unsuccessful attempts to launch the kite into the air in the morning sunshine. The child's grandfather perhaps, Möller thought vaguely.

The search had exhausted almost thirty of Möller's fifty-five years. While he was, he reflected, closer to his quarry than perhaps he had ever been, the woman in the nursing home might yet deny him.

She had been there, in the shadows, since the day he'd stepped off the ferry from Bergen, watching him. He had known of her presence almost immediately, but until now, had failed utterly to understand her true identity and thus her motive. Had he done so then, he might by now have had the object that he sought in his possession, he reflected bitterly. Or have had the pleasure of killing her in pursuit of it, but he'd had no idea. Even on that night in Shoreditch, when he had left her for dead in the middle of Luke Street. No idea of how close he had come.

Möller looked over his shoulder and up toward the first floor window. She was there. Watching him still but now she was afraid.

BUILDING 41

Even at a distance he could see it in her movements. The same fear he had seen in her eyes, through the hotel window and as Carmichael and the idiot Stammers had assisted her from the hotel to their car.

The years had not been kind to her and were about to become less kind still. Because now, thanks to his source, he knew. She had used the idiot Stammers and Carmichael - her own flesh and blood - to locate the body of her former colleague. Had they known that she was using them? Had Carmichael been manipulating the museum curator too? It was, perhaps, an overly Machiavellian notion but it appealed to him nonetheless. He was looking forward to discovering just how resourceful the Carmichael bitch really was, though a certain amount of caution was in order. He had underestimated the woman who had called herself Rosemary Sellers. He was not about to similarly underestimate either of these women again.

That she had ostensibly set Stammers the task of finding the log reader's body meant that she'd had some pressing need to discover the remains of her old friend. Most likely, she had assumed that on the night she'd gone missing, Watts had been carrying the object. Or at least some evidence of its whereabouts. But there had been nothing. He had personally searched both the cell and the mummified body. Arthur Wallington, the man who, believing her already dead, had left her there, had taken nothing from her. He had been too much of a coward to take a keepsake. Möller's tenure as Max Banks-Wallington's driver had provided him with the opportunity to make certain of it.

Either the old woman had been mistaken, or Stammers and Carmichael had indeed recovered something. Something that he had missed and that they were concealing. The alternative - that none of these scenarios were correct and that the old woman knew nothing of the object's whereabouts - was not one that Möller was willing to entertain.

The sound of his mobile phone interrupted his thoughts. He removed the phone from his pocket and answered the call. 'You are later than we agreed,' he said, in German, listening impassively to the response. 'You will continue.' He listened again. 'Good. You have done well mein schönes parteigenosse*.' He listened once more and then ended the call.

Elsie Sidthorpe. The old woman was the key, as she had always been. Günther Möller stood up, turned and walked towards the entrance to the Southwold nursing home.

Elsie Sidthorpe had been watching him from her bedroom window for most of the last hour. He had appeared there again last night, shortly after she had returned with Ellen from the funeral in London. Ellen hadn't stayed. She had made some excuse and left, almost immediately. They had continued to argue about Harry's proposed search for his mother. The presence of the man on the bench outside meant that this was the very worst thing that Harry could be doing, though he didn't know it. Neither Harry nor Ellen were aware, even of the man's presence, let alone the history that linked them together and the threat that he posed to them all.

Her only option had been to try to influence Ellen to dissuade Harry from taking the search any further, but the attempt had backfired, as she might have anticipated that it would. Ellen had always been a defiantly independent young woman. If there was one thing that Elsie should have learned about her great niece by now, it was that telling her what to do or what not to do was likely to have precisely the reverse effect. But the risk was great and, if Ellen was unwilling to dissuade Harry, then Elsie's only option was to seek to deal directly with the man outside. A man who had now climbed to his feet and was staring at her. She tried to swallow but her throat was so dry that she had to stifle a cough. She stepped back from the window instinctively to prevent him observing her weakness.

* My pretty party member.

BUILDING 41

She had known that this moment would come, ever since his escape from the tunnels below Belsize Park Underground Station. Indeed, she had feared it across the many years that had passed since their last meeting in the narrow lanes behind the National Union's offices in Shoreditch. That she could barely recall the incident was testament as much to the severity of the injuries he had inflicted on her, than to the passage of time, though more than a quarter of a century had passed since the assault. Still, she didn't need to recall it to be afraid of him. The scars she still bore, physical and mental, were enough.

Until the incident at the hotel she had been uncertain of the watcher's identity, though she had suspected it with a creeping and crippling fear that had dominated her every thought. Spotting the watcher's presence had been easy enough. Years of experience had taught her to recognise such things. Natalia had dismissed her agitation as mere paranoia. The delusions of a failing mind. Elsie allowed herself a smile. Her body might be failing but her mind was still sharp, whatever her doctors had told them. Although it was certainly true that the sudden appearance of the face in the hotel window - his face - had shaken her.

Gunther Möller. Whenever she thought of him, she was transported again to the lanes behind the old NUGB offices in Shoreditch. She wondered whether the young couple who had discovered them knew that they had saved her life. Or cared. London had become a cold hearted, impersonal place where people existed cheek by jowl, in ignorance even of the names of those who lived beside them. Where elderly men and women might die and their bodies lay undiscovered for weeks or months before even the most disinterested of neighbours might be compelled by the stench to complain to the Council.

London. The great, sprawling city where she had lived and worked for more than thirty years and the city where she had almost died. Elsie closed her eyes and saw the face of Flora Jackson. That she had recovered from the attack was due, in no small part, to the retired nurse who had, so selflessly, offered her shelter. Flora Jackson had insisted that Elsie make the North London flat her home for as long as she needed and had cared for her tirelessly. In the end, it had been almost six months before Elsie had felt strong enough to return to Wangford, the tiny Suffolk village on the outskirts of Southwold, which had subsequently become her home.

The little sixteenth century cottage on Wangford's main street had belonged to her parents. They'd bought it when she was three years old. She remembered the holidays she had spent there with John her brother, and her younger sister Edie. These were, she reflected, the only truly happy memories she could summon of a mother and father who, having rapidly lost interest in their children, if indeed they ever had any, had dispatched them to boarding school at their earliest opportunity.

Still, it had been her parents, or rather her father, who had ultimately provided for her long term security when, during the summer of 1957, he had rolled their little Austin Healey two-seater off the road at Sommières in Southern France, killing himself and her mother instantly. By then, Elsie had been their one and only heir. John had died in the fighting in Italy in 1945 and poor Edie, of a brain tumour in 1951. Elsie had inherited not just the Wangford property, but another house in the New Forest that had belonged to her mother's parents, and a very much larger and grander house in Kensington which, on the face of it, had been their family home but had never once felt like it.

She had always detested the Kensington house. It had been a cold, heartless place that her parents had bought more as a trophy to their success, then a place in which to live. When she had inherited it, Elsie had immediately put it on the market and, when it sold, invested the proceeds. Along with her salary, the investment had made her a wealthy woman. Something from her parents, at least, for which she could be thankful.

BUILDING 41

Prior to her forced retirement, she'd used both the Wangford and the New Forest properties as bolt holes. Places to which she could retreat when she needed to lay low, which the nature of her work had made necessary on occasion. When she was working in London, she had preferred to stay at Claridges. The lavish hotel was outrageously expensive but, what she couldn't claim on her expenses, she had paid for herself. It had been worth it. She had come to adore the place. Had it not been for the assault, she might happily have become a permanent resident there.

Her eyes flitted, involuntarily, to a photograph on the table beside her bed. It had been taken in the dining room at Claridges. The only such picture that she possessed. She reached down and touched the frame, fondly. It had been a double life, in every sense of the phrase. One life, as an agent in London and the other as an ageing village spinster. Which of these personalities was truly hers? She had spent most of her life playing one part or the other.

While she had been away in London, as far as the community in Wangford was concerned, she had been working for the Foreign Office. When she'd retired to Wangford full time, they'd accepted her back and, until her frailty had prevented her from managing the cottage's steep, narrow stairs, she had lived a peaceful life among them.

But it was always a peace that she knew might be shattered at any moment. By the man who had now found her. By Günther Möller, the renegade German, who had arrived in Britain with a false identity and a purpose that it had taken her many years to discover, though even now she by no means knew it all.

His true identity had been confirmed when, having been raped in a most sadistic fashion by Jimmy Dobson, Liz Muir had recovered a number of documents from Dobson's flat that had identified him as Günther Möller, a man wanted in Germany for his involvement in a string of bank robberies and the brutal murder of a policewoman. By then it had been too late. Having pursued Liz Muir through the streets of North London and out into the

Hertfordshire countryside, the post office van she had been driving had exploded in a field beside the A1 and Möller/Dobson had disappeared, seemingly altogether.

It had been revealing that her former masters had apparently shown such little interest in finding him. She had long suspected that he was being protected by elements inside the Service. The same elements that had been working against her and who had, in the end, forced her retirement. But it was the injuries that she had sustained at Möller's hands that had ultimately left her powerless to counter him and, for a time, after her return to Wangford, she had all but given it up.

If her life was about to end, then there had, Elsie reminded herself, also been happier times. While she would always look back on 1977 as the year when Möller had very nearly killed her, it had also been the year when her niece, Eleanor, who lived just a few miles from Wangford with her husband Stanley Carmichael, had given birth to a baby girl. From the moment baby Ellen had been introduced to her great aunt, there had been a bond between them that, over the years that followed, had become unbreakable and in which they had both taken such delight. The relationship that they shared was the great joy of Elsie's life. A joy that ought to have been sufficient, Elsie knew.

But it had not been sufficient. Rather, the guilt she had born, since the day when Martha Watts had failed to arrive home, and a determination to put right the wrong that she had been so certain was the cause of her friend's disappearance, had continued to haunt her, long after her retirement to Wangford. So sure had she been that Martha had taken the secret with her to London, and so certain was she that Martha had paid for it with her life, that understanding Jimmy Dobson's purpose had become something of an obsession.

She now knew, of course, that she had been mistaken about her friend's disappearance. That Martha had been murdered by Arthur Wallington, who had discovered her, purely by chance, sitting on an upturned crate in the deep level air raid shelter below Belsize

BUILDING 41

Park. That having attempted to rape her and believing her already dead, Wallington had dragged her to the tiny room where her mummified body had been discovered sixty years later. It had been an error, Elsie reflected, that had cost lives and very nearly the lives of those she held most dear.

Her actions, all those years ago, had been reckless but the repercussions had seemed endless. "Like tossing a stone into the ocean, the ripples of it seem to go wider and wider" she had once told Liz Muir. "It has brought me and others nothing but anguish".

More than anguish. It had cost several men their lives. She would never be able to forget the scene in Ronnie Warren's living room where the sailor had been tied to a chair and tortured so brutally. She had often wondered what, if anything, he had revealed before Möller had so callously murdered him.

Warren's murder had been by no means her only failure. She had failed to protect Liz Muir, who had relied on her. A failure that had seen the young agent's family torn apart and for which, her children - Harry and Kate - were both still paying the price.

Worst of all, perhaps, was her decision to enlist Harry's help in the search for Martha Watts. Triggered by Möller's reappearance as "Stephens" and the knowledge that her physical frailty meant that she could not renew the search or hope to counter him herself, Harry's letter had presented her with an opportunity that in the end she had been unable to resist.

Harry. Her mind drifted back to the little boy who she had, as soon as her recovery had allowed it, watched occasionally from a distance. Playing in the park with Kate, his sister. Flora and Simone Jackson and their great friend from Claridges, Alphonse Richelieu, had come to her aid. Though Harry had never suspected it, Alphonse and the Jacksons had watched over him tirelessly. In particular, for any sign that Dobson/Möller had made the connection between the boy and Liz Muir. But of Möller there had been not the slightest sign for the whole of Harry's teenage years and into his young adulthood. Harry had grown into a fine young man, undoubtedly pained by his missing mother, but free, at least, from any immediate threat from Möller.

It was a pain that, unbeknown to Harry, she had shared and for which she held herself responsible. The only answer, she had long concluded, was either to beat Möller to his quarry or to ensure that it remained undiscovered.

If Harry's appointment to a position at Bletchley Park had seemed like a coincidence, for coincidence was what it was - she had played no part in it at all - then his search for the Park's veterans had offered her the perfect opportunity. The plan had not been without risk and she had spent many weeks arguing with herself about it. In the end though, she had posted the letter and a train of events had unfolded that had, once again, run out of control. Once again there had been terrible and unforeseen consequences, not just for Harry and the young men who had helped him but also for Ellen. Dear Ellen. Exposing her to such extreme danger had never been her intention. It was, perhaps, the worst of all her failures.

A gentle tapping on her door, roused her from her thoughts. Her stomach twisted.

While setting Harry the task of finding Martha Watts and his discoveries in the tunnels below Belsize Park had answered many questions, Möller had, disastrously, evaded capture once again. With Möller at large but still ignorant of the link between Harry and Liz Muir, and with Harry unaware of the nature of Möller's true quarry, it would be safer for them all, Elsie had reasoned, were it to remain lost. For as long as Möller stayed away and posed no further threat. As the weeks following Martha's funeral had turned into months, Elsie had begun to hope, beyond hope, that the ripples from her actions might finally have run to ground.

Another knock and, this time, a voice. 'Elsie? It is Natalia. Can I come in?'

BUILDING 41

Once again, she had erred. This time, however, would be the last time. If he threatened them again, he would force her hand. This time she was prepared.

Elsie reached for the handle of the drawer to her bedside cabinet. Her hands were shaking so violently, that it was a struggle to slide out the drawer. When finally she had removed it, she carefully emptied its contents onto her bed. Then, turning the drawer over, she worked loose four tiny catches and released the false bottom, beneath which were two items, one in an envelope and the other, larger object wrapped in silk. She removed them swiftly, refitted the false bottom, re-filled the drawer, and slotted it back into place.

'Are you alone?' she called out, noting the tremor in her own voice.

'Yes, but there is a visitor for you. He is waiting downstairs'

She took several deep breaths to calm herself. 'Come in, would you please Natalia,' she called out, trying to prevent her voice from faltering. 'I have a favour to ask of you.'

CHAPTER NINETEEN

Elsie sat by her window, with a blanket across her knees, staring out into the late morning sunshine. Möller was a monster. A violent beast of a man who had killed repeatedly in pursuit of that which he sought. She had never been a match for him physically, of course, and now her advanced years and frailty made even flight impossible. While her professional alias had, until now, served to conceal both her identity and her interest in him, he had evidently discovered her true identity at last. Since she could not run, she had no choice now but to face him.

She was not, though, completely without resource. Möller's reappearance had changed the game but the game was not yet lost. While she had, since the events of a little less than a year ago, been unwilling to make any move that might again threaten the safety of Ellen and Harry, or put others at risk, Möller might very well be about to force her hand. If he did, then she had an insurance policy. Or two, she reflected. One was the envelope she had given to Natalia, along with the accompanying instructions. The other was tucked beneath the blanket across her knees. Still, it was an effort to stop her hands from shaking on the cold metal.

There was a knock on the door.

She waited.

The door opened.

'Your visitor,' announced the Russian nurse.

BUILDING 41

'Thank you, Natalia. Please show Mr Möller in,' Elsie replied, without turning away from the window. The view across the fields was such a lovely one. Even with the dreadful water towers. 'Would you leave us please, Natalia?'

'Are you sure?' the young nurse replied, an edge of uncertainty to her voice.

'Yes, I'm sure. Thank you.'

'Very well, but if you need me, you will please use the bell?'

'I will.' She waited until she heard the click of the door. 'Sit down, Mr Möller,' she said, still without turning. She heard him walk towards her and pull out the chair that she had positioned for him.

'I would like to say that it is a pleasure to see you again,' Elsie said, when finally she was ready. 'Visitors are usually such a delight. Alas, they are not as frequent as they once were.'

Möller said nothing.

'In your case, however, I had rather hoped that our last meeting might have been our last,' she said, turning to face him.

He had changed. Certainly since their last meeting. Hardly surprising given the passage of time. But also since the pictures she'd seen of 'Stephens', the Banks-Wallington's driver. He was heavier set, she observed. Broader and more muscular. His neck was thicker too. In fact it was so thick and his shoulder muscles so pronounced, that it was difficult to work out where his neck finished and his head began. The most marked difference of all was that he had lost all of his hair. His baldness startled her momentarily.

His smile was cold. 'Did you really think that we would not meet again?' he said, as though the idea amused him. 'We have unfinished business, Elsie Sidthorpe. Or shall I call you "Rosemary Sellers"?' he added.

'Either will do,' she said, lightly. 'As for business, tell me something Mr Möller, what makes you think that I can assist you?

Or,' she added, with a steely tone, 'that I would choose to, were the means even to be at my disposal?'

Möller stared at her. 'I have little doubt that you have the means. The question is whether you will exercise them through choice or by force. It amazes me that you have, until now, preferred to put the safety of others at risk. It would be unfortunate were they to come to further harm.'

The threat was barely concealed. She did her best to ignore it. 'You seem to imagine,' she said after a moment's thought, 'that I have the faintest idea where the codebook is. That is why you are here, I take it?'

He said nothing.

'Mr Möller,' she said, letting out a long sigh. 'If I knew the whereabouts of the codebook, do you not suppose that I would have recovered it by now? And that having recovered it, taken steps to have the contents deciphered?'

The German smiled. 'Perhaps you already know what the book contains. If you do not, then I have no doubt that your former colleagues do. It serves their purposes and yours, perhaps, for the book to remain hidden.'

It was an interesting statement. If Möller was right that the faction inside the Service, the existence of which she had long suspected, knew of the book's contents then how did they know? How could they? While she had not, in the short time it had been in her possession, examined it closely, the contents had been encrypted, presumably using German Naval Enigma. It had been taken by Petty Officer Warren, in 1941, directly from the wireless room aboard U-110. While it was entirely possible that he had bragged about it on some other occasion, at the time and outside Bletchley Park, there hadn't been a man in Britain who could have deciphered it. The book had remained in his possession until November 1944, when she had so recklessly relieved him of it. It had been in her possession for a matter of hours only, before Martha had discovered it among her things. If nothing else, Elsie was certain that it had not been recovered. Why else would Möller have been allowed to remain at large?

'What makes you say so?' she said, intrigued but without any real expectation that he would provide an answer. Instead, she was still considering the possibility that the faction within the Service had indeed known of its contents. Perhaps they had always known.

'Why else would you have worked so tirelessly to keep me from its discovery?' he said.

The flaw in his logic was obvious and startling. Had they wanted to keep him from the book, it would have been a simple thing to have removed him. Officially, her own purpose had been to monitor the activities of a suspicious foreign national. Though, unofficially, she had suspected a connection to the codebook, principally as a result of his interest in Ronnie Warren. Why else would Möller have tortured and killed the retired petty officer? Far from trying to thwart him in his search for the codebook, Möller had been allowed to remain at liberty, presumably in the hope that he might lead them to it. 'Then I am afraid that I am going to have to disappoint you on both counts. I know nothing of the book's whereabouts. Nor do I have the faintest idea of its contents.' The latter, at least, was something approaching the truth.

Möller snorted. 'It was you who took the book from the sailor. Do not deny it.'

'I do not deny it. Taking the book was an act of recklessness on my part. Something I have regretted ever since.'

Möller stared at her icily. 'You will tell me what became of the book.'

She held his stare. 'I will not. Because I do not know. I returned to Martha's cottage by the canal on the night I took it, a good deal worse for the wear. The following morning Martha, who I believe you have met in death at least,' she said, observing him dispassionately, 'told me that she had found it among my things and had returned it to Ronnie Warren. I had no reason to doubt it then. We both have good reason to doubt it now.'

'Which is why you sent Stammers to do the job you could no longer manage,' he sneered. 'If what you say is true, you had sixty years to locate the book and he was the best that you could do?'

The mention of Harry's name made her tremble. She said nothing.

'I took you for many things. But not a fool.'

'I asked Harry Stammers,' she said shakily, 'to search for Martha because I wanted to know what had become of my friend. He was already engaged in the search for veterans of Bletchley Park long before I met him.'

Möller began to laugh. 'Perhaps that is so. But if you believed that Watts had lied to you about returning the book to Warren and had, instead, taken it with her to London, you cannot seriously expect me to believe that the task you set Stammers wasn't in fact motivated by your hope that the discovery of her remains might have revealed if not the book itself, then at least some clue as to its whereabouts?'

In this respect, at least, his reasoning was sound but she was not about to concede the point. 'I do not care what you believe, Mr Möller. In any event, no trace of the book was found. So where does this get us, regardless of what you assume to have been my motive?'

'Unless, of course, Stammers did discover something in the tunnels. Or perhaps I should say unless *they* discovered something.'

She instinctively tightened her grip on the object beneath the blanket. If he noticed it, Möller showed no sign. He was fishing. He had to be. 'You know perfectly well what they discovered,' she said, desperately trying to mask her growing anxiety. Möller had snatched Ellen's bag in the car park at Barnet Hospital, after the incident in the shelter lift shaft, in the hope that it had contained the small leather purse that Harry had found in the darkness.

Möller stared at her.

BUILDING 41

'As you know, all that they discovered was a purse. It contained a small amount of money and a train ticket. From Bletchley to London. It was the ticket that led them to conclude that Martha had been there and, ultimately, to locate her body. There was nothing else.'

Möller continued to stare. 'Glückwünsche,' he said suddenly. 'You lie exceptionally well. You would have made an excellent Nazi.'

She observed him dispassionately.

'But I am afraid that you are playing a losing game. If you will not tell me, then I will have to pursue the matter with Stammers and Carmichael directly.'

He was watching her reaction.

'Perhaps I will start with Ellen. She escaped me once before. She will not do so again. I will enjoy extracting the truth from her. Possibly as much as I enjoyed extracting it from Liz Muir before she blew herself to pieces.'

Elsie turned her face towards the window to cover her relief and surprise. Möller's assumption that Liz Muir was dead might explain why he had never discovered Ted and the two children. Nor indeed, made any link between Harry and Liz Muir.

Elsie had never discovered the true extent of the depravities that Möller had inflicted on her. Nor did she need to. Their impact on her had been devastating, not least in convincing Liz of the deadly threat that he had posed to Ted and their children. Ultimately it had been this that had led her to choose exile. If, as now appeared evident, Möller had accepted her death, then her decision was exonerated. It had served to protect them all. Until Elsie's decision to involve Harry in the search for Martha Watts had brought him to Möller's attention. While Möller had apparently failed to make the link between Harry and Liz Muir, if what Ellen had said was right, then Harry might yet reveal it through his ill-timed search for his mother. Elsie could not allow that to happen, for all their sakes.

'You would be foolish to attempt any contact with Ellen,' she bluffed. 'She is being watched carefully by the security services, as she has been since your escape from Belsize Park. Go anywhere near her and they will have you.'

It was a bluff wholly without effect. Möller simply laughed at the attempt. An empty laugh, without any trace of humour. A laugh that chilled Elsie's heart.

'Then perhaps you'd like to explain how it is that I was able to watch you eating Sunday lunch. How it was that I was able to watch them bundling you into their car and to follow them to Leighton Buzzard.'

He was watching her reaction.

'Yes, I know where they live and I know where Ellen works. The car that she drives. I can take her anytime that I wish and, believe me, when I do take her, I will take her in every way possible. Until she screams. I especially like it when they scream,' he said, enjoying the impact that his words were having on her. 'Now I will ask you again, old woman,' he said with undisguised malice, 'what else did they find in the tunnels?'

The scenes that his words had conjured in her mind had served only to strengthen her resolve. 'You are sick, Möller. A sick animal,' she said with something approaching hatred. 'Like a sick animal, you really should be put out of your misery. It is something that I could and should have done a long time ago. As ever, you underestimate me.' With that she drew the gun from beneath the blanket and aimed it at his chest.

Möller did not so much as flinch. Instead, he stared at her icily.

She glanced up at the clock on the wall behind him. 'Before you arrived, I instructed the nurse who showed you in, that if I did not ring my bell twenty minutes after your arrival, to call the police and to give them your name. Or I should say names. Those twenty minutes just ran out. There is a station in the town. It should take them no more than a few minutes to arrive. If you make any attempt to leave, please understand that I will certainly kill you.'

Möller stared at her but still he did not move.

BUILDING 41

'I am, as you said, an old woman. I do not expect to live more than another few years. Do you imagine that I care if I spend them in prison, safe, as I would be, in the knowledge that you could pose no further risk to those who I love? Neither will I pretend that your death would not bring me a certain amount of personal pleasure. Do not test me, Mr Möller.'

He moved. Not so quickly as all that, she observed. Because as had been the case on the previous occasion they had met, he was a big man and big men move more slowly than lighter men. Quickly enough, however, to avoid the shot. And of course she was older and her reflexes slower. In the instant before she fired, he had dived slightly forward and to his right, onto the floor. As the revolver recoiled in her hand and the bullet hit a blue glass vase that had been arranged on her sideboard, shattering it into a myriad of tiny pieces, he erupted toward her. With one hand he grabbed her wrist and, with the other, reached out and took the gun from her easily. The pain in her arm - the same arm that he had smashed before - took her breath away. He stared at her and grinned, but it was a grin that was short lived. Because in the distance they both heard it. The sound of sirens.

'Go ahead,' she sobbed defiantly. 'I am old and tired. Killing me will do you no good. Your precious codebook is beyond you, Günther Möller. You will *never* have it,' she wheezed with the last of her defiance, 'I have made sure of it.' And in her agony she knew, as the words left her mouth, that once again she had erred.

'I don't think so,' he spat. Then he struck her with the butt of the gun.

*****

Smith sat down beside her. After a short pause, the Russian handed him a small plain brown envelope. He emptied its contents into his hand.

'You said that he would not harm her,' she said eventually. 'That she would be safe.'

'Neither of us knew that she had a gun,' he said, matter of factly, his attention on the single key now resting in his palm. 'Or that she would try to kill him. She was lucky.'

They were sat on the middle of three benches on a wide green, in the shadow of a square church tower.

'Lucky? Are you mad? Did you not see what he did to her?'

'I did not need to see it. She was lucky that he did not set out to harm her. That he did so was due entirely to her provocation.'

'Elsie is eighty-two,' the Russian fumed. 'Eighty-two. He could have killed her. It is a miracle that he did not. Do you even care?'

Her reaction was understandable but, as far as Smith was concerned, somewhat disappointing. 'Your eighty-two year old just tried to blow a man's brains out using an unlicensed firearm. If she recovers, she is going to have a lot of explaining to do. She is hardly the innocent you seem to believe her to be.'

'Where is he now?' the Nurse fumed. 'Why did you allow him to escape?'

Smith said nothing.

'You told me that we were protecting her. Now I think that you were using her. That, if she survives, you will go on using her. Until you get what you want.'

Smith remained silent.

'What is it that Elsie is hiding?' she continued. 'The same thing this Möller wants, perhaps? You hope that she will reveal it? Is that what this key is?' she said, gesturing toward the object in his hand.

Smith smiled. 'Well done. You're a natural, Natalia. If a little naive. You must learn to detach yourself from these emotions.'

She stared at him, her eyes still smouldering.

'Now tell me more about this,' he said, holding up the key.

She said nothing.

'What instructions did she give?'

'She told me to pass it to Harry, in the event that anything happened to her.'

'With a message?'

BUILDING 41

The hesitation was for no longer than a split second but it was a hesitation nonetheless and he noticed it.

'She told me to tell him to trust nobody but those he loves.'

He snorted, 'And what else?'

'Nothing else. That was all.'

He didn't believe her but no matter. He turned the key over in his hand. 'Here,' he said, tossing it to her.

She caught it.

'What do you make of it?'

She stared at him.

'Natalia, you are an intelligent young woman. You have correctly deduced that Mr Möller and I are competing to find an object, to which we had both hoped that Elsie might in time lead us. Möller's strategy failed because he underestimated his opponent. It was a failure that very nearly cost him his life. Unfortunately for Elsie, however, her strategy was similarly unsuccessful.'

She looked away.

'How old are you Natalia?' Smith said, after a moment's pause.

'What has my age got to do with it?' she shot back.

'How old?'

'I am twenty-seven.'

Smith smiled. 'Which makes me forty-two years your senior.'

The expression on her face told him that she was surprised.

'I have been watching Elsie Sidthorpe for longer than you have been alive. By a considerable margin, as a matter of fact. Do you imagine that I would have invested so much time and effort in watching her had I cared nothing for her welfare?'

She shrugged.

Smith sighed. 'Had I been able to prevent him from assaulting her, I would have done so,' he said in a gentler tone.

'You expect me to believe this?' she said, turning to face him again.

'Elsie knew the risks. She was, in her day, one of our most experienced operatives. I am sorry. Truly sorry that she was hurt.'

'Sorry?' That your task may be more difficult, perhaps. But for Elsie, no.' She shook her head. 'I do not believe that you are sorry at all.'

Smith said nothing.

Natalia turned the key over in her hand.

'What do you make of it?' Smith asked, watching the Russian carefully.

'Make of it?'

'Yes. I would welcome your opinion.'

She snorted. 'It is old.'

'And the engraving?'

She shrugged. 'A number.'

'But no maker's mark.'

'What is it that you want from me?' she said, suddenly. 'I know nothing of this,' she said, thrusting the key out towards him.

He declined to take it. 'What I want, Natalia, is Elsie's message. All of it.'

'She gave no other message.'

He could have tried to wring it out of her. Frightened her into revealing it. One mention of bundling her on a plane back to Domodedovo Airport, on the outskirts of Moscow, might have been enough. But Natalia was a principled young woman and she might just have chosen to go, rather than bend to his will. It was not a risk that he needed or wanted to take. Yet. She had the trust of Sidthorpe, Stammers and Carmichael. A trust that could be exploited, if handled correctly. Besides he liked her. She reminded him somehow, of himself when he was younger. Very much younger. 'In that case, I would like you to follow Elsie's instructions,' he said, evenly.

Her surprise was self evident. 'You want me to give the key to Harry Stammers?'

'Yes. I want you to do exactly as Elsie instructed.'

The two of them locked eyes.

'Very well,' she said, breaking eye contact, slipping the key into her pocket and getting to her feet.

'And Natalia?'

'What is it?'

'Be careful. Remember that Möller is a very dangerous man.'

For a moment, she looked uncertain. 'You think he will come after me, why?'

'It is possible that Elsie mentioned you. If so then he may be wondering whether she confided in you. He may decide to pursue this with you himself.'

'You should not worry. What could happen to me while you are protecting me?' she said with biting sarcasm.

But he did worry. He worried a very great deal.

CHAPTER TWENTY

Ellen pulled the Saab over and I leapt out, intending to remove the cones that had been placed across the drive to prevent cars parking immediately outside the Southwold nursing home. In the event, Natalia appeared in the doorway, carrying a large bunch of flowers. Chrysanthemums. I recognised them because Ted used to grow them in our garden at home. Each plant would have a cane pushed into the ground beside it with an upturned plastic cup on top filled with newspaper. It was supposed to stop earwigs getting into the flowers. It didn't work. Whenever he brought flowers into the house they always seemed to harbour several of the nasty little creatures. Which was why, when I held out my hand, it was with a certain amount of trepidation.

'They are for Elsie,' Natalia said softly. She seemed close to tears. 'They are her favourite.'

I found myself hugging her. She felt as fragile as a bird in my arms. 'You didn't have to do that,' I said, releasing her. 'They're beautiful. Elsie will…' I hesitated.

'I wanted to do something,' she interrupted. 'It was all that I could think to do.'

I smiled, weakly. 'I'll put them in the boot. Come on,' I said, taking her by the arm and leading her across to the car. I opened the nearest of the rear passenger doors and she got in. Then I stowed the flowers in the boot and got into the car beside Ellen.

BUILDING 41

'I am so sorry,' Natalia was saying, tearfully, as I pulled the car door closed. 'That this terrible thing has happened.'

I looked at Ellen who was clearly struggling to contain her own emotions. She nodded but said nothing. In fact, she'd said very little during the drive up from Leighton Buzzard. I wasn't sure whether it was the shock of receiving the telephone call from the police, or the revelations at The Three Locks. I knew that she was struggling, not just with the notion that Elsie might know a great deal more than she had been letting on, but that she might be at the middle of it all. 'We'd better get going,' I muttered. It was the best that I could offer in the circumstances.

'There is something I must give you,' Natalia said, as Ellen pulled the car out in to the road. 'But not here.'

I turned, craning my neck against the safety belt so that I could see her. 'What is it?'

'Can we wait? Until we are away from here?' Natalia said, scanning the fields to our right and the buildings to our left.

We turned left and passed a little garden with a stone sculpture and a blue plaque. While the plaque itself was visible, its dedication was not. I couldn't help but wonder about it. As if I didn't have enough to think about.

Natalia waited until we had cleared the high street. Then she removed an object from her jacket pocket and handed it to me.

'What is it?' Ellen said, glancing across towards me. It was the first time she'd spoken since Natalia had got into the car.

I did not reply. Instead I held up the key so that Ellen could see it.

Ellen stared for a little longer than was comfortable.

'Elsie said that if anything happened to her, I must pass it to you.'

Which was puzzling because it had been Elsie who had asked to keep the key, in the first place. We had discovered it during our first foray into the shelter, but none of us had been able to come up with any link between the key and Martha Watts. When Elsie had asked for it, I hadn't really given it a great deal of thought. But I was thinking about it now. 'Did she say why?'

Natalia stared at me. 'She said to tell you both that he has returned, that you are in great danger and must trust no one.'

'Stephens.' The name tasted sour in my mouth.

'Or Jimmy Dobson,' said Ellen.

Natalia looked confused. 'The man who attacked her?'

I nodded.

'His name is Günther Möller.'

We were, by then, on the edge of the town, heading north towards the A12. 'Möller?' I said, surprised. 'Are you sure?'

'Yes. When I told Elsie that she had a visitor, she told me his name. He used the same name at reception. Günther Möller.'

I looked at Ellen. 'What do you think?'

'I think we should hear the rest of Gran's message.'

'Was there more?' I asked, turning back towards the Russian.

Natalia nodded. 'Elsie told me to ask you something, Ellen.'

'Me? Ask me what?' Ellen replied, sounding surprised.

'She said to ask you: - "Do you remember raven's car?"' The Russian nurse pronounced the last two words awkwardly.

'Raven's car?' Ellen replied, slowly. Like she was trying to make a connection.

'What the hell is a raven's car?'

Ellen appeared lost in thought.

'There is one more thing,' added Natalia when Ellen said nothing more. 'When Elsie said that you should trust no one.'

I turned and looked at her over my shoulder. Her expression was impenetrable.

'I think that this should include me.'

'What do you mean?' Ellen said, obviously shocked. 'Elsie trusted you. That's good enough for us.'

'Thank you for saying this Ellen but I'm afraid that it is not true. Elsie was very careful to choose words that I would not understand. She trusted me to deliver them, perhaps. She did not trust me with their meaning.'

'Elsie speaks very highly of you Natalia. You should know that. She takes a great deal of comfort from your friendship,' Ellen said, her eyes fixed on the road.

'Thank you,' Natalia said, simply.

But Natalia was right. Had Elsie truly trusted her, then she could have passed whatever message she intended, plainly. Why not just tell us about the relevance of the key, about the identity of Möller/Dobson/Stephens, about her own identity? Why not explain the whole damn thing? The truth was that Elsie had seen fit to tell none of us the truth, including Natalia. 'Evidently, she trusts you as much as she trusts us,' I said, without thinking. 'Right now, Natalia, you know as much we do about the real Elsie Sidthorpe.' I regretted saying it as soon as the words had left my lips.

'Harry.' Ellen exclaimed. 'That's not fair. She's still my Gran.'

There was an awkward silence.

'I'm sorry,' I apologised. 'I really didn't mean that the way that it sounded. This whole bloody thing is doing my head in.'

'Elsie has her reasons perhaps,' Natalia interjected. 'She is also a woman who loves you very much, Ellen. And you Harry. Both of you. Whatever she has done. She wants only what is best for you. I have no doubt about this. So please. Listen to her words. Trust no one.'

'So come on, what the hell is a raven's car?' I'd been dying to ask her. Natalia's insistence that we avoid discussing the meaning of Elsie's message in front of her was puzzling but she'd been absolutely adamant. In the end, we'd spent most of the journey in silence, each wrapped up in our own thoughts. Ellen was dreading what we'd find when we arrived at the hospital. I could tell. With Elsie in intensive care and the prognosis uncertain, I think we all were.

Ellen and I were seated in the cafeteria at James Paget Hospital, on the outskirts of Great Yarmouth, drinking coffee and trying to come to terms with Elsie's battered face, the tubes attached to her and the police officers who had refused to leave us alone with her, even though they knew who we were.

'It's not a what. It's a where,' Ellen said, gloomily.

'A place?'

Ellen nodded. 'A village in North Yorkshire. Ravenscar. Between Scarborough and Whitby. Gran didn't come with us on many family holidays but she did come on that one. I was ten or eleven, I think. 1985 or '86. Something like that.'

Elsie had looked like she'd been hit by a small train. Or a baseball bat. Seeing her brought new meaning to the term "black and blue". Ellen had turned so pale at the sight of her that I thought she was going to keel over. Natalia hadn't looked much better. Miraculously though, Elsie was at least still alive.

'Any idea why she wanted you to remember it?' I said, trying to keep the conversation going.

'I don't know.' The hot coffee was putting some colour back into Ellen's cheeks.

'She must have suggested it for a reason. Was there anything particularly memorable about the holiday?'

Ellen smiled weakly. 'Loads. It was the one and only time we ever went on a camping holiday, for one thing.'

'Camping?' I was surprised. Elsie didn't seem to me like the kind of woman who would have surrendered herself willingly to the indignities of life in the great outdoors. 'Elsie went camping?' I said, smiling in spite of the solemnity of the moment.

Ellen nodded 'Actually, you know, Gran dealt with it better than any of us. She was quite resourceful in those days. Mum was completely useless, of course. Afraid of the dark. Can you believe that? I must have been the only child in the world who had to comfort their mother when the lights went out.'

BUILDING 41

I'd met Ellen's mother half a dozen times by then and it didn't surprise me in the least that she was afraid of the dark. She was a mouselike woman, who would skitter away and hide in the kitchen at the slightest sign of trouble, and quite often without it. About as unlike Ellen as it was possible to be.

'The thing that I remember most was dad losing his keys. We'd gone exploring. Dad had an old map of the area that showed some ruins, so we'd walked up there me, dad and Gran. I can't remember why mum didn't come. She'd probably gone shopping or something.'

'What sort of ruins?'

'I'm not sure now. Dad did tell us. Wartime, I think. He'd looked it all up. He was very keen on that sort of thing. Always fancied himself as a bit of an archaeologist. Anything remotely historic and we'd be off on some adventure or other. Great fun when we were little kids but by the time I hit thirteen it was just embarrassing.'

I wasn't sure that Ellen was describing the same man I'd met. Mr Carmichael had recently retired from the accountancy firm that bore his name and at which he'd been a partner for a little less than forty years. Had I been describing him, "adventurous" would not have been my adjective of choice.

'Anyhow, at some point, Dad realised that he'd lost his car keys,' Ellen continued. 'Without them, we'd have been stranded. We searched high and low for them but there was absolutely no sign and then the light began to go, so dad went back to the campsite to make sure that mum was all right. Gran volunteered to spend the night with me at the ruins so that we could resume the search at first light. She found a couple of bales of straw in one of the old buildings. We used them to make a kind of sofa and Gran built a fire. We fell asleep watching the flames dancing. Well I did, anyway. It was absolutely magical. I will never forget it.'

I tried to picture them both, but when I thought of Elsie all I could see was the car crash face I'd just seen in intensive care. *What kind of a man could do that to a woman in her eighties?* As I thought it, a voice in my head told me to stop kidding myself. I knew exactly what kind of man Möller was. He was the kind who could kidnap a young woman, tie her and gag her, shut her away in some godforsaken hell hole, one hundred feet below London and leave her to die. The kind of man who could blow Tomasz Dabrowski's brains out and dump his body in Aldenham Reservoir with a bagful of bricks for company.

That Elsie had tried to kill him had shocked us both. We'd been aware that a firearm had been discharged - the police officer who had called Ellen to tell us that Elsie was in hospital had told us that much. I reckon he'd had to because, by the time we were half way to Southwold, news of a shooting in a Suffolk nursing home had been all over the local radio. The reports contained little detail and the police had told us less still, so Ellen and I had both naturally assumed that it had been her assailant who had discharged the weapon. But, as we made our way into the hospital, with very little idea of what to expect, one of the reporters from the press pack outside had thrust a microphone in Ellen's face and asked her what she knew about the gun Elsie kept under her pillow - she didn't know anything about it, obviously - and whether we'd ever seen her fire it, which was plainly ridiculous.

'Did you ever find your dads keys?' I said, still trying to keep the conversation going.

'Yes.'

'You did?'

'When the sun came up the following morning we started searching among the ruins again and I remembered that dad had stumbled on a loose flagstone, just inside the main building. When we retraced his steps, I noticed a gap between two stones and when Gran and I lifted them, we found a cavity under the floor, at the bottom of which were dad's keys. Gran let me climb down to fetch them. It was quite a drop. Four or five feet. I was a skinny little thing in those days but quite athletic,' she said smiling, briefly.

It was the first time I'd seen her smile since The Three Locks.

BUILDING 41

'Now why doesn't that surprise me?' I said, honestly. It didn't surprise me at all. Ellen is one of the fittest women I know.

'While I was down there, I noticed that the cavity seemed to slope downwards and to run off, under the walls of the building, in the direction of the other buildings. Like a secret passage, I guess. It was dead exciting. I was dying to explore it but there was no way that Gran was going to let me. She said it was too dangerous.'

Watching her, I could well imagine the excited little girl that she would have been. She still had a flame of youthful excitement in her eyes sometimes, although there were bags under them now through lack of sleep. At that moment, I just wanted to take her in my arms and make all her troubles go away. I reached out and took her hand.

'I love you, Harry,' she said, suddenly tearful.

'I love you too, sweetheart' I said and I meant it. I did. I watched a tear trickle down her cheek. 'This is one hell of a mess isn't it?'

She nodded and sniffed.

'Do you have any idea, any idea at all what the fuck is going on?' I said, shaking my head.

She shook hers too, laughed and let out a sob at the same time.

'Me neither.'

I found her a tissue and she wiped her eyes. 'It's like you said at the pub the other night, Harry.' She blew her nose. 'It is all linked.'

I nodded. It was. 'But by what?' I ran my hand through my hair. 'I can't help wondering if we're being blinded by all the detail. You know, the can't see the wood for the trees thing? Missing the obvious.'

Ellen screwed up her face. She was thinking.

I waited. I didn't want to interrupt whatever was going on in there.

'Gran said that we are in danger,' she said suddenly, staring at me as if I could tell her why.

I played dumb. Actually, at that moment, I wasn't playing it.

'Why us, Harry?'

I must have pulled a face.

'I mean, whatever Möller's problem is, if that really is his name, his issue is with Elsie and not us, surely. So why are we in danger?'

'Because we screwed Max Banks' plans for world domination last year?' I offered.

'Well, yes I know we did that, but Banks isn't the missing link that pulls this all together, is he? It's something else.'

I could see where she was going. If all of it was linked by one, overarching story then like all stories this one had to have a beginning and an end. In all probability, Max Banks was a chapter in the middle somewhere. What we needed was the introduction. Before it was too late and we found ourselves featuring in the thrilling conclusion.

'Something that triggered all of this,' she said, echoing my thoughts. 'One single event. Everything has a beginning.'

She was right, of course. 'Supposing that Elsie has something that Möller wants,' I said suddenly. 'Something she is refusing to give to him.'

'Like the key. It must be significant or why else would Elsie have passed it back to us?' Ellen drained her coffee cup.

'You know, I've been thinking about the key. Do you remember when we were all brought up from the tunnels at Belsize Park, I was interviewed by two…' I hesitated. 'Well one of them was a police officer. I am not sure about the other one.'

'Yes, vaguely.'

'One of them seemed very interested in what else we had found in the tunnels. Do you remember? He gave me quite a grilling?'

She nodded.

'I denied finding anything. I don't really know why, to be honest. I just had a feeling about him.'

Ellen nodded again.

'Well, I think I saw him. At the funeral. I think he was in the crowd when that bastard reporter stopped us…' As I was talking, I could see that Ellen's attention was being drawn away by something or someone behind me. 'I think his name was Smith.' I said as I turned my head. Natalia had approached the table and was standing a couple of feet behind me, staring.

'Hi Natalia. You okay?'

She hesitated. As if she was about to say something but had thought better of it. 'There are people here to see Elsie. The police won't let them. I thought I should bring you, Ellen.'

'Who are they?' Ellen said, glancing first at me, then back at Natalia.

'They are called Jackson.'

Something rang a bell in my head.

Ellen looked blank.

'Flora I think. And Simone,' Natalia added.

Simone. Jackson. The bell was now a wailing siren. I was on my feet before I was even aware of it. The woman who had looked after us prior to my mother's disappearance. In whose flat I'd met, as a seven year old boy, a woman with piercing blue eyes called Rosemary. The same woman whose battered face we'd just seen in intensive care.

'Harry?'

I stared at her, momentarily lost for words. There were too many connections firing in my head. 'Simone,' I said eventually. 'Aunty Simone,' I added excitedly. 'Come on.' I held out my hand.

Ellen leapt to her feet.

'Where?' I said to Natalia.

'They are waiting in the reception. Unless they have gone.'

'Shit. They'd better not have,' I said, grabbing Ellen's hand and pulling her after me.

CHAPTER TWENTY-ONE

It was the strangest of reunions. As we tore through the swing doors into the reception and waited for Natalia to catch us up, I spotted them. Two black women. One seated. She had grey hair. Clearly very elderly. The other, somewhat younger. Perhaps in her sixties. Tall. Standing and arguing with a uniformed PC. I didn't hesitate. I walked straight towards them with Ellen still in tow.

The younger of the two women spotted my approach. She stopped arguing with the PC and put her hand on the other's shoulder, as if to steady herself. Both women stared at me. I recognised neither of them. I think I had expected to and the fact that I didn't left me feeling suddenly uncertain.

'Harry,' said the elder of the two women.

I really didn't know what to say.

'And you must be Ellen,' the older woman said. 'I'm Flora Jackson.'

Ellen shook her hand.

I followed suit. On autopilot.

Ellen held out her hand to the second woman.

'Simone. Simone Jackson.'

'We're old friends of your great aunt,' said Flora Jackson, obviously noticing our confusion.

BUILDING 41

Simone was staring at me, her eyes full of tears. 'I'm sorry,' she said, shaking her head. 'It's been a long time since I saw you, Harry. Well properly, anyway.' The tears trickled down her cheeks.

'You are Simone? Aunty Simone?' I said awkwardly.

She nodded. 'We were so afraid when we heard,' she said.

'Heard?' Ellen replied.

'About the shooting. It was on the news. We knew that it would be Elsie, but they wouldn't tell us anything. So we just got in the car.'

Simone had taken hold of my hand.

'I'm sorry. We really shouldn't have come. We were so afraid for … Elsie that we…' Simone glanced from me to Ellen and back again. 'Is she… I mean, we're not… They wouldn't tell us.'

'She is alive,' I said. 'Unconscious. They're not sure yet what the prognosis is. He hit her pretty hard.'

Flora Jackson had covered her mouth with her hands.

I'd suddenly become aware of our surroundings. It was as if until that moment the room had been completely still and silent, save for the Jacksons. As though suddenly someone had thrown a switch and the place was full of people and sound again.

'Look, we can't do this here.' I turned to the young PC. 'Is there somewhere we could talk in private?'

He looked around. 'No idea, mate.'

Mate. What is wrong with people that they cannot use the word "Sir"? The kids who serve at the McDonalds drive-through in Leighton Buzzard were always calling me "mate" or "pal" or worst of all "bud". I'd promised Mike that the next time it happened, I was going to roll down my window and punch them in the face. But needless to say I wasn't going to smack young PC Mateyboy, regardless of how much he deserved it. 'Do you think that you might try to find out? Please?'

He stared at me for a moment longer than was comfortable and then sauntered off in the direct of the reception.

'Harry?' Simone squeezed my hand. 'It is so good to see you. Are you well? Apart from this, I mean.'

I smiled. 'I am…' I hesitated. I tried to think about how I was feeling and failed. 'Trying to understand what the hell is going on.' I looked across at Ellen who was looking as bewildered as I was feeling. I reached out and pulled her towards me. 'We both are.'

At that moment PC Mateyboy reappeared. 'You can use the overflow waiting room.'

I looked around. 'Which is where?'

He stared at me.

I stared at him.

After a few seconds of pointless staring he gestured towards the far corner of the room. 'Over there, mate.'

I could have. I really could. In fact, I almost did. But, for once, good sense prevailed.

Ellen helped Flora to her feet.

And then I remembered Natalia. There was no sign of her.

'Do you know where my mother is?' It was the only question that really mattered. Perhaps I was being selfish but, right at that moment, I really didn't give a damn.

'No, Harry. I'm afraid not.'

But… It was obvious that there was going to be one. 'But you do know that she is alive?'

Simone hesitated. 'Yes, I do know that she is alive,' she answered at last.

I let out a breath. 'Have you seen her?' These were the questions I needed to ask. The questions I'd always needed to ask.

'No. The last time I saw Liz was the day that she left you and Kate with us.'

But now that it had come to it, it was as though the questions were asking themselves. Like my mouth was on auto pilot. 'So, how do you know that she's still alive?' I heard myself saying.

BUILDING 41

Simone closed her eyes and kept them closed.

I was trying not to think about how I was going to feel if Simone's answers were not the answers I wanted to hear.

She opened her eyes and stared at me. 'I can't tell you everything, Harry. You have to understand that. I'm sorry. I can't.'

'Why not?'

She looked me straight in the eye. 'I made Liz a promise. I won't break it. Not for you. Not for anyone. Not now. Not ever.'

It was like a punch in the guts. Here was someone who could, if she chose to, tell me many of things that I wanted and needed to know.

'Liz loves you Harry. She always did and she always will.'

'It's a funny kind of love, isn't it?' I said, my mouth still on autopilot. 'That leads a mother to abandon her children and stay away all these years.'

'No. It isn't,' Simone said patiently. 'It is a most courageous and committed kind of love. Your mother believed that all of your lives would have been at risk had she stayed.'

'Why?'

'I can't tell you that.'

'So, she just walked away.' Even as I said it, I knew how it must sound. I was speaking like a child. Like the child I had been when my mother left. Like the child part of me was feeling.

Simone sighed.

'Ted was given the opportunity to go with her, wasn't he?' It was Ellen who had rescued me. She took hold of my hand.

Simone and Flora Jackson exchanged a silent question and then Simone spoke. 'Yes,' she said, simply. 'He was offered the chance to start again but he refused it.' She shook her head. 'He was a very stubborn man but, in fairness to Ted, Liz had not been honest with him. Not by a long chalk. I would imagine that he felt terribly betrayed.'

'She told him that he was not my father. Didn't she?' I couldn't help the accusation.

Simone seemed to struggle with the weight of that. 'So I gather,' she answered quietly.

'Do you know who is?'

I felt the collective intake of breath.

This time, when Simone looked at her mother, Flora appeared to have no answer. 'Liz never told us and it was not my business to ask,' Simone said, like there was going to be another *"but"*. She looked from me to Flora to Ellen and back again. 'There was only ever one man. Apart from Ted, I mean. There was only one other that it could have been.'

'Wait,' I said, getting to my feet. I walked away, towards a window. It overlooked an overgrown courtyard. I stood there, gazing downwards but seeing nothing. Why the hell did it matter who my father was? He had played no active part in my life up to that point and there was no reason to suppose that he'd ever play a part in it. He had simply been the man who had provided half my genes. Nothing more. But it did matter. It mattered a very great deal.

'Come on.' Ellen said, appearing at my side. She took my arm and led me back to the seat beside Simone.

'Are you sure you want to hear this?' Simone asked, gently.

I nodded. 'Yes. I am sure.'

'Your mother loved him very much, Harry. Too much. It was a ruinous love that, for Liz, was like a wildfire that she could neither control nor extinguish. Like a drug. An addiction. It caused her, and those around her, a great deal of anguish and misery.' She paused. Like she was waiting for me to digest her words.

'Go on.'

'She loved Ted. Don't you ever think that she didn't. Because I know that she did. A much gentler, thoughtful and, in many ways, deeper kind of love. But her obsession with…'

'Who?' It was all I could manage. 'Who?' I insisted.

'His name was Peter Owen.'

BUILDING 41

Peter Owen. Peter Owen, ex-NUGB leader. Now serving a long sentence at Her Majesty's pleasure.

'Owen?' I laughed, slightly crazily. 'You have got to be kidding.'

Simone was watching my reaction.

I don't know why it was so difficult to believe. Why not Owen? She had clearly been working with him. So he was a notorious, right wing nutter who had tried to bomb London and blew a hole in a Hertfordshire field instead. She could have fallen for him. What the hell did I know? 'But that's ridiculous.'

'I'm sorry, Harry. It must be hard to take in.'

Connections. They were firing in my head again. Jimmy Dobson, who had worked for Owen. Now Günther Möller. The man who had pistol whipped Elsie and put her in hospital. Again. *Elsie Sidthorpe aka* 'Rosemary. What was her surname?' I said, thinking out loud.

All three women stared at me.

'Rosemary. That was the name that Elsie was using at the time, wasn't it?'

Simone looked like she'd just been slapped.

'She was there. At your flat. I remember her,' I added.

'It wasn't Simone's flat,' Flora Jackson broke in. 'It was mine. I took Rosemary in after your mother and Simone rescued her. We looked after her until she was well enough to return to Southwold.'

'Rescued her?' It was Ellen who had asked it. 'Rescued her from what?'

'She'd been found in the street, Ellen,' said Simone. 'Battered half to death. She didn't regain consciousness for over two months. When finally she came to, she was unable to speak. When we found her, she barely even knew her own name. Your mother,' she said, turning to face me, 'was convinced that Rosemary's life was in danger. So we rescued her from the nursing home where they'd put her and took her to mum's flat.'

'Why was she using a false name?' Ellen asked. 'Why did she call herself "Rosemary"?'

'At the time, we had no idea that it was an alias.' said Simone. 'As far as we were concerned, she was Rosemary. Rosemary Sellers.'

All four of us were quiet then. Each with our own thoughts.

'You said that she had been assaulted,' Ellen said, eventually.

Simone nodded.

'Do you know who assaulted her and why?'

'It was never proved. But his name was Jimmy Dobson. He was…'

'Oh, we know all about Jimmy Dobson,' I interrupted.

'You do?'

'We know that last year, when we first ran into him, he was using the name "Stephens".'

Simone said nothing.

'We know that his real name is very probably Günther Möller,' Ellen added.

'Was it him - this Günther Möller - who attacked her again?' Simone asked.

Ellen nodded.

I was watching Simone's reactions.

'Do you know why he attacked her?' My guess was that she did know. 'Why all this is happening?'

Simone glanced at Flora and then shook her head. 'No.'

She was lying. I was just about to accuse her of it when Ellen saved me, again.

'But you have your suspicions?'

Simone stared at her but said nothing.

'Simone.' Ellen said, reaching into her pocket. 'Before she confronted Möller, Elsie gave this key to her nurse.' She had pulled the key from her pocket. 'You met her earlier. She is called Natalia?'

Simone nodded.

'Elsie asked Natalia to pass the key to us, along with a message, in the event that anything happened to her.'

BUILDING 41

'May I?' Flora asked, holding out her hand. She took the proffered key, examined it carefully and then passed it to her mother. 'What was the message?'

'She told Natalia to warn us that "he" had returned and that we are in great danger.'

'Was that all?'

'No,' Ellen replied. 'She warned us to trust no one.'

Which was presumably why Ellen had omitted to mention Elsie's reference to their holiday in Ravenscar.

'Do either of you know anything about the key?' Ellen asked, addressing both women.

They shook their heads without hesitation. My guess was that on this occasion at least, they were telling the truth.

Flora placed the key in my hand.

'Elsie was obviously talking about Günther Möller, but do you know why she thinks he is a danger to us?' Ellen asked.

The two women said nothing.

'Look,' I interjected, beginning to lose patience. 'Günther Möller is a dangerous man. We all know that. He has assaulted Elsie, twice now. We know that he is more than willing to use extreme violence to achieve his purpose, whatever that is. If there is something we should be doing to stop him, then we need to get on and do it. Before he turns his attention to us. Which Elsie seemed to think was imminent. If you have any idea at all that might help us, now would be a very good time. Otherwise, I suspect that we might be shortly joining Elsie in intensive care. If we're lucky.'

Simone stared at me. 'I'm sorry,' she said. 'I can't tell you any more.'

'Can't or won't?' I said, daring her to deny it.

'Both,' Simone shot back. 'I don't know why you are in danger and I won't speculate about it. Had Elsie wanted you to know more than you do, then she would surely have told you herself.'

It was Ellen who provided the breakthrough argument. 'Actually Simone, there's a flaw in your logic. Elsie obviously wanted to warn us and to suggest that we do something with the key. Or else why ask Natalia to pass it to us, along with the warning about Möller?'

'So why didn't she tell you directly?' Simone asked.

'Because,' Ellen replied confidently, 'she didn't wholly trust Natalia. I think she was taking her own advice and trusting no one.'

Simone said nothing.

'Gran has her secrets,' Ellen continued. 'I know that. And no doubt, in normal circumstances, she would have preferred that her secrets be kept. But do you really think she would choose to keep them now if, by so doing, our lives would be endangered? Because I don't. Not for a second. So if you know anything that might help us, Simone, as Harry said, now would be a really good time.'

We waited.

'Rosemary never confided in us directly,' Flora Jackson began.

All three of us stared at her.

'When I took her in, she could barely speak. Alphonse would sit with her for hours and Liz too when she could…'

'Hang on. Who is Alphonse?' I interrupted.

'He was one of Rosemary's closest friends,' she said, flashing her daughter a sad smile. 'He became a very great friend of ours also.'

Simone nodded.

'He died in 1990,' Flora continued.

'I'm sorry,' I said, regretting the question.

'It was a long time before Rosemary was able to put her memories back into any semblance of order. Her confusion distressed her greatly. There was something she felt she needed to do. Some error that she was desperate to correct. She would pace back and forth, muttering under her breath and occasionally arguing with herself. Sometimes, I'd walk in on her and she wouldn't even know I was there. Alphonse used to say that I should not listen but I couldn't help myself.'

'Did you ever find out? What is was that she felt she needed to do?' Ellen asked, as if reading my thoughts.

'She'd taken something. And no,' Flora said, holding up her hand. 'I didn't ask and she never told me. But whatever it was, people had suffered, I do know that. I listened to her tearing herself apart with guilt…' Flora's voice trailed off.

I was thinking. About whether this might have been the beginning that Ellen and I had discussed. 'Did you get any sense of when this was?'

'I think so. Rosemary talked about several people. A man called "Smith".'

Ellen and I exchanged glances.

'And somebody for whom she had been "too late". She'd say it over and over again and often break down in tears. It sounded like something pretty awful had been done to him…'

'Because of this thing that she had taken?' Ellen asked, quietly.

'Yes. I think that is what she believed,' the older woman replied.

'Okay, but how does this help us with the timeframe?' I interjected.

'Rosemary mentioned one name, more than any other.'

'What name?'

'Martha. Whatever it was that she had taken, Martha was involved in some way. I am sure of it.'

'Which means that she must have taken it prior to Martha's disappearance,' I reasoned.

'On November 10, 1944,' Ellen added.

'I think Rosemary believed,' Flora continued, 'that Martha had tried to make amends for her in some way. I know that she blamed herself for Martha's disappearance.'

'Meaning what?' I said, thinking out loud. 'That Elsie thought that Martha had the object with her when she went to London? And that someone had killed her for it? But we know that didn't happen. Martha was murdered by Arthur Wallington.'

'We know that now,' Ellen corrected me. 'But we only discovered it last year. Poor Gran spent most of her life carrying around a whole heap of guilt when, in truth, she was in no way responsible for Martha's disappearance.'

Poor Gran. I could buy that to a point. But I was having another, more uncomfortable thought and it wasn't doing much to enhance my sympathy for Elsie.

Ellen was staring at me.

I ran my hand through my hair. 'You're not going to like this.'

'What?'

'When she asked me to investigate Martha's disappearance…' I hesitated.

'What are you trying to say?'

The look on her face told me that she knew exactly what I was trying to say. 'Maybe Elsie wasn't being entirely honest with either of us, Ellen,' I said, trying to avoid voicing exactly what I was thinking.

Ellen had paled. 'No. Gran just wanted to know what happened to her friend. She and I discussed it many times.'

And then a truly horrible thought occurred to me.

Ellen must have seen it in my eyes. 'What?' she said, like she really didn't want to hear any more.

'Think about it,' I said gently. 'If she believed that Martha had taken the object with her to London, that Martha and others had suffered because of it, and if she knew that Möller was searching for it, then she also knew that by asking me to investigate Martha's disappearance there was a chance that I would encounter Günther Möller first hand. Which, of course, I did. We both did.'

Ellen was shaking her head. 'I don't believe that and I can't believe that you think that of her.'

'So why didn't she tell us? Because she must have known…'

'Hang on,' Simone intervened, coming to Ellen's aid. 'Now listen to me, Harry. Yes, Elsie has her secrets, but there is no way in this world that she would have deliberately put either of you in

BUILDING 41

danger. Many years had passed since Jimmy Dobson's assault. As far as any of us know, she had heard nothing further from him in all that time. She must have thought that the time had come when she could safely resume the search. She told you that she was desperate to discover the truth about Martha's disappearance and I am sure that she was. Perhaps, secretly, she also hoped to right a great wrong that she believed she had committed. But that is very different from deliberately putting you in the path of danger.'

'Let he who is without sin, cast the first stone,' said Flora Jackson.

I wasn't convinced. Elsie had asked me to look for Martha Watts when, in truth, I'd been looking for something else. That something else had brought Möller down on us, like one of the four Horsemen of the bloody Apocalypse.

'Exactly. Gran would never have asked you to look for Martha if she'd thought for a minute that you would be in danger.'

'I'm not saying that she deliberately put us in the path of danger, Ellen...'

'And I'm not saying that when she asked us to find Martha, a part of her wasn't also hoping that we'd discover some clue about whatever it was that she had taken. Has it occurred to you,' Ellen said after a short pause, 'that perhaps we did.'

The key. We had discovered it in the tunnels below Belsize Park. Elsie's interest in it had always seemed curious. Now, faced with the prospect of a confrontation with Möller, she'd chosen to pass the key back to us with an indecipherable message about...

'The key,' Ellen said out loud. She was staring at me. 'Think about it, Harry. All of it.'

She was right. The key. I still had it in my hand. I stared at it. Was this what Möller had been seeking? If the key was the answer then, it struck me suddenly, what we needed now was to understand the question.

CHAPTER TWENTY-TWO

It had been three days since Elsie's admission to hospital and we were still no nearer to discovering the relevance of the key. Ellen had stayed in Southwold, in case Elsie's condition worsened. The blow to Elsie's head had caused minor internal bleeding. There was a very real chance that, this time, she was not going to make it. We both knew it.

If she died, then the police investigation would become a murder enquiry and the newspapers were going to have a field day. The media was already making the most of it. According to The Mirror, it was the first time a gun had been discharged "inside a British nursing home". Sure. Like gunfights in nursing homes elsewhere were commonplace. But The Sun's "YOUR ZIMMER OR YOUR LIFE!" headline was going to take some beating.

I didn't much like leaving Ellen in Southwold but the place was crawling with police and the truth was that she was probably safer there than back in Leighton Buzzard with me. I'd argued with her, but Ellen had made it absolutely clear that with Elsie's life hanging in the balance, she was going nowhere.

I would have been more reluctant had Natalia not offered to put her up. After the reunion with Flora and Simone Jackson, I'd found her sitting on a bench outside the hospital's main entrance. I'd gone out for a cigarette. She'd seemed troubled. Like she had something on her mind. When I'd mentioned Ellen wanting to stay

BUILDING 41

in Southwold for a few days, in order to be close to Elsie, the Russian nurse had immediately offered to help. Maybe she was she trying to compensate for Elsie's mistrust, which she seemed to have taken very much to heart. In any event, I was mightily relieved. There was no way that I was going to leave Ellen on her own in some motel.

According to Ellen, Natalia had a beautiful little terraced cottage in Southwold called "The Teepee" high up on East Cliff, overlooking the sea. How she could afford it on a nurses salary, I had no idea. Property in Southwold was not cheap. Fortunately, Natalia had been due to take some leave and had been able to negotiate to bring it forward meaning that Ellen was unlikely to be on her own. Still, I didn't much like being away from her. I worried about her incessantly.

If the conundrum concerning the key was frustrating, it was the Jacksons' revelations concerning Peter Owen that had been occupying my thoughts. I'd spent every evening trawling the internet for every scrap of information I could find on Owen. This was easy enough up to the point of his conviction but, in the years that had passed since, interest in him had evidently waned. For the last fifteen or so, there had been practically no word of him at all. I couldn't even discover where he was incarcerated. I did however, discover that his ex-wife's name was Emma. She'd divorced him shortly after he was convicted, had reportedly won a very favourable settlement indeed and was now a resident of Sandbanks in Bournemouth. I had already thought about trying to contact her and then thought better of it. I could't see Emma Owen falling over herself to welcome her former husband's long lost, bastard son.

Later that morning, I was due to be making a presentation to a group of visiting dignitaries on the work of Hut Seven, which had led on deciphering Japanese naval codes. I could have done without it, in all honesty. Especially since the Major was due to deliver the introduction. He was bound to get half of the details wrong. If he did, I'd have to re-write my presentation on the fly, in order to avoid contradicting him and making him look completely foolish.

Before that, Jane had somewhat mysteriously asked to meet me at the roundabout between D and E-blocks. There'd been an edge to her voice when we spoke on the phone, so my guess was that she had discovered something. On my arrival back from Southwold, Jane had asked to borrow the key. I'd dropped it in to her at the bungalow the following morning. Although she had a habit of discovering the impossible, I wasn't really expecting a breakthrough this time, short of Elsie waking up and telling us what the hell was going on. The key had probably been sitting there on the tunnel floor for sixty years. Even Jane was going to struggle to find the matching lock.

I made sure that I'd emailed the presentation over to the mansion office, picked up my jacket and stepped out into the corridor. I didn't get very far before Petra Neufeld appeared from one of the store rooms. 'Where are you going?'

What? Like I needed a pass? 'I'm meeting Jane and then I've got the Japanese presentation over at that mansion,' I said, betraying my irritation just a little.

She smiled. 'I will come with you.'

As much as I liked her, Neufeld was hard work. I was going to have to be direct. 'Not on this occasion, Petra. I think Jane wants to talk to me in private. If you don't mind?'

'Oh. Sure. I will get my jacket and come down with you anyway. I think I'll take a walk.'

I stared at her. She was annoying, without meaning to be. 'Fine,' I said. 'The lake is looking lovely today. You could be round it in ten minutes.'

Neufeld nodded. She followed me out onto the metal stairs, our feet clanking on the steps as we descended. At the bottom, I pulled out my cigarettes. 'Smoke?' I said, offering her one.

'Sure,' she said taking a cigarette.

'Light?'

BUILDING 41

She nodded and grinned.

What was it with her? I held up my lighter and struck a flame. She cupped her hands around mine. I could smell her perfume.

No sooner had she lit the cigarette than she started to cough. That cough that afflicts non smokers who try a cigarette for the first time.

I stared at her. 'You do smoke?' I said, as soon as she had finished coughing.

'No,' she said, brightly. 'But I'd like to.'

'You're nuts,' I said shaking my head. She was. Barking.

'See you later,' she replied, turning and making her way toward the lake, the cigarette between her fingers. I stood and watched her as I lit my own cigarette, inhaled and blew out a long column of smoke. 'What the hell is it with you?' I said, under my breath.

I walked up towards the old tennis courts at the top of the Park, turned right past Hut One and found Jane sitting at a wooden table behind Hut Three with a large map spread out in front of her.

'What's this then?' I said, casually.

'What does it look like?'

She was evidently in good spirits. 'It looks like a set of site plans.'

'Well done. That's some intellect you've got there.'

I smiled and straddled one of the wooden bench seats. 'Well, this is nice.'

'Do you want to know what I've found, or don't you?' Jane said, caustically.

'Why not?'

'Fine. Then speak when you are spoken to and keep your answers focused on the matter in hand. Clear?'

'Clear.'

'Tunnels. What do you know about them?'

'Tunnels,' I echoed. 'You mean in general, or here at the Park?' I knew the rumours. I also knew that not a single tunnel had ever been found, despite all the surveys.

She gave me a withering look.

'I know that not a single tunnel has ever been found,' I offered.

'There's a first time for everything.'

My scepticism must have shown.

'Elsie's reminder to Ellen about Ravenscar,' she said.

'What about it?'

'Ellen found her father's keys in a cavity beneath the floor. When she climbed down to get them she found what appeared to be the entrance to a tunnel.'

'So Ellen says but what's that got to do with…'

'Just answer the question,' Jane interrupted.

'Yes, she did.'

'The ruins at Ravenscar were built in nineteen forty-one. Note the year please.'

I did. 'Nineteen forty-one. Check.'

'Excellent. Ravenscar is a disused radar station.'

'Radar. Check.'

Jane stared at me. 'Now you're just being irritating.'

'Sorry.'

'Okay. Now take a look at this and tell me what is significant about it,' Jane reached into the breast pocket of her blouse and handed me the key from Belsize Park.

'Jane, I've looked at this a thousand times. There's nothing significant about it. It's a bloody key.'

'Look again.'

She'd said it like if I didn't, she'd punch me in the mouth. So I looked again. It took me a while to see it. Ridiculous because, once I had, it was obvious. I smiled. 'The number.' On the key's bow. '41B' I read out. 'Forty-one. Same year that the radar station at Ravenscar was built.'

BUILDING 41

'Correct. Gold star,' said Jane, sarcastically. 'So, we have found a link.'

I pulled a face. 'Well, hardly…'

'Now examine the plan in front of you, if you would please,' she interrupted.

I looked at the map. 'What am I looking for?'

'Another link, Harry.'

I looked up at her and pulled another face.

'All right. Try looking for the magic number.'

I had not the slightest idea what she was talking about.

Jane shook her head. 'All that money invested in a university education.'

I looked again. 'Nope. No idea what you're on about.'

'Oh, for the love of God. All the buildings on the site, huts and blocks are either numbered or are allocated a letter code, are they not?'

'Yes.'

'Dear Lord,' she said, shaking her head.

I grinned at her. 'You're getting very religious, all of a sudden.'

'Is it any wonder, when I am surrounded by heathens?'

'Charming.'

'Let's try one last time, shall we? All the blocks have letter codes. So no number forty-one there. The huts don't go up as far as forty-one. So that leaves the smaller brick buildings. So try looking for a building numbered "41".'

Building 41. I'd never heard of it. 'Is there one?'

'Yes,' Jane sighed. 'There is. It is right there,' she said pointing at the plans.

I looked closely. 'That's… over there, right?' I said, peering over my shoulder.

'Correct again. Well this is going well.'

I grinned.

'It's the little building at the side of G-block. Just beyond the old bicycle shelters. Disused and semi-derelict like all the buildings are over there.'

I was trying to visualise it. 'That building with that weird thing on the roof?'

Jane folded her arms and smiled. 'It is an old direction finding antenna.'

I looked at her, blankly.

'A bit like radar. Not quite the same but close enough. Too close to be a coincidence.'

'I know what a direction finding antenna is.' I was staring at her and she was enjoying it. Radar. Building 41. Tunnels. Connections.

'Look at the key in your hand again, Harry.'

I did.

'It is a Bletchley Park key. I've checked. Standard wartime issue. They were cut on site.'

'You're kidding?'

Jane was looking smug. 'Stamped with the relevant building number.'

'Are you sure?' It was a stupid question. She wouldn't be saying so, if she wasn't sure.

Jane nodded. Still smug.

Martha Watts had taken a key from Bletchley to London and had lost it in the tunnels below Belsize Park. Almost certainly, when she'd been dragged unconscious through the tunnels by Arthur Wallington. 'Why 41B?' I said, suddenly. It's a tiny building, no doubt with a single door. Number forty-one surely? If there is a 41B then there must be a 41A. Stands to reason.'

'Perhaps there is more to Building 41 than meets the eye,' Jane said with an edge of excitement in her voice.

It took a moment for the penny to drop. 'You're not serious?' I said incredulously. 'Oh, come on.'

'Martha needed somewhere to hide something for a few days, while she was in London.'

BUILDING 41

'Well I know that, but...'

'Remember Ravenscar. That's what Elsie said. Think about it. Secret wartime location, *check,*' she said, mimicking me. 'Key recovered from below ground, check. Forty-one, check. Radar, check. Tunnel entrance?'

I ran my hand through my hair. I could buy it to a point. After all, had Martha needed to find a bolt hole, then Bletchley Park had been just about the safest place in the country. It was the tunnel thing that I was finding hard to swallow.

'Well don't just sit there, man. Let's go and have a look.'

I looked at my watch. 'Can't,' I said. 'Presentation to do up at the mansion. Jaa mata*,' I said smugly.

'Watashi wa matsu koto ga dekimasu**,' Jane replied.

I was thinking *'Why do you always have to be so fucking clever?'* as I got to my feet. I wasn't thinking it for long though. Because, as I turned, I caught sight of a figure disappearing into the alley between the huts behind us. I only saw her for a split second but there was no mistaking her. She was wearing a black leather jacket.

---

* 'See you later,' (in Japanese)
** 'I can wait.'

CHAPTER TWENTY-THREE

Friday, November 10, 1944

'Come on!' Martha yelled over her shoulder. 'McFarlane will be furious if we're late.'

'I don't care,' Elsie called back. 'Not one bit. I simply cannot walk any faster.'

Had they caught the park bus it would have taken them in through the main gate and deposited them outside the mansion, but by the time they'd made it to the stop, the park bus had been and gone.

'It is entirely your own fault. If you hadn't taken half an hour to put your face on, we wouldn't have had to walk from the station,' Martha said, glancing back.

'Don't. Just don't.'

Martha observed her friend. Even though she was rushing and slightly red in the face there was not a hair out of place. 'How do you do it. Elsie. Just tell me that?' Martha said, when Elsie had caught up.

'Do what?'

They were approaching the gate. Martha checked her watch. It was eight-thirty. The last of the morning shift girls were queuing to have their papers checked. 'Get absolutely plastered, spend the night in somebody else's bed, dress yourself in yesterday's clothes in the morning and still manage to look like Margaret Lockwood.'

'Breeding, darling. It is in the blood. Though the Lord knows who put it there because it cannot possibly have been either of my beastly parents.'

They joined the end of the queue. Apart from Roselyn Bettis from Hut Four, who was at the front and who waved at her enthusiastically, Martha knew none of them. 'Your blood must be one hundred percent proof by now,' Martha quipped, waving back at Roselyn. 'Honestly Elsie, if you ever manage to spend an evening in a public house without drinking everyone under the table, I will personally give you a piggyback to Bletchley.'

The two young women stared at each other and then burst into laughter.

'You do know that you were absolutely steaming?' Martha added, disapprovingly.

'I will have you know,' Elsie announced, altogether too loudly, 'that I was in full control of my faculties.' She dropped her voice to a whisper. 'Poor Petty Officer Warren. Did you see his face when you told him that his services would not be required. So far as my faculties are concerned, I rather suspect that he was hoping for a guided tour.'

Martha flushed. 'Yes, he did look a little,' she hesitated 'disappointed.'

'Deflated, darling. He was positively deflated.'

They both giggled. Martha couldn't help herself.

Thank God it wasn't raining. It was cold, but at least the sun was shining. And then they were at the front of the queue and Martha realised, with a jolt, that she didn't recognise the soldier on duty.

'Papers?' he said, smoothly.

She swallowed and handed him her identity card.

She had never once been searched on entering the Park and, in truth, she had not even considered the possibility that it might happen. Until now. How could she have been so thoughtless? If the soldier asked to see inside her bag, she might very well be done for. She was already rehearsing an explanation. Or trying to. Because, try as she might she could not think of any way to explain away the contents of her bag.

His expression was impossible to read. 'Good morning... Miss Watts,' he read out loud from her card.

She smiled at him, trying to make herself relax. 'Good morning,' she said brightly.

He handed her back the card. She stepped past him, holding her breath.

'Just a minute...' the soldier said, suddenly.

As she turned to face him, her heart had already stopped beating. She was sure of it. But he wasn't even looking at her. 'Elsie Sidthorpe,' he had exclaimed, as Martha turned. 'Well, I'll be damned.'

Martha felt a wave of relief wash over her, but she was sure that her cheeks were glowing like a beacon.

'What are you doing here?' he was saying, clearly delighted. 'Teddy?' he called out, over his shoulder.

One of two soldiers standing beside the gate house, turned and started to march towards them briskly.

'Hello Jack,' Elsie was saying. 'What a wonderful surprise.'

Martha watched them greet each other. *How wonderful it must feel, to be that popular,* she thought. Although on this occasion it was just as well that neither of the men were paying Martha the slightest attention. She turned and, without further hesitation, walked away as casually as she could.

Martha glanced up at the clock on the wall for the umpteenth time. She'd been watching it all morning.

'Do stop clock watching,' Elsie whispered. 'It is driving me to distraction.'

BUILDING 41

'Sorry,' Martha mouthed, silently. 'I promised Gerry Gorbold I'd run an errand for him at half twelve,' she whispered. 'If I can get away,' she added.

'Gorbold?' Elsie looked surprised. 'Whatever for?'

Martha's eyes darted toward the far end of the hut where, seated at his desk, Bob McFarlane was engrossed in a pile of papers, looking for all the world like the university professor that he used to be before he was press-ganged and sent to Bletchley. McFarlane was a Scot by birth and a decent enough sort of chap, but if there was one thing that he could not abide it was what he called "idle chatter".

'They've lost a whole batch of spares,' Martha whispered, watching McFarlane for any sign that he had heard them. 'Reg was telling me about it yesterday.' She turned backed towards Elsie. 'Apparently Gorbold will be for it unless they're found.'

Elsie was looking like she really didn't care.

'Reg is really quite worried about it, you know. They all are. They'd hate to lose him.'

'Surely Reg doesn't think it would come to that. Gorbold's been here since the beginning,' Elsie said, looking only slightly less disinterested.

Reg really wasn't her type at all and Gorbold, who must have been sixty-five if he was a day, was not even on Elsie's radar. Martha nodded. 'Apparently. They're missing almost two hundred pounds' worth.'

'Two hundred pounds?' Elsie mouthed, portraying her astonishment.

Martha nodded. 'The thing is, I think know where they are.'

'You do?' Elsie stared at her, suddenly very interested. 'How?'

Martha tapped her nose and smiled. 'So after I left you at the gate this morning, I went to see him.'

'You went to see Reg?'

'No, you idiot, Gorbold.'

'Oh,' Elsie mouthed.

Martha reached for her bag and carefully removed a bunch of keys, watching McFarlane as she did, but the Scot did not stir.

'You have never got old Gorbold's keys?' Elsie's eyes lit up. 'We could have some fun with those.'

'Shhh,' Martha hissed. 'And no.'

'But...'

'Absolutely not,' Martha added, firmly.

'Spoilsport,' whispered Elsie.

'The thing is, Gorbold doesn't want it known that he's looking for two hundred pounds' worth of spares.'

'Well, one can imagine why,' Elsie observed.

'So I offered to go and have a look, for him.'

It was at that point that McFarlane looked up from his papers. The Scot stood up and slowly made his way towards them, pausing occasionally to look over the shoulder of one or other of the girls as he passed, or sometimes stopping to give instruction or make some more lengthy comment.

Martha stuffed the keys back into her bag, put her head down and waited.

'You can get off for lunch now if you wish, Miss Watts,' McFarlane said, when he'd drawn level with their desk.

Martha glanced at the clock on the wall and then back at McFarlane. 'Thank you, Sir. I will.' She stood up, grabbed her bag and her coat from the coat stand and, with a meaningful wink in Elsie's direction, opened the hut door.

Martha drew her woollen coat about her tightly and fastened the buttons. It had been fine when they'd arrived at the Park that morning but the sky had since clouded over ominously and the morning's gentle breeze had turned into a surprisingly bitter wind. It whistled between the huts, sending those few hardy souls foolish enough to have stepped outside, scurrying for cover, which suited Martha's purpose. The fewer people there were to observe her, the better it was going to be for the activity she had in mind. She

BUILDING 41

turned right and took the narrow passage between two huts, crossed over the roadway and made her way toward the bike sheds and the little building beyond, nodding casually at the few hardy souls she met on the way.

Her target was an odd little brick building that stood on its own beside the roadway. It was made conspicuous by a most peculiar contraption on the roof. It looked rather like one of those concave mirrors you sometimes see at fairgrounds or amusement arcades. The kind that make your reflection look impossibly thin. Or was it fat? Martha could never remember. Reg Woolley had explained the purpose of the device to her once. Something about planes and radio signals. Most of it had gone straight over the top of her head. Quite literally, if she'd understood even the half of it correctly.

Gorbold happened to have a key to the little building because his team had been installing a pair of teleprinters in the building's communications room. Although the work was not yet finished, according to Reg, the team had been called away to the main teleprinter hall. Since the little building had not yet been commissioned, it was unlikely to be occupied. Really just as well in the circumstances, because it was the building's secondary and somewhat more clandestine purpose that was the reason for her visit.

Martha had no business knowing the building's secondary purpose. She doubted very much that Gorbold knew it. Very few of the Park's staff did. Reg certainly didn't. While not exactly a secret, it was supposed to be known only to those who needed to know and Martha wasn't one of them. Elsie knew, of course. There wasn't much that Elsie didn't.

Fortunately the entrance to the building faced away from the roadway. That and the fact that the rapidly deteriorating weather had, seemingly, persuaded most of the Park's inhabitants to stay indoors meant that she was unlikely to be observed from the roadway at least. The same could not be said for G-block, however, which overlooked the little building almost directly. As a precaution she readied the keys, so that she wouldn't be standing in the doorway, fumbling with them any longer than was absolutely necessary.

She passed the building, then suddenly turned to her right, skirted the building's perimeter, turned right again and found herself standing in the doorway. She didn't hesitate. She inserted the key, opened the door, entered the building and closed the door behind her, all in one smooth motion. Then she counted to ten, opened the door slightly and peered out. There was no sign that anyone had observed her. She closed the door, locked it and, standing with her back to the wall, let out a particularly long breath.

There was very little natural light inside the building, due to the blackout boxes on the windows. They could be raised via pulleys but she thought it best to leave them closed. In the gloom she could make out a row of big, heavy looking radios on the benches toward the back and, above her, what looked like a large motor, presumably for turning the device on the roof. She was tempted to turn on the lights, but instead, waited for her eyes to adjust to the darkness. While the risk that the lights would be seen from outside was slight, the consequences of discovery would be anything but. The thought of it sent a tremor of doubt into her legs. *Come on. Come on. If Elsie and the others can do this, then so can I.*

Martha knew about the building's secondary purpose through Roddy and Johnny Merchant from Hut Four. Johnny even had his own door key. How he had obtained it, Martha had no idea and didn't want to know. Elsie had never seemed bothered in the slightest about the risk although, to Martha's knowledge, they'd never accessed the facilities in broad daylight as Martha was now about to attempt. She tried to steady her nerves. If she was right about the location of the spares - and she was almost certain that she was - then at least Mr Gorbold would be grateful. It was a secondary concern but of some comfort at least. On the other hand, if she was discovered… It didn't bear thinking about. She tried to

BUILDING 41

banish the thought from her mind but her hands were shaking as she reached for the handle of the door into the side room.

It was unlocked. The teleprinter boys had probably forgotten to lock it. They were an undisciplined lot. Hence, Martha imagined, the missing spares. Reg had said that, whatever the outcome, heads were going to roll but that if the spares were recovered it might at least be the right heads rather than Gorbold's.

She entered, noting the teleprinters that were lined up, side by side, along one wall, at the centre of which was a wooden desk. She approached the desk, slid open the top drawer, removed some papers and then the drawer's false bottom as she had observed the others doing on the occasions they had used the facility together. Inside the small compartment was a single key. She removed it, replaced the drawer's false bottom along with the papers and closed the drawer.

Then she walked to the far end of the room, located what appeared to be a key operated switch on the wall, inserted the key and turned it. There was a dull clunk. She knelt down and ran her hand across the floor until she had located the lip of the trap door. As she lifted it, she was momentarily blinded by the lights that buzzed on, illuminating the stairs that fell away into the depths.

Martha checked her watch. She had a little less than twenty-five minutes. She removed the trap door key and made her way down the concrete steps as quickly as her shaking legs would permit. She should, perhaps have closed the trap door behind her, but she detested tunnels and the thought of being shut in, more so, so she took the risk and left the door open.

The steps descended steeply for perhaps twenty feet and then opened out into a narrow concrete lined passageway, no more than six feet wide, which ran in a roughly south-easterly direction. According to Johnny, who claimed to have explored the entire network, there were several branches, including one that went as far as Bletchley Station. Martha knew about the entrance in the cellar at The Belles public house, since this was the one that the four of them had used to get back into the Park, after hours. Johnny had said that another working entrance came up in the basement of the Park's main stores. She was banking on Johnny being right.

The original intended purpose of the tunnels was unclear. There was no evidence that they were in regular or even irregular use, officially anyway. Johnny had reckoned that the project had been abandoned. In fact according to Johnny, one branch that appeared to have been intended, given its direction, to link to the drying rooms below B-block, had not even been completed - it simply ended in a rough dead end.

Fortunately, the lighting system had been installed, at least in the main tunnels, where switches had been fitted every ten yards or so to illuminate the next section of tunnel. Martha threw the first switch. A row of the new style fluorescent tubes buzzed on.

In the now illuminated tunnel Martha was able to examine a door in the wall opposite the stair well but when she tried it, the door was locked. She tried the key from the trap door but it didn't fit. She checked her watch again and felt a surge of anxiety. She was running out of time. She moved swiftly along the tunnel and quickly came to a second door. This time a key had been left in the lock. She said a silent prayer of thanks, turned the key, opened the door and smiled. Beyond it, was a small space. Really no more than a shallow cupboard. It contained what appeared to be a row of electrical switch gear and a fuse box. She had no idea of their purpose. Nor did she particularly care. Above the switches was a shelf on which was a row of cardboard boxes and a first aid kit. Martha removed the bag from her shoulder and took out the note book. She reached up and tucked it behind the box furthest to her right. Then she closed and locked the door, removed the key and, fishing her purse from her bag, dropped the key in the purse, slipped the purse in her bag and slung the bag back over her shoulder.

BUILDING 41

Satisfied that her first task was complete, she moved swiftly now, almost running along the tunnel throwing light switches one after the other. After little more than five minutes she came to a branch and took the left turn that Johnny had said led to the stores basement. It ended in a flight of steps. She smiled and made her way up the stairs, stopping at the summit. The stores were closed between 1230 and 1315 hrs. She listened. Satisfied that there was no one on the other side of the door, she reached out and pulled a lever in the wall. The lever sprung the trap door above her head. She climbed the remaining steps and stepped out in the basement of the Park's main stores. She looked around trying to get her bearings.

Martha had been to the stores several times and had, on occasion, visited the basement, collecting stock for Mr McFarlane but she'd had no idea at all of the location of the tunnel entrance, even though she'd known from Johnny that it must be there, somewhere. It had been on one such occasion, less than a week before, that she'd come across several large boxes at the back of the store. When she'd looked inside them it was rather obvious that they had been mislabelled. Presumably deliberately so. The electronic valves and other parts they contained would be worth a small fortune on the thriving black market. She had considered reporting it to the Quartermaster but, in the end, had decided not to involve herself, a decision that would, assuming that she could relocate them now, be fortuitous, at least for Mr Gorbold.

She had worried that she might struggle to find them again but, in the event, relocated them without difficulty. She pulled the boxes out and ferried them up, one at a time, to the stores main desk. There, she found a requisition book and scribbled a note to the Quartermaster to the effect that the boxes were for Mr Gorbold who would be in to collect them shortly after 1315 hrs.

Having completed the task, Martha ran. Back down the steps from the stores basement, along the tunnel, switching lights off as she went and finally back up the steps into the little building with the strange contraption on the roof. She shut the trap door, put the key from the switch back into the compartment in the drawer and, just as her watch showed 1pm, stepped back out into the wind that had now been joined by sleet. She closed and locked the door behind her and walked swiftly away from Building 41, greatly relieved and looking forward to her weekend in London. Because tonight Martha Watts was going home.

CHAPTER TWENTY-FOUR

Wednesday, May 4, 2005

I was going to have it out with Neufeld. Whatever was going on with her, there was a limit and she'd just exceeded it. In the end, though, I didn't get the chance because the Hut Seven presentation went on a lot longer than I had expected, due entirely to the Major's presence. By the time I got back to the archive, Neufeld had apparently gone home for the day.

I was sitting at my desk, contemplating calling Ellen, when the phone rang. It was Jane. She still wanted to take a look at Building 41. I'd been thinking about Jane's rationale all afternoon. Although it made some sense, I was still dubious about there being any tunnel.

There had been rumours of tunnels beneath the Park for years and it did seem entirely feasible that a place like Bletchley might have had some kind of shelter or bunker below ground to offer extra protection in the event of an air raid, both to the Park's secrets and its staff. There had even been a couple of digs. One at the bottom of a stair well in the north-east corner of B-block, adjacent to the old green hut now used by the Park's resident radio society. During the excavation, the diggers had broken through a brick wall at the bottom of the stair well, but all they'd succeeded in doing was damaging the building's foundations. As a result, the block's basement had flooded with three to four feet of water every winter since. Of a tunnel there had been not the slightest sign.

In fact, despite all the effort, not one shred of hard evidence for the existence of the suspected tunnels had ever been found and, perhaps more significantly, not a single veteran had ever come forward who was willing to admit to ever having set foot in a tunnel of any kind at Bletchley Park. So to say that I was not overly optimistic would have been an understatement. Still, I agreed to go and take a look at Building 41. I didn't really have anything to lose.

I picked up the telephone on my desk and dialled Ellen's mobile number.

She answered her phone almost immediately. 'Where the hell have you been?' she said, obviously upset.

'Are you OK? How's Elsie?'

'I've been trying to get hold of you all day.'

Shit. I'd switched off my mobile for the presentation and had completely forgotten to switch it back on again. Mostly because I'd been thinking tunnels. I put my hand in my pocket, pulled out my phone and turned it on.

'I'm sorry. I've been stuck in a presentation all afternoon.'

Shit. Eight missed calls.

'What, so you couldn't have called me during a break?'

She was right. I could have called her. I should have called her.

'I'm sorry.' I thought about making up an excuse and then thought better of it. 'I spent most of the day trying to steer the Major away from creating a diplomatic incident with a party of visiting Japanese dignitaries, and the rest of it trying to decide whether what Jane told me this morning might actually have some merit. She's got a theory about…'

'Yes, I know,' Ellen interrupted.

'You know?'

'I spoke to Jane earlier.'

BUILDING 41

I should have guessed that she would have. 'Right. Well, she wants me to…'

'Yes, I know. She told me.'

Jesus. Maybe we should just have Jane move in with us and be done with it. I thought it, but I didn't say it. 'Right.'

'So what do you think about this Building 41? Could there be a tunnel beneath it?'

'I don't know,' I said doubtfully. I told her about the rumours and the fact that nothing had ever been found.

'It's worth a look though, right?'

'Sure. Why not? We're not exactly falling over ourselves with leads, let's face it.'

Ellen said nothing.

'Are you all right?' I said after a pause.

'No. Not really,' she said, sounding suddenly vulnerable.

'Why? What's the matter?'

'I want to come home.'

I was surprised. She'd been adamant about wanting to stay near to Elsie. I was wondering what had changed. 'Then come home.'

Suddenly, Ellen was sobbing.

'Hey. What's the matter? Has Elsie taken a turn for the worse?'

'No. No she's… if anything, she's stabilised. It's looking a bit more promising.'

'That's great.'

'Yes, I know.'

'Then what?'

'I don't know how to explain it.'

This really wasn't like Ellen at all. 'Explain what?'

'There's something not right here, Harry. I don't know what it is. I don't know what the hell is going on. Something is just not right.'

'Not right in what way? What do you mean?' We'd agreed that she'd come home if there was the slightest sign of Möller or any kind of trouble.

'I can't put my finger on it.' She hesitated.

'Maybe you're just over tired. It's been one hell of a week.' I hadn't meant to sound dismissive, but that is how it sounded and Ellen picked up on it immediately.

'I'm not making it up, Harry,' she said irritably.

'I didn't say you were. I just meant…'

'Don't you dare tell me I'm imagining things,' she snapped.

'I wouldn't. I'm not,'

'God knows I've supported you often enough when you've had a feeling about stuff.'

She was right. She had. 'Look, I'm not… I'm just saying…'

'And I'm being followed.'

'You're what?'

'I'm being followed and the house is being watched. I mean, Natalia's place. I'm sure of it. Last night there was a car outside.'

'I should hope so,' I said feeling relieved. 'Elsie was involved in a shooting, Ellen. The police will be watching you like a hawk, for any sign of Möller and, if they aren't, they bloody well should be,'

Ellen said nothing.

'What?'

'It wasn't the police.'

'How do you know that?'

'Because I called them and they denied it,' she hesitated. 'Well, all right, they didn't exactly deny it, but they didn't admit it either. If it was them Harry, and they're watching me for my own protection then why not just admit it?'

I thought about it. She did have a point. 'Maybe, its just procedure.'

There was a pause. 'Harry, can I ask you something?' She didn't wait for my permission. 'Why is it when you get a feeling about something, I believe you without question. I've even given it a fucking name.'

I was getting worried about her now. Ellen rarely used the 'f'-word. When she did it meant that she was stressed.

'But,' she continued. 'I get a feeling and you look for every reason you can think of to dismiss it.'

Very stressed.

'I'm not dismissing it. I'm just trying to reassure you.'

'Yeah? Well maybe I don't need your reassurance right now. I'm not a fucking five year old.'

Shit. This conversation was going rapidly downhill. 'I'm sorry, love,' I said, trying to sound conciliatory.

'Oh, for fuck's sake.'

I could feel my own temper beginning to rise. 'Look, if you're telling me that you're not comfortable with something there, then that is good enough for me. I'll jump on the scooter, pick up the car from home and come and get you. If I'd had my way, you wouldn't have been there in the first place. Staying in Southwold was your idea.'

There was a silence.

'Then there's Natalia,' Ellen said, in a slightly softer tone.

'What about her?' I asked, trying to keep my voice calm.

'She's evasive.'

'In what way?'

'In every way. She'll happily talk about Elsie all night long. In fact, she's been asking me so many questions about Elsie that at times its felt like an interrogation. But ask her about herself. How she can afford to rent The Teepee. About what she's doing in England. About her family. And she's just evasive. I've been staying with her for three days and I know nothing more about her than I did a week ago.'

I thought about Natalia. Her reaction to passing us Elsie's message and the thing about not being trusted had been strange. As though she might be having some sort of crisis of conscience. 'What's with her and Petra Neufeld?' I said almost to myself.

'Neufeld? Your new researcher?'

I was impressed that she had remembered. 'Yes.'

'What about her?'

'She's a fruit cake. I caught her spying on me and Jane today.'

'Spying?'

'When I went up to see Jane this morning. To hear her big reveal. It was probably nothing.'

'About Building 41?' Ellen asked.

'Yes. When I got up to leave, I'm sure I caught a glimpse of Neufeld disappearing around the back of Hut Three.'

'Why would she have been spying on you?'

'I don't know,' I said, honestly.

'What the hell's going on Harry?' Ellen said after a moment's silence. 'It is like nobody is telling us the truth. Not Natalia, the Jackson's, the police. I hate to say it but I don't even know who Gran is anymore. What the hell is going on?'

She was right. It was bewildering. Everything around us seemed to be nothing but smoke and mirrors. 'Trust no one. That's what she said, Ellen. I'm beginning to think that it was good advice.'

'I know but we can't do this on our own, can we?'

'I'm not sure that I know what it is that we're supposed to be doing. But I tell you what. Whatever it is, we should be doing it together. I'm going to come and get you.'

There was a silence. 'All right. But look, Natalia is taking me up to James Paget this evening. How about you check out Building 41 with Jane and then come and pick me up in the morning? Can you take a couple of hours off to drive over? I can be ready as early as you like?'

'I'd rather come tonight.'

'Really?'

'Yes. Really. I don't like you being over there when we're both feeling like this.'

'I'll be fine. Look I'm sorry for losing it. It's just all the worry. I can wait until the morning. Honestly. I'll be fine.'

I thought about it. 'No. I tell you what, I will check out Building 41 with Jane. She's chomping at the bit and, to be honest, so am I. Let's face it, Jane is usually right about stuff.'

BUILDING 41

'OK.'

'That's not going to take more than an hour or so. Then I'll jump in the car and drive over. If you are still up at the hospital I'll pick you up from there. Otherwise, I'll meet you at Natalia's place. I can be there by...' I looked at my watch. 'Say, half nine?'

'Great. That sounds great.' The relief in her voice was self evident. 'Be careful in Building 41. Don't go falling down any holes.'

I laughed. 'Don't worry. We won't find any holes. If it was going to be that easy they'd have been found already.'

'Good. But still be careful.'

'I will.'

'Thanks Harry. I love you.'

I knew that she did. Even when she was pissed off with me, I knew it.

*****

'Well if it ever needed a key it sure as hell doesn't need one now,' I said, looking at the broken doors. They looked like they had been jemmied open. Probably by vandals forcing their way into the little building to strip it of anything valuable. Security on this side of the Park was lamentable. Most of the derelict buildings had been looted and vandalised years ago.

'They can't be original,' said Jane. 'Doors like that wouldn't have lasted five minutes in an air raid.'

She was right. These doors had been mostly glass. There were six, now empty panels in each. Hardly suitable for a wartime building. 'Guess so,' I said, stepping gingerly over the threshold and feeling the broken glass snap and crunch beneath my feet.

Inside, Building 41 was a complete mess. The roof had been leaking quite badly in places and mother nature had already gained a foothold here and there. Left unchecked, my guess was that she'd have the whole place pretty much under her spell in another season or two.

'Look at this,' said Jane, running her hand across a patch of wall plaster on which the grey/green paint had begun to peel in a most elaborate fashion. It looked as though the wall had been delicately camouflaged with thousands of tiny green leaves. They crackled as Jane ran her hand over them and tumbled, in tiny pieces, to the floor.

'I hate seeing these buildings in this state,' I said. And meant it. It was a disgrace that so much of the Park was being allowed to disintegrate. Right under our noses. 'It gets to me.'

Jane said nothing.

Across the back of the main room was a wooden bench that had collapsed. Above us was what looked like the remains of the mechanism that must have once turned the direction finding antenna on the roof. Part of the ceiling had fallen in, exposing the rotting wooden rafters that held the mechanism in place. I wondered how much it weighed and what the odds were of it collapsing in the next hour. Because I sure as hell didn't want to be beneath it when it did.

The room that we had entered was, maybe, ten feet square. The only place for a tunnel entrance was in the floor. I pushed away some debris with my foot. Solid concrete.

'No trapdoor then?' said Jane.

'Concrete. No trapdoor. No tunnel,' I said, a little gloomily.

'Let's try in here,' Jane suggested, indicating a doorway to our right. I followed her into the side room. It was in a marginally worse state than the main room. Here, the roof had collapsed altogether in one corner, revealing patches of sunlight through which rain had evidently been pouring for an indeterminate period but long enough to give a buddleia sapling a fighting chance at survival among the debris. Somehow it had managed to gain a foothold in the deteriorating concrete floor. I stood and marvelled at the hardiness of the thing.

BUILDING 41

'More of the same,' Jane said staring at the floor. 'Solid concrete.'

She was right. If there ever was any kind of entrance way, which looking at the floor I doubted, it had subsequently been buried beneath a layer of concrete.

We explored the room in silence. It didn't take us long. There wasn't much to see.

'What do you reckon this is?' Jane called out, just as I was beginning to lose interest.

I turned. 'What?' I walked across to her. 'Light switch?'

Whatever it was had been painted over, several times.

'With a keyhole?'

I looked more closely. What we were were looking at appeared to be some kind of key operated switch. I tapped it with my knuckle. It sounded hard and brittle. Bakelite. Or possibly some other kind of early plastic. In the centre of it, barely visible under several layers of old paint was the slot for a key. Jane stared at me.

'What?'

She raised her eyebrows like I was supposed to know what she was thinking. It took me a few moments to catch up. 'Yeah, well there's no way we're finding that out anytime soon.'

'You're sure about that, are you?' she said, with that cleverdick face I had come to know and hate.

'That,' I said examining the switch again, 'is completely clogged with paint. You're never going to get our key in there.'

'Oh ye of little faith,' Jane said, pulling a set of screw drivers from her pocket.

She removed the smallest screwdriver and put the others back in her pocket. While Jane set to work on the switch, scraping away little flecks of paint from the key slot, I explored the room again. I wondered what equipment had been here. The only signs of it were the electrical sockets and trunking gullies that ran along the top of the bench and up the adjoining wall, presumably to feed wires through to the room next door and maybe out to the antenna on the roof.

'I need something smaller,' Jane announced, looking at me over her shoulder. 'Paperclip?' she added hopefully.

I put my hand in my trouser pocket, fished around a bit and pulled out, among other things, a paperclip.

'You have your uses,' she said, grinning.

While Jane applied the paperclip I bent down to examine the buddleia more closely. That it had managed to survive in a concrete floor was a miracle of nature. Somehow it had forced its roots into what, originally, was probably no more than a hairline crack. Having done so, it had set about the business of widening the crack, forcing its way deeper in search of water and sustenance. The gap in the concrete had widened in places to perhaps an inch. Certainly no more. I ran my finger along the crack.

'Oi. Percy Thrower. You do have the key I take it?'

I hesitated. I wasn't sure what I was seeing. 'Eh?' I turned round. Jane was holding out her hand.

I stood up, fished around in my other pocket, took out the key and handed it to her.

'What do you reckon?' she said, staring at me.

I pulled a face.

She readied the key. 'I name this switch...' And then she pushed the key into the slot. '41B?' she said. Or tried to. Because the key didn't fit. Not even close.

'It's just as well then, isn't it?'

Jane turned towards me. I so wish I'd had a camera. The expression on her face was priceless. 'What is?'

I grinned. 'Would you like to know where the trap door is?'

CHAPTER TWENTY-FIVE

'You should have seen her face,' I said, reliving the moment and enjoying it all over again. 'It was an absolute bloody picture. She had been so utterly convinced that the key was going to fit.'

'I bet,' Ellen replied, finishing the coffee we'd picked up from the garage and placing the empty cup into the holder in the door of the Saab.

'Let's face it, there aren't many things that Jane doesn't do well, but failure is one of them.'

'I hope you didn't rub her nose in it,' Ellen added, disapprovingly.

'Err.. Yes I bloody did.'

'Oh, Harry, honestly.'

'Hey. When was the last time I got one over on Jane Mears?'

Ellen shrugged.

'I'll tell you when. Never.'

'You two are like school children.'

I couldn't really argue with that.

'So, this trap door you found. When do you think…'

'Hey, hang on,' I said, interrupting her. 'I didn't say that it was definitely a trap door. It could just as easily be a manhole cover or even a drain.'

'All right. But when do you think you're going to be able to lift it to find out?'

Which was a more complex question than I suspected Ellen realised. 'Depends.'

'On?'

'On whether we do it the official way or the unofficial way.'

Ellen turned and stared at me. The light from the street lamps illuminated her face in pulses as we passed them by. 'What do you mean?'

'Well if we do it officially, we'll need permission. Not just from the Major, but probably from the trustees and maybe from the Council. You can't just go into one of these buildings with a Kango and start digging up the floor.'

'So how long is that going to take?'

'How long's a piece of string? The Park is notoriously slow to authorise anything and, if it has to go to the trustees, there's no telling that they'll even agree. Since the last dig in B-block wrecked the damp course and flooded the basement, they've developed a bit of an aversion to tunnel hunting.'

'Understandably.'

'Which adds to the case for doing it unofficially.'

'All very well if you find something. What if you find nothing? I mean, you find a manhole or a drain. How is the Major going to take to finding a hole in the floor of one of his buildings?'

'He'll want to throw me down it, that's how he'll take it. So if we take the unofficial route, it will have to be done after hours. If we find nothing, we blame the hole on vandals. If, and when, it gets noticed.'

'I don't know Harry. Supposing you're discovered? You might have celebrity status, but you're not bullet proof. Could you lose your job?'

I shrugged.

Ellen was thoughtful. 'Do we have a choice?'

I said nothing.

'I mean, if the answer to all this is down there. Somewhere. Then can we afford to ignore the possibility of locating it?'

BUILDING 41

I waited. I wanted Ellen to come to the same conclusion that I had come to.

'Gran wants us to discover it. I'm certain of that. Otherwise, she would not have passed us the key and the message. Whatever this object is, Möller wants it and is prepared to kill for it. When I think about what he did to her...' Ellen's voice trailed away into silence.

I reached for her hand.

'Sooner or later Möller is going to turn his attention to us. Gran clearly thought so.'

'If he hasn't already,' I said quietly.

Ellen faced me. 'What do you mean?'

I tried to keep my eyes on the road. 'When I got back to the house this evening to pick up the car, I finally got to meet our neighbour.'

'Did you? Which one?'

'Charlie. His name's Charlie.'

'And?'

'And I was right about him keeping an eye on the place.' I risked a glance at her. 'According to Charlie, we're being watched.'

'We're always being watched,' Ellen said dismissively. 'Bloody paparazzi...'

'Except for one thing,' I interrupted. 'This guy doesn't carry a camera.'

'Oh come on,' Ellen said, sounding nervous.

'He's seen him three times. Same bloke. First time, the day we got back from Southwold after Elsie had her turn. We pulled up outside and a car turned in to the flats across the road. As we were opening the front door, Charlie reckons that a man appeared in the alley opposite and watched us enter the house.'

Ellen said nothing.

'Second time. A couple of days later. Charlie can't remember which day. Wednesday or Thursday, he thought. You went off to work in the Saab. The same man, pulled out behind you.'

'I would have noticed,' Ellen said dismissively. 'What was he driving?'

'Beamer. Dark grey or black. Charlie wasn't sure.'

Ellen hesitated. 'I would have noticed...' But she was uncertain. I could hear it in her voice.

'Last time. The day before the funeral. Early. Charlie had got up to let their dog out. As soon as he opened the back door she went nuts.'

'I vaguely remember that,' Ellen said.

'You do?'

'Yes. I couldn't sleep. I remember the dog barking.'

'He says that he put his head over the gate and caught a glimpse of the same man disappearing down the alley. He hauled Daisy back in - that's the dog's name - and went to the front window. Same car. A dark BMW pulled out from the flats across the road and drove away. He was going to call the police.'

'So why didn't he?'

I thought about it. 'Don't know. He didn't say.'

'Great.'

I waited.

'We don't know it was Möller.'

'You're right. We don't.'

'How did Charlie describe him?'

'Big. Broad. In his fifties maybe. Bald. Not very tall.'

'Great.'

It was Möller. I had little doubt about it.

'That's all we need,' Ellen added.

'Which makes this a little too urgent to do officially doesn't it?'

Ellen said nothing.

I risked another glance. Ellen was staring ahead. 'Are you all right?' I squeezed her hand.

'Trust nobody,' she said suddenly. 'That's what Elsie said. Trust nobody. You've got to do this, Harry and nobody can know about it. If Möller discovers that we're onto something, God knows what he'll do.'

'I know.' The thought had crossed my mind.

'You can't tell anyone. Just you, me and Jane. Mike, of course. Nobody else.'

I waited.

'In fact, no one must even suspect. If word gets back to Möller then none of us will be safe. And it's not just you and me. You know what he's capable of. He could easily take Mike or Jane, or anyone else who is close to us.'

Which was exactly the conclusion I'd reached.

*****

I'd no idea of the time but my phone was playing "Girl On The Phone". I could see the phone flashing on the cabinet beside my bed. I reached out, grabbed it, pressed the answer button and put the phone to my ear. I didn't recognise the voice but it was female. 'Who is this?'

Quite without warning, the room was flooded with light and Ellen was speaking.

'Yes? Who is this?' I repeated.

Ellen's face came into focus. 'Who?' she mouthed. Looking worried.

I pulled a face, like I didn't know. For a moment, I really didn't. And then it clicked. Neufeld. What the fuck was Neufeld doing calling me in the middle of the night? What the fuck was Neufeld doing with my mobile phone number? 'What do you want? It's...' I hesitated, looking for my watch.

'Half past two,' said Ellen. 'What's wrong? Who is it?'

Even half asleep I could hear the stress in Neufeld's voice.

'Put it on speaker phone.'

'What?' I was trying to listen to Neufeld and Ellen at the same time.

'Oh, for God's sake, give it here.'
I handed Ellen the phone and pulled myself up onto my elbows.
'Harry? Are you there?'
Now we could both hear her.
'Yes. What's going on?'
'I'm in trouble.'

CHAPTER TWENTY-SIX

However fast I drove, it was going to take us at least twenty minutes to get there. I hoped to God that Neufeld was going to be all right.

'This is crazy. Do you even know where we're going?' Ellen said, irritably.

'Yes.' I hesitated. 'Roughly.'

'Roughly,' Ellen echoed.

'So, I'll call her when we get closer. I couldn't just leave her. You heard her.'

Ellen sighed. 'I didn't say that. Will you please slow down?'

I glanced at the dashboard. I was doing eighty-five. I backed my foot off the accelerator.

'What I don't understand,' Ellen said suddenly, 'is why Neufeld?'

I had been asking myself the same question.

'I mean, why not one of us? Jane, maybe?'

'He's being careful,' I said, thinking out loud. 'In case we're being watched.' I glanced in my wing mirror. I could see nothing but darkness. Good luck to anyone who might be trying to follow us along the bypass, with their lights off.

'I don't know. Something about this just doesn't feel right,' Ellen said.

'Why?'

'Well, are you sure about her?' Ellen asked. 'You said yourself that she was spying on you and Jane. That she's been behaving oddly. Has it occurred to you that this might be a trap of some kind?'

I turned towards her. 'What are you saying? That the two of them are working together?'

'Maybe.'

'Oh, come on. You heard how terrified she was.' I was playing the scenario through in my head. We arrive to find them both waiting for us. Möller, gun in hand. But, as nutty as Neufeld might be, I just couldn't think that of her.

'So why was she watching you?' Ellen persisted.

I'd been thinking about that too. 'I don't know. Not for sure. Which is why I'm going to have it out with her.' I hesitated. 'But do you know what I think?'

I waited for her reply but Ellen said nothing.

'I think she's one of those people who just enjoys wrong footing people. You know, who gets off on it? You must have come across people like that?'

Ellen snorted. 'Not really.'

'Oh, come on. People who like to shock. Behave unpredictably. Keep you guessing about what they're going to do next.'

Ellen said nothing.

'It's a power thing. A way of getting the upper hand. There's probably nothing more to it than that.'

'Well, it sounds very annoying to me,' said Ellen, flatly. 'I'm already beginning to dislike the woman and I haven't met her yet.'

If I'd been hoping that Ellen and Neufeld were ever going to be best buddies, I had a feeling that I'd just blown it. Neufeld was intriguing. Plus, she did have a fantastic arse. Which, thinking about it, was probably something I should keep to myself.

We'd turned onto the A5 and were heading north. 'Hang on,' I said, straining to see the road sign up ahead. 'I think we come off here.'

BUILDING 41

'Are you sure?'

'Nope.' But I took the exit anyway and followed the signs for the town centre.

'Have you considered what we're going to do if he is waiting for us, whether aided by Neufeld or not?' Ellen said suddenly.

I had considered it. I just hadn't come up with any definite ideas. 'He won't be,' I said like I was confident about it.

'You know that, do you?'

'He'll be long gone,' I persisted.

'I don't know Harry. Something here just doesn't feel right.'

I wished that she'd stop saying it. That was twice now. I turned Neufeld's words over in my head. She'd said very little about what exactly had happened. Little more than that he'd been waiting for her when she'd arrived home. If she'd been making it up she was a bloody good liar.

I drove on for another ten minutes. I eventually broke the silence. 'Right, there's Pink Punters, up ahead.'

'What the hell is Pink Punters?'

'It's a gay and lesbian night club.'

'You are kidding.'

'No, I'm not.'

'In Bletchley?'

'Gay people do actually exist outside of Brighton, you know. Now it should be over the canal and first right. The station is up there on the left. I think.'

We went over the canal and I turned right.

'Don't you think you should slow down and maybe switch off your lights?' Ellen whispered.

Why in God's name was she whispering? Möller might be hiding somewhere up ahead, but he sure as hell wasn't sitting on the back seat. My eyes strayed involuntarily to the rear view mirror. 'Why?'

'In case Möller is waiting for us.'

'He won't be.'

'He might be.'

'You've been watching The Bill again haven't you?' It was a poor attempt at humour, but at that moment I wasn't at my best.

'What number did she say it was?'

'37b. There,' I said suddenly and slowed the car. 'On the left. There's a light on upstairs. See it?'

'Yes.'

I pulled the car over and stopped. It was a tree lined suburban street like any other, with semi detached houses on either side, most of them with gates and off road parking. Number 37 had evidently been converted into flats. I switched off the ignition. Then the lights. We both sat in silence. I pulled my mobile out from my pocket and called Neufeld's number. 'Petra? It's me. We're outside.' I hung up. 'Come on,' I said to Ellen. 'She'll buzz the door.' I undid my seat belt and got out. Ellen followed suit. Neither of us spoke.

I opened the gate and we both walked up to the door. It buzzed as we approached and we went inside. Neufeld's flat was on the first floor. We climbed the stairs in near darkness. Evidently the light was out. She was waiting for us at the top of the stairs but we didn't get a proper look at her until we'd stepped into her flat.

'Oh my God,' Ellen gasped, just before I caught sight of Neufeld's face. She had turned towards me. Her bottom lip was split and badly swollen and the left side of her face was already bruised. By morning my guess was that she was going to look like she'd been five rounds with Frank Bruno.

'Are you sure you're all right? I really think we should take her to casualty, Harry. That might need stitches,' Ellen said, turning back towards Neufeld.

'It is nothing,' Neufeld replied, dabbing her lip with a cold flannel that Ellen had retrieved from the researcher's bathroom.

BUILDING 41

'I can't believe that he did this to you,' I said, honestly. 'This whole business has nothing to do with you. I'm so sorry that you've been caught up in it.'

'Who is he?' Neufeld said. 'He is German, of course.'

I exchanged glances with Ellen. 'Yes. His name is Günther Möller. Or at least that is what we believe.'

'You don't know?'

I shook my head. 'Not with any certainty, no. He has used several aliases, but…' I stopped myself and glanced again at Ellen. She glared at me. *Trust no one.*

'We think that he is the same man who kidnapped Ellen, during the search for Martha Watts,' I added.

'The MP's driver?'

'Yes.'

'He says that you have something that belongs to him.'

'I think you should sit down,' Ellen interrupted. 'I think we all should.'

Neufeld's living room was sparsely furnished. There was a dining table, around which were arranged four chairs. We each pulled a chair and sat.

'Do you have this thing?' Neufeld asked.

'No, Petra. We don't. In fact we don't even know what it is,' I said honestly.

'But you know of it. You are searching for it. That is why you went to see Jane, yesterday?'

Trust no one.

'What did he want from you, Petra?' Ellen interrupted. 'Why was he here?'

Neufeld turned to face her. 'He seemed to think that I might know where you are looking.'

'What did you tell him?' I asked.

She stared at me. 'I told him to go fuck himself. Do you think that he would have done this to me,' she said, touching her face gingerly, 'if I hadn't?'

'I guess not,' I conceded.

'Why were you spying on Harry and Jane, yesterday?' Ellen asked, making little effort to conceal the accusation.

'I was curious.'

Ellen didn't believe her. I could see it in her face.

'I am still curious,' Neufeld said, looking me straight in the eye.

'It is none of your business,' Ellen said, with a little more force than was necessary. 'You need to stay out of it.'

'It was none of my business, perhaps. Until this man Möller broke into my flat and tried to smash my face. It is my business now.'

She had a point. Neufeld was not the first person to find herself dragged into the conflict with Günther Möller. She and I had that much in common. I'd had no idea, the day that Elsie had asked me to investigate what had happened to Martha Watts, that a year later I'd still be dealing with the fallout. 'Look, Petra. I'm really sorry that this has happened, but Ellen is right. You'd be better off staying out of it. The less you know, the safer you'll be.'

'Why did you call us?' Ellen interrupted.

We both stared at her.

'Why didn't you just call the police? You didn't call them, I take it.'

'No,' Neufeld replied simply.

'Why not?' Ellen persisted.

Neufeld hesitated. 'Because of this. Möller gave it to me as he was leaving.' She put her hand in her pocket, removed what looked like a photograph and handed it to me. 'I want to understand how much of a threat he is. I need to know. I want you to tell me.'

It was of a picture of a young child, standing beside an elderly woman.

'Who are they?' I asked, afraid of the answer.

'The child is called Mathilde. The picture was taken outside her school in Rüdesheim in Germany, where she lives with my mother.'

BUILDING 41

I waited.

'Mathilde is my daughter. He says that she will be taken if I go anywhere near the police.'

Ellen had paled.

I swallowed. 'Möller is a serious threat, Petra. If he has threatened you. If he has threatened your daughter, then you need to take it seriously. Very seriously indeed.'

CHAPTER TWENTY-SEVEN

Möller threatening Neufeld was a clincher, as far as I was concerned. This thing was spinning out of control again. He was more than a threat. He had once again embarked on a course of violence and intimidation in order to discover the whereabouts of whatever it was that Elsie had taken. It was evident that he knew that we were searching for it, which made us a target, along with anyone who was unfortunate enough to have associated themselves with us. Whatever it was, we needed to find it quickly. Elsie had warned us that we were in danger. By threatening Neufeld, Möller had provided all the evidence we needed that the danger was imminent.

'What if there is nothing below Building 41 Harry? What then?'

Ellen had pulled the Saab into the car park on the slip road that led to The Three Locks and we'd walked down to the canal. I'd found a bench overlooking the lock and ordered us coffee.

'Then we're screwed,' I said bleakly. I was still not confident that we would discover anything. 'Building 41 is our only lead. Möller suspects that we're looking. I don't know how. Maybe Elsie gave it away.'

Ellen started to protest.

'I'm not saying deliberately. Who knows what he beat out of her.'

Ellen relented.

BUILDING 41

'We need to move quickly. Before he realises that we've got any sort of lead. If he thinks we've found it - whatever it is - or even that we know where it is, he'll move more definitely against us. There are just too many people at stake here. You. Me. Jane, Mike. Neufeld. Your family. Her family. He could take any one of us and, if he does, we'd have no choice but to hand the key over to him and tell him everything we know.'

'What if you find it? What then? I mean, I'm not sure that I understand any of this. So we discover this...,' Ellen hesitated 'object? What if it means nothing to us? What are we going to do with it?'

I don't know why she was looking at me. I had not the slightest idea. I ran my fingers through my hair.

'Maybe we should just throw in the towel. Give the key to Möller and tell him that we want nothing more to do with it. It was never really anything to do with us, was it?'

It was an option. It had always been an option. We were at risk because of Elsie. It was her battle. Not ours. I looked at Ellen and held her eyes. 'You're no more ready to let Möller win than I am, are you?'

Ellen shook her head. 'No.'

'I didn't think so.'

Ellen sighed. 'Whatever Gran took, she spent half a life time trying to prevent him from discovering it. She's entrusted us with this. For a reason. I just wish I knew what it was.'

Amen to that. Elsie was asking us to put our lives and the lives of those around us at risk. Again. It would have been kind of nice to know why.

'She is still my Gran. I can't let her down.'

Which might have provided Ellen with a motive but, in all honesty, it wasn't doing it for me. I just didn't trust Elsie anymore. I couldn't trust her. Not after the secrets that had already been revealed. Elsie had known about my mother. She'd probably known about her all along. Yet she had never said a word. I was going to find it very difficult to forgive her for that.

'She must have had her reasons,' Ellen said, as if reading my mind once again. 'I'm not defending her, Harry. I'm not. But if she could have, she would have told you. I'm in no doubt about that.'

I frowned. 'Jesus, if anyone else tells me that they know what happened to her but can't tell me, I'll strangle them. Ted. The Jacksons. Elsie. It seems as though everybody knows but me.'

Ellen said nothing.

'In the end, it boils down to whether I've got the balls to find out, doesn't it? Because it is all linked. Somehow. Elsie. Martha. My mother and what happened to my family.'

Ellen nodded.

'Tom. Mike. Marcus's terrible injuries. This whole thing. It all goes back to Günther fucking Möller.'

'What in God's name did she take?' Ellen said suddenly. 'And what has it got to do with Möller anyway? If she took it in 1944, then unless he's a lot older than he looked the last time I saw him, he probably wasn't even born in 1944. Have you thought about that?'

I had. Like Ellen, I had no answer. 'Whatever it was, it is important enough for him to kill for. That's for bloody sure.'

We drank the remainder of our coffee in silence. I watched a pair of swans floating along the canal, poking their bills into the water and greedily filling their beaks with weed. 'Apart from Möller, there's only one other person who knows,' I said after a few minutes. 'And unless she stages a miraculous recovery, she's not going to be telling us any time soon.' I looked at my watch. 'Where the hell are they?' I said suddenly impatient. 'They're late.'

Ellen was looking over my shoulder. She smiled.

'Who is?' said a voice, from behind me.

I turned. 'You are.'

*****

BUILDING 41

'What about Neufeld?' It was Jane who had asked the question. The two of them - Jane and Mike - had bought themselves drinks at the bar and had joined us beside at the table overlooking the canal. I'd outlined the events that had unfolded at Neufeld's flat. Jane seemed unimpressed. Evidently she'd already made up her mind about the German researcher.

'My guess is that she'll be on a plane back to Germany, by now,' I answered.

'You think so?' Jane said, looking like she didn't.

'Well wouldn't you? If it was your six year old that Möller had threatened?'

'Maybe,' Jane replied. 'Unless, of course, I had just handed you a heap of bullshit.'

'Oh come on.' I made no attempt to keep the irritation out of my voice. 'Ok. So you don't much like her. Fine.' It wasn't really fine. 'But don't you think you're taking it a little far? Möller put her teeth through her bottom lip. How do you make that up?'

Jane stared at me. I could tell what she was thinking but I was having none of it.

'Whatever,' Jane said, without breaking eye contact. 'But if we're doing this tonight, we do it in complete secrecy. Just the four of us. No Neufeld. Got it?'

'For Christ's sake. He threatened her daughter. What more do you want?' Jane was beginning to seriously piss me off.

'And you take precautions,' Jane said, ignoring me. 'You need to make absolutely certain that you are not followed to Bletchley.'

'How am I going to do that?'

Jane stared at me. 'Is there a back way out of your place?'

I glanced at Ellen. 'Kind of.'

'Kind of?' Jane repeated. 'Meaning?'

'Over the wall at the bottom of the garden. Into the industrial estate.'

'Is there any possibility of being seen from the street?'

I thought about it. 'Unlikely.'

'Good. Then that's the way you leave. Mike and I will pick you up.'

'Where?'

'Give me a landmark, a mile or so away from your house.'

'A mile or so?'

'You can walk can't you?'

I stared at her. 'The church. In town. We can take the alley off Grovebury Road and walk through the park,' Ellen said.

'Good. Do you normally leave a light on at night?'

'Yes,' replied Ellen. 'In the downstairs hallway.'

'So leave it on. Do what you normally do.'

'What about tools?' I asked. 'We're going to need a pick axe. A cold chisel. A couple of spades. Torches. Maybe ropes. I can hardly cart that lot through the bloody town park.'

'There are tools in the old generator house beside E-block.'

'You know that how?' I asked.

'I know that because I looked. And before you ask, yes, I do have a key.'

I raised an eyebrow.

'I'd already decided. If you'd bottled it, I was planning on digging up the place myself.'

CHAPTER TWENTY-EIGHT

Four o'clock on a Saturday afternoon and I didn't know what to do with myself. Eighteen months ago and I'd have been in the garage working on the Lambretta or in the East Stand at Underhill watching The Bees go down to another glorious defeat. Instead, I was sat in front of the computer screen, googling Peter bloody Owen. Again. There was plenty of historic stuff. Pictures of him. Material covering the activities of the Nationalist Union back in the seventies. Video clips of NUGB demonstrations and counter demonstrations. Grainy footage of long haired men in flared jeans waving Union Jacks. Black Brixton kids with afros being dragged away by uniformed policemen. None of the riot shields and gear that gets deployed nowadays at the drop of a brick. It was like another world. Strangely little about the '77 bombing, though.

An incident like that should have been sensational. It would certainly have been sensational had it happened last week. It would have been all over the newspapers and social media. Maybe a Panorama special. Endless interviews with Jeremy Paxman on the meaning of it all. Maybe a public enquiry or two for good measure. But the reporting of the '77 bombing seemed muted in the extreme. Reluctant. As though the media had been told to play it down. The trial was barely reported at all. Jane was right. All the main NUGB heavies seemed to have been quietly spirited away. Shuffled off into obscurity, never to surface again. Except, of course, that

Jimmy Dobson aka Stephens aka Günther Möller had surfaced again. Twice now.

   The more I thought about that, the more puzzling it seemed. Dobson had clearly been involved with Owen and the NUGB. As their Head of Security he'd evidently been their number one thug. If he hadn't been directly involved in the bombing, then he must surely have been a key witness. He'd clearly been caught up in at least one murder enquiry. Knowing even the little that I knew about him, it seemed entirely plausible that he had murdered Karl Dixon, the young lad who had very probably been taught by my mother. When she wasn't working for Owen. Despite all that, it seemed that he'd been allowed to disappear. Only to pop up last year as Stephens, Max Banks's henchman, to kidnap Ellen, blackmail Tom Dabrowski into attempting my murder and then blow his face off when Tom fouled up. He'd shot Mike in the woods not far from Little Wymondley and exchanged gunfire with Jane in the tunnels below Belsize Park in an attempt to prevent Ellen's rescue. Then to pop up again to assault Elsie and threaten Petra Neufeld's daughter, Mathilde. Möller might not be public enemy number one, but surely to God he'd done enough to have had his collar felt. The bloody maniac seemed to be immune.

   Of course, Möller wasn't the only one to have used an alias. Elsie had been born Elsie Sidthorpe and had certainly been using that name in 1944 when she was at Bletchley Park, and yet by 1977 she had apparently become Rosemary Sellers. Now she was Elsie Sidthorpe again. Even my mother had been Liz Stammers for seven years by the time she'd been working for Owen. And yet there she was as Liz Muir. Staring out from the photograph with Peter Owen, looking like she wanted the ground to open up and swallow her. I'd managed to get through my 34 years as Harry Stammers. What was it with these people?

   We had to find whatever it was that Elsie had taken. Linking all of these people, places and events together. Martha Watts. Bletchley Park. Rosemary Sellers. Liz Muir. Belsize Park. Peter

BUILDING 41

Owen. Right-wing nutters. Bombs. Murders and attempted murders. Günther fucking Möller. It was doing my head in.

Which is how I almost missed it. A brief reference, buried on a left wing website, revealing, albeit in a piece that amounted to little more than a string of wild conspiracy theories, that Peter Owen had been quietly released from prison in 1998. If it was true, then Owen was out there. Had been out there for the last seven years. Doing god knows what. I wondered whether he even knew that he was my father. I wondered whether I was his only offspring. I might have a whole second half-family out there. But that was about as far as I got with thinking about it. Because at that particular moment the phone rang and Ellen appeared in the kitchen door way looking… I'm not entirely sure how to describe how she was looking. "Stunned" doesn't quite do it justice.

'It's the hospital,' she said breathlessly. 'Gran has regained consciousness.'

'I'm not having you go alone, Ellen. Not with Möller stalking us. It's too risky. We'll have to shelve the dig for tonight. Besides, if we can talk to Elsie we might be able to discover whether there really is anything below Building 41 without having to lift a pick axe.'

'Forget it. The hospital said that she is very weak and needs complete rest. We can't go bowling in there demanding answers. It may be days before we can talk to her properly. If we have to tell her anything at all, we're telling her that it's all fine. We're all fine and there is nothing at all to worry about.'

I stared at her. 'Fine.' It wasn't fine. Not really. 'But it's still not safe for you to go alone.'

Ellen stared at me. 'I'll have to. You can't delay the dig. Right now, only you, me, Jane and Mike know about it. If you move quickly, there's a chance that you can do this before Möller catches up with us. Before he knows anything about it. I'll call Natalia.'

'Natalia? You don't even trust Natalia,' I protested.

'I didn't say that I don't trust her.'

'You said that she was evasive.'

Ellen stared at me. 'I was overwrought. So Natalia didn't want to talk about her background. That's not a crime. I'll call her. I'm sure she'll come with me to the hospital and, if need be, she'll put me up for a couple of days.'

I looked at Ellen doubtfully.

'At least I won't be on my own. Okay?'

I carried on looking at her doubtfully.

'Harry, we need to do this. I need to go to Elsie. You need to find out what, if anything, is below Building 41. If we delay, we'll put everything at risk. If we move quickly, we might just gain the upper hand. For once.'

I said nothing.

'Please?'

'All right.'

CHAPTER TWENTY-NINE

Petra Neufeld stood at the window of the empty flat, watching the house opposite for any sign of movement. Since Harry and Ellen had returned from their excursion to the canal-side pub, there had been no sign of either of them. She felt the telephone in her pocket vibrate. She removed it and pressed the answer button. 'Neufeld.'

She listened. 'This morning. They met Mears and Eglund. At a local pub. They drank coffee and talked. For about an hour.'

She listened again. 'No. The waitress said that they fell silent when she served them. She heard nothing.' She paused. 'Wait.'

The door opposite had opened. Neufeld stepped back from the window. 'Carmichael is leaving.' Neufeld watched her walk to her car and open the boot. 'An overnight bag, perhaps.' she said, in answer to the question. She waited. 'Very well.'

Neufeld grabbed her crash helmet and ran for the stairs. Carmichael's Saab was already moving. The black Triumph motorcycle came to life at the first attempt. Neufeld pulled out, three cars back and followed the Saab southwards towards the bypass.

They had pulled into a service station. Neufeld watched Carmichael park the Saab and get out of the car. She was a good looking woman. Not so tall as all that, but well proportioned.

Slightly muscular, as though she worked out regularly. Neufeld had admired her physique when she and Harry had come to the flat.

She took off her helmet, locked it to the Triumph and watched Carmichael walk across the car park to the service station's main building. Stammers was a lucky man.

She followed her, at a discreet distance, pushing her way through the glass doors and scanning the faces of those inside, spotting Carmichael easily, heading for the toilets. Neufeld smiled.

She picked up a Coke and a copy of Motorcycle News from a branch of WH Smith and, having paid at the checkout, positioned herself so that when Carmichael emerged, she would not be seen.

After a few minutes, Carmichael reappeared, glanced around and then headed for the Costa Coffee. Neufeld watched her pay the barista.

Getting close to her was going be a minor risk only. Carmichael might have been expecting to be followed, but presumably not by a female, leather clad biker. She watched as Carmichael was served and found a vacant table. Fortunately there was another, immediately behind her. Neufeld approached the table casually and slid onto the seat. They were so close that, incredibly, Neufeld caught the scent of Carmichael's perfume.

Neufeld had guessed, correctly as it turned out, that the background noise level might be a blessing in disguise. Because when Carmichael made the call home, she had to raise her voice to be heard. Not by much, but it was enough to ensure that Neufeld heard almost every word.

She didn't wait for Carmichael to finish her coffee. As soon as Carmichael had ended the call, Neufeld got to her feet and walked briskly away from the table, still with her back to Carmichael, before doubling back and heading for the exit. She glanced backed towards Carmichael once, who was still seated, and then exited the building.

BUILDING 41

Less than five minutes later, she had taken the next exit, ridden across the bridge, re-joined the A14 and was nudging 85mph back towards Bedfordshire and Leighton Buzzard.

A little under two hours later, Ellen was manoeuvring the Saab into a space at the James Paget Hospital. 'Are you sure they didn't mind you taking the afternoon off?' she said, glancing across at the nurse.

Natalia shrugged. 'I swapped shifts. They don't care as long as the shifts are covered.'

Ellen scanned the car park as she got out of the Saab. It was vast. Hundreds of spaces. Most of them occupied. People walking to and from their cars. It was impossible to tell whether any of them were watching. But if she'd been followed, she reasoned, she'd have noticed. She had been paying close attention.

'You think we're being watched?' Natalia said, staring at her from the opposite side of the car.

It was Ellen's turn to shrug. 'Maybe.' She turned and clicked the central locking.

Natalia had walked around the car. 'By Günther Möller?'

'I don't know, Natalia.'

They started to walk toward the hospital entrance. She was thinking about what she was going to say to Elsie. She'd told Harry that she'd no intention of questioning her until she was properly recovered, but that hadn't been the whole truth. Or any part of the truth, really. The point was that she hadn't wanted Harry there when she did.

'What makes you think this?' Natalia pressed.

Even if Harry had been wrong about Elsie's purpose in asking him to look for Martha Watts, he was right that she had exposed him to Günther Möller. That was bad enough. But it had also become evident that she had been hiding the full truth from them all along and from Ellen, most of her life. Ellen wanted to know why. It was a matter, firstly between the two of them. As much as she loved Harry, this was a conversation she needed to have with her great aunt alone.

Natalia said nothing more while they negotiated a crossing, both dashing across the road to avoid an oncoming ambulance. 'If not Möller, then who? The police perhaps?' she said when they had reached the other side.

Ellen stopped in her tracks and faced the Russian nurse. 'Look, what is this Natalia? The third degree?'

Natalia looked at her blankly. 'Third degree. What is this third degree?'

'You know perfectly well what I mean. When are you going to stop play acting, Natalia? When are you going to start telling the truth?'

For the first time, Natalia looked flustered. 'The truth? What truth am I not telling you?'

They had stopped outside the main entrance to the hospital.

'I tell you what,' Ellen said, flatly, 'you tell me how you can afford The Teepee on a nurse's salary, and I'll tell you exactly what I think.' She watched the nurse's reaction.

There was a flash of anger in her eyes, quickly masked. 'I worked for some wealthy people in London before I came to Southwold. They pay me so well, I have some money.'

She had sounded hurt. Real or feigned? It was impossible to tell.

'I use my money to live in a nice house. Is that a problem for you, Ellen?'

Finished with a challenge.

'No. It's not a problem for me, but I'll tell you what is? Secrets and lies, Natalia. Secrets and bloody lies. I am sick to death of them.' Ellen was close to tears. She hadn't meant to let her emotions get the better of her, but they had.

Natalia said nothing. Instead, she stared. It didn't seem to Ellen that there was any defiance in her silence, but rather just a whole heap of pained indecision. As though inside her head there was an argument raging. Ellen could see the battle lines laid out on the

BUILDING 41

Russian's forehead. It was Ellen who surrendered first. 'I'm sorry. I didn't mean to shout at you. It's not you. I…' she hesitated.

'You don't need to apologise. It is nothing. You are upset.'

Ellen had removed a tissue from her pocket and was dabbing her eyes to stop her make up from running. 'Let's just go in. Shall we?' She grasped the nurse's shoulder. 'I'm sorry.' She tried to smile. 'I need to see Elsie.'

They entered the hospital, made their way to reception, and within a few minutes, Ellen was seated beside her great aunt's bed.

CHAPTER THIRTY

Sunday, January 12, 1958, Near Rüdesheim, West Germany

It was cold. So bitterly cold that his finger tips stung when he rubbed his hands together. He could barely feel his toes at all, as he pushed the wooden train across the stone floor.

'Boy! Throw some wood on the fire. I'm as cold as a well digger's balls.'

He glanced toward the hearth. The fire had died to little more than a smoulder. He was afraid to tell his father that there was no more wood in the basket.

'Boy! I said wood! Do you hear me?'

Mama reckoned that it had been the coldest winter in ten years. He didn't know about that. He could only remember three or maybe four but he'd certainly never known a winter like this one. Snow, half way to the tops of the windows in the morning. The Stegbach, the river that ran across the fields behind the village, to Geisenheim and down into the big river, frozen solid. No way to get to school, had the school been open, which it wasn't. No work for Mama. Which meant that they went hungry more often than not. 'But Papa…'

'Shhh Günny,' his Mama interrupted. 'Leave that and come,' she added, pulling him away from the toy train. 'There is some in the

BUILDING 41

out house. Let us put on our coats and boots and bring some for the fire.'

His father grunted and took a long draught from the bottle that had been resting on the chest beside his chair.

The wind in the yard outside was icy. It tugged at his coat sleeves as they as they fought their way across the yard toward the little outhouse that doubled as both the water closet and a wood store. His mother threw open the door. The logs were stacked in a pile behind the door. Or what was left of them. He didn't think they'd last much longer.

'You may as well use the toilet while we are out here,' his mother said. He watched her studying the wood pile, the worry etched in lines on her face.

He shook his head.

'Go on,' she instructed.

He shook his head again. 'It is too cold. My pee man will fall off.'

She smiled. 'Get on with you,' she said fondly, turning to take a log from the pile, but gasping as she did and clutching her side.

'Mama? Are you sick?' He said, afraid.

Her eyes seemed glassy and vacant.

'I will go fetch Papa,' he said, now properly frightened.

She caught hold of his arm and shook her head. 'No,' she said, breathing in sharply through her nose and exhaling though her mouth. Her breath was a cloud of wispy white vapour that sailed up toward the ceiling like dragon smoke. 'No,' she repeated more steadily. 'Just give me a moment and I'll be fine.'

He could see that she was in pain and not for the first time. It made him angry. 'Why does Papa do nothing?' he said indignantly.

'You know why,' she reproached him gently.

'I know what people say behind our backs. They say that he's a drunk. That he is not right in the head.'

The slap across his face stung like crazy and made his eyes fill with tears.

'Don't you ever say that about your papa. If that is what people say then they are ignorant pigs. Your father was a hero of The Reich. Trusted by the Führer, himself.'

He stared at her in defiance. Determined to prevent the tears in his eyes from rolling down his cheeks like a baby, he held them there by force of will. 'Then why must we never speak of it to anyone? Ulrich is always boasting that Herr Holtzmann fought on the Eastern Front.'

'Holtzman,' she said scornfully 'is a filthy communist. A traitor who cares nothing for the Fatherland. Your father fought for the Führer. Here,' she said, handing him a log from the pile. 'You just remember that.'

'Then why does Herr Holtzmann drive a Borgward, while we must walk? Why does Ulrich have fine clothes and books, while we have nothing but rags?' he said, holding out his arms to illustrate the point.

His mother stared at him. He didn't think he'd ever spoken to her like this.

'Enough of this,' she said, sternly, but there was a hint of something in her voice. He could hear it. It made him feel good.

'We must feed the fire. Or we will all freeze,' she said, handing him another log.

'We may as well freeze,' he said, bravely.

'I said enough.' She pushed past him with an armful of logs and shoved open the door with her elbow. 'Now come.'

He tramped across the yard behind her, the half frozen slush crunching beneath his boots.

They entered the house. He waited by the door while his mother disgorged her pile of logs in a heap beside the hearth before returning to him. 'Here,' she said, taking the logs from him. 'Take off your boots.'

'Hurry up,' said his father. 'Do you want me to freeze?'

His mother was loading the fire with logs. 'Günny wanted to know why Herr Holtzmann…' she said the name like it was acid in

BUILDING 41

her mouth, 'drives Ulrich to school in a Borgward while we have to walk.'

'Mama!' he exclaimed.

'Herr Holtzmann,' his father scoffed. 'You would rather you were a Holtzmann would you, boy.'

'No, Papa,' he replied honestly. For all their comforts, his mother was right. Herr Holtzmann was a pig and Ulrich was a show off.

'Come here, boy,' his father gestured, roughly.

He hesitated. His father had been drinking. The drink made him scary. He'd be nice one minute and nasty the next. A word out of place and he'd tan his backside. Or worse.

'I said come.'

He glanced at his mother. She nodded reassuringly. 'Go on. I'll warm you some milk.'

He approached his father cautiously.

'Here,' his father said, indicating that he should sit on the arm of the chair.

He did it. His father smelt of beer and sweat.

'So, what's this about the Holtzmanns?'

He shrugged.

'Have you been fighting with Ulrich Holtzmann?'

He shrugged again. 'Maybe.'

'I hope you thrashed him.'

'He says bad things about us.'

His father snorted. 'And what do you say?'

'I tell him that he's nothing but a filthy Red.'

His father laughed. 'Well good for you, boy.'

They were silent.

'Tell me the story Papa.'

His father picked up the bottle, drained it and placed it back on the chest beside his chair.

'Tell me about our real name. About the submarine and how you came to hurt your leg. About the King and the British traitors and how we are going to make them pay, one day.'

His father was staring across to the now roaring fire.
'Tell me about the codebook.'

CHAPTER THIRTY-ONE

I lit a cigarette, inhaled and let the smoke out through my nose. Ellen had called about an hour before I left. They'd only seen Elsie briefly and were back in Southwold at Natalia's place. *The Teepee.* What the hell was that all about?

The square in front of the Church was deserted. The Golden Bell had been closed for an hour or so, I guessed. The only sound was the whistle of the breeze in the trees around the church and the whine of a train in the distance. Probably the late train up from London.

By the sound of it, nothing much had been said between Ellen and Elsie. Ellen had adhered to her plan of saying nothing to distress the old lady. Although she'd said that they were going back tomorrow. By then, if everything went to plan, I hoped that we'd know what was below Building 41. If everything went to plan, which until that moment, at least, it had. And then I heard the sound of footsteps. I turned and stared at the approaching figure in open mouthed disbelief.

'Harry.'

Neufeld. She was dressed in black leather. Like she'd just stepped off her bike. 'What the hell are you doing here?' Jane was going to go ape shit.

'I followed you.' She said it matter of factly. Like it was a perfectly reasonable thing to be saying.

'What? Why?'

'I'm keeping an eye on you. In case you get into trouble.'

I was having difficulty keeping a grasp of reality. 'I thought you were going back to Germany.'

'What gave you that idea?'

What was she playing at? What did she think had given me that idea? 'Möller? Your daughter?'

'Mathilde is fine. My mother has taken her to a safe place.'

'And what do you mean you're following me? How did you follow me, for fuck's sake? I left by the back door. It's the middle of the night.'

Neufeld smiled. 'I was watching. You came to your front window. With your coat on. When you didn't come out of the front, I guessed you were leaving by the back. I was right. Too obvious Harry. You should be more careful.'

I stared at her. 'Look, I don't know…'

'Harry. There is something you should know about me. I am not a victim. I have never been a victim and I don't intend to become one now. When this man, Möller did this to me…' She touched her face. 'And threatened Mathilde, he was trying to make me into a victim. He will not succeed.'

I snorted. 'You've no idea what you're dealing with.'

'Do you?'

'I've got a bloody good idea.'

'So tell me.'

I stared at her.

'I did not ask to become involved in this, Harry. I came to England thinking I would be studying at Bletchley Park. Intrigued by the story I had read about the famous Harry Stammers.'

I could feel my resolve beginning to waver. The trouble was that I liked her. I just couldn't help it.

'Now I find myself in the middle of the story.'

'You're not *involved,* Petra, and this isn't a story. You don't want to be involved. Go back to Germany. Do yourself a favour.' I

BUILDING 41

pulled another cigarette from the packet I'd fished from my jacket pocket.

Neufeld held out her hand.

'You don't even smoke,' I said, exasperated.

'I do now. I like it. I like you. In any case, you need my help. If Möller had been watching you, it might have been him here with you now. Instead of me.'

I gave her a cigarette and held out my lighter.

She cupped her hands around mine as I struck a flame. She put the cigarette to her mouth and inhaled. 'What you're looking for. This thing that Möller wants that is important enough to him that he is willing to threaten my daughter. I want to know why. I want to know what it is.'

I thought I'd try one last time. 'Why, for fuck's sake? He's killed for it already, you know. We're not messing about here. Möller is dangerous. I mean, seriously dangerous.'

'You ask why? You of all people should know. We're researchers, you and I. We encounter a mystery and we want to understand. To solve the puzzle. The harder it becomes the more we want to know and the further we will go to get to the truth.'

She was right about that. I heard the sound of a car in the distance. *Shit.*

'Your friend Jane, perhaps?'

I stared at her. 'She is going to have a bloody fit,' I said, shaking my head.

'But you will convince her. To take me with you.'

'You don't know Jane,' I replied, watching the car approach with a sinking feeling in my guts.

We had driven to Bletchley in silence. I'd thought that Jane was going to turn around and drive away again at the sight of Neufeld. It had been Mike who had stopped her. I'd seen the smirk on his face. I think he was enjoying my discomfort. Jane had pulled off

Sherwood Drive onto the building site that ran across the top of the Park's northern boundary.

'Where are we going?' I said, breaking the silence.

'Through the front gate,' Jane said with heavy sarcasm. 'Where do you think we're going?'

'I don't know. That's why I asked,' I replied, not even attempting to mask my irritation.

Neufeld and I were sat in the back of Jane's Volvo. I was sure I could see Neufeld smiling lopsidedly in the darkness, her bottom lip still badly swollen.

'There's a gap in the fence behind G-block. We can get into the Park from there.'

Jane drew the Volvo to a halt and we got out. The land had been cleared but not much else. A new housing estate was going up. Apparently. We trudged through the mud in single file. How I managed to avoid falling arse over tit in the darkness I'll never know. I had stashed several torches in the bag slung over my shoulder, but Jane didn't want us to use them until we were out of sight of the road. Not that there was anyone about. It was after one in the morning.

Pretty soon we picked up the Park's perimeter fence. It didn't amount to much. Mesh panels joined together with rusty steel clamps. The darkness seemed to envelop us as we progressed. I was glad that Jane knew where we going, because I sure as hell didn't.

We eventually found the gap in the fence, and stepped through opposite a back entrance into derelict G-block. The block's doors had been torn from their hinges. Presumably by vandals in search of something of value to nick. Most of the internal metal work had already been stripped. I was amazed they hadn't taken the metal window frames. It was probably only a matter of time. We skirted the Park's northern boundary and eventually found the little roadway that led southwards towards the roundabout between D and E blocks. Building 41 was up ahead on our left.

BUILDING 41

'You and Mike wait here,' Jane said, as we neared our destination. 'Me and Evel Knievel will go and get the tools.'

We stopped alongside Building 41. Jane held out her hand.

I stared at her.

'Torches, dipshit. Unless you've got night vision goggles.'

Mike sniggered.

I took the torches from my bag and handed them out.

'Don't go waving them around,' Jane said, like she thought me an idiot. 'Come on,' and with that Jane and Neufeld trudged off into the darkness.

'Nice one Harry. Springing Neufeld on us was a masterstroke,' Mike said, once they were out of earshot.

'I did not spring her on you. I had no bloody choice. She sprung herself on me. I didn't ask her along, you know.'

'Hey, I'm not complaining. She has livened up proceedings no end. Besides, what a backside.'

I tried to make out his face in the darkness

'I am just glad it was you and not me,' Mike said.

'Yeah, thanks Mike.'

I couldn't see whether he was smiling, but I knew, somehow that he was.

'You are sure that Neufeld is OK?' he said in a moment of seriousness.

I thought about it. 'Nope. I haven't got a bloody clue, mate. But what's new?'

Mike said nothing and I felt a pang of guilt. 'Look, thanks for talking Jane round.'

'No problem, bud.'

I clasped his shoulder. 'Come on.'

I switched on my torch and we made our way around the little building and in through the broken door.

'Nice place,' Mike said, as we stepped inside.

'Mind your footing. The floor is pretty uneven. It's over here.' I led the way into the side room. 'We'd better clear some of this junk.'

We spent a few minutes clearing debris. It wasn't long before Jane and Neufeld returned. They were carrying a pick axe, a couple of spades and an old canvas tool bag. Neufeld looked a little subdued. I reckoned Jane must have had a word. Or twenty.

'Here,' Jane said, handing me the tool bag. 'Your new friend can help you. Mike and I will keep watch.'

I waited for them to disappear. 'You all right?' I said to Neufeld, handing her a spade.

'Sure.'

'She gave you a hard time?' I said, sympathetically.

She shrugged. 'No. But she threatened to tear my head off if I betray you.'

I smiled weakly. 'That's Jane for you.'

'It is not a problem. She's your friend. We could all do with somebody like Jane looking out for us.'

There was no arguing with that. I pulled out a cold chisel and hammer and started to chip away at the floor around the trap door. If it was a trap door and not a drain cover. It took about twenty minutes. When I had finished the job, I stood up. 'Do you want to fetch them?'

Neufeld disappeared and returned seconds later with Jane and Mike. We all stared at what had been revealed in the floor.

'What do you reckon?' I said, grinning. Because it didn't look like a drain cover to me.

'I reckon you're going to have one hell of a job lifting that,' Mike replied.

'Use the pick axe to dig out a hole and then lever it open,' said Jane, with just a hint of excitement. Which, knowing Jane, was the closest to real excitement I was going to get out of her.

It took a few minutes to excavate a hole big enough to insert the tip of the pick axe under the edge of the hatch cover.

BUILDING 41

'Ready?' I asked when I was.

'Get on with it. We haven't got all damn night,' Jane replied.

I pulled and heaved but the thing would not shift.

'You'll have to dig around the edge some more. Break whatever is holding it down,' Mike said.

They all stood and watched while I dug a trench along one side of the hatch, swinging the pick axe high enough to do the job, but all the time painfully aware of the noise I was making. Just as it seemed that I had done enough, I heard the sudden sound of a dog barking. It sounded like the Hound of The Bloody Baskervilles. I stood stock still.

'Kill the lights,' said Jane through gritted teeth, switching off her torch. Mike and Neufeld followed suit.

We waited in silence. There it was again. The dog sounded even closer.

'I thought you said there wouldn't be any guards,' I hissed.

'It must be a visiting patrol. On the look out for vandals.'

'Well they're about to strike the bloody jackpot,' I whispered.

'Just shut up, will you,' Jane growled back.

If there were dogs outside, I thought about throwing Jane out there to deal with them. She didn't look like she'd have had much trouble.

We waited. Nothing. We waited some more. Some more barking but this time a little more distant.

'Stay there,' Jane said suddenly and disappeared out through the doorway. She returned a couple of minutes later. 'They're in D-block. Far end. I could see the lights from their torches.'

'What do you reckon?' I said, doubtfully.

'Just get on with it,' replied Jane, turning on her torch.

I tried the hatch again. The damn thing just would not budge.

'Let me try,' Neufeld offered.

Jane snorted.

Neufeld ignored her. She selected a corner, inserted the tip of the pick axe, readied herself and then heaved. The hatch began to move, slowly at first but just enough for Neufeld to push the pick axe in a little further. When she heaved again the hatch lifted. Mike handed his torch to Jane, he and I stepped forward and together we hauled the hatch up and over.

Jane didn't need to illuminate what was below in order for us to see. If it was a shaft, the way was blocked by brick rubble.

'Shit,' I said out loud.

'Man, if that is a stairway, it's going to take us hours to dig that lot out,' said Mike, voicing what we were all thinking.

*****

Ellen ended the call, slipped the mobile phone into her pocket, reached for her cup and drank the remainder of her coffee slowly. *Neufeld.* Ellen wished to God that she'd been there. She wished that she was there now. Whatever Harry thought of her, Ellen didn't trust her. *Trust no one.* That's what Elsie had said. That's what they had all agreed.

In his defence, it didn't sound as though Harry had been given much choice. Neufeld had followed him. Even Jane had been forced to concede that, like it or not, Neufeld was involved. Their only alternative would have been to abandon the dig, but what then? Neufeld would not have left it at that and they'd needed to move quickly.

At least Jane had been right about Building 41. While they had not yet found the tunnel, despite having removed, according to Harry, around eight feet of rubble, the stairway had to lead somewhere. *Remember Ravenscar.* That's what Elsie had said. Reminding her of the cavity beneath the floor of the derelict radar station. Where she'd found her father's lost keys. Now they had found another cavity, this time below Building 41 at Bletchley Park. Exactly as Elsie had intended that they should. But to what end? What were they looking for? Of the two people who knew the answer to that, Günther Möller was surely not going to tell them. Which left Ellen's great aunt.

Elsie had slept for most of the half an hour or so they'd been with her last night, waking only briefly and smiling weakly when she'd recognised Ellen's voice. Ellen had fought back tears of relief. But if Elsie remembered anything, either of the events that had put her in hospital, or of the key and the riddle she'd passed to them via Natalia, then she'd given no indication of it. And who was to say that Elsie would have any recollection of it? The consultant, who they'd seen briefly at the hospital last night, had been infuriatingly noncommittal about the likely prognosis. Would they ever learn the truth about Elsie's former life or discover the secrets that she had guarded so carefully and at such cost all these years? Or like Harry, was she too late? Would Elsie take her secrets to the… Ellen stopped herself. She couldn't think that. She wouldn't think it.

'More coffee?'

She had been only vaguely aware that Natalia had joined her. She turned and watched the Russian nurse take the coffee pot from the stove. 'Yes. Please.' She started to get up.

'It is okay. I will fetch it. Then I will make us some breakfast.'

'Not for me. I don't think I could.'

Natalia walked across to the table at which Ellen was seated. It almost filled one end of the tiny kitchen/dining room. 'You are worrying about Elsie,' she said, pulling out a seat.

Ellen nodded.

'Me, also,' Natalia said simply, slumping down into the chair. 'At least she gets better. She is awake now, yes? That is good.' She reached across and filled Ellen's coffee cup.

'It's not just Elsie. I'm worried about Harry. About all of us,' she added. 'This man Möller is a monster. What worries me most is that he seems immune to the attentions of the authorities. He seems to be able to do entirely as he pleases.'

Ellen saw the Russian's reaction to her words. Once again, she was struggling with some inner argument. Or was she again being unfair to the nurse? What was it about her manner that made her so difficult to trust? Ellen felt a sudden pang of guilt. 'What I said outside the hospital last night,' she said, catching the nurse's eyes and trying to hold them. 'I'm sorry, Natalia. It was unfair. I should not have said it.'

Natalia's face flushed. She looked away.

'I really didn't mean it,' Ellen persisted.

'You do not need to apologise,' the Russian said, still without meeting her eyes. 'You have much on your mind.'

'Yes I do,' Ellen agreed. 'But that doesn't justify the things that I said. You've been such a good friend to Elsie and to all of us. Elsie trusts you, Natalia. You have done so much for her. I should trust you too.'

'But you don't?' Natalia said quietly.

Ellen hesitated. She didn't want to offend the Russian but it was the truth. No matter how unfair it might seem. 'Can I ask you something?'

Natalia nodded.

'When you gave us the key and the message from Gran, that we should trust no one…'

Natalia looked away.

'You said that this should include you. What did you mean, exactly?'

'I meant that if Elsie had truly trusted me she would not have hidden the meaning of the words.'

'I know that, but there was more to it than that. Why would Elsie not trust you?'

Natalia shrugged again. 'Perhaps it was the wrong words I speak. English for me, it is difficult sometimes,' she said.

It was obvious to Ellen that it was an excuse, but what was not obvious was why. 'I want to trust you Natalia. I could certainly do with a friend right now and so could Elsie. Gran is in great danger.

BUILDING 41

I can't be here all of the time. I need to be able trust the people around her.'

'I would never do anything to hurt Elsie. I have done always what I can to keep her safe. To do what I thought was right.'

Which was true, Ellen didn't doubt it. 'I know you have.'

'I swear this on my mother's life.'

'You don't need to do that,' Ellen said, shaking her head. 'But it is obvious,' she added, deciding to risk a more direct approach, 'that there's something more that you are not telling me. The truth, Natalia, that's all I'm asking for.'

'The truth,' the nurse snorted. 'Nobody tells the truth in this…' She sighed, apparently unable to find the word.

'You're right about that,' Ellen said, smiling ruefully. 'This whole damn thing is a nightmare.'

The two women were silent.

Ellen decided to push her again. 'There is something that you are not telling me, isn't there?'

The nurse stared down at her hands.

'Is it Günther Möller? Is he threatening you?'

Natalia shook her head.

Ellen stared at her. 'Then someone else?'

The nurse said nothing.

'Natalia for God's sake. If someone else is threatening you…'

'Nobody is threatening me, Ellen.'

'Then what?'

Natalia hesitated and then appeared, suddenly, to make up her mind. 'When I came to Southwold, I was working at the nursing home and living in a room at The Bell in Walberswick. Sometimes, I worked behind the bar. The money at the nursing home, it was not enough to find a better place to live.'

Ellen stared at her.

'The landlord said that he knew someone who could find me a better place. If I work for him.'

The truth at last but Ellen knew that she needed to tread carefully. 'Doing what?'

'He wanted me to watch Elsie. To report on her progress. Tell him if there was any trouble. In return, he said that I could live here,' she said, spreading her hands.

'You agreed?' Ellen said, trying to keep her voice neutral.

'Yes. I like Elsie and this is a good place. Much better than the rooms at The Bell.'

'Well, yes but did it not worry you? I mean, what reason did this man give for his interest in Elsie?' If it hadn't worried her at the time, Ellen thought, then it was evident from her expression that it was certainly worrying her now.

'He said that Elsie's work, before she came here to live, had been dangerous. That she had made many enemies. He wanted to be sure that she was safe. To protect her. That is what he told me.'

'Did you believe him?'

'Yes,' the nurse said, simply.

'But you don't believe him now?'

Natalia shook her head. 'No, I do not. I think he lies. I think he has used me, Ellen. Like he is using Elsie. Like he is using you and Harry.'

'Using us, how?'

'He is watching you. He has eyes and ears in many places. He hopes that you will lead him to what he wants.'

'You think that there are others watching us?' *Neufeld.*

'Yes. I cannot be certain, but I believe so.'

Ellen had assumed that if the German researcher was working for anyone it was for Günther Möller. Perhaps she'd been mistaken. Ellen stared at the nurse. 'Do you know what this man wants from us?'

She shook her head. 'No. This he does not tell me, but it is very important to him. He has been watching Elsie for a very long time, I think.'

BUILDING 41

'Do you believe that Günther Möller wants the same...' she hesitated, 'thing?'

The nurse nodded.

Both women were silent.

She needed to warn Harry and Jane. If Neufeld was also feeding information to Natalia's employer, then it seemed almost certain that he already knew about Building 41. 'The key,' Ellen said suddenly. 'Elsie's message. Did you tell him?'

The nurse bowed her head. 'I am sorry.'

'You told him about Elsie's message?' She had already admitted spying on Elsie, but still the revelation came as a blow.

'I showed him the key and told him about Elsie's warning. That is all.'

'What are you saying? That you didn't tell him about Ravenscar?'.

'No. I didn't tell him.'

Ellen snorted. 'You expect me to believe that?' she said, shaking her head.

'It is the truth.'

Did it make any difference? If he knew about the key. If Neufeld had also betrayed them.

'He promised me that Elsie would be safe. Said that he would protect her. He lied.'

'Who is this man, Natalia?'

'We have men like him in Russia. Powerful men. Dangerous men. You must be careful.'

'Who is he? What is his name?'

Natalia stared at her. 'Smith,' she said, quietly. 'He calls himself Smith.'

CHAPTER THIRTY-TWO

Smith parked the Mercedes, got out of the car and walked purposefully towards the hospital entrance. It was a dreary morning. Grey and raining half heartedly. The kind of fine rain that soaks you in no time at all. He pulled his coat about him and picked up his pace.

Inside, the hospital foyer seemed unusually quiet. An elderly male patient was seated in the waiting area, just inside the main doors. He was wearing a dressing gown and slippers and was reading a copy of The Sun. 'Good morning,' the elderly man said, nodding at Smith as he passed by. Smith ignored him. He approached the receptionist. 'I am here to see a patient. Elsie Sidthorpe. She has a private room. Charnwood Ward.'

The receptionist tapped away at her computer keyboard. 'Your name is?'

He put his hand into his inside pocket and flashed her his Service card.

She looked at it over the top of her glasses. 'Home Office, eh? Who are you then? James bloody Bond?' she said, grinning like she'd said something funny.

'Smith.'

'Smith? What, like John Smith? Sam Smith? Give us a clue love, would you?'

'Just Smith. Mister Smith, if you must.'

BUILDING 41

'If you'd like to take a seat Mr Smith, I'll give them a call.'
He stared at her. 'I'll wait. If it's all the same to you.'
She returned his stare.
'Do it now.'
'Jesus. Which charm school did you go to then?' she said, reaching for the phone. 'There's a man here to see Elsie Sidthorpe,' she said when the call was answered. 'Home office. Says his name's Smith. Mr Smith. Shaken not bloody stirred.'
Smith stared at her.
'First floor,' she said, hanging up. 'West corridor, next to Ward 11.'
'I know where it is,' he said and turned away.
'Have a nice day,' the receptionist called out.
He ignored her.

She had become aware that somebody had entered the room. Perhaps a nurse or a doctor, come to prod or poke her again. It had been good to see Ellen last night, although she had been groggy from whatever drugs they'd been pumping into her to lessen the pain in her neck. They had helped her to sleep, at least, although she'd woken several times in the night and had called for the nurse. When the nurse had appeared, she had noticed the uniformed policeman outside the door. Until then, she'd been only vaguely aware of the events that had triggered her admission to hospital, although she had not the slightest idea which hospital. In the hours that had passed since, she had managed to reassemble her thoughts into some sort of order, fearing, as she did, that once again she might have failed. She needed to speak to Ellen. More than anything or anyone else. 'Ellen?' she said, suddenly opening her eyes.

Whoever had entered the room had opened the curtains. She could see a blurry figure, silhouetted against the light flooding into the room through the window. 'Ellen? What time is it?'

The figure walked towards her bed. She tried to focus and to push herself up onto her elbows. The movement brought a stab of pain from her wrist and she winced, her head slumping back against the pillow.

The blurry figure pulled up a chair and sat down beside her bed. She had closed her eyes and waited for the pain to subside. Her visitor said nothing. She opened her eyes again, slowly.

'It is a little after ten, in the morning.'

It was a voice that she recognised, even before her vision had come into something approaching focus. 'What do you want?' she said, weakly.

'I wanted to see how you are.'

Smith. He had aged considerably since their last meeting. She tried to remember when it had been. 'Really. Well now you have seen.'

'Indeed.'

Her throat was dry. Why were hospitals always so warm and airless? She glanced across at the water jug on the table beside her bed. 'Would you call the nurse, please. I would like to sit up.' She coughed, self consciously. 'Perhaps a drink of water.'

'No need,' he said, getting to his feet.

She felt him push his hand behind her back, ease her up and tuck the pillow behind her shoulder. His touch was gentle enough, though doubtless less so his purpose.

'Here,' he said, pouring some water into a glass and handing it to her.

She took it with the stronger of her hands.

Smith sat back down.

'Why are you here? You are going to tell me, I take it?'

He smiled. 'I am here to offer you my help.'

'Help?' She attempted to laugh but it became another cough. She took a second sip of water. 'It is a little late for that.'

'Nevertheless…'

'How exactly do you propose to help me?' she interrupted him.

BUILDING 41

Smith sighed. 'Do you know how long I have been watching you, Elsie?'

She was tired. So tired. She closed her eyes.

'Over forty years,' he said, without waiting for her reply.

Forty years. Half a lifetime.

'I wasn't the first. We have been watching you since your Bletchley days. Did you know that?'

She tried to remember. Their first meeting. It seemed so long ago.

'As a matter of fact, it was at our suggestion that you were recruited. Not mine, of course. Before my time.'

He was watching her. Trying to gauge her reaction.

'We hoped, even then, that you might lead us to it.' He hesitated as if deep in thought. 'Tell me, Elsie,' he said suddenly. 'Was it you who took it from Petty Officer Warren? Or was it Martha Watts? I have often wondered.'

'I'm tired. Say what you came to say and then go,' she said, hoping to dismiss him but knowing that he would not be dismissed so easily.

He smiled. 'Secrets. Do you ever tire of them?'

She waited.

'You were, in fact, in no position to lead us to it. You knew no more about the book's whereabouts than did we. That is the truth of it.' He smiled again. 'To think of it. All those years, and despite our very best efforts, you and I. To say nothing of the efforts of Günther Möller.'

The mention of his name brought her scattered thoughts into focus. 'Finding the book is your obsession. Not mine.' She said without emotion. 'Although I concluded long ago that, to be attracting such interest, it must contain some great secret indeed.'

'We wish simply to ensure that it does not fall into unsympathetic hands. In the interests of national security, of course.'

She snorted. 'I wonder, was it ever the national interest that you sought to protect? Or your own?'

She noted the flash of irritation in his face.

'The point...'

'Yes, why don't you get to the point,' she interrupted, angrily.

'The point is that Möller seems to have concluded, from your confrontation with him, that Harry Stammers is searching for the book. Something you said, perhaps?'

You will never have it. I have made sure of it. With the memory of her words, came a wave of fear and a sense of helplessness. It was so intense that, for a moment, she was unable to speak.

'Don't blame yourself, Elsie. However, you must realise, surely, that you are no longer able to counter him. That the frailties of old age have caught up with you, as indeed they must catch up with us all in the end.'

'Möller is mistaken,' she croaked. 'Harry knows nothing about the book.'

'Oh come now, Elsie...'

'Leave me alone. I am tired,' she said, cutting him off and closing her eyes again.

'Harry is a resourceful young man,' Smith persisted. 'He has more than proved his worth. However, when it comes to subterfuge, he is simply not a match for Günther Möller. You must surely accept that. As for Ellen...' He hesitated, leaving his words hanging.

She opened her eyes and stared at him.

'They are playing with fire, Harry and Ellen. Whether they know it or not. How much longer do you suppose that Möller will wait?'

'Wait? Wait for what?'

He was watching her. 'You, more than anyone, know what Möller is capable of. You cannot protect them, Elsie.'

She needed to warn them. Needed to see Ellen... She closed her eyes again. *So weary.*

'Without our help, they are at Möller's mercy and, as you know, mercy is not a concept that comes easily to Günther Möller.'

'What do you propose then?' she whispered.

'A bargain.'

She waited.

'Whatever you think, our aims are not so dissimilar to yours.'

'Really?' she said, rallying. 'You are taking me for a fool if you think that I do not know what your aims are. Who you really work for, Smith.' She almost spat the name. 'Who you have always worked for. I have nothing in common with you and your kind.' She said, daring him to deny it.

Another flash of anger.

'This bargain' she said, making no effort to mask her scorn. 'Get on with it and save me the platitudes.'

'Very well. I wish firstly to ensure that the book does not fall into Günther Möller's hands. This is an aim which I would have thought that you and I both share. However, perhaps where our aims diverge is that neither do I wish it to fall into the hands of anyone who might have the means to decode the book's contents. Harry Stammers, for example.' He paused.

She said nothing.

'That Harry and Ellen are searching for the book is in no doubt…'

She began to protest.

'You passed him the key and, no doubt, some message as to the book's whereabouts. Do not deny it,' he said, interrupting her. 'While the search is conducted, they will have the benefit of our full protection. If it becomes necessary, Günther Möller will be…' Smith hesitated, 'neutralised,' he added, apparently satisfied with his choice of words . 'Once it is discovered, and in return for our protection, you will instruct them to hand the book to us.' Smith fell silent.

Harry and Ellen knew nothing of the book. They could not possibly know. However, if they had interpreted the message that she passed to them correctly and were, as Smith claimed, searching for it, then they might have it soon enough. 'Not so much of a bargain then, as the surrender of the book. As for this protection you offer, tell me Smith, was I also supposed to be a beneficiary? Because, from where I am sitting, it rather seems as though Günther Möller is more than capable of evading you.'

Smith inclined his head in acknowledgement. 'I am sorry,' he said, meeting her eyes. 'Genuinely. Our assessment was that he would not harm you. In that, we were mistaken.'

'A mistake that very nearly cost me my life.'

'Your doing,' Smith shot back. 'We had no idea that you possessed a firearm. Let alone that you might try to use it against Möller. Had you not done so, he would not have attacked you. He was watching you, as he has been watching Harry and Ellen. In the hope that one of you will lead him to the book. Which I am rather afraid they are about to. We can prevent this, Elsie. You must see that.'

'Then prevent it. If you are so sure that Harry and Ellen know of the book and are searching for it, then Möller is of no further use to you. Neutralise him now.' She watched his face. 'As I thought. He continues to evade you, doesn't he? Have you any idea, any at all as to his whereabouts?'

The flicker of annoyance in his eyes told her that he did not.

'Make your decision Elsie. We will take the book in any event. Harry will not be permitted to decode it. Not that he is likely to get that far. If you hope to save Harry and Ellen the pleasure of encountering Günther Möller first hand, what other choice do you have?'

CHAPTER THIRTY-THREE

I yawned and looked at my watch. It was 11.30am. I'd managed about three hours sleep. I yawned again, sat up and groaned. Just about every muscle that could ache, did ache. We'd shifted a huge amount from the stair well below Building 41, piling the bricks and other rubble in a heap in the main room. There was much still to do before we stood any chance of breaking through into the tunnel below, if indeed the tunnel itself was not full of yet more rubble. The problem was in part, man power. While Mike had done his best, his injuries from a year before had limited his usefulness and while Jane had worked like a trojan, the truth was that she was not exactly built for heavy labour. Neufeld's presence had been a godsend. She had hauled more than the rest of us combined, me included.

I limped to the bathroom, turned on the shower taps and waited for the water to run hot. Jane had been infuriated by the German's presence. I could understand her reluctance to involve her, but we'd had no real choice and Neufeld had more than proved herself. Surely, even Jane could see that now. I stripped, and stepped under the shower, stretching my arms and enjoying the sensation of the hot water on my still aching shoulder muscles.

On Sundays the Park closed to visitors at four o'clock, but we'd agreed to hold off resuming the dig until nine. Building 41 was reasonably well hidden from the view of the neighbouring properties, but it would be far safer under the cover of darkness. One call to the police from a concerned neighbour and the dig would be over.

I stepped out of the shower and was still drying myself when I heard the phone ring. 'Shit.' I dropped the towel, dashed for the stairs, and made it to the phone in the kitchen before whoever was calling had hung up.

'Hello?' I was naked and dripping water all over the kitchen floor.

'Ellen?'

*****

I pushed the Lambretta up onto her stand, took of my gloves, undid the chin strap and took off my helmet. Jane appeared in the doorway. I walked across to her as casually as I could, determined not to look back towards the street. She greeted me and we went inside.

'Well?' she said as soon as the door was closed.

'Couldn't tell.'

'Why the hell not? You've got enough mirrors on that bloody thing.'

'There was a big bike. Half a dozen cars back. But it wasn't there the whole time. Or at least if it was, I couldn't see it. There was nothing behind me when I pulled up.' I followed Jane into the kitchen.

Mike was seated at a large oak table. 'All right, bud. Nice coat,' he said, evidently admiring the parka.

'Make the most of it. You only get to wear it once.'

Jane rolled her eyes. 'So, what did she say? Did she swallow it?'

I shrugged. 'Who knows with Neufeld? I'm still not convinced, you know.'

Natalia's revelations concerning Smith and the Russian's suspicion that there might be others watching us was one thing, but

BUILDING 41

there was nothing actually linking Neufeld to him, nor any real evidence that he had us under surveillance, courtesy of Neufeld or otherwise. It had been Jane's idea to tell Neufeld that we were postponing the dig. That there had been a change of plan and that I was instead intending to drive to Southwold to see Elsie with Ellen.

'For the record, I am not convinced that she's working for this Smith character either,' Jane said, surprising me. 'But I never trusted her and I trust her even less now. Whether she's working for him or not, she's up to something.'

Sidelining Neufeld was all very well, but we were going to struggle to shift the rest of the rubble from the stairwell below Building 41 without her. I shrugged. 'If you say so.'

Jane stared at me. 'We can't afford to take the risk, Harry. If Neufeld is working for him, then he already knows about Building 41.'

Which was pretty much what Ellen had said.

'Our only hope is to fool Neufeld, and anyone else who might be watching us, into thinking that we've given it up for now, draw their attention away if we can and get to the bottom of that stairwell before anyone realises it.'

I could not think of a better plan. 'I just wish I knew that we are supposed to be looking for.'

Jane held up her hand. 'Let's hope that Ellen is able to find that out when she speaks to Elsie. One step at a time.'

I nodded, reluctantly.

'Ready Mike?'

'Sure,' Mike replied, getting to his feet.

I took off my parka.

Jane was watching me. 'What size waist are you?'

'What?'

'What size waist are you?'

'Fuck off. He's not getting my bloody Levis as well.'

She just stared at me.

305

'We're both wearing jeans,' I objected.
'Different colours. Not even close. What size?'
She was enjoying this. 'Thirty-four.'
'Great. Mike's a thirty-two. Get them off.' She was smirking. 'You too, Mike.'
'What am I going to wear? I'll never get into a thirty-two.'
'Mike's got some track suit bottoms.'
'Track suit bottoms? Sweet Jesus, no.'
'You needn't worry about your shoes, fat boy. Mike's got a pair of brown desert boots exactly like yours. I'll go fetch them and the tracksuit bottoms while you two boys get down to business,' she said, turning and disappearing back out into the hall.

Mike started to unzip his jeans. 'In for a penny,' he said, grinning.

I took off my jeans and handed them to him. 'You going to be all right driving the Spitfire?'

Using the Spitfire, which had been garaged at Jane's since our move to Leighton Buzzard, had been Jane's idea. It was either that, or the Lambretta and there was no way I was letting Mike loose on the scooter.

'Sure,' Mike said. 'Why wouldn't I be?'

'There's no synchromesh on second gear. You'll have to double declutch.'

Mike shrugged.

I wasn't really thinking about the car. I was thinking about the last time that Mike had volunteered to be the driver for us, albeit that he had been the watcher rather than a decoy. A few hours later he'd been found in a ditch beside the B656 in Hertfordshire with a bullet hole in his shoulder and another through his foot.

'It was my right foot,' he said, as if reading my thoughts. 'It's fine with the accelerator.'

I nodded. 'I hope they're right and this time it's Neufeld and not Möller. She's going to be mightily pissed when she realises you're

BUILDING 41

you and not me, but I really can't see her pumping you full of bullets.'

'Yeah, thanks bud,' Mike said, like he hadn't taken much comfort.

Jane had reappeared in the doorway. 'Christ almighty. Have you got a pair of stocks stuffed down there, are you just happy to see me?' she said, staring at my groin.

I marched across to her, snatched the tracksuit bottoms and held them out in front of me. 'These are a crime against fashion. If either of you ever mention this to…'

'You're going to look so good in those and a pair of desert boots,' Jane interrupted. 'Here,' she said, tossing Mike his shoes. 'Now are we all set?'

Mike was grinning again. He was one of the people who seemed perpetually cheerful but probably wasn't. People like that never really are. 'Game on,' he said like he was off to the seaside for the day. Which I guess he was. Kind of. When he was ready, we followed him out, across the hall and through a door into the garage.

'I hope to God she starts,' I said nervously. The Spitfire sometimes didn't. Especially if she'd been garaged for more than a couple of weeks.

'The bloody thing better had,' Jane said like she was going to hold me responsible if the she didn't.

'Here,' I said, handing Mike my sunglasses. 'Don't forget the hat, and keep them on until you're safely inside Natalia's place.'

'Relax, bud. It'll be cool.'

He unlocked the door and lowered himself into the driver's seat.

'Remember to come off the A1 at Wyboston,' I reminded him, like he'd be bound to miss it if I didn't. 'It's signposted to Cambridge. Then it's…'

'The A14. I know,' he interrupted.

'Have you got your mobile?' Jane asked, looking worried for the first time.

'Got it.'

She shoved me out of the way, leant into the car and kissed him. 'Take care.'

He looked at me over her shoulder and winked.

'For God's sake stop grinning. You're supposed to be me. I don't do cheesy, OK? In fact, I don't do grinning at all. Cheesy or otherwise.'

'Call us, if you spot anything,' Jane added. 'In fact, just call us. Even if you don't.'

'I will.'

He inserted the key into the ignition, checked the gear stick for neutral and turned the engine over. She coughed but didn't start.

'Try her again. The petrol's probably evaporated from the carb. There should be plenty in the tank.'

He tried again and this time she caught. I exhaled.

'Well, don't just stand there,' Jane said, gesturing toward the door.

I retreated into the hall, well out of sight of the road.

I heard Jane haul open the garage door, Mike rev the engine and he was gone, tooting the horn as he pulled out of the drive. I listened as Jane closed the door behind him.

'Any sign?' I said as she appeared in the doorway.

She shook her head. 'Now we wait.'

'For what?'

She stared at me. 'We just do. Okay?'

I shrugged. 'Where did you park the Volvo?'

'I didn't. Mike did. He went out about ten minutes after you called. Parked up in Sainsbury's, walked back on foot and came in through the back garden. The way we'll be leaving in about…' She glanced down at her watch. 'Ten minutes.'

I stared at her. 'Do you think this is going to work?'

She shrugged. 'Depends.'

'On?'

BUILDING 41

'On whether Neufeld believed you, she has been watching us and thinks you and not Mike just drove away in your car. And on how much rubble we can shift in the next few hours.'

CHAPTER THIRTY-FOUR

'You are kidding?' I was struggling to take Jane's suggestion seriously. We'd collected the car from the supermarket where Mike had left it and were on our way to Bletchley.

'It's the safest way. If we go in the back way while the Park is open, we'll be seen. We can't risk it. If we go in through the main gate with you in the passenger seat and the gate is being watched, we'll blow Mike's cover. Not even you can be in two places at once.'

Jane was adamant and I couldn't fault her logic. 'What about you? You're just as involved as I am.'

'Maybe so, but it's not that unusual for me to pitch up at the Park on a Sunday.'

'What are you going to do with the car? Someone is bound to notice if it's still in the car park when the gates are closed.'

'So, I'll leave at four. Just like I normally would. Then I'll park up somewhere and come back in via Alford Place. It'll be safer once the Park has closed.'

'You could have bloody warned me.'

Jane glanced at me, irritably. 'I could have, but I didn't, okay? Now quit moaning, will you? I'll pull over when we're out of town. '

Which is what she did. After I'd tried to argue about it a bit more.

BUILDING 41

'You'll be in there for no more than ten minutes or so.'

If Jane was trying to reassure me, it wasn't working. 'I just hope that your bloody boot isn't airtight.'

'Of course it's not airtight, you idiot. Now stop whining and get in.'

At least she'd emptied it, or Mike had. It was still bloody uncomfortable and pitch black when she closed the boot lid.

If it was ten minutes, it felt more like thirty by the time that the car came to halt and she opened the boot lid. The light blinded me. I held my hand up over my eyes.

'Hurry up or you'll be seen.'

I clambered out of the boot. She'd parked on the slip road, by the old bicycle shelter. Building 41 was the next building along.

'There's a gap in the fence. We used it last night when we retrieved the tools. Go. Quickly. I'll park around the back, by the Bungalow and make my way back when I can.'

I glanced across towards the huts. There were several people walking away from us in the distance. Towards the old tennis courts opposite Hut One.

'Move,' Jane almost shouted.

I moved. I found the gap in the fence as Jane pulled away in the Volvo, and made my way into Building 41.

The main room was over half full of rubble. I hadn't realised that we'd shifted so much. What the hell were we going to do with the rest? Much more and we'd be unable to get in and out. I clambered over a pile of bricks, went into the side room and pulled up the trap door. There seemed little point starting without Jane. It was going to be much more efficient to hand the rubble up in an old bucket we'd discovered in the bushes outside. I took the dozen or so steps down that we'd cleared and started to sort through the tools that we'd left at the bottom. We had, in fact, hardly needed them. It was a case of pulling the rubble out by hand, piling it in the bucket and heaving it up the stairs.

Jane reappeared after about five minutes. She handed me down a pair of gloves that she had pulled from her bag. 'You first, and try to keep the noise down. We've got a couple of hours until the Park closes. Until then, we do not want to be overheard.'

I pulled on the gloves. 'Who was on the gate?'

'Stan Coombes.'

I nodded. 'Good. He's a lazy bugger. He won't venture up this far.'

I'd already started pulling out bricks and lumps of concrete and loading them into the bucket. 'What are we going to do with this lot, once next door is full?'

She stared at me. 'I don't know.'

'I thought you had everything planned.'

'Shut up and keep digging.'

*****

Mikkel Eglund parked the Spitfire opposite The Teepee. He pulled the hat low over his eyes, got out, locked the car and walked swiftly towards the cottage's powder blue front door. He didn't look back. It was an effort not to limp. His foot was aching like hell, but he managed it. He knocked once.

Ellen opened the door, threw her arms around his neck and kissed him full on the lips. 'Just in case,' she whispered in his ear. She glanced over his shoulder. 'Come in.'

He stepped inside and closed the door behind him.

'Well? Were you followed?'

'I didn't think so. Not until Stoneham. After that, there was a big bike behind me. Kept dropping back. I'd say it was Neufeld. She followed me into Southwold but I lost sight of her when I hit the high street.'

'Mike, this is Natalia.'

The Russian nurse had appeared in the doorway through to what Mike guessed must be the kitchen.

BUILDING 41

'Hi.' He removed his sunglasses and held out his hand as she approached. She shook it, awkwardly.

'How did you manage in the Spitfire?' Ellen asked.

'It was okay. That is one bad-ass clutch.'

'Yes, I know. I hate that clutch. Harry always drives whenever we take her out.' Ellen had moved to the window. She peered out, through the nets towards the cars parked opposite and the sea beyond. 'No sign. Do you think she's out there?'

'I reckon so,' Mike replied. 'I ought to call Jane,' he added pulling his mobile from his pocket.

'Can I get you some coffee?' Natalia asked.

'Sure. Black, no sugar,' Mike replied, searching for the number on his phone and hitting the call button. 'Jane? It's me. I've arrived.'

Petra Neufeld leant against the white steel railings that ran along the cliff top, away into the distance and down towards Southwold pier. Waves were crashing over the wooden groynes that sloped gently down into the sea. It was windy here on the clifftop, but the afternoon sun was shining brightly. She closed her eyes for a moment, enjoying the warmth on her skin. She'd stashed her biker's gear in the Triumph's back box. Unusually, she was wearing jeans and a pale green tee-shirt. They were more or less the only clothes she possessed that were not black.

She glanced back towards the cottage. The little sports car that she'd followed from Leighton Buzzard was parked, two cars up from Ellen's Saab.

'Enjoying the sunshine, Petra?'

He had appeared as if from nowhere. It took her seconds only to realise that he had come up the flight of steps from the beach, just a few yards to her right.

'What are you doing here?' she said glancing from left to right.

'Oh come on. Sun, sea and Southwold. What is there not to like?'

'I am not here for the sunshine,' she said, tersely.

'I thought you Germans liked nothing better than a deckchair and a towel.'

She ignored him.

'I see that Harry has arrived,' he said, nodding towards the Spitfire.

'Yes.'

'And Carmichael? Is she inside?'

'Yes.'

'You have seen her?'

'Yes. She greeted him at the door. It was quite…' She hesitated.

'Touching?'

'Nauseating.'

He smiled.

'You seem pleased with yourself.'

'I am. It appears that Elsie Sidthorpe has seen sense at last.'

'Meaning?'

'Meaning that by the end of the day, Stammers and Carmichael will be working for us, if not exactly with us.'

'I don't understand.'

'Elsie and I have come to an agreement.'

She waited but he volunteered nothing further. 'Why am I here?' she said suddenly. 'If you knew that Harry was coming here to see Sidthorpe, you could have waited for him yourself.'

'Because, I need you to help me fulfil my side of the agreement.'

She studied his face but, as usual, he was not giving anything away. 'My help? How?'

'In a few minutes, Carmichael, Stammers and Natalia, Elsie's nurse, will leave for their meeting at the hospital. When they have gone, you will enter the cottage with this.' He held out a key.

She took it.

'Where you will wait for Möller to join you.'

'Möller?' she exclaimed, turning to face him. 'He is here in Southwold?'

BUILDING 41

'Oh, yes,' he said, his eyes fixed on the door to the cottage. 'In fact, he is probably watching us at this very moment.'

It took a few moments for his comments to register. 'Bastard.'

'Stay calm. Once you are inside, you will find a gun. It is hidden in the bathroom. Behind the bath panel. I would retrieve it quickly, if I were you. When Möller enters, you will kill him and make your escape. You will return to Bletchley, to collect your passport. A car will be waiting. I have booked a flight for you. First class, I might add. To Munich. And do not even think about running. Möller will be unlikely to forgive your betrayal and knowing him as well as we both do, you will no doubt agree that while he remains alive, for you, there will be no hiding place.'

'You bastard,' she spat.

'Think about it Petra. By killing Möller you will solve your problem as well as mine.'

For a moment, she considered walking away.

'Goodbye Petra, and thank you. For your assistance. Rest assured that your masters in Germany will receive a glowing report.'

With that, Smith turned, walked toward the steps down to the beach and slowly sank from view.

CHAPTER THIRTY-FIVE

We'd been digging without a break for two hours when I heard Jane's phone. I could see her through the hatch. I strained to listen. The news from Southwold sounded good. Mike was evidently satisfied that Neufeld had taken the bait and followed him there. 'Well?' I called up, when she'd ended the call.

'They're about to leave for the hospital. Mike's pretty certain that Neufeld followed him, which means that we were right about her. He's worrying about how much longer he can keep up the pretence though, if she's still watching them.'

On realising her error, which she surely would eventually, it was going to take Neufeld no more than two, maybe two and a half hours to make it back to Bletchley. If she was working for Smith, or Möller for that matter, it would take her a damn sight less than that to report the oversight. 'Damn it. We need to shift this more quickly. What's the time?'

Jane looked at her watch. 'Ten to four. The Park will be closing in ten minutes.'

'Are you going to move the car?'

'I really wish I didn't need to. We can't afford to waste any time.'

'We could gamble on Stan not checking. He probably won't.'

'We could,' she said, evidently undecided.

BUILDING 41

'What's the worst that can happen?' I was thinking out loud. 'He sees your car, checks the office, finds you not there and wonders why you left it there overnight? Is that such a big deal?'

'I guess not.'

'Decision made. Let's get on with it. It can't be much further.'

'I hope not, because there's very little space left up there,' she said, glancing over her shoulder.

*****

Neufeld stepped back behind the white building on the corner, as Harry, Ellen and Natalia emerged from the little cottage on the other side of the green. Harry was still wearing his coat, despite the mild weather. And a Breton cap?

If Möller was watching her, she had seen no sign of him. Had Smith been bluffing? She knew that he hadn't. He'd staged everything with typical precision. She cursed herself again for not anticipating him. Smith was a first class shit. He'd left her with no other option than to do his dirty work for him. A task that was not without risk. She took another look. They'd hurried across to the car. Why the urgency? Harry was limping. She peered at him. Something about his gait was not quite right. The realisation, when it came, hit her like a brick. She backed away, and leant heavily against the wall. Then she looked again. He was climbing into the back of Ellen's Saab. She concentrated on his face, which was partly obscured by the hat and a pair of sunglasses. 'Sohn von einem Weibchen!' she hissed through her teeth.

Somebody had just climbed into the back of Ellen's car but it wasn't Harry Stammers. Mikkel Eglund? They were pulling away. She watched the car until it had turned and disappeared from view. If Stammers hadn't come to Southwold where was he? Then that hit her too. 'Son of a fucking bitch,' she repeated, this time in English. Bletchley. They had not postponed at all. They were at Bletchley Park. Right now.

She stepped out, scanned the buildings ahead of her and ran across the green. She needed time, but time was the one thing she didn't have. She let herself in with the key Smith had given her and ran to the back of the cottage. Was the bathroom upstairs or down? 'Shit,' she muttered, turning and running for the stairs.

Smith had been duped too. Perhaps if she told him. She reached into her pocket for her mobile. But what difference would it make to him? Möller had, at last, outlived his usefulness. Why Smith had not already taken him out... The thought had barely registered when the answer replaced it. Ultimately it had been the menace of Möller that had forced the old lady to submit, finally, to Smith's will. It had always been the menace of Möller. Without it, none of this would be happening. Harry would not, at this very moment, be hauling bricks and rubble from the stairway below Building 41. She would not be about to confront him. Always the threat of Möller.

She made it to the top of the stairs. There were three doors. She ran from one to the next until she found the bathroom. They'd used a decoy. Something, or someone had prompted it. Who? Harry and Ellen had fallen for the feigned attack by Möller, she was sure of it. It had been the threat to her non-existent daughter that had convinced them. It could not have been Smith because he had known nothing about the decoy. Unless that too had been part of his plan.

She could tell Harry now. Call him and tell him what he was looking for. Warn him about the arrangement between Sidthorpe and Smith. Tell Harry that she was about to confront Möller. Maybe kill him. But would telling him make any difference?

She tore the panel from the side of the bath. As she did, she heard the sound of breaking glass. Möller. He had come for her. Exactly as Smith had said that he would. She knew what kind of a man Möller was. What he would do to her. She ran her hand along the underside of the bath. She could hear him. He was in the house now. Footsteps on the stairs. Seconds. Her hand touched cold steel.

BUILDING 41

She snatched the gun, clambered to her feet and backed away from the door.

Möller exploded into the room, his face distorted with rage. 'Verräter!' he yelled at her. 'Traitor!' and before she could so much as think about pulling the trigger, he was on her. He had smashed the gun from her hand with a single blow to her wrist and grabbed her by the neck with the other hand, lifting her off her feet and ramming her against the bathroom's rear wall. The gun had skittered away, out of sight.

'Wait,' she choked, shaking her head violently in a vain attempt to loosen his grip. 'It is not...' She was coughing. Her vision, blurring. With immense effort she brought her knee up, hard into his groin.

He gasped, his hold slipped and he took a step backwards.

'Wait,' she wheezed. 'I was set up. It's not what you think.'

'Liar.'

'It's not him,' she coughed again. 'It's not Stammers. He's not here. They fooled us.' She saw him glance in the direction of the gun.

'What are you talking about?'

'It's not him,' she repeated. 'Somebody else was driving the sportscar.'

He began to move in the same instant that she dived. *The gun.* She saw it and then he was on her, the weight of him crushing her face against the floor boards. She saw him reach for the gun and take it.

He stood up, panting. 'Face me, bitch.'

She turned. She felt the blood on her face. Tasted the iron on her lips. 'He's not here. Stammers. Whoever it was driving his car. Whoever has gone with them to the hospital. It wasn't him.'

He took a step towards her.

'Stammers knows where it is. He is searching for it. Right now. I can show you where. Take you to him. There's no time. We must move quickly or he will have it,' she pleaded.

He grinned and stamped on her ankle.

She felt the bones crunch under his boot. She screamed in agony. 'Where?'

'He'll have it in no time,' she sobbed. 'He may already…'

He stamped again, twisting his boot like he was squashing a beetle. 'I said, where?'

She screamed again. Her foot felt as though it was on fire. She thought of Harry Stammers and she wanted him to have the codebook. Wanted him to decode it. Wanted the secrets it contained plastered over every newspaper in Europe. Most of all she wanted Möller beaten. 'Fuck you,' she yelled. 'Fuck you to Hell.'

'Wrong answer,' he said, grinning. Then he pulled the trigger.

*****

His failure to anticipate Neufeld's betrayal had been a serious error and one which, Günther Möller knew, might cost him dear. Unless he moved decisively and without delay. Neither had he anticipated the intervention of the man with whom he'd seen her talking, so carelessly, on the clifftop. His continued interest in the codebook was no great surprise. But his failure to apprehend him, or to obstruct him in any significant way, had long since convinced Möller that, like the old woman, he was a spent force. It had been another mistake that he was not about to repeat.

If Neufeld had been correct that Stammers was about to recover the book, or that he might already have it, then there was only one course of action left open to him. Möller turned into the hospital and drove the length of the car park. It took him minutes only to locate the Saab. He parked the BMW several rows back, turned off the engine and waited. With Carmichael here in Suffolk, they had as good as handed him the means by which he would force Stammers to give up the codebook. Once it was in his possession, the icing on the cake was going to be dispatching them both.

CHAPTER THIRTY-SIX

'They can't discharge you, Gran,' Ellen said, staring at her great aunt in disbelief. 'You're not strong enough.'

They'd been at the hospital for almost an hour before being allowed in to see her. Mike had long since retreated to the cafe. When finally she and Natalia had entered her room, Ellen had been dumbfounded to find Elsie already seated in a wheelchair with her coat on.

'I am perfectly fine,' Elsie said, hesitating. 'A little sore perhaps, but I can be cared for just as well elsewhere. Natalia will make sure of that, won't you dear?' she replied, glancing towards the nurse.

'No she won't,' Ellen interrupted. 'It is out of the question. Only a few days ago they were warning us that you might not...' Now it was Ellen's turn to hesitate. 'That you could be in here for weeks,' she corrected herself.

'Nonsense,' Elsie replied, dismissing the argument with a wave of her hand.

'It is not nonsense, Gran. You were unconscious for six days. A blow like that could lead to all sorts of complications.'

Elsie sighed. 'Ellen, dear. I appreciate that you mean well, but if there were going to be complications, then I rather think they would have complicated matters by now, don't you?'

Ellen tried to think of another, more compelling argument.

'With a little rest I will be as fit as a fiddle.'

'What about the police? Surely they...'

'Will not be pressing any charges,' Elsie broke in. 'They are entirely satisfied with my explanation concerning the firearm.'

'They're what?' Ellen said, involuntarily glancing towards the door and the policeman waiting outside.

'The gun was an heirloom belonging to my father. From the war. I had always assumed that it had been decommissioned. I had absolutely no idea that it would function as a firearm, and least of all that it was loaded with live ammunition.'

'I don't believe it,' Ellen replied, shaking her head.

'But the police did. It was the serial number, you see. They traced the weapon back to the Parachute Regiment. Did I never tell you that my father was a Para? He took it as a trophy when he was demobbed, the damned fool. Can you believe that he kept it in his bedside cabinet?'

'No,' Ellen said, staring at her. 'I can't. In fact I do not believe a single word of it.'

'I found it there when I cleared the house, after he died. It has served me perfectly well ever since. I have asked them to make a proper job of decommissioning it and to return it to me forthwith.'

'I don't care. I'm not...'

'Natalia,' Elsie said, ignoring Ellen's protestations. 'I wish to have a private word with Ellen? Would you mind awfully?'

'You wish me to wait outside?'

'If you would be so kind, Natalia. Thank you.'

Ellen stood, staring at her great aunt while the nurse left the room.

'A word in your ear,' Elsie whispered, as soon as she was gone.

Ellen glared at her. 'What?'

'A word in your ear.'

Ellen hesitated before taking several steps forward and bending to listen.

BUILDING 41

'There is much that we need to discuss,' Elsie whispered. 'But not here. I have reason to believe that the room has been bugged.'

Ellen stood up. 'You what?'

'Tush tush,' Elsie interrupted.

Ellen stared at her and then lowered her head again. 'Bugged by whom?' she whispered.

'His name is Smith. He works for the Security Services. You must believe me.'

There was a knock on the door. Ellen straightened. A male orderly had entered the room. 'Your ambulance Miss Sidthorpe. I will take you down.'

'That will not be necessary, young man. Ellen will take me, won't you dear?'

'Yes. It's all right,' Ellen said, addressing the orderly. 'We can manage.'

'The ambulance is waiting for you in the bay outside the main door.'

'Thank you.'

Ellen waited for the orderly to leave. 'You're sure about this, Gran?'

'Quite certain.'

Ellen swallowed. It had been her great aunt's use of a name that had convinced her. Smith.

*****

'Quiet! I heard something,' Jane whispered.

I froze. 'Shit.' She was right. Movement. 'Can you close the trapdoor?' I whispered.

Jane shook her head but said nothing.

If it was Möller we were finished. I bent down, picked up a brick and handed it to her and then bent down and picked up another. We both stared upwards.

A figure appeared at the top of the stairs. With the light from the hole in the ceiling behind him it was impossible to make him out. I hefted the brick in my hand like I meant it.

'What in God's name are you two doing?'

It took me a moment only to recognise his voice. 'Stan?'

'Jesus. Where the hell does that go?' Stan said, peering down the stair well.

I dropped the brick.

'We think we may have found the entrance to a tunnel,' Jane said, beating me to it.

'Well, bugger me. Nobody tells me anything.'

I'd taken half a dozen steps towards him, squeezing past Jane who had evidently decided to let me take the lead. 'Well, no. On this occasion, I don't suppose they would have.'

'Why's that then?'

I glanced back at Jane who tilted her head in assent.

'Because nobody knows.'

He stared at me.

'Nobody knows, because we haven't told them. In fact, I'm not here at all. I'm in Southwold.'

'Why?' he said, with more than a hint of suspicion.

'You got any cigarettes?'

'What?'

'Cigarettes. I'm out and I'm gasping.'

We'd made much better progress with Stan on board. He was surprisingly fit for a slightly overweight bloke in his fifties. Plus he'd found us an old wheelbarrow. When it was dark enough, we'd be able to shift any excess rubble to a patch of ground around the back of D-block. It was, according to Stan completely overgrown with brambles. It would be possible, so he said, to dump a great deal of rubble there without anyone noticing it. In the short term, anyway.

BUILDING 41

'How much further down do you think it goes?' Stan said, puffing like a train.

I gazed upwards. We'd descended about fifteen feet. Maybe more. 'I have absolutely no idea,' I said, stretching my arms. 'I hope to God we're almost there. I'm not sure how much longer I can keep this up.'

'Typical bloody mod,' he said, grinning. 'Bunch of bloody fairies, the lot of you.'

I smiled weakly. As well as being exhausted, I was feeling guilty. I'd spun him a yarn. As close to the truth as I could, without revealing the possibility that at any moment we might be confronted by a gun wielding Nazi maniac, intent on our destruction. I'd thought about telling him. Jane and I had argued about it while he was above ground, but in the end, I'd relented. Jane had been right. With my energy waning fast, Stan's help was a lifeline. If he'd taken flight we'd have been done for.

'Here. What's this?' Stan said, suddenly. 'You got that torch?'

I walked across to where I'd dropped it, picked it up and handed it to him, almost too tired to care. He switched it on and shone the light at a patch of brickwork. 'Just what I thought.'

Jane appeared on the stairs above us. 'What is it?'

Stan stared upwards, towards her. 'It's a lintel. That's what it is.'

I was trying to work out why this was of particular significance.

'The kind of lintel that holds up a wall,' Stan said like it should have struck a chord.

It didn't. I stared at him, too tired to think straight.

'God almighty. The kind of lintel you'd install across a cavity,' he said, grinning.

Jane had come down the stairs and was kneeling beside him. The two of them were pulling more rubble away and tossing it against the opposite wall.

'Well, well,' Stan said, after a few minutes frantic digging. 'Would you look at that?'

I peered over his shoulder. A gap had opened up below the lintel. I sank to my knees with exhaustion. Jane was suddenly in front of me, looking like she cared, which made a change. 'Are you all right?'

I shook my head, unable to speak.

She threw her arms around me and pulled me towards her. She'd never done that before. Not that I could remember, anyway. I was watching Stan over her shoulder. He had laid down in the rubble and was shining the light into the gap. 'Yup,' he said, peering back at me. 'It's a tunnel all right. They must have chucked this lot down here when they closed it up. Looks to me like it runs away in the direction of the mansion.'

Jane had sat back on her haunches, holding my shoulders. 'Come on. One last effort and we're there.'

Where were we exactly, I wondered.

*****

'Are you going to tell me what is going on?' Ellen said, her eyes flitting involuntarily toward the Russian nurse. Natalia had said nothing since they had clambered into the ambulance. She was sitting on a narrow bench at the rear of the cabin, her eyes downcast.

Elsie hesitated. 'There is much that we need to discuss but…' Her voice trailed away.

The three women were silent.

'You know,' Natalia said, breaking the silence.

'That you have been keeping Mr Smith informed?'

The nurse nodded.

'Yes. I know,' Elsie replied, her voice even.

'Always, you have known this?'

'No. Not until this morning. Although I had long suspected as much.'

BUILDING 41

'This morning?' Ellen interjected. 'What happened this morning?'

'I received a visit from Mr Smith. He seemed altogether too well informed.'

'I am sorry,' the nurse said, looking down at her hands. 'I thought that I was helping to keep you safe. This is what he told me.'

Elsie sighed. 'I'm sure he did, but altruism was never Smith's forte.'

Natalia looked puzzled.

'An unselfish concern for my welfare,' Elsie explained. 'Smith has his own, more selfish reasons for wanting to keep me under surveillance.'

'I know what you must be thinking. But it was never... I mean, I never...' Natalia stammered and fell silent.

Elsie smiled, weakly. 'What is done is done.'

'I think we can trust her, Gran,' Ellen piped up. 'She told me this morning. About Smith. I think she'd been trying to tell me since the day she passed us the key and your message.'

'I would have told you sooner, Ellen. I wanted to,' Natalia pleaded. 'But I was afraid. We have men like him in Russia also. Powerful men...' She fell silent, her head bowed.

'This Smith,' Ellen said, turning to her great aunt, 'who is he?'

'He works for the Security Service,' Elsie replied. 'He is, or was at least, a very senior officer. Certainly more senior than I.'

'You worked together?'

'Never. We worked for the same organisation. But never together. Smith had his own allegiances. We did not then, nor do we now share them,' Elsie said, holding Ellen's gaze.

Ellen nodded.

'Where is Harry? Why is Mike here?'

'Your message,' Ellen said, by way of reply. 'Harry has found the entrance to the tunnel, but it is full of rubble. He and Jane are excavating it now. Mike came here as a decoy. They were being watched.'

'Watched?' Elsie said, a trace of alarm creeping into her voice. 'By whom?'

'Her name is Petra Neufeld. She is a researcher at Bletchley. We're pretty certain that she followed Mike here, thinking that he was Harry. That was the plan, anyway.'

'Neufeld. It is a German name.'

Ellen nodded, catching her great aunt's train of thought. 'We don't know who she is working for. We don't really understand any of this, Gran. We don't even know what Harry is meant to be searching for.'

Elsie glanced sideways at the nurse. Then, as if making up her mind, turned back to Ellen. 'Harry is looking for a book. I took it from a sailor in 1944. Martha and I met him, the evening before she disappeared. I had no idea of its significance and it was in my possession for a matter of hours only. Martha told me that she had returned it to him. By the time I realised that she had not, Martha was already missing. I feared then, as I did for many years afterwards, that the book had been the reason for her disappearance.'

Ellen was staring at her great aunt, trying to put the pieces of the jigsaw together in her mind. 'You blamed yourself? You thought that Martha had been trying to protect you?'

Elsie nodded. 'And I was right about that, even if I was mistaken in the belief that she had taken the book with her to London and that by doing so she had put herself in danger.' Elsie sighed. 'It was the key, you see,' she continued. 'After you brought it back from Belsize Park, I realised my mistake.'

'You recognised it?'

Elsie nodded. 'Martha ran an errand on the day she left for London. It was an unconnected matter and I had no idea that she had gone into the tunnels. Until Harry produced the key.'

BUILDING 41

Ellen was still playing catch up. 'What is so important about this book?'

'The sailor had taken it, as a trophy, from the wireless room of a captured U-boat in 1941. It was an act of sheer foolishness on his part and, indeed, on mine when I stole it from his bag. However, to my very great regret and shame, he paid for the misdeeds of us both with his life.'

'He was murdered?' Ellen said, recalling the discussion with the Jacksons.

Elsie nodded. 'I am afraid so.'

'By Günther Möller? He wants the book? That's why he did all those terrible things as Jimmy Dobson back in the seventies and as Stephens last year? Because of a book?' Ellen said, like the very idea of it was preposterous.

Elsie nodded again. 'Yes, Möller's purpose in coming to Britain was the recovery of the book.'

Ellen hesitated. 'But why? What on Earth does this book contain?'

'Code. Almost certainly Enigma enciphered code. As to its meaning…'

'Wait a minute,' Ellen said suddenly. 'Is that why Harry's mother had to leave them? Why they were offered protection? Did she know about this codebook? Is that why you didn't want us to look for her?'

'No,' Elsie said wearily. 'Harry's mother knew nothing of the codebook.'

Ellen looked at her doubtfully.

'She had been working for Smith. She was offered protection because she had been forced, by Smith, into working under cover on a case that brought her into contact with a man called Jimmy Dobson…'

'Aka Günther Möller,' Ellen interrupted.

Elsie smiled but it was a smile that was short lived. 'She suffered terribly at Dobson's hands. She foiled him in the end, along with the organisation she'd been brought back into service to infiltrate. And, by foiling them, saved a great many lives. But Dobson escaped. Or perhaps Smith allowed him to escape because, as you say, Dobson's real name was Günther Möller and Möller's continuing freedom served another purpose.'

Ellen opened her mouth to speak.

'The point is,' Elsie interrupted her, 'that whether by Smith's design or not, Möller was at large. Had he discovered that she was still alive and that she had a family, he would have used them against her. They were all in the most terrible danger. That is why she went away, Ellen. Möller had to believe that she was dead. It was the only way.'

Ellen had paled. 'You know where she is, don't you?'

Elsie met her eyes. 'Yes,' she said after a pause.

'You've always known? Even before I met Harry? Since he was a child? You've known all along?'

'Yes. All along. Since the day she escaped from the burning van that she'd driven out into the countryside, preventing the deaths of Ted Stammers and, perhaps hundreds of others. I have always known it.'

'Why?' Ellen said, ashen faced. 'Why didn't you tell him?'

'Because I swore to her that I would not. That I would never reveal her whereabouts to Harry. Don't you see? Not while Günther Möller remains at large. She is convinced that so long as he believes that she is dead, they are safe. She sacrificed everything for them. It was her only concern. It is all that she cares about still.'

CHAPTER THIRTY-SEVEN

Mikkel Eglund climbed into the Saab, pulled out of the parking space and drove the short distance around to the front of the hospital where the ambulance was waiting for him. He pipped the horn as he approached the waiting vehicle. The ambulance flashed its hazards and slowly pulled away. They'd agreed that Ellen and Natalia would ride in the back of the ambulance with Elsie and that he'd follow them back to Southwold. Which was just as well because he hadn't the faintest idea where he was going. He'd paid no attention during the journey up from Southwold. He followed the ambulance out toward the road and turned right with them.

Neither did he have much idea of what was going on. Having finished his coffee he'd wandered up to Elsie's ward to find the three of them - Elsie, Ellen and Natalia plus a very worried looking young police constable - already assembled in the corridor. The policeman was still arguing with them, trying to persuade them to wait for an escort but Elsie was having none of it. The poor bloke had looked like a rabbit caught in headlights. As they'd disappeared down the corridor Mike had heard him using his radio to report their departure.

Mike reached into his pocket, pulled out his phone and with one hand managed to select Jane's number and press the call button. He held the phone to his ear and listened to the ring tone. No reply. He waited for the message announcement. 'It's Mike. We're on our way back to Southwold from the hospital. Elsie has discharged herself. I'm following behind in Ellen's Saab. Don't worry. I'm cool. We're all fine. Call me when you can.' He hung up. But he wasn't cool or fine. He was worried. Jane would certainly have had her phone with her. It was unlike her not to answer. Especially in the circumstances. So why hadn't she? He ran several scenarios through his mind. None of them made him feel any less worried.

They'd been on the A12, travelling south, for about twenty minutes, when up ahead the ambulance indicated left. As he approached the junction, he noted the signs and followed them onto the Southwold Road. He tried Jane's number again, and again got no reply. He was fiddling with his phone, trying to bring up Harry's number when a car appeared in his rear view mirror. It swerved out, into the opposite lane and overtook at speed. Mike instinctively hit the brakes and dropped back, thinking that the car would pull into the space between the Saab and the ambulance. But it didn't pull in. It continued past the ambulance and swerved into the emergency vehicle's path. Before he'd registered what had happened there was a blaze of brake lights and the ambulance had screeched to a halt.

Mike dropped the phone and hit the Saab's brakes again, pulling up hard a matter of yards from the emergency vehicle's rear. A figure had appeared beside the ambulance driver's door. Mike recognised him instantly. Günther Möller raised his arm and there was a flash. The unmistakable blast of a gunshot.

Mike stared.

A second shot. Both fired into the ambulance. Möller had turned and had started to walk towards the Saab. He was grinning and holding the gun out in front of him.

'Shit. Shit. Shit.'

There was a third flash. The Saab's windscreen shattered.

Mike jammed the gear stick into reverse and hit the accelerator.

Another flash. The bullet hit the bonnet. Mike saw the spark from the ricochet.

BUILDING 41

He pushed his foot down to the floor, craning his neck to see over his shoulder. Without warning, the Saab began to veer. He tried to correct it but it was going to be impossible at speed. He hit the brake. The car spun, tilting so hard that, for a moment, he thought that it might roll over. He looked over his shoulder toward the ambulance. There was no sign of Möller but a car had pulled out from in front of the stationary ambulance. The same car that had overtaken them. A black BMW.

Mike's first thought was that Möller was going to come after him but the car manoeuvred up onto the verge and Möller got out. He paid the Saab no heed. Instead he approached the ambulance, opened the door and dragged something bulky from the cab. It was the ambulance driver's body.

Inside the stationary ambulance, Elsie had heard the unmistakable sound of a gunshot. Natalia had instantly thrown herself from the bench seat to the floor and had started to scream. Ellen had come to her feet and was already moving towards the rear doors.

'Ellen, wait!' Elsie cried out, trying to get up from her chair. But she was too weak.

Another shot.

'Get down onto the floor,' Elsie ordered.

Ellen hesitated.

'Now, Ellen!'

Ellen sank to her knees.

Two more shots. This time more distant.

Möller. There was no doubt in Elsie's mind that it was him.

The roar of an engine.

'Oh my God. Mike!' Ellen cried out, struggling to regain her feet.

'Wait.' She made an effort to grab Ellen's arm.

Ellen turned.

'Listen to me. There is nothing you can do.' She held her eyes.

Natalia had crawled into a corner, where she was sat, hugging her knees. 'He is going to kill us. We are all going to die,' she sobbed.

'No, we are not,' Elsie said, trying to keep her voice calm. 'He will want to use us. We are of no value to him dead.'

The whine of a car reversing away, into the distance.

'It's Mike,' Ellen said, straining to hear. 'Please God, let him get away,' she pleaded.

The sound of another engine. This time closer.

'Quickly,' Elsie hissed. 'Do you have your phone?'

They heard a car door and then felt the ambulance tilt to one side.

'Yes!' Ellen thrust her hands into her pockets.

The ambulance lurched again.

Ellen produced her phone.

'Wait until we are moving, or he will hear you,' Elsie whispered.

The ambulance began to reverse, then turned sharply and pulled away. The sudden movement had thrown Ellen off balance. She steadied herself with an outstretched arm.

'Keep your voice down or he will hear you. Call Harry,' Elsie instructed.

Ellen dialled the number and waited. 'There's no reply.'

'Leave him a message.'

'I can't. He doesn't use his message service. Never has.' She hung up.

'Then text him.'

'What shall I say?'

'Tell him that Möller has us. That he must find the book.'

Ellen began to type out the message but her hands were shaking so violently that it was slowing her progress.

'Hurry, Ellen.'

Ellen nodded.

BUILDING 41

'It has a soft red cover and a white paper label. Tell him about the doors. In the tunnel. One of them will be 41B. Tell him to use the key,' Elsie added.

Ellen tapped out the words and hesitated. Then she tapped out another short sentence. 'Done.'

'Has it gone?'

'Yes.'

'Now delete it, quickly.'

In the cab of the ambulance, Günther Möller was listening to the emergency vehicle's transceiver while reflecting on Petra Neufeld's words and the identity of the driver of the Saab, which had disappeared at speed, away into the distance. He would, undoubtedly have called the police. Möller figured that, in a rural area such as this, it would take the police ten to twenty minutes to get to the scene and longer to summon a helicopter. But there had, as yet, been no indication from the radio that the ambulance controllers were aware of the hijacking. He was still listening when, over the ambulance's audio system, Möller heard the telltale warbling of a mobile phone signal.

Without warning the ambulance drew to a shuddering halt. The sudden braking sent Ellen sprawling to the floor. The phone slipped from her grasp, hit the side of the cabin and came apart in pieces.

'Natalia! Quickly!' Elsie cried out.

But as the nurse reached for the body of the phone, the rear doors of the ambulance flew open.

'Stay quite still. All of you.'

Möller was facing them, a gun in his right hand.

Ellen whipped around to face him. 'You bastard. If you've killed Mike...' she spat.

Möller grinned. 'So it was your Norwegian friend. I thought so.'

Ellen stared at him but said nothing.

His grin faded. 'You,' he said, waving the gun at the nurse. 'The phone. Bring it to me.'

Natalia hesitated.

'Now,' Möller yelled.

Natalia clambered hurriedly to her feet, her eyes wide with fear. She retrieved the phone and approached him.

He snatched it from her trembling hand. 'All of it.'

She turned and retrieved the battery.

Möller held out his free hand.

She passed it to him.

'Now you two,' he said, brandishing the gun at the two ambulant women. 'Empty your pockets… No, wait,' he commanded. 'Better still, take off you shoes, your jackets and your jeans. Toss them to me.'

'What?' Ellen was staring at him, her eyes wide.

'Quickly. Or I will shoot you,' he said pointing the gun at the nurse, 'where you stand. You can keep the rest of your clothes on. For now,' he added, leering at Ellen.

She hesitated.

'Do as he says,' Elsie said, in low, even tones.

Möller watched them while they both undressed. When they were done, he added 'Now her bag and her coat,' he said, pointing the gun at Elsie. 'Quickly. We don't have all day.'

Ellen helped her great aunt out of her coat and threw it to him. And then the bag.

'I take it that I do not need to search you, old woman.'

Elsie observed him coldly. 'No. I do not carry a telephone.'

'If I find that you have lied, she will die,' he said, again pointing the gun at the now half-naked and cowering nurse.

Elsie said nothing.

'Good. Enjoy the rest of the journey.'

He slammed the rear doors.

'Bastard,' Ellen spat after him.

BUILDING 41

The three women said nothing until the ambulance was moving again. It was Elsie who broke the silence. 'The message,' she whispered. 'Did you delete it?'

Ellen stared at her and then slowly shook her head.

CHAPTER THIRTY-EIGHT

'I need a cigarette,' I said, clambering to my feet. 'And something to drink.'

Jane looked me up and down.

'I don't care. I'm completely shagged. Before we go down there,' I said, peering at the gap that Stan had dug out beneath the lintel.

She nodded. 'You look terrible. There's a bottle of water in my bag. Up there,' she said gesturing towards the open hatch. 'Just inside the door.'

'Thanks.' I turned and climbed the stairs. I found Jane's bag, reached for the bottle, took a swig and then another. Then I found Stan's cigarettes, pulled one from the pack, lit it and took a long draw.

It was odd, but now that we had found the tunnel, I didn't feel elated. I wasn't feeling anything. Maybe I was just too damn tired. Tired of the dig. Of Möller. Neufeld. Elsie. The riddle of my missing mother. Peter Owen. Tired of the whole damn thing.

I found a space and eased myself slowly down onto the pile of bricks. As I relaxed, my thoughts turned to Ellen. I realised, with a sudden jolt of anxiety that we hadn't heard from them since Mike's arrival in Southwold. I stood up again, fished around in the pockets of Mike's now filthy tracksuit bottoms and found my phone. I stared at the screen. There was an unopened text message and a

BUILDING 41

missed call. I opened the text message, began to read, felt my legs give way and sat back down heavily.

'Harry?'

Jane had appeared in the doorway. 'I thought I'd...' She stopped mid sentence. 'What's wrong?'

I stared at her.

'Harry?'

I held out the phone and waited for her to read the text message. 'What the fuck are we going to do, Jane?'

She looked at me, ashen faced. It was the first time I'd ever seen Jane close to tears. 'Mike,' she whispered. 'Where's Mike?'

*****

Mikkel Eklund jammed the gear stick into first and put his foot down hard on the accelerator. For a moment the car lost traction. He fought to regain control, as the car spun to the right in a tight semicircle. All he could think of was Möller. The man who had, less than a year before, shot him twice and left him for dead. For a crazy moment he considered turning the car around and ramming the ambulance but it would be crazy, he realised. Möller was armed and more than capable of killing them all.

He drove northwards, heedless of his speed, back towards the hospital, without any clear idea of what he was going to do next. Should he call the police, or Jane or both? He glanced across at the passenger seat. The phone had slid onto the floor. He could see it in the passenger footwell. He reached for it blindly with one hand, the other on the steering wheel and his eyes fixed on the road ahead. He was sweating with the effort of it. He glanced down and willed his hand to grab the phone. When he looked up again, the Saab had veered onto the wrong side of the road and another car was hurtling towards him. He hit the brakes, felt the steering go rigid and then slack and the car begin to roll. He heard the wailing sound of a horn. Of breaking glass. Grinding metal. And then he was upside down, slammed forward and the world went black.

Smith got out of the car and ran across to the wrecked Saab. The driver was partially suspended, upside down, by the car's seat belt. He'd recognised the Saab in the seconds before the crash and had assumed the driver to be Stammers. But it wasn't Stammers. The driver was Mikkel Eglund. He hauled open the twisted door. Blood was running from Eglund's nose. Which was a good sign. It meant that his heart was still pumping.

Smith stood up. What was Eglund doing here and, more to the point, where was Stammers?

Eglund groaned.

Smith knelt. 'Where are they?'

Eglund opened his eyes.

'I said, where are they?'

'Who the fuck are you?' Mike spat.

'I'm your guardian angel. Now where are they?'

The Norwegian put a hand to his face and touched his nose. 'Fuck.'

'I'm going to ask you one more time. You answer and I will consider helping you out of the car. You don't and I walk away. Now where are they?'

Eglund groaned. 'Möller has them. He hijacked the ambulance. He shot the driver. His body is back there,' he said, glancing back along the road.

Smith stood up.

'Hey, wait a minute. I thought we had a deal.'

Smith turned and began to walk towards the Mercedes. There was a thud.

'Fuck,' Eglund had grunted.

Smith turned. The Norwegian had clambered from the smashed Saab. Miraculously, and apart from the blood on his face, he appeared largely unhurt.

BUILDING 41

'You got a phone?' Smith called out.

'I did have,' Eglund replied, glancing back at the wreck. 'Before you totalled my car. I guess it's in there somewhere.'

'Find it. Call 999. Ask for the ambulance service. You need to get your face checked out.'

Eglund had begun to limp towards him.

Smith stopped and turned again. With blood running from his nose onto his coat Eglund looked like an extra from Night Of The Living Dead.

'The phone will be toast. You can't just leave me here,' Eglund spluttered, holding his nose.

'Oh, I can. Believe me.'

'Yeah, but come on. You haven't even told me who you are. I'll need your details. You know, for the insurance claim? Hey,' Eglund added, narrowing his eyes. 'You do have insurance?'

Smith stared at him. 'I don't have time for this,' he muttered.

'Then take me with you and we can discuss it on the way.'

'On the way where?'

'On the way to wherever you're going.'

Eglund was now standing in front of him, pinching his nose.

'I don't know where I'm going yet.'

'Cool. A mystery tour. Game on.'

Smith smiled. 'Funny.'

'There's plenty more where that one came from.'

'Maybe you'll be useful.'

'Maybe I will. You decide. I'm not in any rush.'

Smith didn't know why he was still smiling. Because, for once, he didn't have a plan. Not even in outline. He turned. 'Get in,' he called over his shoulder. 'And try not to bleed on the seats.'

CHAPTER THIRTY-NINE

The ambulance came to a halt. Ellen glanced at her two companions in turn. There was a short pause and then it moved again, briefly and stopped.

'Do as he says,' whispered Elsie. 'Try not to antagonise him. Remember, both of you. We're worth nothing to him dead.'

Ellen nodded.

'We'll be swapping vehicles. He can't use this. They'll spot us too easily.'

'Where will he take us?' Natalia whispered.

'I don't know. My guess is that he will have planned for this kind of eventuality. Maybe not for this particular scenario but kidnapping one of us was always a possibility. He'll have a safe house.'

'Maybe this is it,' Ellen said.

Elsie shook her head, doubtfully. 'Too close.'

Ellen was watching her great aunt with a growing sense of incredulity. Gone was the mentally frail eighty-two year old who, no more than a week ago, had been battered half senseless by Möller. In her place, was another woman entirely. A woman whose face, though still bruised from the encounter, showed no sign of fear and whose eyes seemed alight with a steely determination to see them win through. Had her previous persona been an act?

BUILDING 41

Elsie glanced at each of them in turn. 'I need you both to be brave.'

Ellen nodded, wordlessly.

'Natalia?' Elsie said, turning her attention on the nurse once again.

Natalia was still shaking. 'I am sorry. I am afraid.'

Elsie closed her eyes. 'We should all know fear,' she said, opening them again. 'It is our friend. It keeps us alive.' She paused.

The nurse said nothing.

'But panic does not, Natalia. Hold onto your fear. Store it away. Let it out, only when you need it.'

The nurse nodded, without conviction.

The three women waited.

*****

Jane had tried to call Mike but his phone had gone straight to the answering service. The same had happened when I tried Ellen's number. I read the message again. I don't know why. I'd already read it a dozen times:-

"MOLLER HAS US - ELSIE ME NATALIA. ALL OK. LK 4 CODEBOOK. RED COVR. WHITE LBL. DOORS IN TNL WALL. 41B. GRAN NOS WHR YR MUM IS. DNT GIVE UP. NOT EVR. LUV U. ALWAYS. E XXX"

Reading it again did nothing but deepen my sense of despair. Möller had them. It was my worst nightmare. I smiled. I actually smiled. Jane looked at me like she thought I was losing it. 'Elsie knows where my mother is. Like it matters. He's got them for fuck sake. If he kills Elsie… If he kills…'

'Stop it. Give me that bloody phone.'

She snatched it from my hand.

'You can't think like that.'

I snorted. 'That's easy for you to say. There's no mention of Mike…'

'Easy?' Jane hurled. 'Easy? You think that makes it better for me?'

I stared at her.

'Mike isn't with them. So where is he? You think you feel worse than I do right now?'

I ran my hand through my hair. 'I'm sorry.'

'He could be anywhere.'

'He's not with them. That's the main thing,' I mumbled.

'So why isn't he answering his fucking phone,' Jane cursed, trying Mike's number again.

I waited.

She shook her head. 'We've got to think. What will Möller do next?'

Which was precisely what I was trying to avoid thinking about.

'He wants this codebook. He will use them to force us to hand it over. Which means that we've got to find it.'

I couldn't fault her logic.

I was smoking another cigarette. 'What does it contain that is so fucking important?'

'He'll contact us. Use them as hostages. And when he does, we'd better have the book.'

She was right about that. Without the book, we'd have nothing to bargain with and we both knew what that would mean for the three of them.

'We need that codebook Harry. Now.'

I nodded. 'Come on.'

We found the bottom of the stairwell empty. Stan had evidently already clambered through the gap between the rubble and the lintel and, if it was big enough for him, it was going to be big enough for Jane and me.

BUILDING 41

'You first?' I said to Jane, my guts feeling like they'd been liquidised.

She nodded.

I found a torch and handed it to her.

She dropped to one knee and peered into the void.

'You need to see this.' Stan's voice drifted up to us.

Jane manoeuvred her body and went down, feet first.

I found another torch and followed her.

The rubble had spewed from the stairwell in an uneven but relatively easy slope. Once I was through, I eased myself part way down on my back. I was still thinking about Ellen's text as I went. I was thinking that Möller could take everything from me. Ellen. Elsie. My mother - if he killed them, I'd have no other means to trace her. I'd have lost them all. Jane and Stan were both waiting for me at the bottom. I stood up. My legs felt like stone.

The torches created a pool of light no wider than a couple of yards, beyond which there was nothing but inky blackness. I raised my torch and the darkness retreated back along the tunnel in, I guessed, a roughly southeasterly direction.

The tunnel wasn't particularly wide. Probably no more than six feet or so. The walls and ceiling were made of concrete, rather than brick. Which surprised me. I found myself wondering about the construction. They must have dug out a trench, lined it with concrete and then covered it over. Like they did with some of the early London Underground lines. It would have involved the removal of many thousands of tons of soil. A project on that scale would surely not have gone unnoticed by everyone stationed at the Park at the time and yet no record of the tunnels, or of their construction, had survived. Where were the men who did the work? I don't know why I was thinking about it. At that moment I didn't really give a shit.

'Hey,' said Jane, shining the torch back up the rubble pile. In the wall, immediately opposite the entrance to the stairwell, was the top of a narrow doorway, the remaining six feet of which was covered by the rubble. 'I hope that isn't door 41B.'

I hoped so too. Because if it was, then even Stan was going to have trouble moving it. I doubted that I had the strength. Not without some serious rest.

Stan had already set off down the tunnel. 'There's another door,' he called back. 'Doesn't look like much. Some sort of store cupboard would be my guess.'

We trudged after him.

'Have you noticed how dry it is down here?' Jane said, sweeping the tunnel walls with her torch.

I wonder now, whether she was trying to divert my attention away from Möller and what he might be doing to Ellen. I glanced across at her.

'Well, have you?'

Being on a gradual slope, water tends to run down the Park, west to east, which is why, breaking through G-block's damp course, in search of a tunnel entrance, had caused the building's basement to flood every winter since, putting the brakes on any further exploration of potential tunnel sites. Jane was right. Running north-west to south-east, across the path of the flow, ought to have made the tunnel damp, at least. But there was no sign at all of any water ingress. 'Yes. I have,' I said, wanting to punch her in the face and kiss her at the same time.

'Ellen's going to be all right, you know,' Jane said, as we approached the second door.

'You think so?'

'Behind that door, we're going to find that fucking codebook. And then we're going to go and get them. All of them. Mikkel Eglund included. I don't know how. But that is what we're going to do. You and me. Together. Got it?'

We stopped, facing each other. I felt a tear roll down my cheek. It felt like my brain was bleeding.

'I said got it?'

BUILDING 41

I nodded.

'Come on you two.' Stan had come back along the tunnel.

'Is there any sign on that door?' Jane said, shining the torch in his face.

'No, but there's a number.'

Jane and I exchanged glances.

'41B'

CHAPTER FORTY

'You two,' Möller barked, pointing the gun at Ellen and Natalia in turn. 'Out.'

Ellen turned and looked at her great aunt.

She nodded. 'Do as he says.'

The two women approached the door.

They were in a barn. The rough barn doors were closed, but daylight shone in through the gaps around the edges.

Möller stepped back.

They jumped down.

'Over there,' he said, waving them away from the ambulance.

When they were out of the way, he reached up and slammed the ambulance door shut. Then he turned to face them.

Ellen swallowed. She felt impossibly vulnerable, standing in front of him in her knickers. She glanced sideways at Natalia. The nurse looked utterly petrified.

For a moment, he said nothing. She could feel his eyes on her naked legs. The look on his face made her skin crawl.

'Stammers is searching for the codebook.' He said it as a statement of fact.

Ellen said nothing.

He sighed. 'I would, in any other situation, have enjoyed extracting information from you… slowly,' he said, grinning. 'It would have been most entertaining.'

BUILDING 41

Her stomach turned.

'But unfortunately time is not on our side. So that particular pleasure must, for now anyway, be postponed. You will therefore answer my questions fully and without hesitation. Otherwise, I will kill her,' he said, pointing the gun at Natalia. 'She is entirely dispensable, even if for now you are not. You do understand that?'

Ellen glanced sideways and then back at Möller. 'Yes.'

'I read your text message to Stammers.'

Her heart sank.

'He is, as we speak, searching for what he now knows is the codebook?'

'Yes.'

'Where?'

'Bletchley Park.'

'That is where the tunnel is located?'

'Yes.'

'But there are no tunnels at Bletchley Park. Even I know that.'

Ellen hesitated.

Möller raised the gun.

'They discovered a tunnel entrance.'

'When?'

'Yesterday. It was full of rubble.'

'How long will it take him to dig it out and retrieve the book?'

'I don't know,' she said, feeling utterly defeated. 'How could I know? I haven't even seen it,' she added, hurriedly.

Möller appeared to be considering her words.

'He may have it already,' she said, noting his reaction with a modicum of satisfaction.

'Then it is fortunate that I have you and the old woman. It will encourage him to bring it to me.'

Ellen said nothing.

'One other matter intrigues me.'

Ellen could feel her naked legs trembling.

'It concerns Harry's mother.'

349

Ellen felt her stomach lurch.

'Did Elsie tell you where she is?'

She stared at him. Afraid to make any reply.

Möller stepped forward and, with his free hand, grabbed Natalia by the hair.

The nurse screamed.

'No!' Ellen cried out.

Möller had whipped her around and was pointing the gun at the side of her head. Natalia was grey-faced and trembling, tears streaming down her face. 'Please,' she begged. 'Please…'

'Silence,' he said icily.

'Harry's mother disappeared when he was a small boy,' Ellen said, hurriedly. 'Elsie thinks that she knows where she is, but she can't possibly…'

'Why?'

Ellen hesitated.

Möller stepped back and kicked Natalia's right leg, just below the knee. The nurse screamed in agony and collapsed to the floor.

'Because she is dead,' Ellen blurted. 'She was killed in a car crash in 1977. Harry knows that,' she lied. 'He's always known it.'

Möller smiled. 'Then why…'

'She meant that she knows where her body is. Where she is buried,' she blurted in desperation. But even as the words left her lips she knew that it was hopeless.

'You're lying.'

'No,' Ellen said, shaking her head. 'You're confusing me.'

Möller raised the gun and pulled the trigger. Natalia had managed to sit up, clutching her right knee. Facing Ellen. The single shot from behind, at close range, blew away her lower jaw, sending a puff of pink spray into the air. The nurse toppled over sideways.

'Wrong answer,' Möller said, without emotion.

Ellen screamed. 'No,' she sobbed, sinking to her knees. 'You bastard. You stinking fucking bastard.'

BUILDING 41

'Liz Muir.'

'No,' Ellen said, looking up into his face, tears streaming down her cheeks.

'I discovered that she was his mother, after our encounter last year. The fool should have been more careful. The radio interview. It piqued my curiosity. It was an easy thing, after that.'

'You're wrong,' Ellen said, still sobbing.

'So Muir is alive. I had not anticipated that, I will admit it,' he said, clearly enjoying her turmoil. 'If I'd known it a year ago, things might have been rather different,' he added, thoughtfully. 'Still, we must each take our chances where they come. Do you not think so?'

Ellen said nothing. She was trying not to look at the nurse's body. Trying not to smell the blood.

'And I intend to take this one, you can be sure of it. Thanks to your carelessness, I can have it all. The codebook, Elsie Sidthorpe, you, Stammers and, as an unexpected but very welcome bonus, Liz Muir.' He grinned broadly. 'Could it get any better?'

When Elsie Sidthorpe heard the gunshot it was as though the sound had punched a hole through her heart. She had cried out, in anguish and struggled to stand, but her legs would not hold her weight and she had slumped back against the wheelchair.

She had known that Natalia's only value to him was as a lever to guarantee their cooperation. Otherwise, she was a burden. An extra body that would slow them down, without any other purpose. Elsie had feared it from the moment they had been taken.

What information had Ellen refused to give him, sufficient to warrant the nurse's murder? There was next to no possibility that Möller had killed Ellen, but still Elsie's heart fluttered at the thought of it. Ellen was undoubtedly his most valuable hostage, by far. While Möller had her, Harry would have no alternative but to bring the codebook to him. To do whatever Möller wished. But evidently, she had not cooperated sufficiently to save the young nurse's life. Elsie bowed her head and said a silent prayer.

She was still praying, when the ambulance doors opened and Ellen appeared, her face grey and slack. 'I'm sorry, Gran,' Ellen blurted. 'I'm so sorry.'

She stared past Ellen at Möller. 'Does life have no meaning to you at all?' she spat.

'Shut up,' he barked.

Ellen had climbed into the ambulance.

'Hurry,' Möller barked. 'Or I will finish her here,' he said, brandishing the gun. He pulled out the rubberised ramp from beneath the ambulance.

Ellen manoeuvred Elsie's wheelchair down the ramp with Möller looking on.

'There would be a certain advantage to shooting you now,' he said. 'And why not? Stammers will cooperate with me fully without any assistance from you.'

This thought had also crossed Elsie's mind. 'Why not, indeed?' she said, bravely.

'Gran? What are you talking about?' Ellen said, horrified.

'But then I would not have the pleasure of watching your face as Harry hands me the book. As well as his, when I kill Liz Muir.'

As he said the words, Elsie Sidthorpe felt her stomach flip. 'What are you talking about? Liz Muir is dead, you know that,' she stammered.

'Not according to Ellen, here.'

'I'm sorry, Gran. I'm so sorry,' Ellen wept.

Elsie stared at her in disbelief.

'Don't be too hard on her,' Möller said, clearly triumphant. 'Although I am bound to say that while sending the text was forgivable, failing to delete it was careless in the extreme.'

'It's my fault. All my fault…'

Elsie bowed her head.

'You will, of course, take me to her.'

BUILDING 41

Elsie whipped her head up, sending a jolt of pain through her neck. 'To who? What are you talking about?'

'Come now, Elsie. The time for such games has passed. Liz Muir. You will take me to her.'

'I will not. Never.'

'Oh, I think you will. It will be the perfect hiding place, until Stammers is ready to deliver the codebook,' Möller laughed like he knew she was beaten.

'You are insane,' Elsie managed. 'There is nothing. Nothing that would convince me to betray her. I would die first.'

'Gran, no,' Ellen pleaded.

'I dare say that you would. I wonder, however, whether your loyalty would survive what I could do to Ellen. The removal of a finger, perhaps. That might encourage Stammers, if indeed, further encouragement proves to be necessary. Or perhaps I could take a few moments to discover the contents of her knickers. Here, in front of you,' he said, stepping sideways and taking hold of Ellen's arm. 'It is a temptation. I won't deny it,' he added, sliding his hand down her back.

Ellen shoved him away.

Elsie stared at him with hatred blazing in her eyes. Had she been thirty years younger, she would have thrown herself on him, abandoning all caution. But she knew that she could not. That there was no possibility of physical resistance.

'Where is Muir? You will tell me.'

Elsie stared at him.

'Now,' he said, still holding the gun and taking a step towards Ellen.

Ellen took a step backwards.

'Hordle. She lives in a village called Hordle. On the southern edge of the New Forest,' Elsie said grimly.

'Excellent,' Möller smiled. 'It appears,' he said, turning towards Ellen, 'that we must, once again, postpone the fun for another time.

You will find your clothes on the co-driver's seat. Retrieve them and put them on.'

She stepped around the nurse's body, avoiding looking at the blood that had pooled around her smashed face.

'Be careful, Ellen. Be very careful,' Möller said.

She walked towards the ambulance and climbed up into the cab. Her mind was racing. She had seconds only. Her eyes darted around the cab, looking for something - anything that she might use as a weapon. And, suddenly, there it was. A chance. She reached over, turned the radio's volume knob down and pressed the power button. She looked around for the microphone, but none was visible. She scanned the controls, reached out and pressed the button marked "TX". She grabbed her jeans and shoes and jumped down from the cab.

'Hordle is in Hampshire, isn't it?' she said as loudly as she dared. 'We'll never make it that far. Not in this,' she added, pulling on her jeans.

'Which would be a problem were we travelling by ambulance,' Möller replied. 'Now hurry. Put your shoes on.'

She slipped them onto her feet.

Möller was watching her. 'Good,' he said, when she was ready. 'Now, outside.'

He followed them to the door of the barn. 'Open it.'

She did as he had instructed.

'The car is to your right. You will help Elsie into the rear seat. Passenger side. You will be driving Ellen.'

She stared at him.

I will be sitting behind you. All the way. One false move and Elsie will die. Do you understand?'

'Yes.'

'Good. Now move.'

CHAPTER FORTY-ONE

'The key, Harry. You have got it?'

I panicked. I was just so utterly exhausted. For a moment, I had no idea where the key was. 'Of course, I've got it. I just...' I stammered, 'Give me a moment.'

'Harry,' Jane said, taking hold of my arm. 'It's all right.'

I stared at her, blankly.

'Have you checked your back pocket?'

I felt a wave of relief wash over me. I'd zipped it into the back pocket of Mike's trousers. It was the only pocket that had a zip. I'd thought it would be safer there. I unzipped the pocket and removed the key.

'Where'd you get that then?' Stan said, like I'd produced a rabbit from a hat.

'It's a long story.'

The number "41" and the letter "B" had been sprayed onto the door in military style lettering. I inserted the key in the lock. The door opened easily. I don't know why I'd been expecting a room but a room it was not. It was a shallow cupboard with a row of electrical switches and a fusebox across the back and a shelf above. On the shelf were three cardboard boxes and an old first aid kit. Jane reached up and removed the boxes, one at a time. Stan shone his torch at each one in turn. The first two contained cleaning materials and some rusting tools. As she pulled out the third, a book flopped down behind. Jane dropped the box like it was hot and reached for the book. It was red, with a yellowing label. We both stared at it.

'Geheim Reichssache,' she whispered.

'Secret Reich Matter,' I translated.

'Stone the crows,' Stan exclaimed. 'Now, ain't that something.'

She turned the cover. Inside, were several pages of handwritten code.

'German naval enigma,' I said, an edge to my voice.

'How do you know it's naval,' said Stan, craning his neck to see over my shoulder.

'The code is arranged in groups of four letters. The German navy used four. Otherwise, it was usually five.'

'What does it say?'

Jane and I both turned and stared at him.

Jane laughed first, but it was infectious. It must have been the stress I guess. Soon, all three of us were howling.

'Jesus. It took some of the finest minds in the world to crack this stuff,' I said, wiping my eyes with my wrist. 'I might be a clever sod, Stan. But even I have my limits.'

*****

Smith drove back toward Southwold with Mikkel Eglund sitting beside him, nursing his nose. Neither man spoke. Smith was thinking that if Neufeld was still alive, which he very much doubted given Möller's continuing presence, there was a slim chance that she might be able to provide some clue as to Möller's intentions.

'How's the nose?' Smith said at last, glancing at his passenger. The front of the Norwegian's coat was covered in blood.

'Feels like someone skewered me with a red hot poker,' Mike replied. 'Otherwise, it has at least stopped bleeding.'

'It's broken.'

BUILDING 41

Mike snorted.

'You're a very lucky man that's all you broke.'

'Hell, yes. It was my lucky day.'

Smith laughed, in spite of everything. 'You'd better lose the coat. You get out of the car looking like that, and people will think that it's the day of reckoning.'

Mike looked down at the blood. 'You don't know what you're saying.'

'It's belongs to Stammers, I take it?'

'Sure does. He is going to be well pissed.'

'Right now, I think that's the least of his problems.'

'You reckon I could use your phone?' Mike said after a few moments.

'Depends on who you want to call.'

'My partner.'

'Jane will have to wait.'

Mike stared at him. 'You were one of the guys who interviewed me in hospital last year, right?'

'That was me,' Smith said, matter of factly.

'Smith, wasn't it?'

Smith said nothing.

They'd arrived in Southwold. Smith followed the road along the seafront and parked the Mercedes behind Harry's Spitfire. 'Don't go anywhere.'

Mike held up his hand. 'I'm cool.'

'Good.' Smith got out of the car and walked across to the cottage.

Mike watched him put his shoulder to the door. He waited until Smith had disappeared inside. Then he put his hand in his coat pocket and pulled out his phone. He'd been holding it when the Saab had overturned. Bizarrely, he'd still been holding it when he came to. 'Jane! I'm fine. No, no I'm fine. But I don't have much time.'

CHAPTER FORTY-TWO

After the discovery of the codebook, we'd climbed back out of the tunnel and made our way over to the bungalow. Stan had gone to check the Park's main gate.

'What do we do now?' I said to Jane as she let us in and switched on the lights.

'You sit, is what you do. While I make us some coffee. Then we'll decide on our next move.'

'I might use the bathroom first. I'm filthy. I can't think while I'm this dirty.'

Jane nodded and headed into the kitchen.

I dropped the codebook on the nearest desk and headed for the bathroom. I went to the sink, turned on both taps and splashed water onto my face. *He has Ellen.* That one single thought kept running through my head like the tolling of a bell. *Möller has Ellen.* He had her and there was nothing I could do about it. *Möller has her.* I stared at my hands. They were shaking. I was gasping. It was out of control. I was out of control. *He has her.* I leant forward, both my hands on the porcelain. And threw up into the sink. When it was over, I looked up and caught sight of myself in the mirror. My face was filthy. Smeared with brick dust and grime from the rubble. The taps were still running. I splashed some more water on my face. It made me gasp all over again. Then I stepped away from the sink, pulled some paper towels from the dispenser

BUILDING 41

and patted my face dry. Somehow I needed to hold it together. Whatever was going to happen next, I needed to face it. With Jane. Like we'd faced it almost a year before. Then, we'd rescued Ellen. Against all the odds and despite Günther Möller. We'd beaten him then. We could do it again. We had to. There was nobody else. Nothing else. I headed back into the office and sat down heavily behind Jane's desk.

Jane reappeared with two cups of coffee and the codebook tucked under her arm. 'You feeling any better?'

'Not much. You?'

She shrugged.

Then her phone rang.

'Mike? Oh thank God. Are you all right? Are you sure you're not hurt? I've been worried to death.' Jane looked like she was going to fall over with relief.

I got up, pulled out a chair and she sat down.

'You what? Ellen's Saab? Jesus Christ. No. We've got it. It's a German codebook. Ellen sent us a text. I don't know.' She paused. 'Smith?'

Smith.

'I don't know. Hang on,' she hesitated and then she handed me the phone.

I stared at her.

She nodded.

'Mike?' I said, like there was no breath in my lungs.

'Hey. Look I don't have much time. I'm with Smith. He's checking out Natalia's place. He doesn't know that I have a phone. I told him I lost it in the crash.'

'Crash?' I said, still breathless.

'Ah, yes. Look, I totalled the Saab. The thing is, we're parked up behind your Spitfire. If I'm quick, I could be away. But it might be better if I stay with him. What do you reckon?'

'Where's Ellen?' It was all I could think of.

Mike hesitated. 'He took them. I'm sorry, bud. There was nothing I could do.'

My worst nightmare. 'Do you have any idea where he's taken them?'

'No. But look, I'm more likely to find out if I stay with Smith, right?'

'I guess.' I looked at Jane.

'I just don't know,' she said, shaking her head.

'For fuck's sake, be careful Mike. Smith is…' I hesitated. What was Smith? Did I know anything about him? 'Just be careful. Don't be a fucking hero. We want you back. All of you.' I added, staring at Jane.

She nodded slowly, her eyes filling with tears.

'OK,' Mike said, urgently. 'Look, I'll call you again. When I can. Tell Jane I love her. Gotta go.'

But I'd stopped listening, because at that point my own phone had begun to ring and I could see the number on the screen. It was Ellen's.

*****

Smith reappeared, grim faced, within seconds of Mike stuffing his phone back into his pocket. He got into the car started the engine and immediately drove away at speed.

'Bad news?' Mike ventured.

'We don't want to be here when the police arrive, which I'd say will be in about three minutes.'

'Why?'

'Why, do we need to be away or why will the police arrive in three minutes.'

'Both?' Mike said hopefully.

'One, because I just called them and two, because neither of us needs to be caught up at a murder scene right now.'

'Murder scene?'

BUILDING 41

'That's what I said.'

'Whose?'

'Petra Neufeld's. Single gunshot to the head.'

Mike stared at him, open mouthed.

Smith said nothing.

'Where are we going?'

'To meet someone and then I might think about letting you make that call.' He hesitated. 'In fact, I might make it myself.'

It was Mike's turn to say nothing. Neufeld, dead. He'd had mixed feelings about her. While he could see the attraction, he'd met women like her before. Women who played games with you. Women with secrets to hide. Ultimately he'd agreed with Jane. She'd not been someone to be trusted. But still...

They'd taken a side street and pulled up outside an off-licence.

'Stay put,' Smith said, getting out of the car, walking two cars further down and getting into the passenger seat of the car in front. Mike strained to see the other occupant but couldn't. He waited. A few minutes later, Smith got out and returned to the Mercedes.

'The police have found the ambulance crew.'

Which was hardly surprising.

'But much more interestingly, they've got an open carrier from the radio of the hijacked ambulance.'

Mike knew enough about radio to know what that meant. Someone had left the transceiver in transmit. 'Is there any sound?'

'Not now there isn't, but there was. They're forwarding me a recording. Just about...' he paused.

His phone beeped.

'Now,' Smith said lifting the phone to his ear and listening. When he'd finished listening, he put the phone back in his pocket. He started the engine.

'Where are we going?'

'Hordle,' Smith said, thoughtfully. 'It's in Hampshire.'

'Why are we going there?'

'Because Ellen is a remarkable woman. When you make that call, you can tell Harry Stammers that Ellen is not only alive but she's thinking on her feet.'

*****

I handed Jane her phone with one hand, grabbed mine with the other and pressed the answer button. 'Ellen,' I said, breathlessly.

'I think not,' said a voice that I recognised instantly and with a deep sense of foreboding.

'What have you done with her, you bastard? If you have so much as…'

'Save the clichés for another day, Stammers. Let's get straight to the point, shall we?'

I said nothing.

'You have the codebook, I take it?'

'Yes,' I said, like the admission was acid on my tongue.

There was a moment's silence.

'As you know, I have Ellen and Elsie here with me.'

I noticed the omission.

'Without wishing to employ another unnecessary cliché, you will follow my instructions exactly. If, of course, you wish to see either of them alive again.'

'Yes.'

'Excellent. First, you will contact no one and especially not the police. If they contact you, you will say that you have no idea why Ellen and Elsie have been taken, who might have taken them or their whereabouts. Is that clear?'

'Yes.'

'You will say nothing about the codebook. You know nothing about it. You discovered nothing in the tunnel. If anyone assisted you with the codebook's discovery you will need to assure yourself of their silence.'

'Nobody assisted me.'

BUILDING 41

'Bullshit, Stammers, but no matter. How you silence your friends is your problem, but silence them you will. Because unless that codebook is delivered to me in complete secrecy, you can kiss goodbye to Ellen. In fact, I'll kiss her goodbye for you,' Möller laughed.

I began to shake. But this time it was with stone cold hearted fury.

'Second. You are going to deliver the codebook to me personally. You will come alone. Do you hear me Stammers? Alone.'

'I hear you.'

'I hope so. For Ellen's sake. Because, I would enjoy hurting her. In fact, resisting that particular temptation has already proved to be something of a personal struggle.'

'Fuck you, Möller. If you so much as...'

'Harry!' Jane hissed. She was shaking her head violently.

I stared at her. She put a hand on my harm.

'Breathe,' she whispered. 'It's all right. Breathe.' She squeezed my arm, gently.

'Where?' I said, through clenched teeth. 'Where do you want me to bring it?'

'Patience Stammers. I feel sure that you're going to find the venue for our little exchange, most revealing. But good things come to those who wait. A maxim which is certainly true in my case. I have waited a very long time for that codebook. A very long time indeed.'

'Where is Ellen? I want to talk to her.'

Möller laughed. 'I think not. Ellen is driving. You do have access to a car, I take it? Your sports car is in Southwold and Mr Eglund appeared to be driving Ellen's.'

'Yes.'

'Excellent. You will drive to Hordle. It is a village in Hampshire. You have,' he hesitated. 'Three hours. That should suffice. When you arrive in the village, you will call me on this number.'

I said nothing. I was trying to work out Hordle's significance, but I'd never heard of the place.

'Is that all clear?'

'Yes.'

'Three hours Stammers.'

The line went dead.

For a moment I stared at it in silence. 'Well, that's it then,' I said bleakly. 'All we can do is give the bastard his fucking codebook.'

Jane looked at me. 'Maybe.'

'What do you mean, "maybe"?'

Jane's expression was impenetrable. 'I mean, maybe that is not all we can do.'

CHAPTER FORTY-THREE

The dark coloured car turned into Cottager's Lane in Hordle and came to a halt on a narrow grass verge opposite a two storey cottage with a low thatched roof. The car's occupants stared out at the building, each with their own thoughts. Even in near darkness, it was a picture postcard of a property, with a rose climbing to the roof on one side of the bayed front door, and a clematis winding up a wooden trellis on the other. The lane's single orange street lamp was partially obscured by a colossal English Oak. It seemed to be leaning toward the lamp, warming its leaves in the fiery light, sending shadows dancing across the front of the cottage in flames of orange and brown. Lavender Cottage appeared to be in darkness, save for a tiny light flickering in a downstairs window. A candle perhaps.

Günther Möller raised his gun and placed it against the driver's neck. 'You have your instructions. Follow them.'

Ellen Carmichael opened the driver's door, swung her feet on to the grass verge and climbed out of the car. She walked around to the front and opened the rear passenger's door.

Möller got out, switching targets from the elderly woman beside him to the woman standing opposite.

Ellen bent down and helped Elsie Sidthorpe out onto the lane. The old woman stood, trembling with the exertion. Together, Ellen and Elsie hobbled across the lane to the cottage's black wooden gate. The two women approached the door.

Möller followed them, lowering the gun but with his finger still on the trigger. He stopped at the window and peered inside. Then he looked at Ellen and nodded. She lifted the iron knocker and rapped on the door three times. After a short delay, a lamp beside the door came on and the door opened slowly, restricted by a chain. A face appeared in the space between the door frame.

'Hello, Liz,' Elsie said, in a strained voice, willing the woman behind the door to sense the danger.

'Rose? Is that you? What on Earth are you doing here? And who's that with you?'

Ellen stepped into the light. 'Mrs Stammers? I'm Ellen. Elsie's…' she hesitated. 'I mean Rosemary's…'

'Ellen? Ellen Carmichael? Yes, I know who you are but what are you doing here?'

'Can we come in, Liz?' Elsie said evenly, 'I'm a little unsteady on my feet. I rather think I need to sit down,' she said, stumbling slightly.

Ellen threw a protective arm around her.

Elizabeth Stammers released the chain guard and slowly opened the door.

Möller had been waiting. He stepped forward, pointing the gun at the woman who was standing in the doorway. 'Good evening, Liz,' he said, evenly. 'Although perhaps "good" is not quite the word, in your case.'

*****

Mike called again about an hour after my conversation with Möller. By then, I was seated beside Jane, in the Volvo, heading south on the A34.

BUILDING 41

'Ellen somehow put the ambulance radio into TX, Harry. It was a smart move. A really smart move. We know where they're going.'

'So do I.'

'You do?'

'Möller called, we're already on our way. Where are you?'

'M25. We've just gone over the bridge at Dartford.'

'No. Mike. Möller made it clear that I am to come alone. No police. If you turn up with Smith, he'll kill them.'

Mike hesitated.

'Can't you stop him? Stall him or something?' I said, quietly.

'No can do, bud.'

'Put him on. Put Smith on.'

I could hear Mike speaking to Smith in the background.

'Smith?'

'Harry.'

'You've got to turn back. Möller made it clear that he'll kill them if anyone interferes.'

'Moller gave you the address?'

I said nothing.

'Harry, did he give you the address?'

'No. I've got to call him when I get there.'

'You have the codebook with you?'

'Smith, please. I will deal with this.'

'Listen to me. What do you suppose Möller will do once he has it? Leave you playing happy families and drive away into the night?'

Happy families.

'I'll convince him. Once he gets the book, he'll have no reason…'

'No reason?' Smith interrupted. 'Think, man. If you do this, he will have the four of you. The people that he most wants to hurt. All together in one place. Unarmed and at his mercy. We're taking about Günther Möller here, Harry. The same Günther Möller who arranged your death in that lift shaft at Belsize Park. The same man who blew away Dabrowski's face, for screwing his plans. Have you any idea how many people Günther Möller has murdered?'

'No,' I conceded.

'No. Neither do I. We lost count.'

I was thinking. *Four people.* Me. Elsie. Ellen. Natalia? Neither Mike nor Möller had mentioned her. *Happy families.* I was missing something. 'Four?'

'What?'

'You said four people. Why would he want to hurt Natalia?'

There was a pause. 'Natalia is already dead,' Smith said flatly.

'What?' A picture of the nurse's face appeared in my head.

'He killed her when they exchanged vehicles. That's three people he's killed today. Don't you get it?'

I said nothing. I was still thinking about the Russian nurse. Dead.

'You really don't know, do you?' Smith said, after a short pause.

'What don't I know?'

Another pause.

'What don't I know?' I repeated.

'The address where Möller has taken them. In Hordle. It belongs to Elsie.'

I knew about the house in Wangford. She still owned it. She'd let it out as a holiday home to a couple from Bristol. Ellen had told me. She'd never mentioned another house.

'So she has another place. So what?' I said, trying to put the jigsaw together but I had no idea what Smith was talking about.

'It is where your mother lives, Harry.'

My mother. The place your mother lives. Lives. I was too stunned to speak. I was thinking about the last time I'd seen her. *Alive.*

'If you go in there with the codebook, he will kill you all. Unless I can stop him. And right now I am the only man who can. He'll kill you, Ellen and Elsie. In front of her. He will make her suffer

BUILDING 41

and then he will butcher her too. Believe me Harry. Günther Möller will spare none of you. He will enjoy your deaths almost as much as he will enjoy walking away with the codebook.'

My mother. Liz Muir. He was bringing us to her.

'He gave me three hours,' I said, like I was reciting the words. 'To get to Hordle and to call him. Otherwise he will start killing them.'

'You're not listening to me. He is going to kill them, whatever you do. You must see that.'

Smith was wrong. I was going to stop Möller. If I died in the attempt. He was not going to harm them and if he so much as touched Ellen... I blocked the thought from my head. We had beaten him before. We would do it again. Somehow. I looked down at the clock on the dashboard. 'We have less than an hour to get there. You must be, what, two hours away? Maybe more? You're too late. I can't wait for you.'

'Harry, please see sense...'

But I'd already ended the call.

CHAPTER FORTY-FOUR

Liz Muir had recoiled from him in abject terror. It had been twenty-eight years since she had suffered at his hands. Since he had subjected her to the most unspeakable horrors. Since he had ripped from her everything that she had held to be dear and in all of that time, she had never forgiven him. Never forgotten. Nor would she ever forgive or forget. He was everything she had feared. All that she had loathed. Returned, to torture her again. To destroy those she loved, after everything she had done to protect them. She had sunk to her knees in front of him. When Ellen had lifted her up, she had barely seen. When she had tied her to one of the old wooden chairs in the dining room, she had felt nothing. She had neither spoken nor cried out. She had simply stared. Watched, as Ellen had tied Rose to the chair next to her hers and as Ellen, had herself, been bound to a third.

'Now, we wait. For the arrival of our guest,' Möller had said, laughing triumphantly.

*****

BUILDING 41

We arrived in Hordle ten minutes beyond the deadline set for us by Möller. Jane pulled up in front of a little row of shops.

'Are you sure about this?'

Jane nodded. 'Just call him.'

'You don't have to do this, Jane. Smith is right. He could kill us all. You don't have to do this.'

'Bollocks. Call him. We're late.'

I sighed, reached for the phone and dialled the number. I listened to his instructions with my stomach in ashes. When he'd finished, I hung up. 'They're in Cottagers Lane at the Everton Road end.'

Jane reached for the sat nav and keyed in the address. 'It's two minutes away.'

'I'm to walk in. Park the car at the bottom of the road and walk up to the cottage. It's the second, on the left.'

'Drop me a little further back.'

I nodded. We got out of the car and changed places. I started the engine and pulled away.

'I just want to say, thank you,' I said, as we turned into Everton Road.

'Shut up.'

'For everything you have done for me and for Ellen. You've been the most wonderful friend.'

'I know. Now shut up.'

'For fuck's sake Jane. I'm trying to tell you how much we both love you. I mean,' I stammered. 'How much I love you. I could not have…'

'I love you too. Both of you. So let's just get this done.'

I nodded.

'And do at least try not to get yourself killed, eh?' Jane said.

'I'll do my best.'

'Good. Over there,' she added suddenly.

I pulled up at the side of the road. Jane got out. She didn't speak or look back. She just walked away. I watched her climb up a low embankment and disappear into the hedgerow that ran along the top.

I put my foot on the accelerator, drove the short distance to the junction with Cottager's Lane, parked up on a grass verge, switched off the engine and got out of the car. So this was it. The moment of truth. I opened the rear door on the driver's side and retrieved the codebook from the seat. Ahead of me, in Cottager's Lane, were Ellen, Elsie, my mother and Günther Möller. Waiting for me. It was a weird feeling. Surreal. As I walked up to the cottage, it didn't feel like any of it could really be happening. That they could be here at all. But I knew that they were. I opened the gate. As I walked towards the door, it swung slowly open. I stood on the porch.

'Welcome to the party.'

I stepped into the hallway. He stepped out behind me and I felt something cold against the back of my neck. Undoubtedly a gun. I saw them immediately. Lined up against the rear of the room into which he had pushed me. It was a beautifully decorated little room with an ornate open fire place, lit by several wall lights and a small oil lamp, perched on the window sill behind the three captives. I could smell the fragrance from the burning oil.

My eyes fixed on Ellen first. She was pale and her face was streaked with tears. She was seated on a chair and looking straight at me. I looked into her eyes. They were filled with fear. I tore my eyes away. Beside her was Elsie. Still bruised from her earlier encounter with Möller. She also stared at me but said nothing. And beside her, a slightly built elderly woman, with grey hair but it was her face that drew my attention. It was slack, her eyes unseeing. Dead. My mother was staring at the wall to my left. She made no acknowledgement of my presence nor gave any indication that she had recognised me. Beside her was an empty chair.

BUILDING 41

'We have been waiting for you,' Möller said, taking the codebook out of my hand. There was a moment's silence. 'Put your arms behind your back. Wrists together.'

I felt him tie them.

'Sit.'

I approached the chair, turned and seated myself awkwardly, my hands tucked between my body and the seat back.

Günther Möller. He had put on weight since I'd last seen him. He was bigger and more muscular. But it was his baldness that was most striking. He had no hair at all. He was wearing a brown leather jacket that looked too small for him and cherry red Doctor Martins. He was clutching the codebook in one hand and a gun in the other.

'No tearful reunion then?' he said, smiling broadly.

No one spoke.

'Nothing to say, Liz?'

He took a step towards her, pointing the gun at her face.

'Leave her alone, you bastard.'

It was Ellen who had spoken. I stared at her, willing her to say nothing more to antagonise him.

'What has she done to you?' Ellen continued. 'What have any of us done to you?'

'What have you done?' Möller laughed.

I noted the edge of hysteria to it.

'Why don't you tell us, Elsie?' he said, turning to her. 'Well why not? You know, better than anyone. What did you do? Tell us.'

Elsie said nothing.

'Tell us,' he yelled.

I was sweating. Wondering about Jane.

'I was twenty-one,' Elsie said, her tone full of bitterness and regret.

I turned my head to face her. She was looking towards Ellen. 'I did something I have regretted every day since. A stupid thing. Not out of any malice. An innocent thing. We were in a pub, near

Bletchley, Martha and I. Celebrating her weekend off. I took that,' she said, glancing at the codebook in Möller's hand. 'From Ronald Warren's kit bag,' she said, looking up at Möller. 'He too had done something stupid. He had taken it from a captured U-boat.'

'Captured?' Möller interjected. 'The crew was massacred. Every crew member but one. Did you know that?'

Elsie shook her head.

'They were mown down, as they emerged from the conning tower. Machine gunned where they stood, their hands in the air. They had been instructed not to resist because their commander had believed that the British Royal Navy would not fire on them.' Möller laughed bitterly. 'He was Kapitänleutnant Fritz-Julius Lettmann. The British took him captive. When he returned to Germany, after the war, it was as an outcast. Shunned by the communists and liberal puppets installed by the Allies, despised by the nationalists as a coward because he'd lost his entire crew. The fools knew nothing of his mission. Of the treachery of your filthy British establishment.' Möller spat the words, like they were vomit on his tongue. 'He died in 1962 when I was twelve years old. He was penniless. An alcoholic and a drug addict. Did you know that, Elsie Sidthorpe?'

'I knew nothing of it,' she said, bravely 'I took the book, without thought. It was a stupid, foolish error. Martha told me that she had found it and returned it to Warren. By the time that I discovered that she had not, it was too late. Martha had disappeared. I was certain that she had taken it to London, to protect me, and been killed for it. She was my best friend. My only true friend, until I met Liz,' she added, turning to towards the woman sitting next to me.

Nobody spoke. I glanced down at my mother's hands. Her tiny wrists had been tied together with what looked like telephone wire. I immediately looked away. She had already begun to loosen her bonds.

BUILDING 41

'After the war,' Elsie continued, 'I thought that I might use the job I was offered to discover the truth about what had happened to Martha and to the book, but I was being used. By elements who knew about the book and hoped that I might lead them to it. When you arrived in Britain,' she said, addressing Möller, 'I did not choose to watch you. I was assigned to you. Did you know that, Möller?'

Möller spat on the floor.

'But always, the same elements who had prompted my recruitment were working to ensure your continued freedom. They hoped, that by pitting us against each other, in a race to discover the book, they might themselves recover it. But, in the end, I became a liability. They used my failure to prevent you from murdering Ronald Warren, as a pretext for retiring me from service.'

Möller snorted. 'Even that did not dissuade you.'

'No. It did not. Your butchery of Warren was an affront to humanity. His death should have been prevented. I should have prevented it. I could not leave it there.'

I glanced at my mother's hands. They were almost free. I readied myself.

'Lucky for you that when I followed you from Excalibur House, I did not know that you were one of the two women Warren had bleated about, or I would have wrung it from you then.'

Elsie's face was expressionless. 'It would have done you no good. I knew nothing then of the whereabouts of the book. Nor of its contents. Though I will confess that, over the years, I have had my suspicions.'

Möller stared at her with hatred blazing in his eyes. 'For someone who claims to have known nothing, you put much effort into keeping the book from me.'

'I sought only to discover the truth. I acted, initially at least, out of guilt. Knowing, as I did, that by taking the book, I had set in motion the tragedies that followed. I sought only to right this wrong that I had caused. If I sought to foil you, it was only to prevent the trail of death and destruction that you left in your wake. And latterly, to protect those who I loved from the threat that you posed to them.'

'Protect them?' Möller laughed. 'Is that why you used him?' he said, waving the gun at me. 'Hid from him your true purpose? Pitted your own flesh and blood against me? Sent them to do your dirty work when you were too old and wrinkled to face me? You're a liar. Your excuses bore me. They are nothing but weasel words. Protect them? Now I have heard it all.'

Möller was unstable. I could see it in his face. In the way he spat his words. While that, in itself, was terrifying enough, it was the fact that he had his finger on the trigger of the gun in his hand that terrified me most. If my mother moved, he might fire the weapon, whether he intended it or not.

'Were you protecting Liz Muir, when she infiltrated the NUGB and destroyed our great cause?' he continued. 'A cause that would have exposed the hypocrisy of your British upper class, a class that you cherish so fondly? Cowards,' Möller said, beginning to pace back and forth. 'Weak minded opportunists and Jews. Traitors. All of you. Is that why you watched while Owen used her?' he said, waving his weapon toward the woman seated beside me.

Elsie stared at him.

'Tell us, Liz. Tell us what did you do?'

I had not expected her to speak. I had expected her to move. I tensed. If I needed to, I was ready to throw myself between them, bound or not. But she did not move. She took a long, faltering breath.

'I never planned it,' she began, staring into the hallway behind Möller's back. 'Never intended any of it. Like Elsie, I was a young woman. Twenty-two when I joined. I'd been offered a chance. To make a difference. To join the fight against the racists and bigots of the Far Right who I despised, utterly. And still do,' she said, shifting her gaze to Möller. 'I took it, willingly.'

BUILDING 41

Möller's eyes were fixated on her, as though he was unable to look away. I risked another glance at her hands. They were free. She was holding the telephone wire to prevent it falling to the floor.

'When I met Peter, everything changed. I fell in love with him,' she said, simply. 'It was like nothing I had ever encountered. A crazy, ruinous kind of love that burned me like a wild fire so that I could neither contain or control it. And yet my whole reason for being with him was to betray him to those who had employed me. It lasted seven years. Not even Rose,' she said, turning toward her old friend, 'could save me from it. When I met Ted,' she said turning towards me for the first time, 'he offered me a way out.'

I stared into her eyes. The depth of the pain I saw in them, brought tears into my own. I felt them trickle down my cheeks.

'You'll never know, Harry, how it tore me apart to lie to him. I was pregnant, you see.'

'I know,' I said simply.

'You do?'

I nodded.

'Ted was such a wonderful man. I thought,' she hesitated. 'I thought that it was my only chance to escape Peter and the ruin of my relationship with him. I left the Service, returned to teaching and moved in with Ted. You were born and little Katie. Such beautiful children…' she said wistfully, tears rolling down her face and dripping into her lap.

'You should have stayed away,' Möller said suddenly. 'Although, I am grateful that you did not,' he said grinning.

Once again, I tensed and for a moment I was certain that she was going to move. But she tore her eyes from him and continued. 'I should have. Yes. But I was forced. Blackmailed back into service by the man who had recruited me, seventeen years before. The man who had seen what loving Peter Owen had done to me. The only man who ever knew that Peter was your father, Harry.'

She was staring at me again. I held her eyes. She glanced, fleetingly to her right. It was an odd movement, as though she wanted me to follow them. I looked away and caught a movement in the corner of my eye. Jane. I stared. Transfixed. She had flitted from the darkness at the back of the house, into the hall way, out of sight.

'His name was Smith,' she said, urgently and in warning.

I tore my eyes away and fixed them on my mother.

'He forced me to betray Peter again,' she said, holding my eyes. Desperately willing me not to look away. 'And then I met, you,' she said, turning back towards Möller. She said it with such hatred that I feared she was going to lunge at him. As if sensing my tension, she turned towards me again. 'I'd taught a young lad who had been murdered, just before Smith approached me and threatened to tell Ted that he was not your father. His name was Karl Dixon. He had been butchered. Stabbed and left to die in an alleyway in Wood Green.'

'The boy was a nobody,' Möller laughed. 'An irrelevance.'

'I was caught, you see,' she said, ignoring him. 'Initially by my desire to discover and expose Karl's murderer, and then by my relationship with Peter. I still loved him. I'd always loved him.'

'Lies. You're another liar,' Möller spat.

He had moved to the space in front of the hallway. It was Jane's best chance. I held my breath. But nothing happened.

'It was as though I was caught by a train of events, that I'd set in motion by accepting the job that Smith had offered me all those years before. When I discovered that Peter was planning to bomb Westminster, my agony was complete.'

Möller laughed. 'Not quite.'

'No, not quite,' she whispered. 'Because I discovered that the van into which they had packed the explosives was going to be driven by a British Telecom engineer.'

It took a moment for the penny to drop. 'Ted?' I gasped.

BUILDING 41

'Yes. I had to stop them. At all costs. I couldn't let Ted die. Not after everything he had done for me. I loved him too, you know. Not the destructive, crazy, uncontrollable love that had afflicted me since I had first met Peter. That had twisted, not just my life, but Ted's and your lives, you and Katie. But I did love him. And I loved you and Katie, Harry. Don't ever imagine that I did not. But when he escaped,' she said, glancing back at Möller, 'I knew that none of us was safe. Would ever be safe while he was at large. He would have hunted me, like an animal. Used you, had he ever discovered your existence, to force me out and then he would have murdered us all. When Ted refused to come with me, I was left with no choice. I'm not blaming him. Who could possibly blame him for hating me? You're right,' she said turning to Möller. 'I was a liar. I'd lied to Ted. Destroyed him. Stole from him everything he ever wanted and deserved. But unlike you, Möller I never acted out of malice. Never. I did what I did and I have suffered the consequences every minute of every day, across all these long years.'

Möller laughed out loud but there was nothing but hatred in it.

'You're inhuman, Möller,' she said, rounding on him. 'An evil, stinking monster of a man. What you did to me was unspeakable. For all those you have murdered and maimed, all the pain and suffering you have inflicted on countless others, you are going to burn in Hell!'

The events that followed were a blur of movement and sound. My mother leapt to her feet and began to turn away. Jane's face had appeared behind Möller, her eyes fixed on something over my right shoulder. Möller raised his arm and, as I came out of my seat, I knew that he would shoot. Jane exploded from the hallway and grabbed his arm from behind. The gunshot, when it came, hit me in the shoulder and blew me off my feet. As I fell backwards, I saw the object that my mother had turned to retrieve. The oil lamp arced through the air, leaving a trail of flaming vapour and oil behind it, like a comet. Möller had turned and hit Jane with the gun so hard, that she had been flung back out into the hallway. He had turned, seen the ignited lamp and had held up his left hand defensively. It was of no use. The oil lamp struck his arm, spewed its contents across his upper body and exploded in a sheet of flame. Möller stumbled backwards into the hall, flailing his arms wildly and the codebook, which he still had clutched in his left hand, in an attempt to swat the flames.

I was struggling to stand, fearful that the fire would engulf the little room, burning Elsie and Ellen who were still bound to their chairs. 'Jane!' I screamed. I could see her laying on the floor behind Möller who was burning like a roman candle, setting light to everything he touched.

I can't in all honestly, recall the order in which the events that unfolded happened after that. There'd been a crashing sound of splintering wood and Mike had burst into the hallway. It had seemed to me that he was instantly ablaze, but I know now that it was the vision of him through the flames that I had seen. Because, as I had learned later, Mike had pulled Jane away, into the kitchen at the rear of the property and out through the rear door. Smith had instantaneously appeared to our right, holding a towel to his face, and had freed first Ellen and then half carried, half dragged Elsie out. I had seen him dragging her body away, like a rag doll, as I lost consciousness.

I came to, laying on my back on the road, Ellen hovering over me, her face covered in soot. The street into which I had been carried or dragged was illuminated both by the flames that were billowing from the roof of the cottage and the blue, flashing lights of the fire engines. Firemen were running too and fro, hauling heavy hoses, spouting streams of water up onto burning thatch. An ambulance woman was attending to my injured shoulder. She held an oxygen mask to my face. 'Jane?' I coughed, as soon as she had removed it.

'She's over there,' Ellen replied. I peered into the distance. A figure was seated on the grass verge wrapped in a blanket.

BUILDING 41

'My mother?'

'Liz is fine. We all are Harry.'

'What about Smith?'

Ellen stared at me and shook her head.

'Dead?' I said, stunned. 'But I saw him dragging Elsie out.'

I later discovered that only one body had been found in the gutted cottage. Smith had vanished entirely. As for Günther Möller, true to her word, my mother had sent him to Hell, where as far as I am concerned, he can burn for all eternity.

Andy Mellett Brown

BUILDING 41

EPILOGUE

Sunday, July 22, 2007

'How long will it take?' my mother shouted, above the clacking sound made by the recently reconstructed Turing Bombe, the only such machine in existence.

We'd come down to the basement of B-block at Bletchley Park to watch the Bombe Team at work. They were all volunteers and keen to assist, sworn as they were to complete secrecy. It was why we were running the machine after the museum had closed, away from the prying eyes of the public. Apart from Lizzie, as I'd discovered my mother now liked to be called, only Ellen, Jane, Mike, and four members of the Bombe Team knew anything of the project.

'It's difficult to tell. It depends on the strength of the crib,' I shouted back. 'They could be here all night.'

'How exciting,' Lizzie said, grinning.

It was exciting. It is always exciting to see and hear the Bombe running at full tilt. To describe something as "awesome" has nowadays become rather meaningless. Another of those Americanisms that Elsie so detests and about which she always complains, so vociferously, whenever I use one in her presence. Watching the Bombe, with its spinning multi-coloured indicator drums, however, can definitely and most accurately be described as truly "awesome". I think even Elsie would agree about that.

'What's a crib?'

'The Enigma operators sometimes got lazy,' I said, by way of explanation. 'They used common phrases, or repeated them, especially if they were in a hurry, as we think our spy on the Irish coast might have been on this occasion. From these errors, it is possible to build a menu. The team uses the menu to set up the machine, the Bombe works its magic and, if we're lucky, we might get a stop.'

Jane and I had been working on the crib for months, often late into the night. We'd analysed what was known about the operating procedures of the Kriegsmarine and German spies in the field. Which, in the case of the latter, wasn't a great deal, it has to be said. In the end it had been the simple realisation that the message had been intended for a specific recipient aboard the submarine 'U-110' and, laughably, that the sender had ended the message with "Heil Hitler", that had provided the breakthrough. Or so we were hoping.

'A stop?'

'Yes. The Bombe will stop if it finds a match. If that happens, they'll try the settings on the checking machine. Over there,' I said, pointing at a much smaller machine to our right. 'It's a lengthy process. Unless the crib is good, the checking machine will just give us gibberish. If it doesn't, then we might be in business. It'll be over to the analysts to work out the rest of the settings. Once we have the settings, then we try the full code on one of the Park's Enigma machines and if we are very lucky indeed, we'll get the original message in clear text. German of course.'

Lizzie's face appeared to cloud over. 'And then what will you do?'

Then what indeed? The deaths of countless men and women were attributable, either directly or indirectly, to the secrets contained in the those few pages of German cipher text. The crew

BUILDING 41

of U-110, who had lost their lives in order to make the original exchange. Petty Officer Ronald Warren, who had been an early victim of Günther Möller. Tomasz Dabrowski, Petra Neufeld, Natalia Varennikov, the crew of the ambulance in which Ellen, Elsie and Natalia had been hijacked. Karl Dixon, who would certainly not have been murdered had Möller not come to Britain in search of the codebook. Günther Möller himself. The authorities still didn't know how many people he had murdered. Or if they did, they were certainly not making it public.

Jane and I had been arguing about an attempt on the code from U-110, ever since she had revealed the copy she'd taken on that afternoon in May 2005, when we'd brought the codebook up from the tunnel below Building 41. Until one afternoon, late the previous summer, sitting in our garden in Leighton Buzzard, she had revealed that she'd taken a copy, I'd had no idea at all. 'Don't you remember?' she'd said, typically enjoying my confusion. 'You left the codebook on my desk while you went to clean up?' I'd laughed. 'Jane, I was so bloody exhausted, you could have pasted the photocopies on the wall and I don't think I would have noticed.'

Quite suddenly, the Bombe stopped. Lizzie and I watched in silence as one of the volunteers made a note of the settings. Three from the front and one from the side. And took them across to a colleague, who tried them on the checking machine.

'What's she doing?' Lizzie whispered.

'She's going to try the settings.'

'But that's not an Enigma machine.'

'No, it's a British Typex. It's been adapted to work like an Enigma. If the settings are right, we'll know soon enough. But don't get your hopes up.'

Had our assessment been that the message was likely to be of historical value only, then I doubt that either Jane or I would have had any qualms about attacking the code. Günther Möller's murderous obsession with the codebook could now be explained by his family connection and a desire to see his father exonerated, at least in his eyes. But that wasn't the whole of the story. Something buried in that code was bigger than Möller and Kapitänleutnant Fritz-Julius Lettmann. It had to be, because Möller's story alone could not explain the actions of Smith and the faction inside the Service to which Elsie believed that he belonged. Why, in particular, had Smith been so determined to prevent the codebook from falling into anyone's hands but his?

Elsie's theory seemed fantastic and it was easy to dismiss it as evidence of her increasing mental frailty. She had deteriorated rapidly in the months after her rescue from Lavender Cottage. With Möller dead and the threat to our safety seemingly lifted, it was though she had finally let go.

It was not, I should add, a purely sad decline. On the contrary, she had been happier than Ellen and I had ever seen her, free as she was of the burden of her knowledge of the codebook and from the threat that Günther Möller had represented to us all. Of course, what she didn't know was that a copy of the book existed, let alone that we might attempt its decryption. Ellen and I had agreed that she would never know.

Of Smith there had been no further sign since his disappearance from the scene of the fire. He had simply vanished without so much as a trace. He had not appeared at the Coroner's inquest into Möller's death, and curiously nor had any reference been made to him in the Coroner's findings. It was as though Smith had never existed.

What worried me, as I know that it worried the others, were the likely repercussions should it come to light that a copy of the codebook not only existed but that its contents might one day be put into the public domain. Though it had seemed fantastic, I had been researching Elsie's theories. The Duke of Windsor's links to the Nazis were well documented. But the existence of any serious plot, within the ranks of the British Upper Class, to topple King George VI and Winston Churchill's Government in favour of

BUILDING 41

reinstating Edward VIII as the figure head of a pro-Hitler fascist state in Britain, seemed to be little more than just another conspiracy theory.

And yet, the more I researched the events in 1977, which had seen Peter Owen - my father - come within a hair's breadth of bombing the Palace of Westminster, the more I had come to wonder whether it might have been more than an act of simple terrorism. If, as my mother maintained, there had been the serious prospect of an NUGB-led coup, following the bombing, then such a coup must have had its backers at the highest level. Could they have been among the same men and women who had plotted the return to the throne of the Duke of Windsor more than thirty years previously? Günther Möller had claimed that the codebook would reveal "the treachery of your filthy British establishment". Could it be that Kapitänleutnant Lettmann, and the long dead crew of the U-boat he commanded, had been engaged in an exchange of intelligence that might, had they been successful, have altered not just the course of the War but the history of Britain? Of this, my mother said - and I had no reason to disbelieve her - she had known nothing at the time of the bombing.

As we stood there hand in hand, Lizzie Stammers and I, waiting for the result from the checking machine, I wondered whether these same elements might still be walking the corridors of power. And if they were, what threat they might still pose should they become aware that the code might yet be broken.

'We have a match.'

I had made no effort to contact my father nor, I had decided, would I ever do so. The news that he had been released from prison had troubled my mother. I knew that she had been thinking about him. I saw it in her eyes whenever reference was made to him in conversation, which was something we had learned to avoid. The human psyche is a strange thing indeed. What is it that engenders in us such feelings of longing for and devotion to another person?

That, regardless of how badly they treat us or how harmful our relationship with them becomes, leads us to such acts of wanton destruction of ourselves and of others? Even of those who love us and who we proclaim to love? On the single occasion, after the fire, that my mother ever spoke of it, she described her inability to escape the fantasy of a relationship that had only ever truly existed in her head. But to be caught so profoundly by such a fantasy. For it to have taken hold of her to such an extent, against all rhyme and reason. Do we all have that potential within us? Or does the fault lie, for some of us only, in our parenting or in some flaw in our genetic make-up?

Whatever had caused my mother's ruinous obsession with him, I had come to my own conclusion that the idea of Peter Owen as my father was, despite the undeniable part he had played in my biological creation, nothing but a fantasy. My father's name was Ted Stammers and, once the anger had abated, I knew that I missed him. That I'd always miss him. Every day.

*****

Elsie Sidthorpe died peacefully in her sleep, at the nursing home in Southwold on August 2nd, 2007. She was eighty-four. Just three days after her death, Jane and I were handed the Enigma rota and pegboard settings for the U-110 code. The following day I watched as Jane punched the characters into one of the Bletchley Enigma machines. Later, on the same day, I translated the text from German to English. We were already agreed, before we read it, about what we would do with the translated code. Ellen's pregnancy, of which I'd only just learned and about which I was, as you might expect, over the moon, had decided it for us.

BUILDING 41

Elsie was buried on Friday, August 17th, 2007, in the gorgeous summer sunshine, beside her great friend and fellow Bletchley Park log reader, Martha Watts. The card attached to the flowers from Flora and Simone Jackson, who stood alongside us at the funeral, was addressed "To our dearest friend Rosemary", which, when we read it, made both Ellen and I smile. I suppose that to them Elsie will always be Rosemary Sellers.

The copy of the original U-110 codebook taken by Jane Mears, and the only copies of the German and translated texts, which we had recovered with the help of the Bletchley Park Bombe Team, was buried with her.

Elsie once said that her theft of the codebook from Petty Officer Warren's kit bag had been like tossing a stone into the ocean, the ripples of it had seemed to go wider and wider with time. It is, I suppose, a great irony that, motivated by our determination to ensure that Elsie's ripples should at last run to ground, and that our child should grow up free from any threat that they might otherwise pose, by destroying the codebook, we had at last accomplished the task that Smith had set out to achieve but was never able to accomplish.

Let us hope that Elsie Sidthorpe and Martha Watts can now both truly rest in peace.

Oh, and if we have a daughter, Ellen and I are agreed that we're going to name her "Martha Rose". They are beautiful names and Elsie would have loved them, I'm sure. If we have a son, then you can rest assured that we won't be naming him "Günther". Or "Mikkel", come to think of it. The state of my bloody parka, he's lucky that I'm still talking to him at all.

Andy Mellett Brown

BUILDING 41

Postscript

After four years of living with Harry, Ellen, Elsie and company, 'Building 41' draws the Harry Stammers Series to a close. As in the first two books in the series, I have again borrowed from a number of historical events and locations in Building 41, including, of course, the building itself which is one of Bletchley Park's lesser known and more unassuming treasures (see below). While I have borrowed from history, as I like to do, please note that all of the characters and events in the book are entirely fictitious. Any resemblance to real persons, alive or dead, is coincidental and not intended. As I did in my last two books, I have included a postscript below, in which I say a little more about some of the places and events referred to in the book. I hope that this will be of interest to some of you.

Building 41

This little brick building sits between D and G-blocks, on the east side of the roadway that runs out onto Bletchley Park's northern perimeter and around to the right to what is now Alford Place. It is on the 'other side' of Bletchley's shameful fence that divides the main museum, run by The Bletchley Park Trust, from the remainder of the site, which includes the very wonderful National Museum of Computing, the home of Colossus, the world's first semi-programmable, electronic, digital computer.

Building 41, like the whole of G-block, is presently derelict and more or less exactly as described in the book (minus the trapdoor in the floor, of course). It is difficult to be absolutely certain about the building's origins or, indeed, its formal designation as "Building 41". There is nothing identifying it as such in any of the documentation I have found and only vague references to the building in the definitive 2004 English Heritage report on Bletchley Park and its buildings [3]. It seems most likely (though I would be happy to be contradicted) that the building is of post-war construction, perhaps having been built after the arrival at the Park of the Ministry of Aviation (later the Civil Aviation Authority) in or around 1947. Externally, the strange shaped rotatable antenna on the roof is the only indication of the building's former use. On the inside, part of the rotation mechanism is still visible (as Harry observes in Chapter 24 - standing beneath it is a slightly worrying experience).

I first came across this otherwise inconspicuous little building while attempting to negotiate the return to the Park of the Milton Keynes Amateur Radio Society, of which I am President. 'MKARS' has a long standing association with Bletchley Park. Indeed, its members had been heavily involved in helping to save it from demolition. Sadly, however, this did not prevent the Society's eviction from the site, in January 2013, by the Bletchley Park Trust.

During the negotiations, reference was made to a "Building 41" as a possible future venue for GB2BP, the demonstration amateur radio station formerly operated by MKARS at Bletchley Park. At the meeting, I remember turning to the Society's then treasurer and saying something like: - "Now wouldn't that make a fantastic title for a book?"

At the time, I had just published 'The Shelter' and was in the middle of writing 'The Battle of Wood Green'. I had the rough plot for the as-yet untitled book three, but for most of the remainder of that year The Battle of Wood Green naturally took priority. It was not until 2014 that I finally paid an unofficial visit to Building 41 (I have since been back on several occasions).

Like all of the remaining derelict places at Bletchley, Building 41 is a tremendously atmospheric building. It wasn't at all difficult to imagine the dramas that might have unfolded within the confines of the building's four walls, or indeed in my imagined tunnel below. I say 'imagined' because, of the tunnel discovered by Harry Stammers and Jane Mears in the book, I am sorry to report

BUILDING 41

that I could find no sign at all. Neither is there any trapdoor in the floor of Building 41, so please don't go digging for one.

While I am on the subject of exploring disused buildings, please note that all of the derelict buildings at Bletchley Park **are dangerous**. Nothing here is intended to encourage you or anyone else to enter them. They are all suffering from vandalism but are very much part of the site's history and of our heritage. They badly need protecting and eventual renovation, which I hope will come soon. If you do enter any of these buildings please be careful and treat them with the utmost respect. Remember the golden rule of urban exploration: - "Take nothing but pictures. Leave nothing but footprints. Break nothing but silence." [8]

Tunnels at Bletchley Park

Rumours have persisted, over the years, of the existence a network of tunnels below Bletchley Park, rather like those described in Building 41. There have, as Harry explains in the book, been various surveys and the occasional test dig. In 2011 I was fortunate enough to gain access to the basement below B-block (on this occasion entirely officially, I might add). This was prior to the demolition of the original classroom hut which was situated directly to the north of B-block and accessed via the block's northern spur, on the site now occupied by Radio Society of Great Britain Limited and their likeness of a Bletchley hut (it is a modern construction). From the adjoining staircase, a locked door leads to a further flight of steps down to the basement and another incredibly atmospheric space. When, that is, it is not flooded. At the foot of the steps, a recess in the brickwork led to suspicions of a blocked entrance to the tunnels. Unfortunately, and again as Harry describes, the subsequent excavation served only to damage the building's foundations, leading to extensive flooding each winter. Of a tunnel, there was not the slightest sign.

In fact, other than the occasional service duct between buildings (for pipes and so forth) no tunnel has ever been found, nor has any survey revealed the presence of any tunnels, nor any veteran ever reported having been into such a tunnel at Bletchley Park. I think that we can take from this that there are very probably no tunnels at BP, as much as I, for one, would like there to be... But you never know.

The Capture of U-110

The first two chapters of 'Building 41' took, as their inspiration, events that in actuality took place in the North Atlantic, east of Cape Farewell, Greenland on May 9, 1941. U-110 was a Type IXB submarine of the German Kriegsmarine's Second U-boat Flotilla, built by DeSchiMAG Weser in Bremen and launched on August 25, 1940. Her home port was Lorient, in occupied France. She was captained by Kapitänleutnant Fritz-Julius Lemp. Lemp was an already notorious U-boat captain, having previously commanded U-30, the submarine that, on September 3, 1939, sank the passenger ship 'The Athenia', killing 112 of her passengers.

U-110 had been attacking a convoy, south of Iceland, when it was spotted by HMS Aubretia. The corvette rushed to the scene and dropped depth charges, forcing U-110 to surface. Whereupon HMS Aubretia was joined by HMS Bulldog and HMS Broadway. Bulldog set course to ram, but thinking that it might be possible to capture the submarine, along with her secrets, Bulldog's commander gave the order to veer away.

Meanwhile, aboard U-110, presuming that the U-boat would go down, taking her secrets to the bottom, Kapitänleutnant Lemp had issued the order to abandon ship (reportedly, he had had coolly announced "Last stop, everybody out", as though conducting a bus in Berlin).

The accounts of what happened next vary somewhat but are perhaps most vividly portrayed in Hugh Sebag-Montefiore's book,

BUILDING 41

"Enigma, The Battle For The Code" [2]. His descriptions of the carnage on the deck of U-110 are not for the faint-hearted: - *"Helmut Ecke, who was standing on the U-boat deck, had seen something even more horrific. The man standing next to him was hit in the head by a shell. It was as if a rifle bullet had cracked open a pineapple at a funfair shooting range. The man's brains were sprayed all over the deck, before his decapitated crumpled trunk collapsed into the water"*.

There is another useful account in Micheal Patterson's "Voices of the Code Breakers: Personal Accounts of the Secret Heroes of World War II" [1] in which he summarises the accounts of Sub-Lieutenant Balme (who led the boarding party) and Ordinary Seaman C.J.Fairrie (both from Bulldog). Sub-Lieutenant Balme's account is readily available, in full, on-line. I relied on it, for reference, particularly in Chapter 3.

After the carnage on the deck of U-110, Lemp and the surviving crew threw themselves into the sea. However, realising that the submarine was not going to be sunk or indeed sink of its own accord, Lemp attempted to swim back in order to scuttle her. It was the last that was ever seen of him.

The capture of U-110 by HMS Bulldog is widely considered to be one of the most important of the War. Michael Paterson writes: - *"The findings aboard U110 were, in intelligence terms, a sort of Tutankhamen's tomb."*[1] As well as U-110's Enigma machine, there were a number of codebooks. These enabled the Hydra code to be broken and read, almost as swiftly by the Allies as by the Germans. From Bletchley, the deciphered U-boat signals could be forwarded to the Admiralty's Submarine Tracking Room and allied convoys routed away.

Today, U-110 lies at the bottom of the North Atlantic Ocean, having sunk on route to Scapa Flow. Fifteen of her crew died in the assault. Thirty-two were interned.

Q-Whitehall

In Chapter 10, Smith is summoned to his controller's office and makes use of a system of tunnels, which he accesses from an entrance in Craig's Court, off Whitehall in London. The existence of these tunnels is known. Oddly, details were published in the January 1946 edition of the Post Office Electrical Engineers Journal. However, their full extent remains classified.

The Whitehall tunnels had (and presumably still have) a dual-purpose, being to serve both as a route for communication cables, secure against bombing, and to be used by military and other official personnel, particularly in the event of gas or biological attack. Construction began as early as 1939 and was completed in 1941.

The tunnels are known as "Q-Whitehall" due to the code assigned to them by the Post Office/British Telecom - "QWHI" - "Q" being the prefix for Government secure installations. At the northern end they connect via a shaft up to the former Trafalgar Square tube station (now part of Charing Cross). At the southern end they connect to a shaft under Court 6 of the Treasury Building, providing a secure route from the Cabinet War Room. Several extensions are suspected, most obviously to the bunker, known as Pindar, below the MoD building and to the Marsham Street Rotunda [7].

As in 'Building 41', access to Q-Whitehall is known to exist, via a lift shaft in the telephone exchange in Craig's Court. There appears to have been further extension in the early 1950's, official documents referring to "Scheme 3245" - the only numbered tunnel scheme ever to have been revealed or located by researchers. Files in the National archives which may relate to the tunnels have been closed for 75 years and will be opened in 2026 [4] [5] [6].

BUILDING 41

References

[1] Patterson, Michael (2007). *Voices of the Code Breakers: Personal Accounts of the Secret Heroes of World War II*. David & Charles. ISBN 0715327194

[2] Sebag-Montefiore, Hugh (2004). *Enigma: The Battle For The Code.* Cassel Military Paperbacks, ISBN 004366625

[3] Monckton, Linda; Williams, Andrew; Grundon, Imogen; Barrett, Nathalie and Morrison, Kathryn (2004). *Bletchley Park.* English Heritage.

[4] Wikipedia, https://en.wikipedia.org/wiki/Military_citadels_under_London

[5] Civil Defence Today, http://www.civildefence.co.uk/secret-tunnels.php

[6] Ian Visits, http://www.ianvisits.co.uk/blog/2009/11/20/more-on-the-secret-tunnel-under-whitehall/

[7] Subterranea Brittanica, http://www.subbrit.org.uk/sb-sites/sites/r/rotundas/index.shtml

[8] http://www.urbandictionary.com/define.php?term=Urban+Exploring

THE SHELTER
THE HARRY STAMMERS SERIES, BOOK ONE
ANDY MELLETT BROWN

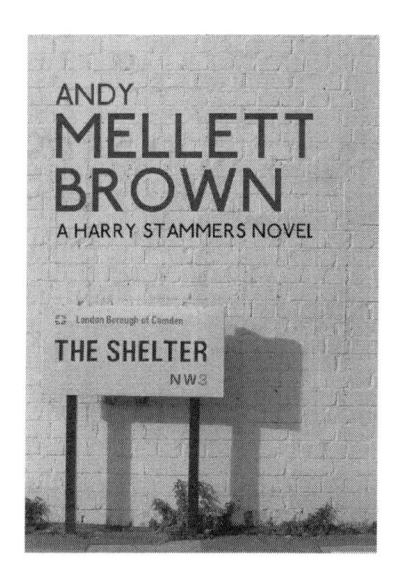

It is 10 November 1944 and a young woman in a woollen coat steps off a trolley bus into the darkness of wartime London and vanishes. Sixty years later, museum curator Harry Stammers receives an intriguing invitation from Bletchley Park veteran Elsie Sidthorpe. Aided by Ellen Carmichael, Elsie's great niece, Stammers sets out to discover the truth about what happened to Martha Watts.

THE BATTLE OF WOOD GREEN

THE HARRY STAMMERS SERIES, BOOK TWO
ANDY MELLETT BROWN

1970'S North London provides the backdrop to part two of the thrilling Harry Stammers series. School teacher and mother Liz Muir believes that she has put her life as an MI5 agent behind her, but when an ex-pupil is brutally murdered at an anti-Nazi rally and the mysterious 'Smith' reappears, Muir is forced back into service and a life built on secrets and lies begins to unravel.

ANDY MELLETT BROWN was born in Harringay, North London and lived there until he was sixteen. He joined Haringey Social Services Department in 1982 and presently works for the Care Quality Commission. He is President of The Milton Keynes Amateur Radio Society, whose members campaigned to save Bletchley Park before MKARS took up residency at the Park in 1994.

Published in June 2013, Andy's first novel, *The Shelter*, has earned him an ever growing and enthusiastic following. *The Battle of Wood Green* is the second in his *Harry Stammers Series*. The third, entitled *Building 41* is out now.

Andy has lived in Leighton Buzzard, Bedfordshire with his wife, Patricia, since 2004.

Meet the author at www.andymellettbrown.com

* Photography by Janice Issitt